D0772388

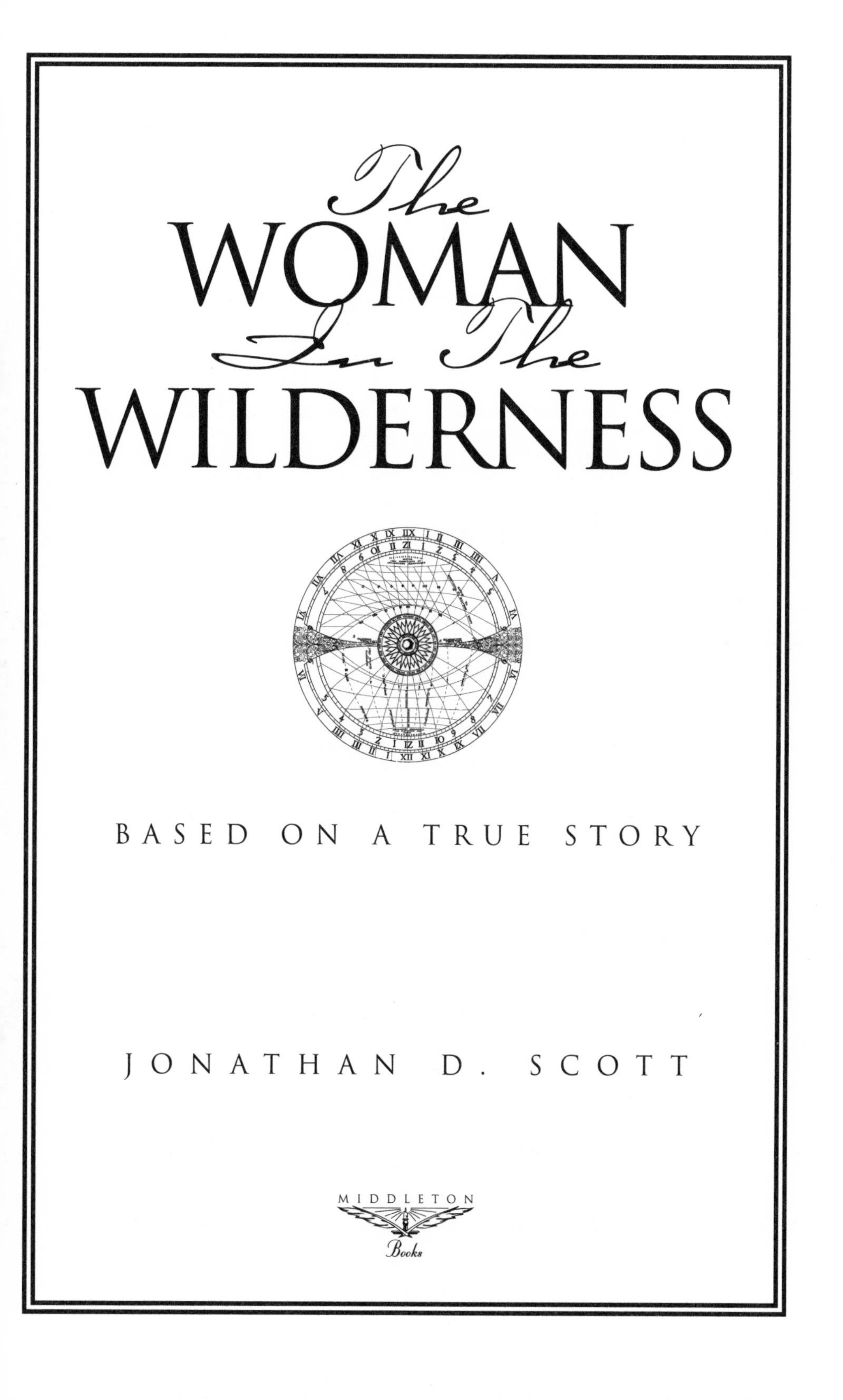

The WOMAN In The WILDERNESS

BASED ON A TRUE STORY

JONATHAN D. SCOTT

MIDDLETON
Books

Published in the United States by Middleton Books,
823 Dana Drive, Coatesville, Pennsylvania 19320
info@middletonbooks.com

ISBN-13: 978-0-9716611-5-8
ISBN: 0-9716611-5-4
Library of Congress Control Number: 20041059

PUBLISHERS CATALOGING IN PUBLICATION DATA

Scott, Jonathan D.
The woman in the wilderness : based on a true story / Jonathan D.Scott.
-- Coatesville, PA : Middleton Books, 2005.

p. ; cm.

"Inside the mystery of America's first mystics."
Includes bibliographical references.
ISBN: 0-9716611-5-4

1. Kelpius, Johannes, 1673-1708--Fiction. 2. Pietists--
Pennsylvania--Fiction. 3. Germans--Pennsylvania--Fiction.
4. Historical fiction. I. Title.

PS3619.C667 W66 2005 2004109659

The text of this book was sent in a typeface called Pietismus,
designed especially for this book.

Front cover design, illustration, and back cover photography by
Jonathan D. Scott

*Diagram taken from the Horologium Achaz Hydrographicum (used with
permission of the American Philosophical Society, Philadelphia, Pennsylvania).*

Dedicated to the memories of

my father, Alan Scott,
a Broadcast Pioneer and a beloved figure
in twentieth century Philadelphia history,

Julius Friedrich Sachse, Litt. D,
whose heroic efforts in the nineteenth century
rescued much of this story from historical oblivion,
and
Johannes Kelpius, *der freien Künste und Weltweisheit Doctor,*
who lived too soon to understand and too soon to be understood.

In Thanks

to Sylvia Pseiffenberger for her help with my German;
to Kelly Griffin and Chris Brown with their help with my English;
to Chris Wentz and Roger Waddell for their technical assistance;
to Dan Allen, David Young, and Elizabeth Shaak for
sharing information at the Valley Green Inn;
to Kaye Brown and Linda Bittner of the Southern Pines Public Libray,
Bruce Gill of Harriton House, Sue Wright of Christ Church, Sue Ann
Prince of the American Philosophical Society, Marion Rosenbaum of the
Germantown Historical Society, the staff of the Historical Society of
Pennsylvania, and especially Jerry Frost of Swarthmore College for their
invaluable help with my research.

"Let us depart from all ceremonies, conjurations, consecrations, etc.,
and with all similar delusions,
and put our heart, will and confidence solely upon the true rock...
If we abandon selfishness the door will be opened for us,
and that which is mysterious will be revealed."

- Paracelsus *(Philosophia Occulta)*

Prologue

Sunday, December 24, 1815
From: Christina Warmer Wüster, Germantown, Pennsylvania
To: Lydia Bielen, Schwenksville, Pennsylvania

My Dearest Lydia,

My eyes are filled with tears this Christmas Eve, but not with tears of sadness, my darling. The tears come from a heart that is filled—over-filled perhaps I should say, since I have had more than my fill in life—of the blessings and the great trials of Life that the Lord puts upon us to help perfect us in His own way.

The things in this box are more than just presents for Christmas. I hope they will remind you of me and of the happy moments we have been allowed to share—for Christmases to come when I won't be with you any more.

I know that these things some may consider trifles. I give them to you not because of their worldly value, but because I know that you, dear, of all my family, with your sweet soul, might cherish them as I have done.

Die Steppdecke—that old tattered quilt—I know it won't warm your body, but I am giving it to you so that one day it may help to warm your heart. Its colors are so faded, but once they were bright. *Meine Groffmutter*, your great-great-grandmother, told me it was made in the Old World and has a blessing sewn into its stitches—what few there are left! I can remember so many Christmas Eves being wrapped up in it. But I give it to you now so that you may have something by which to remember your *Grofftantchen*, your Great Aunt, and perhaps be blessed by the Old World woman who made it, too.

Inside the envelope is a little gold charm, with a six-sided star like the ones that are worn sometimes by the Jews. It is real gold, my dear, so please treasure it and keep it safe! I don't know from whence it came, with its strange design and magical symbols. Perhaps your father can take it to someone who can make it into a necklace for you. If you wear it to bed some night, maybe you can discover its hidden secret in a dream.

Lastly, my darling, wrapped in the quilt you will find a tattered old hymnal. This sad-looking book, with its torn cover, is the greatest treasure of all if your soul is pure and stalwart enough to delve into its mystery.

I know very little of the life of the one who composed these verses, but of his soul I could write volumes. Therein was a deep sadness that was not really a sadness at all, but water from the very same fountain that rises in my heart tonight. To drink from that fountain is the reward of Life, with its dazzling wonder of Love between the Creator and His Creation.

The composer's name was Johannes Kelpius and he came from far away, a long time ago. His life is a mystery, but this much I know—once he came to stay in the house of my grandmother.

She was about the age you are, my dear Lydia, my *Groffmutter*, Christiana, and it was near the time of *Heiliger Abend*, Christmas Eve. Herr Kelpius had come across the sea to live in the woods in the Wissahickon Valley, along the ridge above the creek. In the dark of night he was brought to our home—sick from a terrible cold. *Groffmutter* Christiana said that she worried for the life of this young man, a friend to her father and to all in Germantown, including the children with whom he shared the blessings of his noble birth and education.

On that Christmas Eve, very distant from this one, she was kneeling beside her bed, praying for their visitor, when she noticed a light coming from the small room beside her own, where lay Johannes Kelpius. When she crept in to look, she saw a woman beside his bed, clothed in shimmering robes.

The Angel turned and smiled at my poor, trembling *Groffmutter* before she vanished. It was from this, *meine Englein*, my dear little angel Lydia, that my own grandmother's soul was spiritualized. She spent the rest of her life devoted to following in the footsteps of Christ—a life that was indeed sanctified by her transformation. She told no one about this but me, and dearest Lydia, I tell you now only because her spirit bids me to share her most cherished secret.

I do not know what power brought Johannes Kelpius to Pennsylvania, or why he came so far from his home, or what tragedies befell his young life. All I know is that while he was a guest in her home, my grandmother's mother copied his hymns (I almost wrote poems!) into this little volume from Herr Kelpius' own manuscripts.

I hope that you will read and re-read these hymns, and that they will bring to you the same kind of solace and exultation that I have found in them. In my life they have transformed me, in much the same way as the glance of the Angel transformed my grandmother—in the same way I hope they may transform you, dearest.

Take them to yourself and hold them gently, as you must needs be gentle with the old book—as if you held a gentle and innocent dove in your hands—in the way I hold you, my dearest Lydia, in my heart this Christmas Eve.

In love eternal,
Tantchen Christina

Part One

Chapter One

Saturday, June 24, 1826
Roxborough, Philadelphia

Lydia felt as if she were doing the most foolish thing she had ever done in her life. She couldn't escape from the image of Mrs. Righter, standing just inside the door of the log cabin, listening patiently as she stammered an apology. "I am so sorry that even though my letter promised I would come last month, I wasn't able...."

"I understand, my dear."

"I've been preparing to go away to teach school in New York."

"Yes, so you said in your letter."

"I have just been so terribly busy that this has been the first opportunity..."

"I regret you have chosen such a threatening day." Lydia followed the woman's eyes to the clouds that hung low over the ridge. Mrs. Righter did not invite her inside the cabin.

"You don't mind if I go back and look around?"

"Dear, please don't go inside the building. I wouldn't want anything to happen to you. If you were hurt, no one could hear you call."

It was not a comforting thought. It had already been difficult, walking the distance from the post office in Roxborough along Ridge Avenue until she reached the grassy lane that led into the Righter's property. She worried about strangers, the durability of her hat, and whether she should have brought an umbrella.

Lydia thanked Mrs. Righter and apologized once again. Then, gathering her skirt, she walked around the cabin, along the garden fence and into the woods. There, the sounds of a warbler and the wind in the woods overtook the sounds of horses on Ridge Avenue. The leaves were showing their silver sides, the most reliable portent she knew of bad weather. This was truly a foolish plan.

It had grown from her strange excitement about moving away from home, and all of the emotions it had evoked. It had taken a great deal of effort to sort through eighteen years of her life, and by the time she uncovered the memories of her great-aunt, she was in need of tears simply to cleanse her heart. It was in that moment of shameful female weakness that she had set herself on this foolish adventure, and she had been too prideful to reconsider it.

She didn't believe in wizardry, in spite of the men at the Roxborough post office.

"They burned in the dark of the moon a cauldron," one stooped man told her in a thick German accent. "Brewing, they were, their black *mittel*, the elixir of eternal life."

Another, equally old, blew a puff from his pipe in her face. "The blood from the heart of a virgin. They needed such blood."

"*Geistes*," said the stooped man, blind in one eye. "Their ghosts be up there still. I myself have seen many times lights moving through the trees." He opened his gnarled hands and made slow circles with his fingers. "*Geistes* I saw. Souls damned to wander without rest."

Lydia forced a smile and thanked the men for their concern.

"Why," the stooped man asked, "they came, so far from their home, to live up in *der wuste*, where no one else would go?"

A middle-aged man with gray side-whiskers doffed a top hat as he held open the door for her. He held his mail to his face and whispered to her as she passed. "Perhaps, Miss, you will permit me to walk with you a moment."

On the sidewalk along Ridge Street, he linked his arm with hers. "The men whose tabernacle you are seeking," he said in an accent devoid of any hint of German, "were members of an ancient fraternal order, the true activities of which have been deliberately concealed by the promotion of such nonsense. They came to

Philadelphia by the command of the Supreme Imperator of Europe to establish a branch of a venerable secret society founded by the thrice-blessed Hermes of Egypt—the *Lampado Trado.*" She looked into his blue eyes, trying to decide if she should be afraid. "The fraternal lodge they established included names that would ring felicitously in the ears of all patriotic Americans. T.J. and B.F," he said, raising an eyebrow.

"Pardon?"

"T. Jefferson and B. Franklin. I can say no more, Miss, other than to warn you that certain matters have remained initiatory not without reason." As he tipped his hat, she noticed the large insignia on his ring.

By the time she had lost sight of Mrs. Righter's cabin, Lydia knew there was nothing to be gained by listening to the echoes in her mind, of wizards or the weather. She was not going to turn around. She followed the path until it ended, and then she just kept going.

And there it was.

She came upon it suddenly, although she felt as if it had come upon her. In the ragged remains of a clearing, beyond what had once been a tall and protective fence, it clung to the form of its original hugeness. It looked back at her through four eyes of window holes set opposite a forlorn doorway.

A chill ran down her arms. She had been drawn to this place by a longing that she couldn't explain to herself. She felt as if she had wanted to come here for her entire life, even before she had ever seen that old hymnal. Perhaps a very long time before that.

The Tabernacle was certainly old; there was no doubt of that. Entangled vines had laid permanent claim on its walls. But the original craftsmanship showed in the symmetry of the pointed logs and their carefully mortised joints. It was still a tall building, even though the roof had caved in, bringing with it something that appeared to be a lookout tower.

What had Johannes Kelpius been looking for in the woods above the Wissahickon?

It wasn't easy to climb through the rotted fence and forge a path through blackberry brambles. She suspected the weeds harbored red bugs or worse. But here she was on the great stone step, not ready to open the door, yet unable to stop. She twisted the old knob, pushed, and squinted into the darkness.

She was devastated by its emptiness. Whatever she had been expecting would have been better than finding nothing. There was something though in shadow, something she could see through the light that filtered through a hole in the ceiling. It looked like an enormous "X," lying against the far wall. Yes it was, rusted and forlorn, a suggestion of some profane symbol. The minister of the Lutheran Church had once spoken on the Deist beliefs of the English patriots, and Lydia shuddered at the thought that this might have been the meeting place for a strange secular society. It was only after her eyes had adjusted to the light that she could see an outline on the wall—a faint image of where the great iron object had once kept the sunlight from discoloring the wood behind it. It was not an "X," but a cross—a cross within a circle—a shape that reassured her this building had been the house of true Christian worship.

Other than the great cross, there was nothing in the bare room but the debris brought in by a hundred years of wind. She would have been content to stay outside and follow the very proper advice of Mrs. Righter, if she hadn't seen a set of stairs that led to a second story. Her curious nature had been considered a vice by her parents, but she credited it for her acceptance into the teachers' college. That same curiosity was also the power—vice or virtue—that brought her now to the doorway of the Tabernacle of Johannes Kelpius. She stepped inside.

The room was large, at least forty feet square. The floor shook as she stepped on it, but not nearly as precariously as the stairs. Fortunately, there was a railing to clutch as she climbed. No one, she remembered, could hear if she needed to call for help.

If the second floor held more risk, it also held more interest. Where the roof had collapsed, gray light shone on a series of open doorways into tiny spaces, too small to be rooms. In the closest one she could see marks of crude vandalism, the proud marks of one who had braved to trespass on profane ground. There was but a single closed door. To reach it meant having to step across a hole in the floor—the ceiling of the room below—but she did, thinking she was exceeding the limits of even her own courage.

There was no handle on the door, no way to pull it open. A breeze blew through the treetops and she heard the spattering of drizzle. As she pushed on the door, the old hinges and jamb gave way and it fell to the floor, nearly knocking her off balance. The building seemed to tremble unless, she wondered, it was she who was trembling. There was nothing inside. Bare shelves lining the walls made her think it had been a storage closet or, perhaps, a library.

There was no doubt that it would soon rain.

She made her way downstairs and back outside, thanking God that she hadn't hurt herself. Her hat had a nice brim in front that would protect her face. Surely Mrs. Righter would invite her to wait inside if it were raining. The old widow might even have an umbrella she could borrow and leave at the Roxborough post office.

She was nearly out of the clearing and back into the woods when she stopped. She thought it was because she heard the call of a bird, a mournful call that made her want to take one last look at the Tabernacle—to paint a picture of it in her memory that she could place with the other articles of her childhood. It was while she stood there, as if she were just waiting to be caught in the rain, that she thought of something.

She couldn't believe she was walking back again through a gap in the fence, back into the Tabernacle and back up those dangerous stairs. She scolded herself, this time for having been so eager to leave. She couldn't bear the thought that she had added to the desecration of what had once been hallowed ground—hallowed, at least, by its creators.

She stepped again over the hole in the ceiling and knelt by the fallen door. When she went to lift it back in place, she could see over a century's worth of dust that had been swept beneath it. In the pile were sticks, more leaves, and some bits of paper. She leaned the door against the jamb and cautiously picked out the papers from the dirt.

They were scraps of an old German Bible; she recognized the style immediately from her own family's heirlooms. But also among them was a very small sheet, less than six inches across. In the diffused light of the hallway, she could see that it was written by hand, with immaculate care. She felt the blood rush into her face.

Seneca de refor

Patria meam transire no possum, ominum una est, extra hanc nemo projici potest. Magnum virtutis principiu est ut doxo; paulatim, exercitatus animus visibilia & transitoria primum communtare, ut postmodum possit derelinquere. Delicatus ille est adhue, cui Patria dulcis est. Fortis autem iam cui omne solum Patria. Perfectus vero qui mundus exilium est.

Anno 1694

In Nomine Jesum

Being wholly and completely assured of the Divine Intention of our undertaking, I resolved to make the voyage to America, with my companions, J.G. Seelig, Daniel Falckner, Henrich Bernard Köster, and thirty-five others, from various parts of Germany, all likewise convinced of the rightness of our journey.

On February 7th, I engaged for them the ship Sara Maria (of good hope), Captain John Tanner, an Englishman, the vessel being hired at a payment of 7£ English silver, which I paid out on board on the day of our departure, the 13th.

With me on this voyage, I have the Dove, which must be protected at all costs, entrusted unto me by Magister Johann Jakob Zimmerman, bequeathed unto him through an immemorial chain of transmission.

Johannes Kelpius of Transylvania

Chapter Two

Monday, March 23, 1685
Segesvár, Transylvania

"Wo bistu mein Täublein?
Mein süffestes Englein?"

Johann stopped for a moment beneath the Choir Room window. When he had been summoned away from the class by the mysterious command of the headmaster, the other boys had been left struggling. The eleven- and twelve-year-old Boys' Choir was sadly discordant. A mourning dove, lost in the fog that had settled over the town, called back to them with its own plaintive song. It was only a matter of months before the children of the Choir would leave their education behind and begin apprenticeships. In the meantime they sang bravely, oblivious of their inability, with all the confidence of children whose futures were as sure to them as the next line of the song.

"Ich sehn mich mit schmertzen
Und ruff dich im hertzen."

The top of the Clock Tower that loomed over the lower city had disappeared in the low clouds. The morning was cold and dark as if it were already close to night. Johann could sense rain, hidden also in the clouds, lurking and waiting.

"Wo bistu mein Täublein?
Ach kom doch mein Englein."

He listened again, able to distinguish the voice of each student, especially the cambiata of the boy who had taken his winter coat. Even now, more than a month later, Johann did not consider him a thief. The boy was admittedly a braggart and a bully, but Johann knew that he attended school by the charity of the town. Besides, the wool coat had always been too large, having been passed down by his own brother Martin.

Johann followed the alley to what appeared to be a dead end but instead led to a hidden passageway. Segesvár was full of such places, built by the Roman armies, and Johann knew most of them by heart. This one, nearest his school, was especially unpleasant. It was thankfully short, but dark, and almost always harbored a puddle of stagnant water. It seemed to be a conspiratorial chamber for every rat in Transylvania.

As he came through the tunnel into the cobblestone lane, he splashed water on his breeches. The street was draughty and a chill ran through him. He fought against the wish that he still had his coat. Not only too large, he reminded himself with a reprimand, it was old, shamefully displaying a tear that his mother was not there to sew. She was the one who had made the coat, but that had been for Martin. Fourteen years had inflicted their inalterable changes on the fabric of the coat as it had on the family.

The lane was quiet, save for the rattling cart of a wool-carder, the tinkling of sheep bells from outside the town wall, and the sad cry of the dove still lost in the fog. It was a dark, but otherwise unexceptional morning in Segesvár, the central city of the district where his father had been the pastor of a small Lutheran parish. The only disturbance in the unyielding familiarity of the scene was a red coach coming up the hill from the city gate. Johann stepped aside and watched it pass. The coats of the horses were so black they glistened with sparkles of dampness. The coach turned and disappeared up the street that led past the ancient monastery church to the Bürgermeister's office inside the Clock Tower. Whoever was inside was undoubtedly a nobleman.

Only once before had he seen a carriage like that. Less than a month before at his father's funeral.

It had stopped behind the tent outside the church in the little village of Denndorf, where a crowd had huddled to mourn the passing of their pastor, the Pfarrer Kelp. A man in a long black coat stepped out of the carriage and stood in the rain, apart from the others. Most of the man's bearded face had been hidden in shadow, but Johann could feel the unsettling force of his presence.

It was a presence that hurt at a time when he thought he already had more pain than he could endure. The man brought with him a bitter wind. The rain turned to sleet, and Johann's winter coat was on the back of some other boy. But neither the cold nor the congregation's pity nor the frightening man who watched him from the shadows were as cruel as the feeling that he was completely alone in the world.

"Gott gebe ihm eine selege Auferstehung." The stranger muttered over the heads of the mourners, interrupting the prayer of the Diaconus who led the service. *God grant him a blessed resurrection.*

"Libera nos a malo," finished the Diaconus. *Deliver us from evil.*

"He must have been a friend of Father," his brother Martin whispered to him when the service ended and the red coach sloshed back up the road to Segesvár. "Father had a great many friends."

But Johann knew that Georg Kelp had lost most of his friends. During the sweet days when Martin had lived at home, the Pfarrer Kelp had been one of the most respected men in the district. Once Georg Kelp had been a welcome guest in the homes of Transylvanian nobility. Once everyone in Siebenbürgen knew his great reputation for piety and kindness. Once upon a time.

Martin had grieved that night. When he returned to Leipzig the next week, leaving Johann in the empty house, he described to Johann in dispassion how he mourned. "I loved Father," he said, stressing that unfamiliar verb as if its sound in their home would be a touchstone that would transmute all the injustices of the past.

Johann had loved his father, too. He cherished the times when the two would ride together to the mountains and look down over the city where they lived. From the clearing on the ridge where they would spend the night, Johann could see the walled city, with the spire of the Clock Tower rising over the steep red roofs. His father told him that Caesar had built Segesvár in the shape of a hexagon—a figure containing occult significance in its geometry.

Segesvár had been a fortress to defend Caesar's empire against the demonic spirits that the Romans believed lurked among the dark trees of the Transylvanian forests.

If it were cool enough and clear enough, Johannes and his father could see the smoke rising from Denndorf, a distance of more than ten leagues from Segesvár. On those special nights when there was no wine for his father to drink, only water from the mountain stream, they would kneel together in the pine needles and pray under the great sphere of stars.

Pfarrer Kelp knew every verse of the Bible from *Genesis* to *Revelation* and could, and would, quote one when something brought it to his mind. Johann would spend his evenings at home patiently outside the door of the study while inside his father sipped his wine and studied Scripture by the light of a candle. When Pfarrer Kelp dropped a mote of approval, it was greater than the lavish praise of anyone else.

Johann did not have the sturdiness of his father and brother. He bore the effects of an infant illness that caused his left eye to appear half-closed in either idiocy or melancholy. But if he were physically so imperfect, he had striven to be perfect in every other way. He was excessively diligent at school, and no one but God knew how hard he strove to become a perfect Christian. Unfortunately, for Pfarrer Kelp there was no such thing as perfection. Leaning beside his father's chair in his study was a stout stick casting a long shadow across the long meandering patterns of wood grain of the floor. Johann never felt more alone than when his father went for the stick. No one was there to protect him—no one but God, and God was on the side of Pfarrer Kelp.

"Johannes, you are a bitter thorn in my life." He had seen his father's hand clenched, his cheeks flushed, his eyes red from wine. Pfarrer Kelp could not abide the excuse that allowing the theft of Johann's coat had been charity.

Him that taketh away thy cloak, forbid not to take thy coat also.

Now, in the chill of the March morning, Johann reminded himself that there would not be many more days this season that he would need a coat. And beyond that—he was unable to consider.

He pushed aside dark images of his future and reminded himself that his immediate concern was reaching the Bürgermeister's office. The Clock Tower began to toll the hour as he reached the top of the lane; the tenth chime as he reached the main street. The center of Segesvár was dark and hushed. The red carriage had stopped on the cobblestones, near the Clock Tower.

A chill ran though him and he invoked the strength of the Savior.

Instead of climbing the stone steps, he crossed the street and climbed the fence into the Bürgermeister's family garden. He prayed again, this time that he would not leave footprints in the wet dirt. He climbed the wooden stairs in the back of the steps, listening.

"I knew him for years," the Bürgermeister was saying, "before he became Pfarrer at Denndorf. An extremely devout and intelligent man."

Johann stepped along the landing, close enough to the back door to look inside. The Bürgermeister was lighting a fire. The other man seemed even larger than he had at his father's funeral. As he turned, Johann could see a portion of his face, fully bearded but clean-shaven above his lip. He had waves of matted gray hair, damp or unclean, that fell around his face to his shoulders. His large gloved hands clutched a three-corner hat. As they had been at the funeral, his eyes hid in the shadows of their brows.

"Kelp never recovered from mourning," the Bürgermeister said. "There were so many who offered to help, but he declined as the years went on. I only hope he and his wife have found solace together at last *im Himmel*, so to speak. Did you know her as well? She was a lovely woman. Hearing her sing was to hear the song of an angel. It was such a pity."

Johann's anger wrestled with his shame.

"*Der junge* Kelp inherited his father's intellect and charm as well as his mother's talent. Our Schoolmaster tells me that his mind is quite extraordinary. Sometimes a little *schwermütig,* poor lad, but with all considered, I cannot begrudge him melancholy. His brother refuses to take responsibility, and I fear that without us the child has no future. As you know, Zabanius, has offered his help in Bavaria."

The stranger took a long step across the room, stopping with his back against the window. When he spoke, a loose diamond of glass trembled from the vibration.

"Where is he?"

"I'm certain he will be here any moment, Herr Graf. The child is very obedient."

Johann pushed himself away from the window. It was true that he knew nothing other than to be obedient. He nearly slipped rushing down the damp steps. On the street he paused only to run his fingers through his hair and to try to rub the wetness off his breeches. He took the stone steps two at a time to Bürgermeister Deli's front door, took a breath to calm himself, and knocked.

"Come in, Johann," the Bürgermeister called.

Inside, Deli was stoking his fire with enormous bellows. *"Grüß Gott, mein junger* Kelp."

Even with his eyes respectfully lowered to the floor, he could sense the gaze of the stranger.

"Count Valentin, I present to you Johann Kelp, son of your friend Georg." Johann bowed. "We have been discussing your future, Johann. The Count has expressed a desire to help you continue your education."

Johann bowed with a sweep of his arm. He had been taught painfully well how to behave in the presence of nobility. "That is most generous, *mein gnädiger* Herr," he said.

"I received a letter from your father's friend, Johann Zaban—Zabanius as he is styling himself now," Deli said. "I believe that with the help of Count Valentin, the three of us will be able to provide the resources for you to attend school next year."

Under the weight of the terrible silence that followed, Johann momentarily lifted his eyes. In the light of the fire, he could see that the eyes of the Count were clouded by a yellowish film. His noble lips were chapped in flecks of white.

Johann turned for reassurance to the Bürgermeister. "That is most generous." His voice trembled repeating his response.

"Schoolmaster reports that you are the most intelligent student in the class. Most intelligent student in all of Siebenbürgen maybe, heh, Kelp? That should impress them at Altdorf!"

"Altdorf, Herr Bürgermeister?"

Deli seemed confused. "That is where you would like to go to school? The University of Altdorf in Bavaria? Is that not what you told Schoolmaster?"

Johann felt his face burn with shame. "Please do not misunderstand me, *meine Herren,*" he said to the floor, "but why do you offer this to me?"

Deli laid a hand on his shoulder. "It is because we wish to help you, son. Because you have a fine, bright future. And because your father, may he rest in peace, was our spiritual shepherd. Was he not, Herr Graf?"

Instead of an answer, the Count cleared mucus from his throat. "Leave us alone, please, Bürgermeister."

"Alone? With the boy?" Deli looked solicitously at Johann, painfully aware of the eccentricities of the aristocracy. "Yes, most certainly, Herr Graf. I must attend to—some other things, of course." He picked up a paper from his desk and walked toward the front door. "Do not be afraid," he whispered.

When the door closed, the Count turned toward the window, his back to the boy. "Were you with Pfarrer Kelp when he died?" he asked.

Johann allowed himself to look at the Count. "Yes, Herr Graf. He fell in his study and injured himself." Against his will, Johann once again heard the sound—the grotesque sound that had made him run down the stairs. He remembered the dumb agony on his father's face as he lay beside his desk, the glazed eyes, the pool of red on the wooden floor.

"Did you pray for his soul?"

"Yes, Herr Graf."

By the time Johann had brought his quilt to cover his father, he knew that the great Pfarrer Kelp was going to die.

"Pater noster..." he had said over him. The pfarrer had opened his eyes long enough to look at his son. Johann's left eye, his sad droopy eyelid, was quivering. *"Qui es in coelis: sanctificetur nomen tuum,"* said the boy.

"Dimitte nobis," the Pfarrer had whispered, barely breathing. *"Debita nostra."*

Johann had knelt beside him in the pool of blood and finished the prayer. *"Sicut et nos dimittimus debitoribus nostris."*

When he could endure no more, when the terror inside overcame his paralysis, Johann ran outside. He ran down the lane toward the steps that led to the neighbors' house. He slammed his fist on the door. A young woman came to answer.

"Johann, what's the matter?"

"Father..." His breath caught in his throat. He just stood on the stoop, hoping the girl could look far enough into his eyes to understand. She saw the blood on his hands and britches.

"Mein Gott," she whispered.

By the time they got to back to his house, Georg Kelp was dead.

"I was with my son when he died," the Count said. "I prayed over him until his soul took flight from Time to Eternity. I could not shed a tear. I was too stricken."

There was a long silence, through which Johann desperately wondered if he should speak. He heard the dove, somewhere outside, cooing again. "I am sorry, Herr Graf," he said.

"Pfarrer Kelp attempted to mitigate the pain of my grief. But it was his death that roused me from the depths of despair. And you, Johann Kelp."

Johann cleared his throat. "I, Herr Graf?"

The Count turned back to face him. Valentin bent low, his breath in Johann's face. In a strange and disturbing moment, Johann saw in the man's yellow eyes a flash of images—strange, misshapen images that belonged only to the secret realms of the Count's dark heart.

The Count, looking back at him as if he sensed Johann's perception, placed a gloved finger against Johann's left eye, the anomaly that had given him a schoolboy reputation for possessing the Evil Eye. "What do you know," the Count asked, "of *The Fame and Confession of the Rosy Cross?*"

"I—I do not know anything at all."

"Many years ago," Valentin said, "a distant ancestor of mine was restoring an abandoned building in Würtemberg when his tools struck something unexpected. In the rubble he discovered a vault that had been hidden for decades. When he managed to dislodge the lock, he found inside a treasure greater than those of kings and emperors. Do you know what that treasure was, Johann Kelp?"

"No, Herr Graf."

The Count traced a great arc through the air. "It was nothing less than the azoth, the most-hidden, that which the base call the Philosopher's Stone. It was the secret that hath the power to transform the basest element into the most sublime, the very formula used by Christ to defeat the ancient enemy of Death. 'What times before hath not been seen, heard, and smelt, now finally shall be spoken and uttered forth!' You see, Johann, my cousin had uncovered the lost writings of Christian Rosencruetz, a man who spent his life traveling the Arab world in search of the *Sofia*, the Divine Wisdom, the doctrine of illumination. This knowledge had been vouchsafed to the world to awaken her from her profane slumber and bring the dawn of the fulfillment of Christ's true church, when the Trumpet of Illyricum shall sound, the future eternity of the seven Hebrew vials shall be opened against the Beast and Babylon the Great."

A log in the fireplace fell, sending a blaze of sparks up the chimney and smoke into the room. The Count coughed and struggled for breath. "The taint of infidelity is in this room," he said. "I cannot remain any longer. Come with me, *mein junger* Kelp."

He placed an enormous hand on Johann's back and led him to the door. They walked together down the steps. Then, without warning, the Count strode ahead, his long steps carrying him down the street from the Clock Tower. Johann ran after him.

The wool cart was rattling back up the lane. Smoke from the fire of a dyer in the next street rose in a twisted column into the fog. The dove repeated her forlorn call. The Count had disappeared. Johann listened—not for footsteps, for there were none—but for the whisper of his own, secret intuition.

He found him, the Count's silver-buckled boots ankle-deep in water, crouched in the passageway that led to the alley. His shadow seemed intent on preventing any light from creeping into the tunnel. "I knew you would be able to find me, Johann," he said hoarsely. "Your inner ear is open to the call of my heart. That Gift shall guide you to many things that others cannot hear. I have something for that ear alone, Johann. *Unser Geheimnis—unser Geheimnis. Our secret."*

Johann felt his heart pounding. "There have appeared," the Count whispered, "great wonders in the sky—a woman clothed with the sun, and the moon under her feet, and upon her head a crown of thorns. Being in the throes of birth and in pain, she cries to be delivered.

"But there appears another wonder in the sky—a red dragon having seven heads and ten horns and seven crowns on his head. His tail draws the third part of the stars and casts them to the earth, and the dragon stands before the woman, to devour her child as soon as it were born."

Johann stepped backward, leaning his thin body away from the pressure of the Count's presence. There was a discomforting familiarity in the strange words and their scent of insanity.

"And she brings forth a man child, who is to rule all nations with a rod of iron. And our child is caught up unto God, and to his throne. And the woman flees into the wilderness, where she hath a place prepared of God." The Count stopped, as if his throat prevented him from speaking. Something splashed in the water at Johann's feet.

"But it was not to be. The dragon is triumphant. My son died before he was a year old. It was my sin—my most grievous sin that I committed against my son's mother and against Nature—that caused Almighty and All-merciful God to take him from us, and from the triumph that had been vouchsafed by the great comet.

"One night when I was on the verge of losing my wits I left the castle on horseback. I rode by the light of the moon, not knowing or caring where I was going. I rode for hours until I found myself in a clearing somewhere in the depths of the mountains. There was a lonely hut from which a trail of smoke rose in the moonlight.

"I tethered my horse to the skeleton of a tree beside the hovel and banged on the door as if compelled to seek the person inside. She was an old Romany woman, a woman of the wilderness, a fortune-teller. There were tears in my eyes as she led me to her wretched fire. Fate, she told me, had foretold my arrival. She took my hand and began to read in its lines that which was concealed to my knowing." He held up a great hand, staring at his unstained glove as if it covered a secret shame. "I asked her to tell me what my own faith forbade me to know, as I could no longer live with the uncertainty of my existence.

"'Thou hast been cursed by God,' she told me. A torment that would consume the life from my bones. Little by little, it would eat away my life until the only welcome respite would be death. There was but one way to remove the curse, a method she would not suffer to speak. I fell upon my knees and implored her to give me the cure.

"When my supplication would not make her yield, I took her throat in my hands. Her old eyes showed no fear, yet in that moment I would have avenged upon her what God had trespassed upon me. 'Take heed, Herr Graf,' she said to me. 'It is by coercion that I tell you this. To be freed, thou must not direct thy murderous thoughts at me, but Christ Himself, to save thyself.'

"I ran from that terrible place in agony. But as I forced my horse through the forest, I could not outpace her voice following me in the darkness. 'When the leaden idol of Christ is dead,' it whispered, 'thou canst find the golden truth of Christ.'"

The Count grabbed Johann's wrist. "You see, Johann, when I heard of your father's death, I understood at last. Pfarrer Kelp, with his doctrines and platitudes, was the leaden idol of Christ, as was my child. You have destroyed your father as I had destroyed my son. We, you and I, who have been left in this vale of tears are now free to pierce the veil of idolatry. Do you understand?"

Johann pulled back his arm. "I understand, Herr Graf," he said, although he was frightened beyond understanding.

"The resources I had intended for my own child were meant not for him, but for you. You and I possess the secret of the *lapis philosophorum.* You will inherit the secret of the spiritual alchemy, I can provide you the secret of material alchemy. I have the power to transform your pitiful leaden life into gold."

Count Valentin reached inside his coat and brought out a scroll tied with a white ribbon. "I have made you my heir," he said. "This paper is the notarized document of testimony. You will go to the University of Altdorf. I will make it possible for you. Upon reaching your twenty-first birthday, you will inherit the assets I had set aside for my son. You may spend them in any way, Johann, as you follow the great destiny that God has ordained for you, for you will bear the weight of the mantle of spiritual greatness."

Johann desperately wanted to go on to school. He no longer had a home in Segesvár. He once dreamt about places where there were libraries, places where educated people discussed Scripture and natural philosophy. But he had buried those dreams in the Denndorf graveyard. Now they were being resurrected, only transformed from dreams into nightmares.

They both stared at the scroll. When Johann took it, it was only because he couldn't think to do anything else. As the paper left the hand of the Count, the man's body heaved with relief.

"I will not live to see the glorious and rosy dawn of your new day, my son. But I must warn you, Johann Kelp, that in the last days, perilous times shall come. Men will be lovers of themselves, covetous, proud, and blasphemous, ungrateful, and unholy. You will come to know trucebreakers, false accusers, and those that will despise you for your goodness. Above all, Johann, beware those who merely have the form of godliness but deny the power thereof."

He wanted to run away. He wanted his mother to come into that dark, wet tunnel and hold him so he wouldn't cry. Instead, it was his father's spirit that came, appearing between the pounding beats of his heart. He looked back to the Count, meeting his gaze at last as a man to another man.

"Revelation," he said firmly, "chapter twelve, one through six. And *Second Epistle to Timothy*, chapter three. Were you not quoting, Herr Graf?"

There was a long silence. From outside the tunnel, far above the city, the dove cooed again. Then, imperceptibly, a sound began to rise from deep inside the Count. It frightened Johann at first, then confused him, then astonished him. Valentin was laughing. He laughed until his entire body shook, scaring the denizens of the tunnel into flight. The man clasped his hand around Johann's fist. "Your Bürgermeister will see that you are taken care of while you remain in Segesvár. Zabanius will arrange for your entry into the University. God will provide the rest."

Johann followed him at a distance as Valentin returned up the street to where his coach was waiting. He watched the Count disappear into its mysterious interior and the driver whip the horses into a trot. He listened to the sounds of hoofbeats down the cobblestone street until they were lost in the morning.

His hand, he noticed, was holding the paper so tightly it was crumpling. He stayed there in the middle of the lane, gripping the scroll, until the return of the wool-carder's wagon made him move. He decided there was nothing to do but return to school.

The alley was quiet and empty of the voices of the Choir. It was only when he was nearly at the school door that something in the corner of his vision caught Johann's attention. It was a flash of movement—a dove perched on the red roof of the schoolhouse. For a long moment he watched the bird, sensing a presence in the tiny eyes that was oddly familiar. He wanted to know what sort of portent she was, and what she had been trying to tell him in the music of her song. Then suddenly, as if summoned by an unexpected destiny of her own, the dove disappeared into the clouds and fog.

Chapter Three

Wednesday, March 23, 1687
From: Augustus Hermann Francke, Frankfort, Germany
To: Daniel Falckner, University of Erfurth, Thuringia, Germany

Dear Daniel,

As clearly as I can see white paper in front of me, I can see dismay on your face, occasioned by the inordinate length of this letter. But I pray you to take the reins of your impatience, my friend, because I promise, if you read carefully my words, the time spent will be infinitely more worthwhile than whatever else might be entertaining you in Erfurth.

I arrived safely in Frankfort a few days ago, the trip having been uneventful. The reason for the visit—as I didn't have the opportunity to tell you before I left Erfurth—was an invitation from the Petersens to celebrate my twenty-fourth birthday with them, and also an occasion to meet some of their acquaintances, the list of whom I expected would include some peculiar characters.

Eleonore Petersen herself, whom you have not met, certainly falls into that said category. As a young girl (then simply Eleonore von Merlau) she apparently had been subject to the most extraordinary visions—the most celebrated of which was the conversion of the Jews and the sublimation of the Universal Church. This, I have no doubt, was what brought her to the attention of my good friend and mentor (you know of whom I speak), Philip Spener, of course. She and Spener have corresponded for years since, the two being of the same generation and of the same mystical outlook.

As for Petersen himself—he is a contented-looking gentleman of surprisingly modern outlook. (How could he not be, having married a character such as Eleonore?) In addition to having been Pfarrer for a parish in Hanover, he has been a professor of literature, and is well traveled. He appears to tolerate his wife's notoriety with good graces. The couple share good health, a more than comfortable life, and each are involved in writing books.

Eleonore took me on a tour of Frankfort today. This beautiful city, rightly named Helenopolis by the Romans, is full of wealthy citizens, the majority of whom are Calvinists and Jews. The Petersens' own home is situated where it has a magnificent view of the Mainz and the stately stone bridge over the same. I have to admit that it was only when my humble wagon plodded up in front of their home that I realized how accustomed to clerical austerity I have become.

Now this afternoon, upon our return from sightseeing, Petersen presented his wife a letter that had arrived by late post, having made its journey all the way from North America. If that strikes you as peculiar, Daniel, it also did me, and so I begged my hostess to explain.

It seems that the Petersens, encouraged to quite an extent by Spener, formed a Pietistic group here in Frankfort back in the seventies. These so-called Saalhof Pietists (they held their meetings in their own parlors or *Saales*, rather than in church) were quite materially blessed—a significant number of members having the means and desire to place some of their wealth at the disposal of some *philadelphian* cause. So, if you can believe me, Daniel, they formed a business they called the Frankfort Company and invested in property in North America. About three years ago—the year we had that terrible portentous winter—a fellow named Franz Pastorius sailed over there as their agent. Apparently he has established a little town he calls Germanopolis, but the expected emigration of German people to an uncivilized, undeveloped world has not taken place as they had hoped. I could not help but think, as Eleonore read aloud Pastorius' complaints, that sometimes an idealistic cleric such as myself might have more business sense than a burgher.

It was only later this evening that I gained insight into some not-so-public events by which such as the famed Petersens might have been inspired to such a venture. So, once again, Daniel, I beg you not to put down this letter half-unread, but bear with me. Something that will certainly peak your interest is about to be told.

It was about 6 o'clock, as the Petersens and I were enjoying the mild spring air and a dusky view of Frankfort from the open window of their *Saal,* that their guests—the presence of whom was my birthday gift—arrived at their door.

I will keep you guessing no longer, dear Daniel; it was none other than the lovely Anna Maria Schuckart. Unlike you, I had not had the pleasure of ever meeting this ravishing creature, but your descriptions of her (which I had thought exaggerated) did not even do her justice. She has the most extraordinary eyes. I believe that her hair, which she had pinned in a manner that allowed several curly locks to fall along the sides of her face, was of a color that Nature has saved only for her. But I need not waste paper or ink providing you with descriptions of things that you know from your own experience.

In addition to the *Fräulein,* we were graced with the company of a peculiar man named Johann Jakob Zimmerman, a gentleman from Hamburg, who, according to his introduction, had been hired by Eleonore to proofread her manuscript, *Conversations With God.* This Zimmerman is a man in his forties with a beard laced considerably in gray and a squareness of features that lends him an air of authority far beyond what one would expect from a mere proofreader.

We feasted on pheasant and imported mushrooms, and Petersen assured me that the wine was the very best vintage. It had been opened on that evening, he proclaimed, on behalf of my birthday, which was quite odd, as likely he knew that his guest of honor refrains from all alcohol. Nevertheless, the atmosphere was quite merry, and I found Zimmerman to be quite well versed in such surprising subjects as mathematics, optics, and the Kabalah. Sweet Anna Maria spoke very little during dinner, but when she did, she grabbed the attention of the entire company.

After the servant had cleared away the dishes, I supposed that the two ladies would retire by themselves, but such was not the case. Eleonore placed her hand upon that of Anna Maria and asked, "My dear, is there a chance that you can sense the Presences?"

The young lady closed her eyes for a moment and replied, "I can, my Lady."

Well, at this Eleonore nearly trembled with excitement and eagerly herded us into the *Saal.* This room seemed more a museum than the sitting room of a retired academic. Two Italian tapestries graced the walls, as did an illuminated Arabic scroll, and an oil painting of peasants' midsummer dance around the flames of the *Sonnenwend feuer.*

We sat down and our hostess closed the window (it now being dark) and put out the lights until only a single candle burned. "To whom am I speaking?" she asked. I was at first confused by the question, and then even more puzzled when the young woman replied, "Anna Maria Schuckart."

"Quite good, " Eleonore replied, and she continued her dance around the room, straightening the lace on the arms of chairs and whatnot. A servant came into the room, lit a fire and then withdrew. "To whom am I speaking?" Eleonore asked again.

"Anna...Maria...Schuckart..." This time the voice of the *Fräulein* sounded faint and distant.

Eleonore settled herself down and we sat listening to the sound of the fireplace. I was nearly losing patience when she asked for the third time, "To whom am I speaking?"

Anna Maria's eyes closed and her head swayed slightly. Her hair looked absolutely golden in the dim light. She opened her mouth and, in a voice quite different from her own, she said, "The Prophet of God."

Eleonore took in a sharp breath and held her hand in front of her mouth. I looked to see how Petersen and Zimmerman were taking all this, but neither one displayed a reaction. "Oh, Prophet of God, we welcome you to our company," Eleonore said to the maiden. "To whom do you wish to speak this evening?"

It took a moment (perhaps the Prophet had to make up his mind) until we heard, in that same peculiar voice, "The Augustine." The three others then looked over at me.

Eleonore's eyes were wide. She tiptoed over to me and, taking me out of the chair, whispered, "Kneel in front of her and take her hands." I did as she bid. Now I must interrupt my narrative, Daniel, long enough to say that her hands felt so soft in mine—her touch so smooth—that I found myself questioning the wisdom of celibacy. But, have no concerns, my friend. My vow to harness the sexual energies of the Elemental Body for spiritual purposes permits me only an aesthetic appreciation of the charms of beautiful women.

She, or rather the Prophet of God, then addressing me as 'Augustus Hermann,' began to speak of my future. "Great trials will be given to you because of your great strength. You are under the protection of God." (I must admit that these were quite encouraging words to hear, and the voice with which she spoke was oddly authoritative.) "With each trial thou facest, thou shalt take a step toward the Eternal. All praise to God!"

I heard Eleonore behind me eagerly add, "Amen!"

"Many children thy future holds," the voice said, and for a moment I wondered if she were able to read my thoughts considering the merits of married life. "The means of support for thy children shall be Divinely provided. Do not lose heart. A great destiny awaits thee." I looked over to Eleonore, who was even more wide-eyed than before. More in deference to her than of my own accord, I bowed my head to the *Fräulein* and said, "Thank you, Prophet of God."

As I fell back on my heels, Anna Maria (or the Prophet) spoke again. "Johanna Eleonore von Merlau Petersen. I call thee." And Eleonore took my place, kneeling in front of the young woman. "Art thou the one whom I have summoned?" the voice asked. (I wondered how this Prophet was able to foretell the future, yet not know who was in front of him.)

"I am she," Eleonore said.

"Johanna Eleonore von Merlau, bring me something that has come from very far," the voice commanded. Eleonore seemed a little puzzled and looked over to Petersen for help. He stood and searched the room for a minute or two, then brought over a small china statue of the Infant Samuel at prayer. Anna Maria took the thing in her hand and felt it as if she were blind. "Nein!" She threw the poor thing across the room, and it shattered against the wall. "Something that came from a distant land. Something that entered this house this day!"

For one brief but awkward moment I feared that she was referring to me, and that Petersen would put *me* in her lap, but Eleonore came to the rescue. "The letter," she said. "The letter from Pastorius. In the study." Petersen withdrew and returned almost instantly with it. He gave it to his wife, who put it into the hand of the *Fräulein.* Anna Maria then gave it the same sort of blind man's touch as she had done to the statue, but this time her head rolled backward and her whole body began to sway. She spoke again.

"There is an egg," she began. "An enormous egg lying dormant in the wilderness of a distant land. No one knows it is there but thee. To this egg comes a Friend of God, and into the egg he places another egg and no one knows it is there but thee. When the time for this egg has come, there emerges from it a bird of immense proportions—a falcon." (At this point, my dear Daniel Falckner, I started to wonder if this was referring to you, but apparently the Prophet changed his mind.) "No, not a falcon, an eagle—an eagle with head and tail feathers as snow. This eagle grows and gains in strength, and from its nest its wings spread across the earth. From its power no nation is safe and even our Fatherland falls victim to the grip of its razor-like talons.

"But heed the rest. It appears the strength of the eagle nothing can surpass. Time has all but obliterated the knowledge of the Friends of God. But within the eagle, unknown to itself, the second egg begins to hatch. Unsuspected, unseen, it waits for its time to come. As the world trembles in fear, the power of the eagle begins to weaken, and from the shell of its body emerges another bird—a dove, the selfsame dove that appeared over the head of Christ. The eagle crumbles into dust and only the dove remains—for the thousand-year reign of Christ has begun."

"Oh, Prophet of God," Eleonore then asked, "is this distant land of which you speak that which you told us to acquire? Is this

Friend of God of whom you speak the same Franz Pastorius whose letter you hold?"

For a quite long time Anna Maria said nothing. She continued to stroke the envelope until she had worked the contents loose, then began to stroke the letter. Her eyes were closed, but they began to twitch as if her beautiful face were being thrown into a fit. "The place of which I have spoken is the self-same land, " she murmured, "but there is another..."

What happened after that was truly astonishing. She cried out and her young body began to writhe in the leather chair. Eleonore took the girl's hands in hers as I had done and repeated, "To whom am I speaking? To whom am I speaking?"

From out of the mouth of the *Fräulein* (as I live and breathe, her lips did not move) came a voice so strange, so incongruous with the delicate face, I can not begin to describe it. "*Eli, Eli, lama sabachthani?*"

Tears began streaming down Eleonore's cheeks. "Am I speaking to Thee, Lord?" she asked. "Art Thou the Lord Himself?"

The fire in the hearth suddenly fell into coals and a cold draught swept down the chimney into the room. "*Vos dicitis quia ego sum,*" the voice replied in Latin. *Thou sayest that I am.*

Petersen rose to stoke the fire. Eleonore screamed and lifted her hands. By the light of the newly rekindled fire I could see her fingers covered with blood. When I went to her aid I witnessed, as plainly as I feel the pen in my hand this moment, blood pouring forth like perspiration from Anna Maria's palms. (This was attested to, not just by myself, but by Petersen and the proofreader Zimmerman, whose subsequent accounts accord with mine.)

By this time events had gone too far, even for Eleonore. "I am not worthy of Thy blood," she sobbed, "I am not worthy," on and on until she collapsed into Petersen's arms.

Zimmerman, unleashing a commanding tone in his voice, went over to the Fräulein and repeated, "Return to us, Anna Maria Schuckart," until I could bear the scene no longer and took my leave of the room.

It has only occurred to me now, hours later, as I sit at the desk in the Petersens' guest room, that the nails that pierced the physical form of the Christ were driven, not into His palms as is commonly represented, but into His wrists. Nonetheless the happenings as I described them did occur, but as to their significance, I will defer judgement for the moment.

But beyond the astonishing features of this evening, I find myself curious about Johann Jakob Zimmerman. Eleonore later confided in me that said Zimmerman is far more than her proofreader. At one time, had been one of Germany's finest mathematicians, a renowned astronomer, as well as a respected minister of the Lutheran Church. What transpired in his previous careers, she did not have any idea, although she seems certain he is in possession of occult secrets. It is rumored that he was, in some unexplained manner, responsible for the recent devastation of Würtemberg by the French army.

I am most interested in determining if any of this is correct. I will be leaving Frankfort on the morrow for Bavaria, where I will remain until summer, delivering a series of lectures on the current revolutionary state of religion in Germany. When I return to Erfurth, I intend to pursue the matter of Johann Jakob Zimmerman and determine if he is the occult genius my hostess would believe him to be, or simply a charming poseur.

As ever will pray &c.,
Augustus Hermann Francke

TRACTATUS
Theologo-Philosophicus,
In Libros tres distributus;
Quorum
I. } de { VITA.
II. } de { MORTE.
III. } de { RESURRECTIONE.
Cui inferuntur nonnulla Sapientiæ veteris, Adami infortunio superstitis, fragmenta: ex profundiori sacrarum Literarum sensu & lumine, atque ex limpidiori & liquidiori saniorum Philosophorum fonte hausta atque collecta,
dedicata
ANNO
CHRISTUS MUNDO VITA.

Chapter Four

Thursday, June 23, 1687
University of Altdorf, Bavaria, Germany

The sun was beginning to drop behind the empty campus buildings. Its disappearance would end the usefulness of the great sundial in front of the dormitory where Johann sat on a bench waiting. It would not matter, as time was gradually losing its meaning. The measured progress of hours and days had become so distorted that Johann felt he was trapped in an eternal psychic miasma.

His eyes hurt. He was always tired, at least until the time he wanted to sleep. Then he would be alert, far too alert, and afraid to blow out the candle and face the darkness. He would bundle the quilt he had brought with him to school and place it under his head. There he would lie, caught in a state between sleep and wakefulness. If somehow sleep came to him, it was a haunted sleep that pulled him back to Transylvania, where he would roam the church graveyard in Denndorf, waiting endlessly in his dreams for someone to return.

What he wanted most of all was to be able to turn himself around—to have enough vitality during the day to accomplish what was ahead of him, then to fall into sleep on a cushion of prayer. The former had been increasingly difficult. The latter was so foreign he could barely recall any feeling of reassurance.

If they had called him melancholy in Segesvár, it was only because he accepted the seriousness of life. But here at the University, struggling with life by himself, he had come to understand what melancholy truly was. It was a blanket that smothered rather than protected, defying him to escape its asphyxiation.

"Something of surpassing importance, Kelpius," is how his teacher had described his offer. Magister Fabricius, the Head of the Department of Theology, had Latinized his own name—and Johann's—after the fashion of learned men of the day. It had been meant as a compliment, but the price had been a constant reminder of his exile from his remaining vestige of family. "You are by far the brightest and most promising of students, Johannes, and I wish to have you assist me in the preparation of an *opus magnum.*"

To co-author a paper with the head of a department was an extraordinary honor for a pupil so painfully young. The treatise would compare an expanse of ancient philosophies with Christian doctrine. But the truth, the truth he could barely endure, was that he was no longer certain of the certainty of Christian doctrine.

In his room he had a stack of books that reached higher than the wooden edge of his bed—Augustine, Thaumaturgus, Tertullian, Meister Eck, Faustus. At the rate he was completing his studies, he would graduate with a Doctorate of Philosophy by the time he was sixteen. With his own dissertation and a collaboration with one of the University's most esteemed theologians, he was assured of a respectable and comfortable career in the Church.

Now he could barely concentrate on any part of it. The ramblings of all the philosophers, despite their eloquence, were unable to bring relief to his emptiness. Instead, when he could no longer endure the torture of hours alone, he would take out the only book in which he found solace.

"I knew the Bible from beginning to end, but could find no consolation in Holy Writ; and my spirit, as if moving in a great storm, arose in God, carrying with it my whole heart, mind and will and wrestled with the love and mercy of God, that his blessing might descend upon me, that my mind might be illuminated with his Holy Spirit, that I might understand His Will and be rid of my sorrow."

Jakob Behmen had lived as a cobbler in the early part of the seventeenth century. Failing in his effort to understand the ways of God, Behmen fell into melancholy, shattered and torn apart.

"I stood, fighting a battle with myself, until the light of the Spirit, a light entirely foreign to my unruly nature, began to break through the clouds and the power of darkness. Then my spirit broke through the doors of Hell, and penetrated even unto the innermost essence of its newly born divinity where it was received with great love, as a bridegroom welcomes his beloved bride."

The revelations that Behmen experienced, or claimed to have experienced, inspired volumes of complex religious philosophy. Some thought them highly original and others highly derivative, but on one point there was no disagreement—the Lutheran orthodoxy saw them as a threat. Yet even after years and years of Church persecution, Behmen would not be silenced.

"No word can express the great joy and triumph I experienced, as of a life out of death, as of a resurrection from the dead! While in this state, as I was walking through a field of flowers, I saw through the mystery of creation, the origin of this world and of all creatures. I learned what is His Will. I knew not how this happened to me, but my heart admired and praised the Lord for it!"

Johann would pass the long hours between yesterday and tomorrow feeling the depths of Behmen's melancholy but helpless to comprehend his ecstasy. He desperately wanted to discuss these new ideas. He would have welcomed the opinion of Magister Fabricius on Behmen's concept of God as *Grund* and *Ungrund*, Being and Non-being, the Foundation and the Abyss—to debate whether the qualities of Nature were keys to mystical union. But stronger than his enthusiasm was his fear. He knew the writings of Jakob Behmen were not appropriate reading for Lutheran Divinity students. They were *suspecta fidea.*

He never had any reason to look for mail—he never received any—and it was only from the prompting of his intuition that he had decided that morning to see if anything lay in the small wooden tray bearing the unfamiliar name of Kelpius.

Pietism,
The Kabalah
and

The Revival of the True Religion of Jesus,
The Christ
An Informative and Uplifting Lecture
By
Augustus Hermann Francke
June 23th, 1687
Seven o'clock
Schwartzhaus, University of Altdorf

It sounded as if it were the sort of event of which the authorities, even at such a liberal university, would not approve. But who else, beside Magister Fabricius, knew that he was still in the dormitory to receive mail? And who would know that he would have nothing to do but face the bleakness of another long summer evening? The great clock struck seven.

The tap of his sandals on the cobblestones echoed across the campus. There was an unreality to the sound, just as there was a desperate unreality to everything about Johann's existence. If he could only believe the feeling was simply the result of long weeks without enough sleep. If only someone would reassure him that it wasn't what he feared the most—that nothing was truly real, least of all himself.

He stumbled as he walked, or he only thought he had stumbled. It was a vision that intruded itself into his awareness. Like the sensations he experienced at night when waking and dreaming collided, the vision was palpable and frightening evidence of the fragility of reality.

He could not have described what he saw. It had entered his consciousness through internal rather than worldly light. What he saw was a threat made as concrete as a stone, hurtling toward him. He could hear it—but not through ears—as it shattered the transparent boundary between himself and darkness. It came without warning and he saw himself its innocent and bleeding victim.

By mercy the vision had dispersed by the time Johann reached the Schwartzhaus. Four adolescent boys were huddled outside the great arched door, gawking at the costly carriages grouped along the street. A thin boy in a tattered yellow cap pointed at him.

"Look at this little Jew-lover," he said, raising his voice. "Go home and suck your mother's *Zitze*."

Johann walked toward the door, keeping his eyes on the ground.

"He wants to learn black magic, Sprogel. He thinks it will give him the big *Schwanz*."

"God will damn your immortal soul, you little *Judenhure*."

A few more steps and he would be past them and up the three stone steps. He forced himself to breathe slowly.

"Hey, look at his eye!"

"He's winking at you, Sprogel. I think he wants you."

Johann felt the boy's spit land on his sandal. He looked up at eyes that were eager to hurt an easy victim. "Is that so, *Scheiffe*?"

A young man in a brown robe stepped between him and the boys. He wasn't much older than the others, but a full head taller. He had a youthful beard, too sparse to cover a complexion hopelessly marred by the scars of ugly blebs. But his dark eyes were clear and his sudden presence on the steps brought the smell of sandalwood and spice. There was an incongruous smile on his face. "'Why beholdest thou the mote in thy brother's eye,'" he said, "'but considereth not the log in thine own?' You lads should be more worried about your own souls than that of my good friend here. I suggest you move along. I am but a licentiate and not yet ordained, but I have the full authority of the Church of Martin Luther according to the Augsburg Confession to excommunicate all of you. You do not want to court eternal damnation, I am sure."

The boy named Sprogel backed away from the licentiate. "I wouldn't go in there, if I was you," he said.

"But you are not me," the licentiate replied. "And I am most heartily grateful to God the All-wise that you are not." He laughed and put a hand on Johann's shoulder. "Let us go inside, brother. I think we have both arrived late."

Johann didn't have a moment to breathe before the licentiate pushed him past the boys and through the door. "Licentiate Johann Gotfried Seelig," the young man said. His hand, like the rest of him, was long and thin. His fingernails were meticulously groomed.

"Danke..." Johann began. An elderly woman in the last row of chairs turned, holding her index finger to her lips. The licentiate walked up the aisle and sat down in the front.

The room was oppressive with sweat and perfume. The lecture hall of the Schwartzhaus was lined with large windows that served only to trap heat. Ladies in the audience were cooling themselves with fans, men with their hats. Johann sat in the rear, next to the elderly lady.

At the lectern stood Augustus Hermann Francke. He was much younger than Johann expected, only perhaps in his early twenties. Flowing blonde hair and oval eyes gave him an elfin appearance. "My beloved friends," he began, "listen to my words this evening, and if you are sincere, you shall find benefit in their wisdom. But I warn you, if you are not of honest and earnest heart, do not meddle in Divine Wisdom. If you rely only upon the form of religion for understanding, you will find nothing but confusion and danger for your soul. Only the deluded suppose that honor is due them because of the satisfactions of their dogma and the understanding of reason. Their pride prevents them from considering what abominable error they set up.

"Reason may be wise in its own sphere and help to Knowledge, but it must never arrogate such Wisdom and Knowledge to itself, as if they were in its own possession. Far superior to Reason is the glory of God, to Whom alone all Wisdom and Knowledge belongs."

There was an evangelical energy in Francke, one that seemed directed more toward provocation rather than instruction. Johann leaned forward in his chair.

"The blessed Augustine wrote that the religion known in his day as Christianity had been practiced prior to the time of the historical figure of Jesus the Nazarene. The Primitive Church was built of neither stone nor wood, but of members of small groups, bound under the direction of adepts, themselves part of a chain of spiritual masters reaching back to the human transition of Christ and beyond."

The elderly woman in the next chair shifted her feet. Chairs scraped against the floor. Johann fought back a reccurrence of his apprehension. Murmurs from the audience filled spaces between the speaker's words.

"The Kabalah," Francke said, "is commonly believed to be a system of Jewish magic. However widespread this notion, the truth is that the Kabalah is an instrument of mystical revelation, originally entrusted to Adam as the immutable inheritance of mankind. It is derived from the word *qibel*, meaning 'to receive,' in reference to the traditions of oral transmission. By its nature, the Kabalah cannot be communicated directly but may be expressed only through symbolism and metaphor. Its knowledge was given to Noah before he boarded the ark. It was used by King Solomon to gain mastery over the elements. Do you think that Jesus of Nazareth himself would not have been heir to these secrets?

"Prior to material manifestation, each soul contains complete potentialities—male and female aspects united together in one being. It is only through forgetfulness, experienced upon natal descent, that these essential aspects are perceived as separate. Thus, the term 'Perfected Man' is a misnomer—the true Perfected One is neither male nor female.

"Because that which belongs to the realm of Truth cannot be expressed in words, the Kabalah reveals that selfsame Truth in symbols, letters and numerals which unlock the mysteries of Scripture. Certain numbers are imbued with both sanctity and power, the number four and its numerical representation in the Arabic system being an example. The number ten, being the sum of four and its predecessors, as one plus two plus three plus four equals ten, then multiplies by four to produce *die Vierzig*, forty, regarded as the Perfect Number."

In the front row, silhouetted against the golden light of the window, Johann could see the back of Seelig, the licentiate. He sat with other robed figures, presumably all candidates for ordination in the Lutheran Church. Their arms were moving furiously, trying to capture each word on paper.

"In the First Era, the manifestation of the Old Testament, Moses wrought miracles upon the external world, the Macrocosm. In the Second Era, the manifestation of Christ, Jesus wrought miracles upon the body of man, the Microcosm. Now, we are witnessing the dawning of the third and final era, where the Holy Spirit has begun to exercise its miracles upon the Soul. Christ will not, as the Church imagines, return to vindicate its sterile dogma, but will reveal himself in the flesh through the medium of certain souls, fully perfected for His manifestation."

A man in front of Johann leaned into the ear of a companion. There was more murmuring in the audience. The lady next to Johann squirmed uncomfortably in her seat. Johann felt a wave of dread. A hand went up and Seelig rose in front. "On behalf of those of us who are ignorant," he asked, "would you expound upon the secret of the Four Men?"

Francke pulled the hair away from his face. "I would remind you, ladies and gentlemen of Bavaria," he said, "that you have come of your own free will, and are welcome to remove yourselves from the influence of the stings of knowledge. In fact, you would do well to avoid a Truth that calls you to be hated by your father and mother for His Name's Sake."

The room fell silent. Francke's mouth curled into a suggestion of a smile. "The Secret of the Four Men," he said, "is derived from an allegory, the understanding of which enables one to make sense of many supposedly obscure aspects of man's nature.

"The First Man is Unconscious Man, born from Adam, but an offspring of the earth. He pursues his own desires, his desire for pleasure, for safety, for aggrandizement of his temporal self. Upon mortal death, this Man is extinguished and returns bodily to the earthly substance of which he is composed.

"The Second Man is Religious Man, who sacrifices the pursuit of worldly satisfactions in favor of the rewards of Heaven. He is more refined than Unconscious Man, as water is more refined than earth. He renounces material trappings and takes on the trappings of his religion. His speech, his manner, his thoughts—he takes on all in accordance with the Law and the Doctrine. To most, this Man represents the highest attainment of humanity. Nothing could be further from the truth, for thus were the Pharisees of old.

"The Third Man is Wise Man. When true wisdom is attained, the trappings of religion are seen for what they are. Wise Man comprehends secrets in Scriptures that Religious Man is too obtuse to understand. For him, the fulfillment of the law is not an end in itself, but a means of refinement of his inner being. As the air, he is pure. As the air, he may be anywhere but be unseen by men. He may be known only by the effects of his actions. Thus were the prophets and the Apostles.

"The Fourth Man is the Perfected One. This Man is no longer bound to the religious path, neither in its exoteric nor its esoteric form. As fire reaches above air, he is beyond law and Scriptures. As fire consumes the fuel that feeds it, he consumes his lower self and becomes a pure light of Divine Power. *'That substance which hath a fiery color, and is penetrating and changing to impure earth, this thou must extract out of the water, that thou mayest have fire obtained from water,'* speaks the Kabalah. When the Alchemist speaks his secret language, he refers to the process by which the water of Religious Man, with all its crudity and bibliolatry, is transformed into the fire of the Perfected One. By his heat, the sick are healed and demons expelled. The man of fire is the true Christian—the Perfected One who is not a mere worshipper of Christ, but one who has allowed Christ to resurrect through his own transformed self."

A man brushed past Johann, hardly bothering to avoid his feet in his rush. First two, then four others rose from their seats and left. The elderly woman turned to Johann, glaring as if his own presence in the room somehow added to the heresy.

"As Christ was born in a stable and cradled in a manger," Francke was saying over the noise, "so is Christ in man ever born amidst the animals in man. The new-born Savior is ever laid in a cradle between the ox of self-will and the ass of ignorance, in the stable of the animal condition in man; and from thence the Herod of pride finds his kingdom endangered, and seeks to kill the child, who is to become the ruler of the 'New Jerusalem' in man. The Church of Luther has become as tainted at the Church of Rome and placed a new Herod upon a throne.

"My good ladies and gentlemen, you must ask yourselves whether..."

Whatever Francke wanted his audience to ask itself, Johann could not hear. Everyone seemed to rise at once, and Johann suddenly found himself swimming against a current of rushing adults. Their outrage frightened him. He was pushed out of the way by someone, a burly man who was whispering something about the burning of heretics. It was an all-too-familiar fear, and for a moment the memory of his father's stick returned to him as the unavoidable pain of disobedience. He thought to run back to his dormitory, to bury Behmen's book where no one would ever find it, and retreat to the hypocritical safety of a faith in which he no longer believed.

Johann was certain he would have left at that moment if the vision had not re-appeared, alive and palpable once again, now transformed into the certainty of a premonition. As the adults swarmed around him, he could feel a blow to his head, as if he had been struck. It was a terrible blow and for one moment he saw the blood return, staining long blonde hair, flowing into oval eyes that sparkled with eagerness in their unorthodoxy. There was still time to prevent it.

The licentiates were at the podium, pressing Francke with questions. Someone used a tinder box to light a pair of lamps. "We have chosen a site on a hillside off the road to Nüremberg," Francke was telling the group. "I have sent someone ahead to gather brush to light the *Sonnenwend feuer.*"

"Magister, would you review for us the correct chants for the ritual?"

"Magister, how am I to know if I am truly perceiving the subtle impulses?"

Johann stood behind Francke, his back against the window. There was a movement in the shadows, made green by the deep magenta of the evening light. He was aware that someone was speaking to him, but the words seemed distant and irrelevant. "Brother," Seelig was asking, "will you join us in performing the rites of Saint John's Eve?"

Johann was unable to speak. Something was coming with blinding speed. It flooded his mind, sweeping away his hesitation in one awful swell. He had no time to call out. Instead, grabbing Francke's robe, he pulled with all his strength. The resistance gave way and they slid together to the floor. Then the window behind them exploded. There was a shower of glass followed by screams. Someone ran shouting into the street. Francke was on his knees, picking shards from his hair.

A voice screamed, "*Böser Feind,*" but Johann didn't know if the curse was meant for the one who had thrown the rock—or for them. Everyone began talking at once. "What is happening?" someone shouted.

Johann knew what was happening. It was exquisitely clear. A line was being drawn through his world, a line that could not be straddled, a line that was forcing him to make a choice. He rose to his feet, still shaken. His head was swimming. Someone helped Francke to stand, while others rushed to gather the Magister's scattered papers. Eventually the confusion died down, and the group found its way out the door, leaving Johann behind with the strewn pieces of broken window.

It took several moments before he realized someone was touching him on the shoulder. He turned and looked up into the dreadfully pock-marked face of Seelig, smiling at him in bright wonderment. "What is your name, Brother?"

Johann reached for the licentiate's hand. "Kelpius," he said. "Johannes Kelpius."

"We are grateful, Brother Kelpius." Seelig led him toward the door. "We are eternally grateful to have you with us."

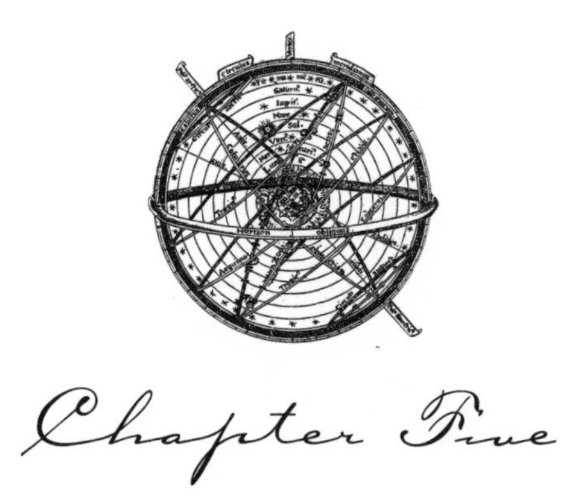

Chapter Five

Friday, September 23, 1687
From: Gotfried von Puffendorff of the Ducal Consistorium, Würtemberg, Germany
To: Reverend Augustus Hermann Francke, Erfurth, Thuringia, Germany

Reverend Sir,

I am writing in response to your request for information regarding the infamous heretic, Johann Jakob Zimmerman, former Diaconus of the Lutheran Church in Bietigheim. I must preface my report with an apology that I know little of your views on the circumstances that led up to recent tragic events here in Würtemberg. I am certain, however, that your devotion to Christ and commitment to the principles of the Augsburg Confession are quite *august* and therefore, I shall be quite *frank* in recounting the entire episode. (If you will pardon this little joke of mine!) I beg you to keep in mind that although some that I am about to write may offend, it is the offense of Zimmerman and not the humble writer of this missive. My responsibilities were only to collect and catalog the evidence.

I was first sent to Bietigheim in the spring of 1684. It is to all outward appearance a quaint and hospitable place, relatively free of vermin, Papists and Jews. The Lutheran *Stadtkirche* is quite an impressive building with an attached tower, built in a likewise impressive manner, reaching a good five stories high with a small windowed room on top. From these windows one can look out over all of Bietigheim, and a great deal further. It was in this same room where Zimmerman implicated himself beyond refutation. But

I am risking running ahead of myself and therein omitting some information that you might find edifying.

I took a room at a local *Gasthaus* along the *Hauptstraſſe* without giving any explanation, either true or specious, for my being there. The owner, a handsome and rather buxom widow, told me nothing about Zimmerman that would suggest she had any idea of the kind of man he really was. In fact, everyone in Bietigheim to whom I spoke reported the most flattering things about the man's character, piety, and intelligence, which they all claimed was second to none in all of Würtemberg.

According to hearsay, this man received his magisterial diploma in mathematics from Tübingen University and has been lauded by a considerable number as one of Europe's most skilled astronomers. After dabbling in the heresies of Copernican cosmology, Zimmerman became more and more involved in mystical speculations. Although we have never met, I am certain you would agree with me, Reverend Francke, that the intellectual mind tends to be too restless to remain content within the Consoling Arms of the Right and True Doctrine.

The reason for the absence of any true assessment of Zimmerman's character on the part of these simple and God-fearing folks eluded me for a time. At first I attributed it to the ingrained morality of the townspeople—that they would loathe committing the sin of gossip. But upon reflection, I recalled no other German town where malicious accusations, true or false, were ever far from the mouths of the people, given half an ear in which to place them.

The next day being the Sabbath, I took myself along with notebook, pen and ink to the morning service conducted by the Diaconus Zimmerman. Now this particular church, built nearly two hundred years ago, is as impressive on the inside as it is from the out. The altar is set back into its own wing, framed by a grand arch. Behind the pulpit rise three very tall arches of stained glass, through which the morning light shines and is reflected off the domed ceiling of the altar.

I had supposed that by positioning myself in the rearmost pew I would be alone and able to take notes on Zimmerman's behavior unobserved, but such was the sway he had over the community that the inhabitants of Bietigheim crowded the church to overflowing. When at last he entered the nave behind the crucifer, the power of his presence brought that entire congregation, vulgar peasants though they were, to a state of reverent expectation. He mounted the pulpit and began to speak.

"Almighty God," he began, "to you all hearts are open, all desires known, and from you no secrets are hid. But those of your people who seek to learn the truth, let them approach with caution, for Your truth accords neither with their doctrine nor their pride in which they cloak themselves in ignorance."

It was due to my own agitated state of mind, or perhaps a trick of the morning light upon the pulpit, but I felt as if the Diaconus Zimmerman were looking directly at me as he spoke these words.

"We shall begin this morning with words from the thirty-eighth chapter of the book of Isaiah. 'In those days,'" he read, "'was Hezekiah sick unto death. And Isaiah the prophet came unto him and said, Set thine house in order, for thou shalt die, and not live.

"'Then Hezekiah turned his face to the wall and prayed unto the Lord, weeping sorely. Then came the word of the Lord to Isaiah, saying, Go and say to Hezekiah, Thus saith the Lord, the God of David, thy Father, I have heard thy prayer, and I have seen thy tears. Behold, I will add unto thy days fifteen years.

"'And this shall be a sign unto thee from the Lord, that the Lord will do this thing that he hath spoken. *Behold, I will bring again the shadow of the degrees, which is gone down in the sundial of Achaz, ten degrees backward.*

"'So the sun returned ten degrees, by which degrees it was gone down.' Thus," said Zimmerman, "did God reverse Time itself, demonstrating His ascendant Power to the faithless generation of Hezekiah."

What followed...well, I once again beg you to keep in mind these words were simply transcribed by one innocent of their heresies.

"Beloved friends, to comprehend the deeply hidden science in this Scripture, one must bring a heart forsworn from slavish adherence to the damnable dogmas of the Church. And though the whole world should account him a scoundrel, and he should lose both honor and goods, nay, and the temporal life also, for the sake of his new choice, yet he must resolve firmly to abide by it."

"Where the way is hardest, there go," Zimmerman continued, "and what the world casts away, take up. What the world does, do not; but in all things walk contrary to the world. So you may, God willing, come nearest the way to that which you are seeking.

"Modern Faith is but an assent to doctrine and an acceptance of its form. Plain true Faith was never weaker, yet the Church cries, saying, 'We have the true Faith,' with a contention which has never been worse as long as men have been on earth."

At this point, my dear Reverend, I found that my hands could no longer transcribe another word, nay, another letter of such blasphemy. My entire body trembled, and I feared that the spirit of righteousness might flee from my bones, never to return. If you find it difficult to read these words of Zimmerman, knowing they came from the pulpit of a Lutheran Church (and so foully directed against that very same Church), you may imagine how difficult it was for me to hear them with my own ears. I was frozen with indignation until outright fury brought me to my feet and led me out the great door of the church, shaking as I gripped my book and pen.

You will readily believe me when I tell you that it took several hours and several frothy mugs of beer, so generously supplied by my hostess, until I was able to face the task that lay before me with anything resembling equanimity. But my duty was clear, and so it was that just before the hour of three I took my leave of the *Gasthaus* and, with sack in hand, made my way down the *Pfarrgasse* toward the rectory.

Providence (and the ancient fathers of Bietigheim) had placed a small alleyway along the street, and it was into this shadowy nook that I slipped surreptitiously to don my disguise. You see, I had cleverly anticipated the need for a ruse, and a rather roguish one I think it was. From my sack I put on a coarse wool robe, hooded to obscure my face. Even more clever was the false moustache I had obtained from a sympathetic theatrical performer from Hamburg. Into my belt I placed my faithful notebook, ink, and pen, ready to record evidence of what I was sure I would discover.

When the door of the rectory swung open to my knock, I must admit I was momentarily startled. The eyes of the woman in front of me, as they took stock of my appearance, were disconcertingly strong. They were the eyes of a woman of exceptional inner strength. Although she was only of average height, her presence made her stature seem greater, as the wave of her brown hair and trim jaw made her beauty seem perhaps more striking than it truly was.

"*Grüff Gott, gnädigste Frau.* Richtorius is my name," I said, glibly slipping into my assumed persona. "Tor Richtorius—a wandering Alchemist who has traveled a long, dry way to drink deeply from the fount of Wisdom."

She studied me for a moment, lingering a bit longer than I would have liked on the area of my upper lip. "If it is a tavern you're looking for, Herr Richtorius," she said abruptly, "I am afraid they are not open for business today."

The meaning of her response eluded me until, chuckling, I recalled the imagery I had employed in my introduction. "I am afraid you have misunderstood me, Frau Zimmerman. What I meant to say was that I have arrived to see Magister Zimmerman—to have him enlighten me with knowledge of the esoteric and occult. I, too, you see, am a follower of the Mystic Way." I gave the woman my most engaging smile, the one that had been working so well on my housekeeper. As expected, she returned my smile, albeit not quite in kind, as hers seemed tainted with what I could only describe as amusement.

"Step this way, Mystic Herr," she said, and she escorted me through a dark hallway to a door at the far end. Upon this she rapped thrice, and we waited until a commanding voice gave permission to enter.

There he sat, smug behind the elegant desk provided him by the very Church he was so wont to slander. Behind him a great window of leaded glass looked out onto a hidden garden. "A gentleman giving the name of Tor Richtorius has come to see you, *mein Gemahl.* He says he has traveled a long way to drink of your Mystic Wisdom."

Zimmerman said nothing. In fact, his eyes did not move from the papers in which he seemed engrossed. His wife politely withdrew, and I was left standing abandoned in the doorway. Not knowing how to proceed in the absence of his manners, I began to survey the room for evidence. Shamelessly mounted upon the dark wall to the right of his immense desk was a painting—a portrait of a robust man staring out of the gloom. The subject looked as if he were a burgher or some sort of merchant. I examined it closely. Attached to the gilded frame was a wooden plaque into which was burned the following epigram:

"If Peter fishes the Jews,
The Weaver enlists Gentiles.
Now both the Cobbler can nurture,
Because with Scripture he combines Nature,
And becomes a Power which Ananias despises."

The scoundrel thrust his head up from his desk. "Jakob Behmen," he said. "You must know him as the Cobbler of Görlitz. He was a simple man to whom God granted a vision of the most hidden secrets of the Universe. In Behmen's writings one can learn to read the mysteries of Life, written into Nature by God. Providing that is, Herr Seeker, one is sincere enough."

Now at this point, Reverend Francke, I knew I had sufficient evidence for the Consistorium. I mean to say, if those words are not proof of heresy, I do not know heresy when I see it. I am certain that you can clearly understand, as did the Consistorium, that Zimmerman was proclaiming that this aforementioned Behmen was greater than the Apostles! It was the words on this plaque, and of course my cleverness in transcribing them, that finally forced the Consistorium to take action.

"What, pray tell, Magister," I asked, slyly glancing at the papers upon his desk, "is the subject of your current intellectual inquiries?"

"It is an exegesis beyond your ability to comprehend, Herr Seeker. It concerns the anticipation of Copernican cosmology in the Scriptures, as revealed by the Kabalah. You must understand, my well-fed friend, that Truth is one, be it the truth of astronomy or the truth of Scripture."

"Magister," I said shuddering at his hubris, "I have a great interest in the meaning of celestial signs. I beg you to show me your instruments of star-gazing."

Zimmerman looked at me for a long and awkward moment. At the time I thought the uncomfortable feeling in my stomach was occasioned by fear that my false moustache had come loose. Little did I realize how soon I would learn the real source of that discomfort.

"Are you a seeker of Truth," he asked finally, "or a seeker of something else?" Of course I had no idea what he meant by this, or how to answer him, and I told him so. "I shall show you what you wish to see," he answered, "but I must warn you that it is not yet dark enough for you to see clearly. It is not dark enough now, Herr Richtorius, but it will be. I promise you, it will be very dark soon. Very dark indeed."

I had no idea about what the man was babbling. By the shadow on the great sundial in the *Hauptstraffe*, it was just the hour of three in the afternoon. What kind of ridiculous talk was this from a man acclaimed as one of Europe's finest minds?

He led me from the rectory through an arched opening into the church tower. Five stories we climbed to a locked door at the end of a dim landing. Zimmerman produced a key, put a hand on my shoulder, and pushed me across the threshold.

Standing in the center of the room that opened in front of me, like some gigantic three-legged insect, stood a great *perspicillum*, or telescope. Glass containers of herbs and liquids of various colors lined shelves. On one table, a book lay open, displaying a hexagon annotated with cryptic symbols. In fact, the same profane symbol had been painted on one wall. This was not the *Sternwarte*, the observatory, of an astronomer. It was the lair of an alchemist.

Brushing past me, he turned his back, and stared out the open windows over the red roofs of Bietigheim. I took the opportunity to peruse his collection—objects so close I could smell the profane odor of their loathsome magic.

"'And there shall be signs in the sun, and in the moon, and in the stars,'" he quoted suddenly, "'and upon the earth distress of nations, with perplexity; the sea and waves roaring; men's hearts failing after them for fear, and for looking after those things which are coming on the earth: for the powers of heaven shall be shaken.'"

"In this room I have set my study of the movements of the spheres," he said, speaking to the sky. "It was here that my calculations foretold the appearances of the recent comets. By applying laws of which you have no concept—such as those pertaining to the refraction of light—I have been able to penetrate mysteries long considered insolvable. What has emerged from this research has taken all my fortitude to endure.

"The End of Days is near, O Seeker. You, lost in your complacent and idle dreams, cannot comprehend the immanence of the nightmare that looms just outside your awareness. My great mentor, Brunnquell, and I are composing a treatise to warn this wayward generation of that which will come upon it as retribution for its errors."

Now in the event that you are unfamiliar with the names of the rogues of Würtemburg, Reverend Francke, I must explain that I fairly leapt from where I stood at the mention of this name. Ludwig Brunnquell was another heretic, a cleric who had been repeatedly warned by the powers of the Duchy to abandon his mystical speculations for the good of Wurtemburg as well as his own soul. Suffice it to say that the scoundrel has since suffered the consequences of his heedlessness.

"It is from supreme vanity that false Babel has been brought forth in the temporal powers of Europe, in which men rule and teach by the conclusions of cunning Reason alone, and have set the red dragon which is drunk in its own pride and self-desire, as a fair Virgin upon the Throne."

At this point the man turned from the window to face me. I had in my hand a small latched box, decorated with a golden six-pointed star embedded into the lid. Upon this star were undecipherable markings of occult aspect. Of course, I had not picked it up with any intention other than simply to aid me in my report. He obviously thought differently, because the mere sight of the object in my possession caused him to lunge forward.

"How dare you have the presumption to touch something about which you understand nothing and deserve to know even less? Give that to me instantly, and if you as much as put one finger to anything else in this room I shall lift you by your seeker's robe and throw you out the window." He grabbed the box from my hand. His face was positively flushed red.

He turned away from me again and for several minutes spoke not. In fact, the only sound I could hear was the afternoon breeze high above Bietigheim and his stertorous breathing as he tried to restore his composure.

"I should not have brought you here," he said at length. "But as you have traveled so far to discover the secrets that lie behind Jakob Zimmerman's power to discern the heavens, it is only fitting that I show them to you."

The man had a strange look in his eyes. A breeze blew into the room, and I was gripped with the fear of being alone in such a place with so obviously mad a man. He brought down from one of the shelves a small object hidden under purple velvet. "The understanding of Truth," he said, "requires both insight and a vehicle. The instrument I am about to show you is one such vehicle. It required more than ten years of searching and my entire estate to acquire it. By the power of its design, I have been able to calculate the planetary time by daylight or moonlight, the moment of sunrise and sunset, the place of the sun in the zodiac and the exact latitude and longitude of my observations.

"Behold the Horologium Achaz Hydrographicum, the sundial of Achaz, by which God has the power to reverse time!"

He pulled back the cloth, and I stared in horror at the profane object. Before me was a brazen plate about twelve inches across, held aloft from a decorated base, and engraved with curious lines, numbers both Arabic and Roman, and the zodiacal representations. Upon its rim was mounted a brazen homunculus—a turbaned man, Moorish in aspect, holding a staff. The top of his staff held fast a thread connected to the center of the plate.

Zimmerman then placed his instrument upon the table in a shaft of sunlight. Turning the rim until the Moorish figure faced north, the shadow of the thread fell upon the line marking the third hour after noon—the precise time. I felt the glare of Zimmerman's eyes upon me. "Does he take me for a fool," I asked myself, "to think that I would be impressed by a demonstration of a sundial?"

"You mistake your blindness to Scripture for reverence, Herr Richtorious—you and the cowards who command your strings. Your presumptions are only evidence of your ignorance. You must learn humility before He who commands the laws of space and time. Behold the miracle of Isaiah!"

The alchemist then poured upon the plate a liquid resembling water that filled its concave surface. As I am a witness for the one true Church of Jesus Christ, I stand by the incredible sight that met my eyes.

Time halted its inexorable progress and, in the remoteness of that ancient tower, reversed itself. The shadow fell backwards from the hour of three to the hour of two.

In that single moment I knew that Zimmerman was not simply a Diaconus who had overstepped the bounds of the Augsburg Confession. I knew he was a magician, who had been controlling the minds of the citizens of Bietigheim and had attempted to control mine by the use of an instrument of Satan.

Before my legs could buckle, I fled. I said nothing more to him, nothing to answer his taunting laughter. I ran down the stairs before he was able to exercise more of his forbidden powers. I had sufficient evidence for the Consistorium. It was never their intention for me to put my immortal soul at risk. Upon returning to the *Gasthaus*, I quickly gathered my belongings and bade a swift farewell to my most kind and toothsome hostess. In retrospect, I now see that her rather startled and confused demeanor was most likely due to the fact that, in my haste, I had forgotten to remove the false moustache from my face.

When I made my report, the Consistorium was most sympathetic. However, at the insistence of one of the more hidebound members, the portion of my story concerning Zimmerman's reversal of time was removed from the report, simply because he claimed it was "too lunatic a tale for any right-minded person to believe." Instead we based our case on three facts, namely:

1. Zimmerman's elevation of Jakob Behmen over the Apostles, as evidenced by the epigram which I had copied into my notes

2. Zimmerman's admitted collaboration with the infamous Ludwig Brunnquell, a convicted practitioner of magic and admitted promoter of the superstitions of Behmen

3. Zimmerman's denunciation of the Lutheran Church and its ecclesiastical establishment, from the pulpit of the same

Shortly after the completion of my report, Zimmerman was summoned to answer to the Consistorium, on behalf of the spiritual well-being of the Duchy. His attitude, rather than one of deference, was one of belligerence—an eventuality that I alone expected. I have to admit to you, Reverend, that although courage is one of my most recognized characteristics, I remained as inconspicuous as possible during the proceedings, avoiding visual contact with the Accused, stationing myself prudently behind the great drapery that graces the Meeting Hall.

Zimmerman conducted himself with such bad grace, it was an insult to the holy office that he held and the scholarly reputation he supposedly enjoyed. He refused all efforts to encourage him to recant, renounce, or in any way revise his views and prognostications. Instead, he claimed that the Ducal Consistorium itself represented the Anti-Christ. He then proceeded to threaten his native country, ranting and raving that Divine Judgment itself would cause a great calamity to befall the Duchy if its rulers took action against him.

What choice did we have but to convict this scoundrel of heresy? Should a man who desires to lead the people from the Lutheran doctrine be allowed a Diaconate of the Lutheran Church? Even his own friends at Court suffered the actions against him.

We stripped the man of his office and banished him, his wife, and children from Würtemberg. Never was the Consistorium so correct, so justified, so Divinely guided, as in taking this action. There was not a dissenting voice heard, other than the wild prophesizing of the destruction of the Duchy by Zimmerman himself. Should the Lord permit me to re-live the entire episode, I would not do one thing differently (save perhaps my several embarrassments with the hostess of the *Gasthaus*).

In answer to your final question, Diaconus Francke, I believe that said Zimmerman subsequently found himself a position in the

School of Mathematics at Heidelberg University, where his involvement in mystical speculations caused him as much secular controversy as it did sacred. I consider the whole affair to be a closed book, as it were. I have, to say it bluntly, no regrets.

There is only one thing, my dear sir, that on occasion still haunts me. Oft times I wake trembling in the night with sweat on my brow, and struggle to banish a persistent superstition from my conscience. I must remind myself, with the firmness one would use with an erring child, that the brutal destruction of Würtemberg by the French—the tragic loss of property and lives, so shortly after Zimmerman was deposed and exiled—was not truly the result of Divine Retribution for his expulsion and not any of my responsibility.

Dutybound in Christ,
Gotfried von Puffendorff, Secretary to the Ducal Consistorium, Würtemberg

Chapter Six

Thursday, December 24, 1691
Erfurth, Thuringia, Germany

It was cold, but the sun was shining through the leaves of the gnarled trees that protected the church graveyard in Denndorf. There he was again, abandoned and forgotten, left to wait for the return of someone who would once more take care of him. And then, miraculously it seemed, he heard his father. "*Grüff Gott,*" said the voice. "I have been waiting a long time to see you again, my son."

Where was he?

Around his shoulders he could sense his old quilt, the one his mother had called the Quilt of Many Colors. He tried to pull it tighter for warmth.

"Don't become cold, Hans," he heard his mother whisper. It was a name no one had called him in years.

Why *was* it so cold? The light looked so inviting, yet he was shivering. And why did his legs ache? The world was trembling. Something was bouncing him around, and he moved away from the brightness of his parents' comforting presence into a lonely darkness. Then it stopped.

The carriage door opened, letting in the flickering light of a lantern. "Erfurth," he heard the driver say. He tried to stretch. The driver reached inside and hoisted out his bag. Once he was outside, standing on unsteady legs, Johannes took in his first view of the ancient city of Erfurth. The cobblestone street was cold and empty, but the distant sound of a choir and candlelight from a dozen windows made it seem almost festive.

"*Heiliger Abend!*" said the driver, showing a nearly toothless smile. Johannes had nearly forgotten. It was the night when the Christian world watches for the appearance of its Savior. Would this man be able to recognize his Savior if he saw him, he wondered. What would have happened if it had been Christ arriving in Erfurth, instead of just a young teacher? He reached into his pocket and handed the man a coin. "*Vielen Dank*," he said.

He watched the carriage disappear into the shadows. For a full minute he stood in the cold wind, trying to wake up to the reality of where he was. Up to that moment, Erfurth had been more a symbol than an actual place. For years, the name had been part of nearly every hushed conversation on the rise of mysticism in Germany. Even in Sulzbach, where Johannes had been living, they talked of Erfurth, and its most famous—or infamous—citizen, Augustus Hermann Francke.

Clutching a piece of paper that had come out of his pocket with the coins, he took it to read by a window that glowed with *Lichtwochen* candelabra. He hadn't planned on it being so late when he arrived or so cold. He stuck the paper back in his pocket and lugged his bag through the streets to a lighted church along the *Mainzehofstraffe*. He walked himself inside, mostly for warmth and protection against the wind. The congregation was standing, crowded to the rear pew, listening to the haunting voice of a soprano leading them in song:

"*Es sterb was sterben muss So seis! Doch krieg ich lufft*
denn was in liebe brennt fürcht keine todes-grufft."

He sensed something in the air—something other than the smells of fir and Yule fires brought into the church in the coats of the worshippers. Instead of devotion, or even merriment, there was a palpable tension. He wasn't tall enough to see over the heads of the crowd, but he could imagine the Pfarrer, surrounded by the decorations of *Weihnachten*, giving the benediction. "*Dominus vobiscum.*"

"Et cum spiritu tuo."

"Ite, missa est."

Then, just as the worshippers were beginning to close their hymnals and gather themselves to leave, the voice spoke again from the nave. "*Sancte Michael Archangele, defende nos in praelio,*" it called. "Be our protection against the malice and snares of the devil. We humbly beseech God to command the Archangel Michael. And do thou, O Prince of the Heavenly Host, by the Divine Power thrust into hell Satan and the other evil spirits who roam through the world seeking the ruin of souls."

"*Deo gratias.*"

The organ blared and the crowd in the rear parted to make way for the acolytes. The Pfarrer, a gaunt man with deep-set eyes, followed them out. Johannes shivered as the procession passed. It wasn't as if he had expected it to be different. He had already heard rumors that the authorities had decided to move against the Pietists, the ones they called the Separatists. Arrests had been made. Francke, it was whispered, had been ex-communicated, arrested, or worse. But Francke was not the only person in Erfurth whose spiritual path led beyond the stone walls of the Church. His own friend J.G. Seelig lived there, too.

Outside the church, in the midst of the worshippers, he once again took the crumpled piece of paper from his pocket and held it under the light of the street lamp.

I can put no more to paper, for fear regarding these things. My Trust is in our higher calling, as is the Trust of A.H.F. If you have the resources and freedom, come to Erfurth in time for Christmas. I have sufficient room and board for us both, and your Presence here is urgently needed. Do not reply. Come. First house on left. Second fl. First door. Rumplegaffe, Erfurth.

Your Brother in Spirit,

J.G.S.

It had become increasingly lonely for him in Sulzbach, a terrible burden even for someone who was all too well acquainted with loneliness. Magister Fabricius had been unable to comprehend his refusal to accept the positions that had been offered. Johannes had thrown away—figuratively and literally—the Doctorate in Philosophy that had been so hard won at such an extraordinarily young age. Since leaving Altdorf, Johannes had devoted himself to efforts that would truly matter, the search for secrets that held humankind's only hope for redemption. He had read extensively of the writings and methods of Raymond Lully, Robert Fludd, the *Carbonari,* the *illuminati* and the other societies that had managed to survive in Europe despite the terror of ecclesiastical oppression. He eventually traveled to Sulzbach to study the Kabalah under the tutelage of the great hymnist, Knorr von Rosenroth.

Then one night by candlelight in his small room, he read Seelig's letter of Francke's activities in Erfuth. It was the eve of his eighteenth birthday, and he knew with inexorable certainty the path that his life would take. He disengaged himself from his studies, packed up what little belongings he had, and left to join Seelig.

His breath turned into a cloud as he asked a boy in the crowd the way to the *Rumplegaffe.* The child led him across the *Domplatz* of the University of Erfurth to the entrance to a dark alley. When they stopped, Johannes turned around, certain he could hear another pair of footsteps on the cobblestones behind them. He reached down to give the boy a coin. "*Fröhliche Weihnachten,*" he said, but the child had taken off down the street. When the sound of his running faded away, there was nothing in the air but the wind.

Shivering, Johannes dragged his bag through the first door and up a flight of rickety stairs. He stopped again, half listening, half fearing there would be no one to answer the door. He took a breath and knocked softly.

"Seelig?" he whispered.

A sliver of light appeared in the darkness and fell across the floor. "Kelpius?"

"*Grüff Gott,*" he whispered back. "I received your letter..."

"You have come just in time. Are you alone?" A tall, thin figure stepped through the doorway and glanced down the stairs. "No one has followed you here?"

"No one, I think..."

Seelig pulled him from the hallway into a bright and warm room. "*Grüff Gott*, my friend. It is good to see you. How was your journey? Here, let me take all your things."

Johannes dropped his bag on the floor, waiting for his eyes to adjust to the light. There were glowing embers in a fireplace against the outside wall, opposite him. "You must be tired and hungry,"

Seelig said. He swept a pile of papers from a wooden stool. "Please sit down."

A small bed to the left was piled with books. In front of the fire, a pillow and a roll of blankets looked as if they had been set out for a guest. To the right, two long and narrow tables against the wall, full of wooden tools and stacks of curly, dried leather. They were the trappings of Seelig's outer life. "Have you been well, Seelig?" he asked. "Have you been...are you safe and sound?"

Seelig had aged. His beard was fuller, covering more of his terrible complexion, and the dark hair that framed his long face fell well across his shoulders. He smiled and waved a hand at his clutter. "My father was uncomfortable when I told him that I had been attending Francke's *Collegia Pietatis*. He turned me out on my own, and ever since I have been earning my way as a book-binder."

He followed the motion of Seelig's hand and then looked back at his friend, studying his face. "That was not what I was asking," he said, sounding harsher than he had intended. "Forgive me, Seelig. It was just that I have heard so many rumors. And then your letter..."

The smile faded. "You must understand first, Kelpius, that it was not my idea to bring you here."

It seemed unnecessarily cruel. "No, Seelig, first you must help me understand. I left my position to come here." He gestured to the bag on the floor. "Everything that I own..."

"Of course, my friend. You will understand. It is only that there are some things more important than personal safety." Seelig pulled another stool from beneath a table and set it near the fireplace. "Come sit, and I will explain." He uncovered a pot hanging near the fire and poured aromatic coffee into two mugs. He handed one to Johannes.

"There was an Inquisition," Seelig said, lowering his voice as if someone else were with them in the room. "They believed Francke was becoming a threat to their authority. People were brought in for questioning and arrests were made." He looked over to the stacks on the tables. "They outlawed our books. Possession of any material not deemed orthodox became a punishable offense. All private gatherings are now under suspicion."

A shudder went through Johannes. He wrapped his hand around his mug. "What happened to Francke?"

"It was September when they moved against him. He had too many friends for them to arrest him. They didn't want to risk the disorder a trial would have caused. Instead, they gave him twenty-four hours to leave the city."

"And he left?"

"He would have been imprisoned and perhaps tortured. He had no choice."

"But you do. Why are you still here? And why—why am I here?"

"This movement we are involved in—you and I, Kelpius—it is greater than anything the Inquisition can prevent." Seelig inched his stool closer. "The Church knew nothing about it, but Francke had formed a secret group—a revival of the ancient Circles of the Elect. We have a new Magister, a mathematician and astronomer from Würtemberg. He read your dissertation from Altdorf and recognized something in your work. When he discovered that you were my friend, he asked me to bring you to Erfurth. He wants to meet you."

"For what reason?"

Seelig took a slow drink from his mug. "He believes you to possess the 'Virtue.'"

Johannes stared into the dark eyes of his friend. "Why does he…?"

"He is a brilliant man, Kelpius. He holds an award from the English Royal Society for his astronomical discoveries. But he is also a Rosicrucian and his knowledge of the Kabalah is more powerful than anyone I have ever met. Anna Maria the Prophetess claims a revelation that he has a chosen place in history."

"And you, Seelig," Johannes asked, "do you believe that he does?"

"You will have a chance determine for yourself." The smile crept back to Seelig's face. "Tonight."

Hours later the two emerged from the *Rumplegaffe* like silhouettes before the street lamp. Johannes felt his heart pounding.

He tried to concentrate instead on the rhythm of their footsteps and the glow of their breath in the cold air. Then he thought he heard it again—someone on the cobblestones. He turned but could see nothing.

"Who is this?" A voice came from the darkness in front of them. "Is this Father Christmas, *Weihnachtsmann,* roaming the streets of Erfurth?"

Seelig stopped, half in the light of the street lamp, and Johannes fell into the shadow behind him. "*Fröhliche Weihnachten, mein guter Herr,*" Seelig said.

A stocky man with a bushy moustache stepped into the light. "Ah, Herr Seelig," he said. "*Grüß Gott.* It is strange to encounter anyone here so late on such a cold night." His black eyes looked past Seelig to Johannes. "I see you have not come out alone."

Seelig was silent for a long moment. "My cousin Hans, from Saxony, Herr Kriebel," he said. "He has come to Erfurth for the Holy Day."

"What is the matter with his eye, Herr Seelig?"

Seelig paused again, but did not turn around to look at Johannes. Instead, he drew a breath that came out like a stream of smoke. "My cousin suffers from fainting spells, Herr Kriebel. That is why we have come out. To take some fresh air. It has been our pleasure to speak to you, Herr Kriebel." He started to move along the street, away from the light. *"Gute Nacht."*

Johannes turned and tipped his hat, but Kriebel followed them.

"I suggest you return home forthwith," Kriebel said. "We have heard that practitioners of the Black Arts are afoot in Erfurth this night."

"We will be on our guard," Seelig said. "Thank you for the warning, Herr Kriebel."

"It is a pagan feast as well as *Weihnachten,* Herr Seelig." The man was on their heels. "It is a time when witches gather to invoke Satan."

"We will be most cautious, Herr Kriebel."

The man took a step in front of them. "Perhaps I should walk with you, Herr Seelig. To make sure that you and Herr Hans get back to your home safely." Johannes heard more footsteps. Kriebel turned. "Who goes there in the dark?" he asked the night.

Someone else was standing near them. "Herr Kriebel," called a voice.

"Who goes there in the dark?"

"Herr Kriebel, a carriage arrived in Erfurth this evening. Someone claims to have seen a man with the features and bearing of..."

"Of whom? Who is speaking?" Kriebel spun his head, trying to follow the sound. His own voice began to quaver. "Show yourself!"

"Get thee to the steps outside the *Stadtkirche*, Herr Kriebel. It is rumored that Augustus Hermann Francke has returned to Erfurth to seek his revenge. I have been sent to warn thee."

"Who says this? Show yourself!"

"Quickly! Make thy way with haste. I must warn others!" There was a sound of footsteps running past. For a moment Kriebel stood still. Johannes could make out the lines of the man's face—his mouth and eyes gaping. A moment later Kriebel turned and ran across the *Domplatz* in the direction of the church.

Then from the silence came laughter.

"He was right," Seelig said. "There are devils afoot tonight. Is that you, Falckner?"

"Come grab my hand," said the voice. "Let us not be seen by the street lamp together."

"I admire your boldness, Falckner. 'Francke has returned to Erfurth to seek his revenge!'" Seelig, imitating the gravity of the other's voice, fell into his own laughter.

"It was pure inspiration that entered into me. I knew that I had to effect a rescue, or else Kriebel would have been tucking the two of you into bed this night. Who is this with you, Seelig? Friend or foe?"

"A friend of mine for years, but eternally a Friend of God. Johannes Kelpius, meet Daniel Falckner."

Johannes felt a hand reach for his own and he shook it heartily. *"Grüff Gott,"* he said.

"Kelpius, the *Wunderkind* from Altdorf?" Falckner asked. "The Magister has been waiting a long time to meet you. Come. We shouldn't stay here any longer. Kriebel may come back looking for his witches."

Seelig pulled Johannes along through the blackness of the night until the three stopped behind a wall, out of the wind. He heard the sound of a flint being struck and in a moment saw a tiny flame ignited. In the instant the young man lit his lantern, Johannes could see his face—pale and handsome, with long curly hair. Falckner's eyes, like those of Augustus Francke, glistened with a mischievous brightness. When the door of the lantern snapped closed, there was only a spray of light on the street. "Come quickly," Falckner whispered.

The three walked silently along a dirt pathway that took them away from the lights of the University campus. Falckner led them through a maze of moss-covered stone walls. Ruins, thought Johannes. An abandoned church or some relic of the old University. Falckner stopped in front of an arched wooden door blocked by a fallen branch. Seelig moved the branch and opened the way through a colonnade into a dimly lit quadrangle.

Several dozen men, draped in robes, stood in a circle in the middle of the cold stone-tiled floor. Their heads moved in unison, swaying from left to right to a hypnotic rhythm. Johannes was frozen from the cold and from fright, but his attention was pulled irresistibly into the dark resonance of their chant.

"*La illaha—il alla—la illaha.*"

Beneath the sound someone was intoning. "I understand…"

"*Nichts,*" came the response. *"Nothing."*

"I intend…"

"*Nichts.*"

"I accomplish…"

"*Nichts.*"

There was something about the scene that was at the same time both strange and strangely compelling. He tried to bring into focus whatever it was, but the shadowy patterns of the swaying heads were making him dizzy.

"I pleasure in…"

"*Nichts.*"

"I boast of..."

"*Nichts.*"

Johannes felt himself led toward the circle, closer to where he could see the edges of light on faces, half-hidden in hoods. "I delight in..."

"*Nichts.*"

"*La illaha—il alla.*"

The droning of their voices fell imperceptibly until finally it was lost in silence. The waves of heads kept flowing in unbroken rhythm, with one exception. Opposite from where Johannes stood, a man lifted his hood. "When the visible is negated," he spoke, "the invisible is perceived." Even with his eyes closed, the determination of the man was clear from the sharpness of his cheekbones, outlined in the light of the brazier. "When self is negated, God is realized."

"*Jesu Christus. Jesu Christus.*" As gradually as the chant of the men had become quiet, so did it rise again, still wrapped in the rhythm of their movements. "*Jesu Christus. Jesu Christus.*"

"When the self is negated..." Johannes heard the words of the leader repeat in his mind. "When the self is negated..." He stared into the face across the circle of heads and wondered why he wanted more than anything to surrender himself to the exquisite extinction wrapped inside the words of their chant.

"I seek..."

"*Nichts.*"

"Naught but the living Word."

The world, his world, overflowed with souls desperately trying to protect, prop up, aggrandize their precious selves. In the hallways of the theologians, in the pulpits of the ordained, in the prayers of the self-righteous faithful, the process was exactly the same—only camouflaged with sanctification.

The Cross. Death. Negation. *Nichts.* He finally understood what had brought Seelig to Erfurth and sustained him in spite of the risks. Here, he realized, he had found the very essence of Christianity. Not a theory to be discussed and discussed again until its very intent was perverted into empty rhetoric.

This is the method, he thought. This is the Way.

The Cross. Death. Negation. *Nichts*. Resurrection. Eternal life. He could feel a subtle vibration as he began to lose sense of his body.

"*Jesu Christus. Jesu Christus.*"

"This is the most exalted and the most holy secret of Heaven," spoke the leader over the rising chant, "disclosed to us by God, revealed in the light of Nature."

Then suddenly and unexpectedly, the man opened his eyes, staring directly at Johannes it seemed, neither surprised nor surmising. But the intensity of his gaze was unnerving, and Johannes wanted to break its contact, to turn to Seelig for reassurance. Instead, it was Seelig who touched his sleeve. "That is the Magister," he whispered.

The Magister and two men at his sides left the circle, which closed as if healing a wound. Johannes watched the three disappear into the darkness, then a moment later he heard footsteps beside him. Seelig took hold of his arm and pulled him along. He could barely walk for his dizziness. His feet seemed to be meshed into the ground, separating and rejoining it like a set of turning gears.

"*Jesu Christus. Jesu Christus.*" Movement of shadows against stone arches. He was rising, losing himself. Farther away. Quieter. Darker. *Nichts*.

"Magister Johann Jakob Zimmerman," a voice said. The flare of the light of a candle being lit. The Magister's face was in front of him.

"*Grüß Gott.* I have been waiting a long time to see you again, my son," Zimmerman said.

They were standing in a small room away from the chanting circle. Another lantern was lit and hung from a hook, throwing patterns against the walls. He stumbled as he reached out to take the man's outstretched hand. He wasn't sure if he were awake or dreaming. "*Grüß Gott.* You must forgive me, *mein Guter Herr.*" He struggled to clear his thoughts. "If we have met before, I have forgotten."

"Your mind is a prisoner of time and space," Zimmerman said. "The illusion of physical death is strong and clouds our memories when we return to earth in different bodies. But the soul retains the knowledge of its history and returns the individual to those with whom it has a common destiny."

"Magister, I present Johannes Kelpius." Seelig's voice came from behind.

"The Transylvanian savant?" A young man with his face half-hidden in a hood stepped next to the Magister.

"*Mein Abgeordneter*," Zimmerman said. "The deputy of our Chapter, the eminent Henrich Köster. Henrich is tutor to the grandchildren of the Brandenburg Privy-councilor. He is also the first man to have purged centuries of translation errors from the German Bible. He is our living polyglot." Johannes extended his hand, which Köster took loosely. "Young Kelpius should make a worthy partner," the Magister said to Köster, "for your intellectual sparring."

Köster removed his hood. His complexion was that of a young man, less than thirty certainly, but his bearing had the confidence of maturity. A slight bump in his nose was exaggerated by the shadow across his face and the angle at which it was raised. He studied Johannes with narrow eyes. "You shall soon find," he said, "that pride in scholarship is a stumbling block here in the company of the Friends of God."

"What Henrich is intending to convey," Zimmerman said, "is that the spiritual perfection we seek is of a different kind than that understood by the world. Like our brethren of the thirteenth century who were made martyrs by the Church of Rome, we reject the ways of Satan and his material world. Our Chapter stands in their name, as a testament to the perennial triumph of the Divine against the Anti-Christ."

"'To renounce possession of all things material, to practice abstinence from all things physical, to work for neither gold nor pleasure, but only for the sake of God,'" chanted Köster.

"The creed of the *perfectii*, the Manicheanans, the Cathars, all those whom the Anti-Christ denounce as heretics, as your own scholarship, Herr Kelpius, has considered so insightfully. As you know, those who could bear the full weight of such a creed were known as the Perfect Ones. It is in honor of their spiritual patrimony we are known as the Chapter of Perfection."

"It is my honor to be your guest, Herr Magister," Johannes said.

"We have no guests," Köster said. "This is not a tea party for dilettantes."

Zimmerman put his hand on Köster's shoulder. "Our activities here are not for the benefit of observers or the curious. The influence of anyone present determines the effect on the entire process. Therefore everyone is a participant in what we do and what we evoke."

"Magister, the hour is nearly at hand." A rough voice belonged to a spectacled old man who seemed to have materialized beside them.

"Elias," the Magister said to him, "I present to you Johannes Kelpius, the brilliant young scholar from Altdorf. Kelpius, meet Elias Burgstaller, the greatest living alchemist in the Christian world."

Burgstaller's spectacles gleamed in the darkness of his hooded face. Johannes went to bow, but the motion made his head swim. "*Grüff Gott,*" he said. "It is an honor to be in your presence, Herr Burgstaller."

The alchemist gave a nod and slipped a wrinkled hand from his sleeve. He touched Johannes lightly on the chin, pushing his head to the left, then to the right. He ran his index finger slowly next to Johannes' left eye and across his droopy eyelid. The pale lines of his lips, Johannes could see as his face caught the light, were moving rapidly and silently.

"We welcome you back into the Chapter of Perfection, Johannes Kelpius." The Magister was speaking. Burgstaller's hand fell back into its sleeve. The alchemist nodded. There was a shuffling noise across the floor. Someone loosened Johannes' hat from the grip of his left hand. "Our circle has no discernable beginning, nor foreseeable ending. It is part of an enduring tradition of adepthood extending back through Adam." Incense was filling the air. The Magister closed his eyes, and Johannes was compelled to do the same. "You will enter into a sublime pact with those that have gone before." He heard the voice speaking softly but deliberately, articulating every syllable. "In doing thus, you pledge to accept and transmit the most ancient and secret knowledge of mankind as an initiate of the Order of the Elect."

"An initiate, Herr Zimmerman?" More shuffling. He didn't know if his words had been spoken loudly enough to be heard, or if they had been only thought. He felt the Magister's hands take his and place them in the posture of prayer, wrapping his around them. It was the way a mother would instruct a child, the way his own mother certainly must have once taught him, long ago.

"Inheritor of a dying world, we call thee to the living beauty. Wanderer in the wild darkness, we call thee to the gentle light. Long hast thou dwelt in darkness. Quit the night and seek the day," the Magister intoned. "Wilt thou pledge thy commitment to the same, without regard to sacrifice, without hesitation, without condition?"

Someone behind him removed his cloak, replacing its worn softness with the roughness of coarse wool. Incense was dancing in the back of his nose, the way it had done when his home had been cleansed of disease. He remembered the smell of incense, lingering carelessly in the air while he lay terrified of the power that could take his mother from him forever.

The Cross. Death. Negation. *Nichts.*

So let die that which must! Yet breathing still am I.

He forced his eyes to open. The Magister stood close to him, his face just inches away. Köster's eyes were closed. The alchemist Burgstaller was lost in the shadow of his hood. The lantern light looked like celestial patterns on the stone walls.

Resurrection. Eternal life.

For what in Love doth burn, will never fear to die.

"I pledge my commitment to the same," Johannes said, "without regard to sacrifice, without hesitation, without condition."

"Welcome back, my son," Zimmerman whispered.

"Let the ceremony of initiation commence," said Burgstaller.

Chapter Seven

Wednesday, March 23, 1692
From: Ludolph Köster, Amsterdam, Holland
To: Henrich Köster, Berlin, Saxony, Germany

My Dear Henrich,

Receiving this letter may come as somewhat of a surprise, but I pray not as an unpleasant one. I have no wish to begin where our last conversation left off, nor will I make reference to Father's letter of November last. What has been done is done, and that which has been spoken, especially in anger, cannot become unsaid. (You know to what I refer.) But I believe that God wants us to set right what has gone wrong, as I am sure you believe also.

Therefore I will not begin in the past, but in the present. This current tale of mine has a curious beginning, or rather not so curious because, as in most matters concerning myself, it starts with a book. In this particular case the book is an original version of *Libri Inquisitionis Tolonsanae*, which I had earnestly sought in order to verify my version of dubious authenticity. For over a year I had made inquiries, it seemed to me all over Christendom. So imagine my surprise to find that an authentic copy could be found here in Holland, in Rotterdam, in the collection of an Englishman—and a Quaker, if you can believe that!

First by way of explanation, in the event you are as ill-informed as I, "Quaker" is not the name by which they call themselves but is a sobriquet given them on the strange supposition that they are subject to agitated states of religious frenzy. In actual fact they style themselves the Society of "Friends," much the same as did the followers of Thauler four centuries ago, and as do members of a certain class of Saracen mystics. The founder of this so-called Quaker religion, an Englishman named Fox, was considered fanatical at least, and possibly deranged by the Church of England. He laid claim to having received some kind of prophecy or vision as to how Christianity should have been practiced for the past sixteen and a half hundred years. I discovered only a little of the precepts of this sect, but I daresay that you, Henrich, even with your Pietistic leanings, will find them as odd as I.

Firstly, these people think all Christian ritual is superfluous and declaim churches as unnecessary. Secondly, they consider Holy Scripture to be inferior to personal experience. Thirdly (this being the strangest of all), they deem any one of their members to be a "minister," requiring only that said member should "minister to others." Of course, this implies that women, the uneducated, even prisoners could rightfully call themselves "ministers" of this peculiar faith.

Naturally you would suppose that it would only be the desperate, the unschooled, and the denizens of the bottom-most rungs of society who would subscribe to such libertine nonsense, and in that, dear Henrich, you would be for the most part correct. So you will well appreciate my surprise when I traveled to the address of one of these Quakers in Rotterdam, only to arrive at an affluent home on the north side of the Wynstraat. Upon my knock, a tall, lean and rather disheveled fellow answered the door. Fearing I had been given misinformation, I asked him if he could direct me to the home of a Quaker gentleman by the name of Benjamin Furly.

He smiled, rather patronizingly I thought, and introduced himself, in flawless German, as Furly himself. "*Grüff Gott*, Herr Furly," I replied in as haughty a manner as I was able to produce, given my shock at being met at such a fine door by the householder himself. "My name is Ludolph Köster. We have a mutual friend, one Symon Jansen, who referred me to you in the matter of the *Libri Inquisitionis Tolonsanae*."

"Please come inside, Herr Köster," he said. He then conducted me into his counting house, which turned out to be more like a university library. The walls were lined to the ceiling with bookshelves, holding volumes numbering well into the thousands. We sat down at his desk, a fine piece of furniture well covered in papers but placed welcomingly by a sunlit window. I could hear, from somewhere above, laughter and crying, as well as an intermittent sound I can only classify as a bizarre type of drumming. "Please, forgive the noise," he begged. "My children."

I looked at him again—his threadbare gray coat and the band of black velvet around his head to contain his hair—and wondered how one man could contain so many paradoxes. It is unusual enough for a merchant to even take an interest in things of the mind, let alone collect such a library, unless, of course, the books were themselves matters of investment and trade. What, I wondered, would such an obviously wealthy man value in the tenets of the Quakers? And, even as a father of young children at such an age (the man appeared well above fifty), what sort of religion would tolerate such a lack of household discipline?

When I realized he had caught me staring thus, I felt ashamed at my lack of manners and moved my gaze down to the paper that had been rolled out over his desk. "Do you take an interest in map making, Herr Furly?" I asked. For the paper was indeed a map, considerably large and well used.

"For several years," Furly explained, "I have been acting on behalf of some property abroad." He removed the weights holding the sheet open and carefully turned it toward me. It showed a section of land bordered on the right by a river. The words "PENN'S" and "SYLVANIA" were written across its breadth. "William Penn, *&c Mitsgaders*" were prominent in the title block.

"William Penn?" I asked. I could have, and certainly should have, bitten my tongue at this point, for my impulses once again took hold of me (as they did when last I was with Father), and I blurted, "Is he not that peculiar Englishman who was imprisoned for refusing to doff his hat before the King?" If I had not known it while I was speaking, it was clear from the look on Furly's face that I had blundered. I recalled that this Penn character was a fellow Quaker to Furly (and another aristocratic one, at that), and realized all too late that, as an agent of Penn, Furly could hardly be unsympathetic with the man.

Furly settled back in his chair. "Herr Köster," he said with an intense sort of calm, "William Penn is one of my trusted associates, a man of honor and integrity, and a Friend of God. In spite of whatever well-meant tales you may have heard, Penn was imprisoned because of the fervor of his convictions. He is the sole proprietor of the largest property ever owned outright by any British subject. And do you have any idea, Herr Köster, what Penn plans to do with this territory? Do you suppose he wishes to declare himself Governor or even greater, and exercise power for his personal glory? Do you suppose that he wishes to realize profit from this land, to further his own interests and comforts?"

I knew not if the man actually wished an answer to these questions, but in fear of upsetting the conditions I thought to be necessary to bring my quest to a successful conclusion, I said rather meekly, "Pray, enlighten me further, Herr Furly."

It has been wisely said that one need be careful for what one prays, in the event he should receive it. It was never more so than in this case, as Furly related to me the entire personal history of said Penn. It seems that Penn's father was an admiral in the British Navy—of particular prominence and a reputation both for good and the reverse, depending upon whomsoever was occupying the English throne.

Young Penn had fallen into deep melancholy as an adolescent (according to Furly), and had been the recipient of a vision. An angel directed him to an itinerant preacher name Loe—a man whom he credits with "spiritualizing" him. Eventually Penn was drawn to the Quaker religion, primarily because it had something to do with acknowledging that "the laws of God live in the hearts of men" or some such ideology. (These mystical concepts you know far better than I, Henrich.) In any event, this commitment led Penn into direct conflict not only with the arbiters of local Anglican law and theology, but also with his headstrong father. (I am not the only one!)

Well, sometime back in the eighties, Penn realized that the English King was indebted to his family due to some actions on the part of the now deceased Admiral, and he (Penn) requested it be repaid by land in North America. This the King was more than willing to do, for I suspect that he, no more than I would, had little idea what to do with countless acres of inaccessible wilderness inhabited by hostile Indians. Well, it seems that Penn did have ideas and had them aplenty.

I thought I should die from impatience, but try as I did to steer the conversation back to the subject of books, Furly insisted on giving extensive account of the plans that Penn (and he, too, I imagined) had for this project of theirs. There is not enough paper in Holland for me to relate even half of Furly's hour-long exposition, but I will tell you enough for you to extract the essence, and in this you will get a sense of both an Englishman's dogged determination and a Quaker's naïve idealism.

The citizens of said province would have complete freedom of religion in practice and in worship (of this I applaud highly!) as well as voting rights for all men, landed or not (I doubt this will ever be workable). Blacks would not be allowed to be brought within the borders of the province (a deterrent to the slave trade), and those already in a state of slavery would be freed after a period of eight years. Penn's city would be a green and wholesome town with wide, tree-lined avenues, built with conscious intent, to avoid the crowded, unhealthy conditions we know all too well here. (Henrich, you should see London someday for yourself.) In short, just as the Quaker tenets themselves are, these and all of Penn's lofty *philadelphian* plans are quite appealing in their own way, but purely ridiculous in the realm of sensibility.

Just when I began to despair that neither Furly nor I would live long enough for him to finish, a sound like thunder coming from the rooms above brought Furly back to Rotterdam. "If you will please excuse me, Herr Köster," he said, rising quickly. "You will find my copy of *Inquisitionis Tolonsanae* along the second to top shelf near the wall on the right. It carries a seal of authentication from Philippus Limborch. You will have to use the ladder to reach it." He left the room, saying, "I shall return in but a moment."

Henrich, I lost no time in locating the volume. Although the cover and binding were identical in every way to mine, it was painfully obvious that I was the owner of a mere copy, one both inaccurate and modern compared to Furly's original. It is difficult to explain, Henrich, how angry and frustrated I felt at knowing that such a rare volume should be in the collection of a merchant who likely had little or no appreciation for the significance of the work. Even discounting the fact that the man was a Quaker and of peculiar outlook, it seemed unreasonable in every way that my long quest should end in such a bitter manner.

By the time Furly returned I was quite prepared to leave. "I do ask your pardon for such a rude interruption," he said and, when I told him that I had already completed my examination of the *Inquisitionis*, he offered, as some kind of compensation, "I have many rare volumes in which you might be interested, Herr Köster. Please, will you not take some time to examine them, also?"

I thanked him with as much warmth as I could muster and, declining to impose further on his hospitality, I took my leave of the Furly household.

To explain what next transpired, I need remind you, Henrich, that Rotterdam is an unusual city, having been built at, rather than above, sea level so that certain districts are accessible only by boat. It was to one of these districts, the Haaringvliet, that I needed to go, it being the home of Symon Jansen, a fellow bibliophile and agreeable friend—the very one, in fact, who had referred me to Furly. But to reach my destination required hiring one of the many flat boats that shuttle the residents of Rotterdam back and forth and are so necessary for the continuation of commerce and life.

While I was aboard one of these boats, I chanced to look down into the canal. It being a clear day, I could see my reflection in the moving water. Now any sensible person who took into account the distortions caused by the action of the boat's oars would have immediately dismissed the sight as a trick of light. I was not able to do so.

You see, Henrich, the reflection I saw in the water was not myself, but a demon that only resembled Ludolph Köster. At first I could hardly move, even my eyes, for the fear engendered in me by the vision. Then, using all my effort, I pulled my attention away and sat as still as a stone for the duration of the trip. The boatman, receiving both a *styver* and an absent look from me, asked solicitously after my health when at last we arrived at Number 40 Haaringvliet.

I was soon revived by the warm welcome I received by old Jansen. I told him that my business with Furly had come to a successful conclusion, and soon we were sharing a wonderful meal that had been prepared for my visit. We spoke of many things, including you, Henrich, and when I told him that you were still employed as special tutor for the grandchildren of the Privy-councilor to the Brandenburgs, he was impressed.

It was only after the meal, when his wife and daughter-in-law left us alone, that he spoke of Furly. "It was quite sad about Furly's wife," he said.

"In what way?" I asked.

"Do you not know? She died only a few months ago."

"I had no idea," I said, feeling a twinge of sympathy for the fellow.

"Yes, it was tragic. Our hearts continue to go out to the children. And to Furly as well. He is the most remarkable man I have ever known."

I could not restrain myself. "Tell me, Symon, what exactly does he do with all his books?"

Jansen took a sip of wine and smiled. "An excellent question, Ludolph. He does not really need them, of course."

"I thought not."

"His intellect, I am sure, contains all the knowledge he has collected in his library."

"Pardon me?" I asked, unsure if Jansen's German were faulty.

"That is what I mean by remarkable. Benjamin Furly is better versed in seven languages other than his native English than I am in my own Dutch. Did you not have the chance to examine his collection?" he asked. "French, Latin, Arabic, Greek, Hebrew. He himself has written some quite erudite tomes in five or six different languages. Many is the time I've discussed philosophy, history, or even literature with him, only to be bested by his command of the material he has read."

I am afraid I stammered. "I...I was not able to stay quite long enough to discover that particular aspect of the man, I suppose. As to his collection, it appeared to me to contain mostly curious books, *suspectæ fidei*, as it were."

"*Suspectæ fidei*?" Jansen repeated, and for the second time that day I felt as if I were facing Father in his disagreeable mood. "Ludolph, you are the last person I would expect to hear decry religious freedom." (How much does he know about me?) "It is one thing to sit within your little coterie and discuss the perniciousness of this or that Protestant sect. It is another to do what Benjamin Furly has undertaken—to use one's wealth and position to defend the rights of those whose only threats to society are their heart-held beliefs."

"I am certain," I told him, "that I have never looked upon things in quite that way."

"I'm certain you have not," he scolded. "Whenever the safety of the Quakers here has been threatened, do you know who publicly demanded that the bürgermeisters and regents take action?" (Dear God! Not more of these questions!) "When anyone with a voice other than the established churches wants to put forth his opinion in print, who provides both the money and means to do so? Who even stood up to his friend Penn against black slavery in North America?"

Jansen went on at some length in this manner, and I endured an increasing sense of discomfort. Finally, as if to offer me a reprieve, the day began to grow dark, and my host's wife, Mariecke, came and lit the lamps. Being exhausted by both my journey from Amsterdam and the day's events, I excused myself and retired to the room my hosts had prepared. However, I was in such a state that I lay awake in bed, turning to and fro for hours until sleep took me at last.

Now, I had omitted to describe that in addition to an excellently comfortable bed, the Jansens had provided me with a small table and chair, and on the former I had placed the copy of Scripture which I always take with me when traveling. That evening, due to my fatigue, I had skipped my evening ritual of Scriptural reading—a fact that alone would account for my difficulty in falling asleep. I mention this only to confirm that I never opened the book after I put it on the table.

And so it was, sometime after I had finally gotten to sleep, that I was visited by a peculiarly vivid dream. I dreamt that I was as I was, lying in a bed at Number 40 Haaringvliet in Rotterdam. In the dream I was awakened by a light shining in my eyes, and I awoke (as it were) to find an illuminated figure at the foot of the bed. Yes, Henrich, it had the mien of an angelic being. She was looking at me in the same manner that both Furly and Jansen had that very day—as if I were guilty of some mortal sin. The censorious look of those two men had moved little in my soul, but the same look, coming as it did from a supernatural creature, affected me to the extreme, and I cried out for mercy. The angel then opened the Bible that lay on the table, indicating with a single finger that it was a book to which my attention was to be drawn. I woke suddenly, my heart beating furiously and feeling overwhelmingly remorseful for all the transgressions I have ever committed, from the most distant to the most recent. I nearly leapt from under the covers and, kneeling in a pool of moonlight beside the bed, begged for Divine forgiveness. It was then that God opened my heart to the discomfort I had caused Father and showed me how scornful I was of you, dear Brother. After all, it was you who defended me when I gave up my life in Father's business to pursue classical studies.

But that was not all.

I must explain, Henrich, something that I had hoped never to have to confess. I understand now only too well that God does know all. The deplorable truth of the matter is, while Furly was absent from his library, I replaced his valuable and authentic book with my imitation, taking the original away with me. I assumed all too readily that it would make no difference to anyone in the world. Yet, by the time the morning sun found me slumped on the floor beside the bed, I understood that there is far more to be considered than this world alone.

A confessional is too small a cubicle to contain the regret that I felt, but I resolved then and there to go forthwith to set right as much as I could of what I have done wrong. Departing from Jansen and his family, I returned straightway to the Wynnstraat and, with my face scarlet, admitted my wrongdoing before Furly. To my surprise and relief, he seemed quite amused by the episode, urging me to keep the authentic copy as a gift (a noble gesture that was quite beyond my ability to accept). He then invited me inside for some coffee, an excellent American variety.

Henrich, I have written you thus, not for pleasure, for my transgressions are difficult to admit, especially to a brother such as you have been to me. As for your own difficulties, such as you had with my adopting the Catholic faith—for this I now forgive you readily. In fact, your influence in my life has been so great, and so beneficial, that I am grateful that I may be able to repay you with some influence of my own.

That morning I spoke at some length with Furly concerning you and the Chapter of Perfection. I told him, in as much detail as I was able, of the persecution which you and the Pietists have faced throughout Germany. I described the increasing threats upon your literature, your gatherings, and yea, even upon your very lives. He appeared more than sympathetic, even expressing a familiarity with, and a type of affinity for, the philosophies of Behmen, Raymond Lull, and others of your mystical heroes.

If, in the near future, you should receive an anonymous offer of help, and even if that offer seem extraordinary, I beg you to consider it well. You have for too long been living in danger. God has given you so much talent and opportunity that you need consider going to extreme lengths to protect yourself. I say this, not speculatively, but as you would prefer, by direct experience. For it was not for my sake alone that the angelic being appeared in my dream.

You see, Henrich, I discovered something else that morning—something that filled me with both a chilling bewilderment and a reverent sense of the majesty of God. To my great surprise, I found my Bible lying open on the desk, despite the fact that I knew with certainty it lay closed when I retired. A single passage stood out prominently from the remainder of the page. The verse was *Jeremiah*, nine, verse 2. Those words, even more than my aching conscience, had given me the impetus to return to Benjamin Furly, because I understood the terrible and awesome destiny that lies open to you.

Oh, that I had in the wilderness
a lodging place of wayfaring men;
That I might leave my people, and go from them!
For they be all adulterers,
and an assembly of treacherous men.

As in duty bound, will ever pray &c,
Ludolph

Chapter Eight

Tuesday, July 4, 1693
Near Detmold, Westphalia, Germany

"Look at him."

"It's the fever that's causing it."

"Geissler, fetch the Magister."

"No! He's resting. Don't disturb him."

Johannes jerked his arms in his sleep as if he were trying to escape from his quilt.

"Find Köster. He's sure to know what to do."

"I'm not looking for Köster."

"Neither am I."

"Geissler, you go. Just be quiet."

Johannes made a sound, muffled but loud enough to jolt him out of his fevered dream. He was covered in sweat.

"Look, he's woken himself up."

"Kelpius, how are you feeling?"

Johannes struggled, first to understand what he was being asked, then to decide if he should tell the truth. "I am awake," he said finally.

"Good thing," said Seelig. "You have been sleeping since yesterday afternoon."

He could hear drumming on the tent canvas. He heard Falckner say, "It's raining."

"Have I been…have you been…?" He tried to clear his mind.

There was a sudden draught of cool air and Köster, followed

by Daniel Geissler, stooped inside the dark tent. "Why has no one lit a lantern?" Köster asked. "Geissler, fetch one from the Magister's tent. And bring me his bag. But, for the sake of Heaven, do not wake him."

"How are you this morning, my friend?" Köster asked Johannes in slow and deliberate English.

"Köster, the fellow is on fire with fever. He doesn't need an English lesson."

"Warm and wet," Johannes answered in English. "*Und naff*," he translated. He pulled his hand out from under the quilt to wipe his forehead. "Is it time to…to break camp?"

"We are not going anywhere today," Falckner's voice said. "The Magister had chest pains yesterday after you took sick. He wants to spend the day resting. And besides…"

A drop of water spattered onto the blanket next to Johannes' head. "I know, it's raining."

It hadn't rained for nearly two weeks, since St. John's Eve— the day before they had started on a journey from which they never expected to return. Who but God, Kelpius had wondered that night, would ever know what they had given up in obedience to the Greater Design? It had been a steady, weeping rain, mourning all the careers that would never be fulfilled, the glorious achievements that would never be attained, the loving families that would never be reunited.

Six months before, Zimmerman had proposed to the Chapter of Perfection a seemingly insane plan. Henrich Köster had received an astounding offer that had been brought to their destiny by the Supreme Will. "*To depart from these coasts of Babylon,*" the offer read, *"to those American Plantations, being led thereunto by the guidance of the Divine Spirit. Seeing that all of you required worldly substance, that you might have a good ship, well provided for you to carry you into those places, wherein you might mind this one thing, to wit your Faith and Love in the Spirit.*" Twenty-four hundred acres had been offered by this anonymous benefactor for a sanctuary, an experiment, and a place for them to make manifest the Final Spiritual Fulfillment of mankind.

From the first time he heard Zimmerman's proposal, Johannes understood the risk and the sacrifice. When he listened to them discuss the idea, he felt almost ashamed at how relatively little would be demanded from him. Most of the members of the Chapter of Perfection, like Köster and Falckner, would be giving up opportunities and leaving behind beloved relatives. But Johannes had already renounced thoughts of worldly success, even the strange fortune that lay waiting in Transylvania for his twenty-first birthday. He had no family in any real sense of the word. He and his brother no longer shared either correspondence or a common surname. What was he leaving behind compared to the others?

A half of a year they spent making preparations. A few, especially those with wives and children, admitted that the plan asked more of them than they could give. But Zimmerman continued to stoke the fires of enthusiasm in the rest, determined to have a perfect number of forty souls to establish a New Jerusalem in a New World. To reach that number meant including some non-initiates like Daniel Geissler, a devoted and eager apprentice whom Köster had known in Berlin. By that rainy night of June twenty-third, there were exactly forty of them, a dozen or so families and the rest single men. And the next day, St. John's Day, had dawned bright and clear as if it were an inarguable sign of Divine Favor for the venture, the practicality of which was anything but inarguable.

Now, two weeks later it was raining again. Geissler entered Kelpius' tent with his long hair soaking wet, holding a black bag in one hand and a small lamp in the other. By its light Kelpius could see a circle of the intent faces of Falckner, Seelig, and Köster. Falckner had let his beard grow, giving his curly-haired head the look of a lion. Seelig's eyes were puffy and swollen, overtaken by concern. And Köster—Köster was smiling in a solicitous way. As Kelpius pulled himself to a sitting position, dizziness overcame him. "We shall have you back to health in no time," Köster said. "Everyone else, leave now. Geissler, see if you can find a blanket to throw over this tent. It is leaking like a sieve."

Geissler hooked the lamp to the tent pole, leaving Köster enough light to search through the Magister's bag. Köster brought out a pen, a vial filled with ink, and a piece of paper. Köster folded the paper carefully and tore off a small square. He checked the point of his pen and for a moment sat with his eyes closed. Johannes could hear his slow and deliberate breathing.

Then suddenly Köster popped the cork from the top of the vial and dipped the pen into the brown liquid. "*De materia proxima*," he whispered, "*ad materia ultima*." With a flourish he scribbled the shape of a six-pointed star—an equilateral triangle with another inverted over it—encircled with alchemical symbols. He turned to Kelpius. "Now take this and eat it."

Johannes took the paper and looked at it. "Eat it?"

"Put it in your mouth, Kelpius. I do not play games."

"Henrich..."

Köster lost his paternal look. "If you want to be cured by terrestrial means, Detmold is only an hour's walk from here. I am certain you can find a barber-surgeon with an ample supply of leeches. Or would you rather I wake the Magister?"

"No, it is just..."

"It is just that you lack faith, Kelpius. You live too much in your intellect. That is why you fell ill."

Johannes twisted his face and folded the paper into clumsy eighths. As deputy, Köster had more than his share of responsibilities. The overland trip to Rotterdam had been difficult enough to arrange. It was at his suggestion that the party had split into two groups to avoid attracting attention. Zimmerman had given him authority to decide how much cargo—how many books, how much alchemical and astronomical equipment—they could reasonably afford to take with them to Pennsylvania. But despite all the authority, Köster still seemed afraid that the others, and especially the young Transylvanian, would forget that he was the appointed deputy.

Johannes looked down at the piece of paper in his hand. Before he put it in his mouth, he turned to Köster. "What about chest pains, Henrich?" he said. "Should you not warn the Magister that he lacks faith, too?"

Köster smiled and shook his head. "Get some rest, young man. Rotterdam is still a long way off." He put the ink and pen into Zimmerman's bag and left, taking the lamp with him.

Johannes was left alone in the darkness of the tent, chewing and swallowing. He wiped his face with his sleeve and lay back down, hoping not to return to his nightmares. He started to count the drips as they fell from the top of the tent. Before ten he was back asleep.

What woke Johannes hours later was not another nightmare. It was a smell—something delicious mingling with the sweetness of perfumed soap.

"Herr Kelpius, would you like something to eat?"

As he opened his eyes, the young *Fräulein* Zimmerman was reaching across to daub his forehead with a cool cloth. He sat up suddenly, bringing his face close to hers. It also brought closer the aroma of her hair. Her eyes were tinged in green, and in the light of her candle they glistened like emeralds.

"Yes, *bitte*," he said when he realized she was waiting for an answer. She set down the candle and picked up a bowl. With a wooden spoon in her slender fingers she brought a mouthful of warm soup to his lips. He took the food as a baby would, staring into her eyes. Something rushed through him, something unfamiliar but so totally beguiling he had no idea how to respond.

"*Bitte*," he repeated, and when she smiled at him, he had no choice but to smile back. He took the bowl and the spoon from her.

"Take care not to spill," she said. He followed her eyes to his quilt. She picked up a corner with her fingers.

"My mother made it for me," he said in between mouthfuls. "She called it the Quilt of Many Colors, like the coat of Joseph. Her own mother had taught her Romany art, and my father told me that there is a secret blessing sewn into the design."

"It is beautiful." The girl stroked the fabric, just inches from his leg. They both stared into the colors—the intricate pattern that seemed to have neither beginning nor end. "Where are you from, Herr Kelpius?" she asked.

"Transylvania...*Siebenbürgen*," he said, giving her the German name.

Maria looked up. She was very pretty, but eleven days of walking along dirty roads had tarnished her charm with dust and weariness. Still, he thought to himself, this was what was meant in the Scriptures as the way to approach the being of Christ—to be as beautifully innocent as a virgin maiden.

"Your mother must miss you," she said. "That is very far away."

He bent his knees, pulling his legs back closer to him. "In truth," he said, "she is further than that. She died, you see, when I was very small. Of the plague."

"Oh, Herr Kelpius," she said, placing her hand on his. "I am so sorry for you."

He felt the blood rush to his cheeks. He moved his hand away and took another spoonful of soup. "Please do not be sorry for me, Maria. My mother and brethren are those who hear the word of God and do it."

Her forehead crinkled.

"Luke, eight, twenty-one," he explained.

She looked at him for a moment and then picked up the candle. "I should be getting back. Shall I tell Mother you are feeling better?"

It was only then he realized that he was. "Yes, much," he said. "What time is it?"

"I don't know. Late. I think I shall leave the tent open. There is more light outside, and the air is very pleasant."

She moved the cloth aside and he looked into the quiet summer evening. There was no sign that it had ever rained except the freshness of the air. "Where is everyone?" he asked.

"They have all left. Everyone save for Mother and Father and little Christoph. And you and me, of course. It stopped raining while you were asleep, and no one wanted to bother you. Henrich, I mean Herr Köster...he was very eager to get on the way. Herr Seelig was reluctant to leave with them. He wanted to be sure you were back to health, and to stay to help us carry our things, but Herr Köster insisted. He desperately wants to be there before the others reach Holland, and he reminded us very forcefully that he is Father's deputy."

"How is your father?"

"He's gone stargazing. Mother is concerned he is not getting enough rest."

Johannes finished the rest of the soup and handed back the bowl. "*Vielen dank*, Maria. Please thank your mother." He pulled off the quilt and slipped on his boots. "It was just what I needed to bring me back to health." He reached to help her step outside, but she had already taken his arm to help him. They stood together for a moment outside the tent, nearly eye to eye. She was two and a half years younger, but just as tall as he was.

"I'm pleased that you feel better," she said.

He looked up to the sky. "I think I will go and find your father."

Maria started back over the little hill that separated her family's tent from his. Then she stopped and turned. "Herr Kelpius," she called. In the lingering light of the summer evening, in her bare feet and white skirt, holding an empty bowl, she looked to Kelpius like the subject of a Flemish painting. "You are not like the others," she said.

Her words, spoken so kindly, shook him as if he were being wakened again. He thought—no, he knew for certain—that she was paying him a compliment. It was not in her nature to do anything else. But he had heard those words too often before, from his teachers, from his schoolmates, from his father. He hadn't expected to hear them from her.

"*Sehr liebenswürdig*," he said. *You are too kind.*

"*Gute Nacht!*" she called and disappeared from his view.

He stood there for a while thinking that he should have said something else.

He walked through the shadowy trees at the edge of their campsite. Zimmerman was bent over in a pasture on the far side of a fence with one eye fixed to his telescope. "*Grüß Gott*, Kelpius," he said. "Do you know how to correct observations for parallax distortions based on distance between the mean line of the observer and the center of the Earth?"

"Yes, Magister, if by that you permit reference to trigonometric tables."

"Of course, Kelpius, unless you have committed those tables to memory; in which case you would be the Magister and I the student." Zimmerman looked at him. "I see that Köster's cure took effect."

"Yes, Magister, but how...?"

"Make allowances for him, Kelpius. Henrich still takes you for an ordinary man, someone who needs drama to help fix his attention. When he was a student in Berlin, he enjoyed demonstrating transformations by using quicklime to create fiery explosions in water. It was no magic of his that healed you. It was Burgstaller's elixir."

"The *Essentia dulcis*?"

"Yes, that's right—the Tincture of Gold. We mix it with a stain that acts as ink. The symbols are purely for an emotional effect. The paper is just a vehicle."

"A vehicle?" Johannes swallowed back the memory of the taste in his mouth. "But does Köster know how to prepare the tincture?"

Zimmerman laughed. "Köster? Not likely. Burgstaller is the current keeper of the formula. He will remain the only living soul with its secret until he bequeaths it to another upon his death. Like the secret of the Philosopher's Stone, this is the way it has been since time immemorial. He gave us a supply to take with us to North America, fortunately for you."

"Yes, I suppose it was." Johannes couldn't keep from staring at the Magister's face, pale and weary. In spite of Zimmerman's reputation for being eccentric and unpredictable, Johannes felt safe within the Chapter of Perfection. And for that reason he had selfish concerns for the health of their teacher and leader.

"How are you feeling this evening, Magister?" he asked.

Zimmerman smiled. "It is Frau Zimmerman who worries over me," he said. "With just cause, sometimes. But at this moment, I have never felt better."

"If you would permit me to say so, Magister, I thought it peculiar that we both became sick at the same time. Of course, I realize that you were not actually sick..."

"Since you say you understand the use of trigonometry in parallax correction, do you know how to calculate the effects of solar cycles on terrestrial energy fields?"

This, Johannes thought, was the way his Magister usually conducted dialogs—suddenly shifting currents, pulling him out of the familiar rivers of thought. It was reassuring to hear Zimmerman sounding more like himself again, even if it were nearly impossible to predict the path of his discourse. "Magister," he admitted, "I do not believe that I have heard of..."

"Of course you never would have. I, myself, developed the system, based on applying Copernican mathematical models to theories of historical concentrations of cosmic energy. The Egyptians, for example, built the pyramids in specific localities to make use of power that is palpable only to those whose perceptions have been refined. The difficulty has been that these fields of power migrate, and there has never been a mathematical basis for predicting their movements. Up until now. Before we left Erfurth," he said, suddenly changing currents again, "I received a letter from Spener. What do you suppose he wrote?"

Johannes knew that no one else but Zimmerman would expect an answer to such a question. He paused, hoping for inspiration. "He thought it unadvised to leave Germany," he guessed. "Despite the dangers of remaining."

The Magister lifted his head from his notebook. "Yes, you are quite right. He suggested we stay in Magdeburg where the authorities are more tolerant and work to establish a new orthodoxy of Pietism. For all his good intentions, Spener is a man of ideas and not experience. He lacks the understanding that we are not running away. He does not comprehend that we are being inexorably led toward something by a power infinitely stronger than fear or hope—for a purpose greater than Spener can imagine."

For a year and a half, Johannes had been listening to Zimmerman's predictions, supported by a multitude of astronomical and scriptural evidence, of the immanent fulfillment of the Last Days. Zimmerman's case had been compelling. There were signs everywhere. The revelations of Behmen and Rosencruetz, according to Zimmerman, were some of the first harbingers that mankind was being prepared for entry into the glory and terrifying awe of a New Age.

And then there was the unexplainable.

For the last few years, no matter where in Germany he was, Johannes had heard reputable eyewitness accounts of extraordinary phenomena. And how could anyone explain what he himself had experienced deep within himself? All his life he had been pursued by voices and visions. The voices had made audible—but not to his physical ears—feelings that were hidden to others. The visions had been sometimes bewildering, sometimes portentous, sometimes profound. They did not come at his bidding and the force with which they came seemed incontrovertible evidence that Divine Reality was far greater than the world of the senses—even than the world of the mind. Logic, philosophy and theology, in comparison to the palpable touch of Sophia, Divine Wisdom, were less substantial than gossamer.

"In due respect, Magister," he said, "I am afraid I do not understand. Could you enlighten me on the relationship of terrestrial energy fields to Reverend Spener's letter?"

Zimmerman raised an eyebrow and began to smile. "For years, Kelpius, I have been attempting to develop a demonstrable system that would account for shifting centers of psychic energy throughout human history. Because the earth is not static and is in revolution around a stellar object which itself is not static, we are in constant motion through the Universe. These complex movements are the cause of the migration of the lines of terrestrial energy. What formerly required a resort to astrology for proof, I have accomplished mathematically.

"I have not taught this science to anyone but Köster. A shift is underway in the energy field that has influenced Europe for several centuries. This civilization is in decline, not simply as a result of immorality and ignorance. It is a cosmic necessity. A new power center will develop, centered eighty-three degrees, thirty minutes to the west. It is not by accident that we have been offered land at this time in that particular province of North America. Just as it was not without meaning that yesterday you experienced physical distress."

"Magister?"

"Yesterday we entered a nexus of negative vibratory energy, moving in advance of the shift of the major arc of the European field."

"That was why we fell sick?"

"Of course, it was very subtle. Only you and I were affected. Compared to what will be coming, it was as a candle flame to a holocaust. You must re-read my *Muthmassliche zeit-Bestimmung*, Kelpius. There has been no guesswork. My calculations have taken into account both empirical phenomena and numerological prophesy. I have been emptied of conjecture and filled with certainty."

Zimmerman put away his book and brought out from his bag an object covered in a velvet cloth. When he lifted the covering from the Horologium Achaz Hydrographicum, the tiny turbaned figure holding the staff gleamed like gold in the zodiacal light of the summer evening. "We have been privy—Achaz and I—to the revelation of that which has been deeply hidden. After generations waiting on the follies of the unworthy, they have made themselves known. Have you read Bruno's *De Immenso et Innumerabilibus*, Kelpius?"

"Yes, Magister."

"*Lucidum, Relucidum, Pellucidum*—we define these as the three principles of creation. As above, so below. A new world, a new man." The magister lifted the bowl over his head, whispering as if only the instrument were worthy of his confidences. "They have spoken to us, to Achaz and I. We will till the virgin soil of an untainted continent, to plant the seeds that will flourish for a thousand years, the fulfillment of the hidden prophesy of Moses. This will be our work, in the wilderness of America, as in the wilderness within ourselves. This is what the Spiritual Authorities have instructed me help manifest. You, too, are part of this work, Kelpius."

"Magister..." he hesitated.

"What is it, son?"

"Magister, while I was sick with fever this morning I...I woke from a nightmare, the sort of dream the Greeks called an *horasis*—a visitation. I thought it might be significant, but perhaps…"

"Perhaps I would like to hear it."

The world was taking on a strange quality as the daylight waned. In the grove of trees, night insects began singing. The sound of cowbells drifted from somewhere in the distance. Nearby, at the bottom of the pasture, a small pond glowed with an indefinable light as the land fell into shadows. "I am uncertain where to begin," Johannes said. "I was wandering through the graveyard beside the church where my father had been Pfarrer. I was searching for him, as if I had been sent there on an errand. I stumbled into a hole in the ground. It was a grave—an open grave." He squeezed his eyes. "At the bottom of the grave I saw my father's corpse. The grave suddenly became filled with water and his body began to float away. I reached out to grab it. I did not want him to leave, even though it was beyond my control. Then…"

"Yes, son?"

Johannes looked back to Zimmerman. "The instant my hand touched it, the water turned into—into fire. Then I woke." He paused to breathe. "Magister, what do you make of this?"

"Do you believe that this is a sign that your father's soul is in torment?"

"I do not know what to believe."

Zimmerman took a lantern, a pair of candles and a small tinderbox from his bag and started a flame. While it glowed, he lit the candles, putting one inside the lantern and handing the other to Johannes. Then, with care, he picked up the Horologium Achaz Hydrographicum. "Kelpius," he said, "take the light and follow me to yonder pond."

They walked silently together through the wet grass. The cool air of night drifted with them down to the edge of the pond. Zimmerman took the instrument, the Dial of Achaz, and slowly filled it with water. "Put the candle into the pond," he said.

Johannes looked puzzled. "That will extinguish the light, Magister."

Zimmerman shook his head. "Light can neither be created nor destroyed. Now do as I ask." Johannes knelt down, and the flame hissed as the wick touched the water. A thin stream of smoke swirled up and vanished into the air. "Now," said Zimmerman, "retrieve the fire."

Johannes looked up, but his teacher's face was only a shadow. "I am not able."

"Listen carefully, son. Your dream was a coalescence of impulses from the future. The death of your father represents the transcendence of your intellectual inheritance. The extraction of Fire from Water is an essential requirement of alchemical transformation. You have read Behmen. '*Who would believe that the Origin of Fire could be in Water?*' Someday you will be able to retrieve the fire you have hidden now. By then you will have reached the stage of Higher Understanding."

The eastern sky was beginning to brighten with the light of a rising moon. From where they stood, it looked as if there were a great conflagration just behind the hills, from the land they had left behind. Staring at the glow, Johannes felt suddenly lost, as though there were an infinite distance between where he was and where he wanted to be.

Watching him, Zimmerman said, "It is difficult to leave home, is it not, Kelpius?"

The night before Kelpius had left Segesvár, there also had been a midsummer moon. By its light he had forced himself to go through what was left of his father's library, to leave behind the books he wasn't able to take with him. His heart felt as if it were an anchor in his chest, trying to hold him against the current of change. From the shelf fell a book, *Epistulae Morales*, written by the Roman philosopher Seneca, a contemporary of Christ. His father apparently had once marked a passage, and the musty tome fell open as he picked it up. The words were written sixteen centuries before, when the ancient philosopher had been banished from his home for a crime he had not committed. Johannes had chanted those words to himself on the journey to the University of Altdorf. And he had chanted them to himself on St. John's Day while he sat alone as the brethren said their tearful farewells to their families.

"'I cannot go beyond my own country; for all is one,'" he quoted aloud to Zimmerman. *"'Into whatever land I come, it is my own. The*

greatest principle of virtue is a mind able to deal with visible and transitory things, then gradually trained to renounce them. Refined is he to whom his country is sweet. Strong is he to whom all countries are as his own. Truly perfect is he to whom the whole world is exile.'"

Zimmerman put his arm around him. It was a gesture of affection Johannes had seen the Magister make with his sons, but he could not remember his own father ever making such a display. The two men started up the hill toward the glimmer of Zimmerman's lantern and the odd three-legged silhouette of his telescope. "Kelpius," he heard the Magister say, "never grieve over the difference you feel between yourself and others. It is neither punishment nor curse. It is a blessing."

Kelpius forced a smile even though it was not likely his teacher could see him in the dim light.

A blessing for whom?

This bitter thought echoed back and forth until he grew worried it would escape from his mind. When they reached the top of the hill, Zimmerman set down the Dial of Achaz on a level spot where the tiny brazen figure waited for the moonlight to cast the shadow of the gnomon across the bowl. Then the Magister stood and rotated the barrel of his telescope in the direction of the bright planets appearing in the eastern sky. "It is a blessing," he said, "for the many that await you in the future."

Chapter Nine

From: Professor Oswald Jones, University of Pennsylvania, Philadelphia
To: Mistress Lydia Bielen, Flushing, Long Island, New York
Saturday, September 23, 1826

Dear Miss Bielen,

I regret that I have been unable to determine the origin or significance of the object you sent. As you suspected, it is genuine gold, and so I strongly suggest that you keep it safe. Apart from any historical or sentimental significance it may have, it would make an attractive object for theft.

It is true that the hexagon is a common symbol used by Rosicrucian and other mystical sects. The six-pointed star is typical of the diagrams found in European alchemical literature dating even as recently as the last century. A colleague of mine informed me that its origin lies with the alchemical symbols for fire and water, being triangles pointing upwards and downwards respectively. The superimposition of these symbols is supposed to be of some occult significance and, I am told, is related to the Masonic symbol of the compass. As I am not a Mason, I am not qualified to judge the truth of these matters.

The evidence that this design was used by the so-called "Hermits of the Wissahickon" is based on local oral traditions of the rites and practices of this supposedly Rosicrucian sect. In fact, so strongly was the hexagon associated with sorcery and the like that the symbol became the source of the "*hexenmeister*" tradition. It was in this way that the word "hex" entered the vernacular as a synonym for the use of black magic. As you probably know, the hexagon was adopted by some of the other "sect" people who followed the Pietists to America, inspired by their search for religious freedom. Variations of the six-sided diagram can today be seen, not simply as adornment for the homes and barns in some Pennsylvania-German communities, but as magical devices believed to protect the inhabitants from subtle elemental influences.

Regarding your question on the transmigration of souls, I do not know if these men held to such superstitions. Many of their mystically-minded contemporaries in Europe did profess a belief in reincarnation. This creed was often used to reconcile Christian redemption with what is called the Doctrine of Universal Restitution. In their minds, a soul who had not accepted the divinity of Christ (or whatever equivalent they held for salvation) would be reborn again and again until, made pure in the grace of God, it would escape death forever. I am curious what prompted your question, and what would give cause to a devout Lutheran young woman to think about such recondite matters.

Neither am I free to comment on the connection between the "hermits" and the "hermetic tradition" that is often associated with freemasonry. Both Jefferson and Franklin were born after the dissolution of the community along the Wissahickon sometimes referred to as the "Woman in the Wilderness." Whether or not these two American heroes were secret Rosicrucians or Freemasons, neither were born in Pennsylvania and so could not possibly have had any association with the German Pietists. As to initiatory Freemason lodges, I am afraid you will never learn anything of their secrets or their societies as women are strictly proscribed from membership.

Unfortunately, in this modern day, there is no longer a single living soul who could give us a contemporaneous account of the men to whom you refer. In the intervening years, Pennsylvania has changed from a wild territory into the great commonwealth that it is today. Some historians, it is true, doubt that the decayed structure along the ridge above the Wissahickon Gorge ever belonged to the "mystics" of whom you speak. There are no known recorded deeds to this property that pre-date the ownership by the Richter (Righter) family. Yet I know for a fact that during the War of Independence, a soldier in a Hessian encampment claimed to have seen the mystic emblem of the cross within a circle which is said to have crowned what he termed the "Cloister of Kelpius."

You see, Miss Bielen, the ways of this world are such that history is, in the main, written by those whose own culture has prevailed. The United States of America is an English country, and in spite of our pride in our tolerance, the stories of other peoples such as the Germans have taken a second (or third) place to the English. This is why Pennsylvania-German schoolchildren may be more familiar with the story of the Puritan Separatists of New England than the Pietists of Pennsylvania.

But we cannot blame those of English ancestry alone for this unfortunate lapse in our history.

There exists today in Germantown a small cemetery upon a hill between High and Haines Streets. The lot is now overgrown with weeds and briars and has become a dumping place for rubbish. This embarrassing sacrilege, which casts such a poor light upon our own German community, is due to supernatural tales surrounding the spot—eerie legends that have given the grounds its romantic name, *der Spuk-bühel*—the Spook Hill. Originally the cemetery had been chosen for its alignment with certain invisible forces that marked it out as particularly auspicious. It was laid out exactly forty feet square and consecrated in the manner of ancient and unknown rites. It is said to hold the remains of several members of The Woman in the Wilderness.

These men were sought out in their own generation as saints, then reviled in the next as wizards of the forbidden arts.

Some fourscore years ago, an English sea captain living on Catherine Street was called upon to make an extended journey to Africa. After the year allotted for the journey had elapsed, his young wife began to prepare eagerly for his return. Another long six months passed without a word of correspondence from anyone connected with the venture. You would certainly understand and sympathize, Miss Bielen, with this young Englishwoman, who was living alone in what was then only a remote colonial town. She grew increasingly distraught, casting herself at last upon prayer as her only source of consolation.

It was at this time that a German woman who ran the bakery at Fifth and Sansom suggested to the sea captain's wife that she seek help from a certain man who was reputed to be able to help when no other assistance could be found. This man, she explained, lived alone in a cabin hidden in the Wissahickon Valley just a few miles from Germantown. Thus the Englishwoman drew up her courage and, in spite of her doubts and her orthodox faith, made her way according to the instructions of the German baker to a remote hut, deep in the forest.

The occupant of the cabin was an old man clad in a long uncolored robe and sandals, a man who wore around his neck a small shell. The sage welcomed her and listened as she told of her distress over her husband's failure to return home and her anxiety over the lack of any word as to his condition. He instructed her then to kneel beside his hearth in prayer to God while he retired into another room, one that was hidden by a curtain. The woman did as she was bid, but long hours began to pass with no further sign of the pious hermit. Finally, her mounting doubts and curiosity drove all prayer from her heart, and she began to suspect that the old man had departed through some back egress, leaving her alone.

Drawing back a part of the curtain, the Englishwoman beheld the magician lying prone in an attitude as in death upon a wooden pallet. Terrified, the woman returned to her prayer, more conscientious than before. After what seemed to her an eternity, the sage re-entered the room. He then explained to her the circumstances that had prevented her husband from corresponding, and reassured her he was safe and sound in London and would be returning home to her shortly. The poor woman was exceedingly confused but grateful and comforted by the words of the hermit.

And indeed those words proved true as the sea captain did return home in due time as had been foretold. His wife was surprised to discover that the reasons for his inability to write to her were exactly as the hermit had told her. But it wasn't until her husband related to her the following incident that she began to understand the significance of what had occurred: On such-and-such a day (the very day when she visited the pious sage in the forest) the Englishman had been sitting in a public house in London when a stranger approached him, saying that his wife in Philadelphia was quite distressed over his long absence and his lack of writing. The captain was surprised at the intrusion but explained to the stranger his reasons for not writing and told him that his ship would be embarking for Pennsylvania forthwith. He described a man clad in a long homespun robe with a small shell hung around his neck.

As an historian, Miss Bielen, it is extremely difficult to assess the influence of those who cared nothing for fame during their lifetimes and even less for what might be remembered of them later. Sadly, I cannot add any further insights into what befell Johannes Kelpius or what became of his reputed Theosophical Experiment.

As Christians, we may claim to prize sanctity for its own sake, but in action we tend to judge a man by the degree and quality of his reputation. Those whose names are forgotten we assume are of little importance. I am familiar with the tale of the English captain's wife, not because of my profession, but because the German baker woman was the mother of my maternal grandfather.

Unfortunately, I have to tell you that it is highly improbable that the gold object you sent was ever the property of Johannes Kelpius. Through the help of a colleague, I was able to determine that the inscription is not Hebrew, but Arabic. There is not a shred of evidence, written or oral, that would suggest there was ever paynim or Saracen influence on any of the German Pietists. In fact, so strongly founded in Christian faith were the Pietists that they would certainly have despised anything associated with a culture that denied the divinity of the Lord.

From the small protrusions on the reverse side, I would propose that the star was used as an inlay, such as one might find ornamenting something of wood. That this is likely is further evidenced by the tiny scratches and creases. It appears that at one time someone pried it loose (rather quickly, I would guess) from where it had been inlaid and attempted to flatten it out later.

I wish you all the best in your endeavors in Flushing and in your career furthering education for American youth.

Yours sincerely,
Oswald Jones

encl.

P.S. The Arabic inscription, scratched as it is, reads either as *el Ward' iyah* or *al Warqa'iyah*. It means respectively either "the rosary," or "the dove."

Chapter Ten

Thursday, August 10, 1693
Rotterdam, Holland

Daniel Falckner stared at the pretty barmaid as she brought a pitcher of beer to the Englishman sitting with them in the sidewalk coffeehouse. "Köster is the one who is best versed in English."

Seelig leaned back in his chair. "Don't bother yourself looking for him. He and his brother left this morning for Haarlem."

"Haarlem? What is so fascinating up there?"

Johannes was leaning against the coffeehouse wall, staring into the face of the town's statute of Erasmus, wondering what the old philosopher would think of his stony immortality. He said, "They believe they are descendants of the Dutch Köster who invented printing."

"I've never heard of him," said Falckner.

"He lived most of his life in Germany. Apparently when this Köster tried to demonstrate his device to the people of Haarlem, they drove him out of the country for practicing black magic."

"Ha!" Seelig laughed. "A story that is all too familiar."

"I thought the Dutch would be more tolerant," said Falckner.

"Well, they must have had some time to reconsider," Johannes said, "at least a few generations later. Henrich says Haarlem now has a Köster Museum in its *Stadt-haus*."

"Kelpius, come sit," said Falckner. "You know a bit or two of English. This Englishman wants to know the reasons why we're traveling to North America. Explain it to him, and perhaps he will share some beer with us."

Falckner pulled a chair from an empty table and Johannes sat down next to the leather-faced man, extending an open hand. "Greetings to you, my friend," he said in English.

"You're a bit of a Prussian pip, now, aren't you?" The man smiled, showing wide spaces between yellow teeth.

Johannes, a little unsure, continued. "We are traveling across the ocean to promote Christian faith in the New World."

"I 'ave me a cousin wot's got a mate," the Englishman said, "who knows a bloke once went to Virginia. Now that's in North America, I'm near certain. 'E said Injun gals go 'round with their brown titties nekid and shakin' fer every white man to feast 'is horny little eyes upon."

The Englishman's gestures conveyed enough of his meaning to Johannes to make up for his odd dialect. Seelig and Falckner, both completely baffled, looked to their friend.

"He says he knows a man who once traveled to North America and became acquainted with Indians," Johannes offered as a translation.

Seelig seemed interested. "Ask him if his friend learnt anything of their spiritual beliefs or practices."

Johannes thought for a moment. "The man of which you speak, was he able to meet any Indians himself?"

"Well," the Englishman said with a snigger, "if you boys'll buy us another round o' beer, I'll tell ye how this bloke sez they gots them native gals to toot them sailor's horn pipes." His laugh was so infectious that Seelig and Falckner joined along.

"We have no money, my good friend," Johannes said with a forced smile. "We are religious pilgrims."

"Pilgrims ye be? Well, that's wot wit the costumes ye got on. I though ye was from some bloody fancy dress party. Well, never ye mind, mates." He slapped Johannes on the back. "I'll share me lot wit ye."

Johannes was struggling to think of the English word for "abstain" when he heard someone in the street calling for Köster.

"Geissler, we're over here," shouted Falckner.

Daniel Geissler ran out of the market crowd and up to their table. "Where is Henrich?" he asked, breathless.

"Gone to Haarlem," Falckner said. "What is the problem? We're not planning to leave for London until the day after tomorrow."

"Wot's smatter wit 'im?" asked the Englishman.

"Then the three of you just come," Geissler said. "It's the Magister..."

Seelig and Falckner stood suddenly, upsetting the table. "'Ey, where ye goin'? Wontcha 'ave a drink?" the Englishman asked.

Johannes felt tightness in his throat. "Thank you, my friend," he said. "We must go." He followed the others in the wake they had left, pushing through the crowded street. At the waterfront Geissler had left a boat waiting for them.

As the boatman rowed them across toward the Haaringvliet, low clouds blew in from the open sea, just beyond the city to the west. The silence of Seelig and Falckner, Johannes knew, was from fear, fear that Geissler might give voice to answers for their silent questions. Instead they sat with their eyes intent on their destination.

Johannes' heart was torn by a sense of disconnection. It intruded on his sense of concentration, his frantic need to stay present in this terrible moment. Helpless, he felt pulled into the currents of his own memory. Something he had left behind, not forgotten, but abandoned. Was he trying to reach back to it, or was it trying to reach him?

He found himself staring into the water. It was darkening along with the sky, and the wind was lifting tiny ripples into imitations of waves. A hundred white rolls, each looking as if it were a scroll of parchment paper held aloft by a gloved hand, skittered across the surface of the canal.

Mariecke, the widow of Symon Jansen, met them at the entrance to her home and paid the boatman. A mourning dove called out from one of the rooftops. As the sound of its cry disappeared, summer thunder rolled across the sky. Johannes listened as he stood at the doorstep, already aware of what he would find inside. In every window the curtains had been drawn.

The drawing room was stifling. It took a moment for Johannes' eyes to adjust to the lamplight, but it seemed more than a dozen people were crowded in the room. Someone was praying.

"*Pater noster, qui es in coelis. Sanctificetur nomen tuum.*" Maria Zimmerman had been sitting near the door. She stood as they entered and took Johannes by the hand. "I am so grateful that Geissler was able to find you," she whispered. He wasn't able to face the green pools of her eyes.

She led him to a room at the end of a hall. As they entered, Frau Zimmerman rose from the chair next to the bed in which the Magister lay. There was darkness around her eyes, and her hair was loose and unbrushed. She embraced Johannes, clutching his arms tightly, almost desperately. "Thanks be to God, thanks be to God, thanks be to God."

"Mother," Maria said. "Let us leave them alone."

Johannes was nearly petrified with fear. He sat down beside the bed, his legs weakening as they bent. The motion of the Magister's chest made a gruesome sound—like the heaving of oars in the canal. "Henrich has gone to Haarlem," Johannes said to him. "He did not know…"

"Kelpius."

"Yes, Magister?"

"Kelpius, will you open the curtains? I wish to have some light." Johannes stood up unsteadily and did as he was asked. "Kelpius," the Magister said again, "open the window." A draught of air, fresh and cool in advance of the coming storm, drifted into the room. So did another peal of distant thunder. "Kelpius, bring me my robe. It is hanging in the wardrobe."

He found it and brought it to the bed. The Magister was propped up, struggling to bring air into his congested lungs. His eyes were open, staring at the ceiling.

"Would you like for me to help you put it on?" Johannes asked.

A half-smile formed on Zimmerman's face. "No, my son. I wish for you to put it on."

He did not know how, but he found himself suddenly on his knees beside the bed. He was using all of his concentrated energy to keep tears from coming to his eyes. His intuition had been trying to prepare him, but he had refused to listen. The robe, the mantle, was the symbol of spiritual authority, of leadership. Of the position of Magister.

"No, Magister. I cannot." His mouth quivered and he bit his lower lip.

"Yes, Johannes, you can."

"The *Essentia dulcis*, Magister. It will restore you to health. Please..."

"No, son. I have asked and have received my answer. Do not think that you are taking the mantle from me so that I may die. I am dying so that you may assume the mantle. A great destiny has been prepared for you. You are the possessor of the Virtue, not I. My portion has only been as a conduit. I have not been worthy of more. Our appointed hours have come, Johannes. Mine to leave, yours to lead."

It was too much, too quickly. "No, Magister!"

"Kelpius, have you forgotten that the first lesson is obedience to your Teacher?"

"But, Köster..."

Zimmerman made a dismissive wave. "Henrich Köster wishes to lead. That is why he must learn to follow. You know how to follow. That is why you are able to lead. Now, son, assume the mantle."

Johannes realized he was clutching it in his hand. He stood unsteadily and wrapped himself in the coarse woolen robe. He blinked back tears.

"Excellent. You will have Maria trim the hem to your height."

"Magister..."

"Please do not regret that we will not be able to perform a ceremony. It is only an empty ritual. I have something far more important."

The curtains flapped as a breeze carried in the smell of the ocean. The water slapped against the stone walls of the house. It was as if the waves were rising into the room, flooding into the body of the Magister, pulling him down.

"Fifteen years ago I was newly a Diaconus," Zimmerman said in faltering breaths. "I fell ill with rheumatic fever. The surgeon in Bietigheim was unable to cure me, and I prepared to die. Frau

Zimmerman and I had just lost our first daughter in childbirth and were still in the throes of grief. From the depths of her broken heart, her prayers for my life were answered in the form of a visitor who had been guided to our church."

Zimmerman paused. His breath fought loudly through the tunnels of his lungs.

"Ludwig Brunnquell," said Johannes.

"There was no one else who could have saved me. Brunnquell was the greatest physician in Christendom since Paracelsus. He restored me to health. It was he who introduced me to the wisdom of Behmen, and opened my inner eye so that I might understand. My soul was spiritualized by his power. What I received from him I have tried in vain to repay with the remainder of my life. But his most important teaching I did not regard, and it has cost so many so much. I have had to pay for their suffering and for my grievous mistake."

"Magister, please..."

"Take my hand, Kelpius. Pledge to me before I die that you will not repeat my mistake. Pledge it to me, Kelpius. Pledge on the Name of the Living Christ."

He took Zimmerman's cold hand. "I pledge, Magister. On the Name of the Living Christ."

"Dear Kelpius, I shall miss you most of all." Zimmerman closed his eyes. "When the alchemist Agrippa was still young, he received a letter from Trithemius, Abbot of St. James at Wurzburg. In this letter was this advice, which Brunnquell confessed to despising, and which I too disregarded due to pride. But you, Kelpius, you must not despise it. You have pledged."

"I have pledged, Magister."

"No, Kelpius, it is thou who art the Magister."

Johannes looked down at the robe. Suddenly he was no longer able to hold back tears—tears that had been unshed for his father and for the mother that he had lost in his memory. They flowed from his heart and from his eyes as if they were waves lapping outside the open window. He turned his face away.

"'*Speak of things public to the public,*'" Zimmerman said slowly. "'*But of things lofty and secret only to the loftiest and most private of your friends. Hay to an ox and sugar to a parrot. Rightly interpret this, lest you be, as some others have been, trampled down by oxen.'*"

Johannes sobbed. His tears dripped from his cheeks to the robe.

"Brunnquell knew it would not be long until the Consistorium put an end to him. His freedom and his life were in danger, even while he stayed with us in Bietigheim. Before he left he gave me..."

Zimmerman stopped and rolled to his side. Thinking he was in pain, Johannes turned to help him, but his Teacher was reaching for something under the pillow. It was a latched wooden box with a gold six-pointed star embedded into the lid. He handed it to Johannes, trembling as he did so.

"Do you know what this is?" His words were barely audible.

Johannes knew, although he could not have explained how. He was holding in his hands a box that contained something so mysterious and elusive that hardly anyone alive believed it actually existed. The realization made him dizzy. He blinked away the tears to clear his vision. When he spoke, he could taste the salt on his lips. "*Al Warqa'iyah,*" he said. "The Dove."

"Yes, my son, it is as you say. Brunnquell received it as payment for healing the daughter of a Jew in Bavaria. It had been in the attic of their home for generations. They told him it had been given to them for safekeeping by Paracelsus himself. The Jews knew only that it was something of value. Brunnquell was terrified it would be found in his possession when he was arrested. He made me promise him an oath I would try to take it out of Europe. We both were aware of the consequences of it falling into the wrong hands. You understand, Johannes?"

"Yes," he whispered.

Zimmerman tried to speak but lost his breath. He gasped, pushing Johannes away. "Three injunctions must you make," he said weakly. "Three injunctions as I have made." He put his own hand around the hand Johannes had holding the box. "First, you must protect The Dove even at the cost of your own life."

What was there for him to say?

"I understand."

"Secondly, you must make certain that before you yourself shall die, you entrust it to one who is capable of understanding. If there is no one..."

"I understand."

"Lastly," Zimmerman's voice fell to a hush. Johannes leaned in closer to where he could smell the stench of death on his Teacher's breath. "You must tell no one of this. No one at all. None of the other brethren. You must understand, Kelpius. It must remain secret. *Unser Geheimnis,*" he whispered.

Johannes could feel himself being pulled away. The present dissolved into the past as the waves of Rotterdam flowed through his memory into one of the hidden passageways of Segesvár. "*Unser Geheimnis,*" Zimmerman repeated. *Our secret.*

He had not asked for this. Just as he had never asked for his education. Or his initiation. But he knew there was another Will working Its way through his life. Long ago he had forsaken hopes of his own in his belief in a greater Hope. He had accepted sacrifice as part of this renunciation. How could he not accept this?

In that extreme moment, when reason had fled and his heart felt turned inside out, he turned to the only resource he had left—prayer.

Fiat voluntas tua.

As he prayed, his mind gradually grew quiet. From the comfort he felt growing inside him, the confused patchwork of his life began to emerge as a pattern—as beautifully beguiling as his mother's quilt.

May Thy Will be done.

The words repeated and repeated as if the human incarnation of Jesus of Nazareth were present, initiating him with a sacred litany.

Johannes found himself again on his knees. How long he had lost sense of where he was he didn't know. It took seven words to bring him back to the sound of distant thunder and the salty smell of the air blowing through the window. Seven words that carried a meaning he hadn't fully understood when spoken by Zimmerman. Seven words that now brought a hundred responsibilities he had not had a mere hour before: *It is thou who art the Magister.*

He could hear Zimmerman singing almost inaudibly.

"'O Becreutzigte Liebe!
Ach nim mich doch mir!
Dass ich immer bleibe,
Ein Geiste mit dir."
Thou Lover crucified!
Oh, take me from 'Me!'
That ever may I abide
One Spirit with Thee.

Zimmerman's eyes were turned upwards, staring intently through the ceiling at a celestial welcome that Johannes could only imagine. He took the man's hand once again in his and kissed it. *"Gott gebe dir eine seilege Auferstehung." May God grant you a blessed resurrection.*

Johannes stood, for the first time honoring the garment he had just put on. He walked to the door and opened it. Crowded in the dark hallway, Frau Zimmerman and her five children stood silently. Their faces were shaded by a thin veneer of composure. The eldest, Johann, had his hand on his mother's shoulder. Maria held the hand of little Christoph, eleven. Johannes looked into the boy's eyes and saw the same confused terror that had filled his own as he had stood beside his father's grave in Denndorf.

The family entered the room and gathered around the bed. Was it a trick of imagination, he wondered as he closed the window against the wind. As he started to pull the curtain, the brilliance of a flash of lightning filled the room. Above his Magister's bed, in a space between moments, he thought he had glimpsed a light—a palpable radiance coming through another window, one that opened to the Invisible World.

"What you have given me," he offered to his Teacher in the silence of his heart, "I could never repay."

It was unbearable—to watch helplessly as the great astronomer and theologian drowned in the sea of his own lungs. Johannes left the family alone. In the hallway the hundred responsibilities flooded back into him. As he reentered the drawing room, everyone's eyes turned. He bowed his head—an acknowledgement that Zimmerman's sufferings were coming to an end. Someone began sobbing.

He motioned for Falckner to follow him into the foyer. "Daniel," he whispered, "I need to secure the services of a reputable agent in London. Then we must dispatch an urgent letter to Bürgermeister Michael Deli of Segesvár."

Falckner's eyes showed no surprise, no difference in the usual brightness of his affection, or any trace of the irreversible change in the quality of their friendship. "Yes, Magister," he said.

Chapter Eleven

Sunday, December 24, 1693
From: Johann Gotfried Seelig, London, England
To: Augustus Hermann Francke, Halle, Saxony, Germany

My Dear Brother Franke,

I have heard through Falckner that you received word of the Magister's death. Although the extreme of our grief has passed, the mean, as it were, lingers on, returning especially on this *Weihnachten*, bringing back memories of past years when we together honored this solemn night. But this year, as the sun turns, we are looking ahead as well as back, and it is in the spirit of both that I have been inspired to write you on behalf of your now twice-orphaned Chapter of Perfection.

Very soon we shall be departing for North America. Magister Kelpius has announced that after the holiday has passed, he will forthwith engage a ship for our transport to Pennsylvania. My heart is heavy knowing that you consider our mission wrongly directed and too perilous to undertake, but recently we have been promised success by a seer of undoubted ability. Your concern for us is truly my only concern. My Faith, in concert with that of the other thirty-nine of us (yes, thirty-nine!), is borne aloft with Hope and Love this bright English Christmas Eve.

You have asked about the fate of our Circle under the guidance of Magister Kelpius. It is my intention to pen a letter conveying some of the unusual (and even perilous) experiences we have had here in the land of the "Angles from Saxony." This way you will not be dependent only upon my opinions, but able to draw your own conclusions as to Kelpius' spiritual qualifications.

We sailed to London last August seventeenth, after we had exhausted our hearts and purses fulfilling the requirements of God and the government of Holland concerning the Magister's funeral. The voyage to London cost us a mere five Dutch styvers per head, but that sum completely depleted our funds. We arrived, therefore, in complete reliance upon His Providence, with no material support save a letter of introduction to a woman of great spiritual repute, supplied to us by our anonymous Dutch benefactor.

Our mutual friend, Henrich Köster, had been trying to teach us the English language as well as English customs, but what we had long suspected was true, *viz.*, that he knew neither one as well as he believed. The sun-filled afternoon we first sailed into the Thames River from the North Sea, our sloop was greeted by shouts from other vessels in the river, "Whores or scholars? Whores or scholars?" It seemed such a strange way to be greeted that I was amused to no end, but our dear Köster began to sputter until he turned crimson. He demanded (in his anger vacillating between English and German) that the captain of our vessel call for an apology or return us immediately to Holland. At the request of everyone else Kelpius intervened, not only between Köster and the captain, but also between Köster and a muscular, red-haired man who seemed to intensely dislike our style of dress. By the time we reached our destination at Black Friar's Wharf, the matter was well settled. It seems there exist along the Thames River two competing groups of mariners, the "Oars" and the "Scullers," and it is customary for sailors to call forth to ships for identification. Thus, from the first, we nearly set Germany to war with England over a matter of misunderstood articulation.

As you know, London is the largest city in Christendom and perhaps the entire world, with nearly a half-million inhabitants. Attempting to understand them has been no small task for us. I have just yesterday come across this statement by one English commentator on his capital. "No city in the spacious universe boasts of religion more," he writes in a pamphlet, "or minds it less."

As far as appearances alone are concerned, there could have been no more indication of the religiousness of Londoners than the shape of the city against the sky. Dozens of spires rise up into the blue, and above the rest, the great dome of the Cathedral of Saint Paul. However, if truth were told, it is not a dome at all. The entire city, St. Paul's included, was nearly destroyed by fire in the 'sixties, and progress to rebuild has been so tedious that even now there is but a skeleton of the dome. As Kelpius pointed out, it is perhaps a sign that we should consider the whole of the English people as a work in progress.

A brisk breeze was blowing that afternoon, refreshing from the air the waste of half a million inhabitants, only a handful of which we actually saw. It being Sunday, the Londoners were tucked inside their numerous doors. We actually encountered more pigs than humans, the former taking advantage of the Sabbath by doing their weekly marketing in the garbage troughs that run in the center of most of the streets.

Köster was of the mind that we should immediately seek out the party to whom we had the letter of introduction, and in this way touched off the first challenge to the new Magister. Kelpius replied that we had no funds and should not take advantage of the hospitality of strangers, but instead find shelter in the lodgings provided for indigent travelers.

"What is the difference between private and public hospitality?" Köster wanted to know.

"The public place may not be as elegant," Kelpius pointed out, "but there we can use what resources we have to administer to the truly poor. Let there be no coercion. May those who wish to find hosts, do so. For me, I choose to follow the path indicated by His Providence until such time as I am led elsewhere."

All of us, the full thirty-nine, followed Kelpius.

Now the English government believes its main responsibility is to protect the rights of property holders. This philosophy holds as its basis the assumption that God judges individuals before, rather than after, life. Thus, a rich man is believed to have been blessed by God, a poor man cursed. So much for what underlies their philosophy. Here is the outcome. In the absence of much secular responsibility, the burden of the unfortunate needy falls to the church parishes, each attempting to do its best to: 1) provide for the physical needs of its local poor and 2) encourage the direst of them to move a few streets away, so that the neighboring parish will be required to take the burden. This perhaps is one of the reasons for the so-called "tolerance" of the English Church toward non-conformity. It may be that it is simply too occupied to care about non-conformity to doctrine.

Now I am smiling at this joke, but not at my next thought, which is of the beadhouse, or lodging place for indigents, to which we were led by Kelpius. By his own intuition he discovered a lane with the auspicious name of St. John's Road. The particular district where the road led us was the parish of St. Sepulcher, the name meaning *das Grab*—an auspicious name in neither English nor German.

Imagine, if you would, a large room in which the brick of the walls is blackened by the smoke of coal. Wooden pallets serve as beds for men who have fallen into disrepute—men who are unclean, uneducated, unhealthy. Many have been maimed with scars. These marks have been given them inside the infamous Newgate Prison, where English judgement (being harsher than that of God) is made permanent. What merchant, what company would hire a man so marked? The answer as you know is none, and thus the best destiny left open to these errant souls is the blackened beadhouse.

You might rightly ask why we did not at this time make plans to depart forthwith to Pennsylvania. I did wonder silently at this, as did several of the other brethren, only not so silently. At the time Kelpius did not provide us with a concrete answer, only saying, "The time is not yet right. God will make known to us when the day has come."

However, in our patience we were not idle. We practiced spiritual exercises in the despondent air of the beadhouse, ministered to the lodgers' spiritual and physical ailments, and undertook a search for the only person whose name we knew in the whole of England. As it turned out, it was one Daniel Geissler, an apprentice tradesman from Saxony, who located the residence of said individual. After making known our presence in London, we were cordially and enthusiastically invited to make our way to a part of the city known as Baldwin's Gardens to meet at last Mrs. Jane Leade, leader of the elusive Philadelphian Society of London.

Like so much of the weather in England, the evening of our appointment was damp, and thick fog had captured the light of the street lamps that glow in every street and alley. However, we were light of spirit, no longer fearing the suspicions of an Inquisition if we walked together in a group. The only exceptions to our number that evening were Maria and Frau Zimmerman who remained with Henrich Lorentz and his wife, Hilde. Frau Lorentz had just been blessed by the birth of a son—a joyous event that returned our number to forty souls! (And perhaps the very same, as I shall later explain.)

We arrived at a very unremarkable home made of the brick that is ubiquitous in London. I believe all of us were comforted by the visible proof of the tolerance of the English Church, tolerance that would permit a mystical society to convene in such an open setting. I did not realize at the time that my exuberance was clouding my perception. I did not understand that opposition in the Path of the Spirit is a subtle and elusive enemy, and may come from many sides and in many forms.

The dozen or so members of the Philadelphian Society were more than politely excited to meet Kelpius, and I supposed that the reputation of our Circle had reached them prior to our meeting. Whether or not what they had heard was true (about us or about Kelpius), it was delightful to our new Magister to be treated with such honor. Having known J.K. for so long, I can say without doubt that it was the first time in his life to be so lavished with attentions. "Dost thou know the hour wherein the End of Days shall begin, Herr Magister?" "Hast thou heard of our Work through thy visions? "Why art thou abandoning the world of man for the wilderness?" &c. Kelpius handled the situation with extraordinary humility and compassion, an attitude which seemed to confirm his rank as a saintly soul to these Englishmen.

As to these particular English (men and women in equal numbers making up their Society), they seemed intelligent, pious, and sincere, with perhaps the exception of a pair of gentlemen whom I shall refer to only as M. and C. Their enthusiasm for our Magister was great, nearly resembling an unnatural attraction, which I suspected (from certain of their mannerisms) they held for each other. They were quite energetic in their efforts to convince us to remain with their Society in London, out of the loftiest of motives, I am certain—perhaps nearly certain. Kelpius himself was unperturbed by their aforementioned mannerisms, either from innocence or kindness, so of this subject I shall write no more.

At the hour of nine, a clock struck and we watched Mrs. Jane Leade descend the stairs, coming into our presence like an angel. She is the Magister (as it were) of the Philadelphians—a woman of tremendous Gifts, inspired by God and Behmen, the cobbler of Görlitz. The depth of her soul was evident in her eyes, which blazed even after having seen seventy Christmas Eves. In fact, it was upon another *Weihnachten,* when she was but a young maiden, that a Divine Voice had interrupted her revels at a Christmas party saying, "Cease from this. I have another dance to lead thee in; for this is vanity." After this visitation, she devoted her remaining life to higher understanding and its promotion among all people. She truly is the woman in Revelation, a righteous lady amidst a wilderness of Anglican spiritual poverty.

The evening ended in a spirit of the purest Love and Harmony among people of different ages, genders, and languages. At the time I was deeply moved by the event, which I took to my heart as living proof of the brotherly love, the *philadelphian* ideal, that both Circles hold as the true state of humankind and the Christian life.

It was that self-same *philadelphian* spirit we brought back with us to the beadhouse. During the following days and weeks we persevered in attending to the needs of the destitute. Falckner and Köster were both conscripted into the service of St. Sepulcher's as teachers to the uneducated adult men. Brother Christian Warmer established a class to instruct in the art of tailoring any who desired to learn a trade. When the senior priest discovered Kelpius' talents, he immediately enlisted him as Honored Guest Choirmaster.

The clergy connected with the parish, although impressed with our skills and erudition, were quite at a loss to comprehend us in the larger sense and would often inquire on behalf of which denomination we were intending to spread the Christian faith in the New World. However, on the whole, they took quite well to us, especially as we (upon Kelpius' suggestion) attended their services faithfully.

So it was with a heart filled with joy and confidence that we returned one evening to the regular convening of the Philadelphian Society. Mrs. Leade being indisposed at the time, it fell to M. and C. to conduct the proceedings. To our surprise, M. announced that he had been recipient to some startling news, conveyed in a vivid dream, or *horasis,* as it is called by the Greeks. It was disclosed to him (he said) by a great winged being astride a pure white horse that the soul of Jakob Zimmerman had returned to earth in the form of the infant Lorentz, as the Magister still desired to lead the Chapter of Perfection.

Furthermore, C. reported that a young Finn man by the name of Shaeffer, who was visiting London at that very time, had vitally important information regarding our plans to travel to America. According to those who knew him, this Shaeffer was a mystic and adept of the highest order. Our mutual presence in London constituted (C. told us) a *coincidence*—an English word coined to describe the situation that obtains when seemingly unrelated events occur simultaneously to produce significance. Shaeffer had expressed a desire to meet with the Magister (Kelpius that is, and not the infant Lorenz) and reveal to him his vision of the immanent future of the Chapter of Perfection. Only three conditions were to be met: 1) that Kelpius was to meet Shaeffer in Southwark (a district to the south of London proper); 2) that Kelpius was to go thither on the evening of the following Saturday; and 3) that Kelpius should arrive dressed in the manner of an English gentleman, and not in the Robe of the Magister.

Now to the first conditions, Kelpius agreed readily, but to the third he said that no genuine adept would be concerned with such superficialities as clothing, and even at the risk of offending this mystic, he would not deign to pose as someone he was not. Upon hearing this, Köster immediately spoke up that he would gladly accompany Kelpius and would not allow a sense of false pride to prevent him from fulfilling the mystic's request. "For who is to fathom," Köster argued, "the hidden intent of one who is guided by the Invisible?" M., being of like stocky stature, arranged therefore to lend Köster suitable raiment and the matter was amicably settled.

Can you picture the astonishment of the lodgers of St. Sepulcher's beadhouse when, on the afternoon of Saturday next, M. arrived in a carriage, bringing with him a bright red silk waistcoat, a pair of black serge breeches, a feathered three-cornered hat, a lace ruffled shirt, and something that appeared to be a medium-sized dog? The latter proved to be only a wig of impressive size, liberally powdered. It took quite some time for Henrich to be adorned in these borrowed items, and the whole episode seemed so similar to a pantomime coronation, that I confess I walked thrice around the cathedral of St. Sepulcher to avoid expressing my amusement.

When the adornment was complete, M. departed, leaving us with a message of regards for the Finnish mystic and directions to a certain coffeehouse along Kent Street, where the aforementioned was waiting to deliver his message. At the moment of departure, Kelpius suddenly asked me to accompany them. As I was neither a Magister, nor dressed as an English aristocrat, I felt unequal to the task, but I complied. A pledge of obedience is a sacred obligation, even if it is to a dear friend.

After we crossed London Bridge (which is not so much a bridge as a city unto itself, lined with shops, jugglers, and determined citizens offering entertainment in the form of their political pamphlets), I began to conclude that the district of Southwark is a distinct part of London, one that had been perhaps cordoned off from the city proper. The appearance of refinement that preoccupies so many Londoners seemed less important on that side of the river, as did the sense of morality in the broad, public sense. Every fourth door is the entrance to an alehouse, and all were well occupied (from the sounds of both song and quarrel coming through the windows). And behind many of the remaining doors are gambling dens, brothels, and even theaters.

Köster, Kelpius, and I made our way toward our destination along Kent Street, despite two awkward facts: 1) that the directions we had been given did not accord with the streets through which we were walking; and 2) that the further our journey took us from London Bridge, the more Köster was attracting attention. "Big wig" was but one of the comments he evoked from the crowd. You may trust me that the other salutations, albeit coarse, were even more amusing. If nothing else, the English have a ready wit.

Köster was becoming visibly uncomfortable at receiving so much attention, quite unusual for him, as his general attitude toward attention is the more the better. He delivered his comments regarding the depravity of humanity in general and the citizens of Southwark in particular, with increasing enthusiasm. At length we came to a street filled with a disorderly queue of men. To the horror of all three of us, we discovered that behind a dilapidated fence lay one of Southwark's most popular attractions, a diversion known as bear-baiting. An unclean and unhealthy animal (not unlike the men of the beadhouse) stood chained to a post while eager participants paid of their wages (or perhaps not their own) to torment the poor beast with a whip or sharpened stick.

Kelpius' face took on an expression of concern, not only for the welfare of the bear, but for Köster, who we both surmised was on the verge of making a vociferous condemnation. So, wisely it seemed, we hastened away with no regard for direction until it finally became inescapably apparent that we would never arrive at Kent Street, let alone the particular coffeehouse we were seeking. In truth, the neighborhood was less than safe for strangers. We were lost and worse—discouraged by the realization we had been victims of intentionally untrustworthy directions.

We found ourselves in a dim street that ended in a blackened wall. Beneath a single street lamp stood a lonely figure who turned as if she had been expecting us. Her face, when revealed by the movement of a brightly colored fan, was one that I shall never forget—fair youth, ravaged by the horrors of Babylon. Her cheeks were sunken, supported only by a thin veneer of red powder that was unable to disguise a scar, the inexorable mark of Newgate Prison. Wrapped in a once-fine shawl, she approached us with her dark eyes fixed upon Köster. "Good evening, kind sir." Her voice was soft and youthful, her teeth blackened by mercury—medicine for the dreaded pox. She ran a slender finger through Köster's wig while he stood, making the same assessments as I. "Are you searching for a lady this evening?" she asked. Her fan brushed his cheek, which turned scarlet at its touch.

"Certainly not, child," he answered in English.

Her reply I shall not repeat. Despite the failings in my knowledge of the English language, I had learnt enough to comprehend the acts she was proffering in highly descriptive terms.

"Get thee hence!" Köster took her wrist and twisted, pushing the Unfortunate to the ground. "Had I indeed been searching for a lady, I would not have found her in thee, for thou art not a lady in any sense. Thou art a being without shame, without decency, and as such not entitled to bear the name 'lady' or any designation of a human being."

"Gor," was all she said, lying still in the shadows beside the alley wall.

"For the good of thy soul," Köster went on, "I am inclined to search for thy parents and rebuke them for permitting such an inexcusable lapse of breeding. In the absence of such possibility, I perhaps should report thee to a constable."

It was the wrong thing to say, even if it had been spoken more from embarrassment than from common sense. Whatever humor the situation may have held, it suddenly fled, and in its place was a cold, chilling silence.

"For the good of *thy* soul," the girl said, "I'd give me your clothes. They'll fetch a better price than any stew could get from the likes of you." She stood up, not chest high to Köster, but pointing to that same chest with a pistol.

Now Kelpius, who had been behind me, stepped unexpectedly into the light, between Köster and the Unfortunate, in line with the pistol's aim. I was frozen, unable to move, as I suspect was Köster.

"'Who are you?" she asked, throwing in the midst of her question an English obscenity.

I had no idea what Kelpius would say, or what was his intention. I was certain that neither the theology curriculum at the University of Altdorf, nor the secrets of the Kabalah, were sufficient to prepare a young Transylvanian scholar for an encounter with a pistol-wielding English whore. I had long considered Kelpius as possessing a soul too pure for the trials of this world, and at that moment was seized with anxiety for the welfare of his body as well as his soul.

"My dear Elizabeth," he said.

Now whether or not the Unfortunate's name was Elizabeth, I knew not, nor how Kelpius knew if it was. One eyebrow beneath black curly locks raised, while the other lowered. I was imprisoned by the sight of her scar, long and brown and caused not by accident or passion, but by the coolness of English justice. "I got a bullet," she said, "that can go through you and still kill His Nibs. That way I won't soil so bad his waistcoat."

"This morning at prayer," Kelpius said, "God spoke a message concerning thee."

"Move, or I kill you now."

"He said that he had a beloved daughter who..."

"Shut your mouth."

"Who would put in danger her immortal soul..."

Her thumb pulled back the pistol cock. "Give me them clothes, or start praying again."

"By committing an act she need not commit."

"Now!"

"For which he sent me to prevent, for His love for thee."

The sound of my heart pounding in my ears is the only thing that I can recall beyond that, until, after a long silence, the Unfortunate spoke again. "What's your meaning?"

"Thou art much loved," said Kelpius. "Thou art an innocent woman, lost within a wilderness of depravity. God understands the misfortunes in your life, and He knows of the insult and suffering you have endured. My friend here is an innocent man and a Friend of God. If you were to cause his blood to be shed, more would be stained than his waistcoat. We are honest travelers, Elizabeth, strangers to your city. I beg you not to take what you need by coercion. Choose to put down your weapon, and I promise my friend will give freely what you ask."

Köster was just as I, compelled by anxious curiosity not to make a move. I extended my perceptive capacity in an effort to sense their thoughts. To my surprise, our Magister seemed not a whit agitated and the Unfortunate just the opposite. "I could kill you right now," she said finally.

"God has promised me thou wilt not," spoke Kelpius.

The light of the street lamp caught the eyes of the Unfortunate. I was not certain if they were, or were not, welled with tears. Slowly she placed her pistol on the ground, not taking her eyes off Kelpius. "Give them clothes to me," she ordered, "as you promised."

Well, Köster complied most willingly, from the feathered hat and monstrous wig, to the silver buckles which he ripped off his boots, beseeching the Unfortunate that we had a long walk still ahead, and that he would apologize earnestly for his previous remarks if she would suffer him to retain his britches, boots and cloak. As they were engaged in all this back-and-forth, I picked up the pistol and hid it under my own cloak. "Trust in God," say the Arabs, "but tie your camel first."

When the Unfortunate had what she wanted, she ran off into the night. Kelpius called out to her as she disappeared, "Elizabeth, come to the Church of St. Sepulcher on Christmas Day. God wishes to grant you a special blessing." I did not understand, nor did Köster, and I am not certain if she even heard what he said.

After that, the three of us somehow found our way back to London Bridge and discovered, to our dismay, that passage across is forbidden from the time of Bow Bells until sunrise. So, despondent that we had been purposely and cruelly misled, the three of us found a sheltered spot by the river's bank and sat down to wait until morning.

"It was only that they loved us wrongly," Kelpius said finally. "More than anything, they wanted us to remain with their society and took offense at our refusal."

"Do not patronize me, Magister," Köster said. "I was taken for a fool by fools and have become a fool in the taking."

"Not at all, Henrich. You were, after all, the one who was guided by Truth. There was a hidden purpose in wearing their clothes. You have helped to rescue a young soul." Köster groaned in self-reproach, preferring to go off and sulk alone by the roaring waters under the London Bridge.

"Do you really believe," I asked Kelpius, "that we have rescued her?"

The Magister said nothing, but lay on the cold ground, staring at the stars. I took the pistol and threw it into the River Thames.

Now, my dear Brother Franke, our friend Falckner has reminded me that the hour of midnight is nearly here, so I must hasten to bring you up to the moment. About a month after the events just described, we were materially blessed by an unexpected donation from yet another anonymous benefactor. Falckner, who has dealt with all the legal issues involved, insists he does not know who has bestowed such abundance upon us, yet I suspect he says this only from a pledge of secrecy.

Be that as it may (as the English say), we have been able to purchase a veritable cornucopia of supplies. London is the most remarkable town in the world in which to spend money. We have discovered untold numbers of books, including the *Philosophia Occulta* of Paracelsus, Galen's *De Simplicibus* herbal, and Rumi's *Masnavi* in its original Persian. We believe the only part of European life that Kelpius is reluctant to leave behind is music, and it was because of this we have convinced him of the need to buy several musical instruments including a small virginal organ to take with us to Pennsylvania.

The Magister moved us from the beadhouse into a great inn nearby with the odd but auspicious name, Turtledove's Rest. Here we are warm at last and living in great luxury for Christmas and the duration of our stay in London. The beadhouse (and its unfortunate residents) received a donation upon our leaving, an amount of twenty English pounds, sufficient for its improvement and operation for several years.

I know you must wonder about the state of our relations with the Philadelphian Society of London. I am glad to report that they are cordial. M. and C. have not attended any of the subsequent meetings at which we were present, and we have not sought them out. Kelpius has, on the other hand, established quite warm relations with many here in London. When he related our adventure in Southwark, he concluded his tale with the following: "We certainly had sufficient cause to be offended with them, yet if we were, where would be the opportunity for growth, and for the love that is founded upon forgiveness from the heart, and forgiveness upon the knowledge of one's own faults?" Although he does not know it, Mrs. Leade will give him (as a Christmas present) a small leather-bound book, suitable for the keeping of a diary or the composition of hymns. I believe that she wishes to make restitution to him for the failings of her erring pair of students.

As to the truth of the mystic Shaeffer, we discovered to our delight that such a one actually exists, and was in fact lodging not two parishes distant from St. Sepulcher's. He visited us here at Turtledove's Rest, and all were able to perceive the extraordinary learning of this young Finn. He was most interested in hearing our reports of the Pietists and the many miracles wrought by God in Germany these recent years. And, most surprising of all, he had indeed been blessed with a precognition of our forthcoming journey.

To Kelpius he vouchsafed the following (in his own words): "*Cherubim would be our companions and protectors in danger, and that this would be a sign that we should accept of Divine assistance, to wit, that despite contrary winds, we shall happily draw ashore in America.*"

By the time you are in receipt of this letter, my dear friend, the Chapter of Perfection will be crossing the sea, departed forever from these lands of Babylon, under Divine protection, sailing ever closer to the pure, untrammeled shores of the city whose very name is a testimony to the highest potentials in us all.

Farewell,
J.G. Seelig

Chapter Twelve

Friday, February 16, 1694
Aboard the Sara Maria, in the English Channel

"Ich sage dieses frëy:
Lafft uns drum nich verzagen.
Die Gottes-Güth ist dannoch neu
Und Höret unser klagen."
What I say to thee is true:
We need not then to despair.
God in His Goodness yet renews
And hears our pleading prayer.

Maria Zimmerman sang as if she were accompanied by a harp and not the shriek of the wind tearing through the rigging. Her faith, thought Johannes, is stronger than the storm.

Their wooden cave had been turned nearly sideways. In one frightening moment, all of the huddled passengers and their cargo had been hurled up against the hull. Geissler, poor Geissler, had caught the full force of the trunks as well as the crate that held the organ, and broken his leg or worse. Now they were trapped in a dark, angled world. The walls had starting weeping seawater. Buckets full of vomit, and who knew what else, had toppled over, sloshing into the cold water swirling around their ankles. Two hanging oil lamps swayed back and forth, casting wild and twisting shadows.

"Auch im Gericht
Gott's herze bricht
Er wird sich unser erbarmen
Als Vater uns umarmen."
In His judgments,
God's Heart relents.
Then we in mercy are relieved,
And in our Father's Arms received.

Johannes' own heart would not relent from its nagging reminder of his responsibilities. To God, the others turned in prayer, but it was to him, their Magister, that they turned with their eyes. Hilde Lorentz looked over to him. She hadn't made a sound when the ship had struck the sand bar. Lying motionless in her arms was her son, the youngest member of their Circle, the baby that the Englishman had told them held the soul of the Magister.

No, he reprimanded himself. It was *he* who was the Magister.

He stood up, unsteadily. His right hand was tucked under his robe, clutching the locked wooden box, inlaid with a golden star. Holding himself with his left hand against the low ceiling, he called over the howling wind. "Let us help one another move out of this water."

Slowly, in a silence that belied the terror of the situation, the passengers climbed over the scattered cargo and each other, toward the high side of the deck. The hatch to the 'tween deck opened, letting in rain and the bellow of a sailor, "Commend your souls to God. We may go down!"

The ship's cannons fired three shots as a distress call. Everyone on board strained to listen for a reply, but Johannes was hearing something else. It was a voice, a strange but distinct voice that he heard in his heart, where the sound of the storm was not able to overwhelm. *"When thou passest through the waters, I will be with thee.*

Fear not; they shall not overflow thee. Tell him thy people shall be saved by his faith."

"Every moment of our life," he called out to the passengers, "whether we are upon land or sea, we are but a heartbeat away from death. This time of danger is but a test. Let us not abandon our faith at an hour when it is required most."

They could hear shouts and cries from the crew in the fo'c's'le, but the forty passengers stayed quiet. He needn't have spoken to them about faith. It was the way they lived their lives. It was the faith of the others on board that concerned him.

A wave suddenly lifted up the *Sara Maria*, leaving the stomachs of the passengers behind, then violently slammed the ship back down. Those who were on their feet fell, including Johannes. The crate that held the organ let out a discordant cry.

He stumbled back over to Henrich Köster, whose face was still masked in shock. "Frau Lorentz is in need," Johannes whispered. Köster looked over to the young mother and nodded obediently. Falckner fell into a heap, with silent tears streaming down his face. "I'm going on deck," Johannes told them, "to speak to the Captain."

It was Daniel Falckner who, too early that morning, had shaken him awake. "Kelpius," he told him, "I have had a premonition of death."

"Go back to sleep, Daniel," he said. He regretted it as soon as he had spoken. Magister Zimmerman used to require them to speak of significant dreams. The Magister's interpretations were invariably odd but always reassuring. And now, simply for the luxury of postponing the responsibilities of the day, Johannes had turned away a friend. His conscience kept him from returning to sleep. After exercises and meditation, he invited Falckner to climb on deck to look at the weather.

The low gray sky had not proven to be the cause of their worry. A contingent of the Royal Impress Gang had boarded their boat allegedly looking for deserters. Captain John Tanner, a lean man with nervous eyes, was arguing with them.

"But these men, they an't even English, they're damn Swedes."

"We're acting on behalf of the King of Sweden."

"But this un's me Bosun, and we got forty passengers to America."

"That's not our concern, Captain."

The *Sara Maria* carried fourteen cannons, but Johannes had learned enough to know that without a full crew their journey would be one of suicide. There was a war being waged in the Atlantic, and merchant ships such as theirs were easy targets for French and even Spanish attacks. He didn't like the way the Captain was shouting. Or the look of the bayonets carried by the Royal Impress Gang.

"Perhaps I may share some information that you would find important." Köster came from behind them and was striding up to the sailors.

"God help us," Falckner whispered.

Beside the uniformed Englishmen, Köster looked almost comic in his plain homespun robe. "Who the hell are you?" someone asked.

"Henrich Bernard Köster of Blumenberg, Westphalia, formerly in the employment of the Privy-councilor to the House of Brandenburg." He extended them his hand. Tanner's clenched into a fist.

Johannes felt Falckner's restraining hand on his shoulder. "Give him a minute," Falckner whispered again. "See what happens."

"I have extensive training in natural observation," Köster said calmly, "and have been watching the members of this crew, scrutinizing their habits and demeanor. These Swedes, gentlemen, have displayed unmistakable symptoms of consumption. You would find them unsuitable for service, and an unprofitable burden. Yonder is another merchant vessel." He pointed to the northeast. "I conversed with their captain before we left London. I have no doubt she harbors a healthy contingent of deserters."

Köster declined the bottle of spirits Tanner offered him later in gratitude. But he enjoyed repeating the whole story in German to the passengers in the 'tween deck. "It came to me in a deep state of contemplation," he told them. "I was prompted to intervene, on our behalf as well as the Swedes'." It was actually a comfort to Johannes to have Köster receive so much attention. Henrich thrived on it, and it seemed to soften his temperament. And from purely selfish reasons, Johannes liked the relief from the pressures of the position of Magister—however temporary it was.

The wind picked up in the afternoon. Seelig and Falckner stayed with him on deck, watching the ship heading through the narrow channel between the English coast and the Goodwin Sands, the shallow banks that lay like death traps just below the stone-colored waves of the Channel. Falckner kept looking over to him, anxious and afraid to speak again of the premonition that was on both their minds.

Wenn du durchs Wasser gehst bin ich bei dir. When thou passest through the waters, I shall be with thee. Fear not; they shall not overflow thee. The words had come to him suddenly, as an intrusion into his thoughts. *Tell him thy people shall be saved by his faith.*

"Kelpius, are you ill?" He shook his head, and forced a smile. He desperately wanted to believe it had been a Divine prompting, just as Köster's had been. Only who would believe him when he doubted it himself? His intuitions spoke out of the silence of his quieted mind, not from agitated worry. And besides, the very last thing he wanted to do was to discount Falckner again. A wave of nausea swept over him, and he looked into the clouds, hoping the sensation would pass. His hands were shaking.

It became bitterly cold. The wind blew harder until it came with the strength of a storm, carrying with it sheets of rain. Johannes found himself torn between the need to reassure the passengers and his desire to remain on deck, watching and praying. He put a long cloak over his Magister's robe and for hours climbed back and forth to the 'tween deck. The passengers, his people, were becoming sicker by the hour from the nauseating motion of the ship. The flux had been bad enough. Only a few days from London it had started, affecting both men and women with constant and shameless diarrhea.

Eventually he asked Seelig to stay below. He wanted to think it was for Seelig's sake, to give his friend relief from the rain and the cold, but he knew it was as just much to avoid the look on the face of Hilde Lorentz. For her, the flux had meant the end of her milk. Without its life-giving properties, nothing else, neither the *Essentia dulcis* nor the subtle healing energies, would save the baby's life.

For Johannes, the most imperative thought was of the small wooden box that he kept hidden among his personal belongings. He went below, avoiding the eyes of his companions, and made his way past the dangling curtains that served as walls. Against a far space by the ship's hull it lay in the dark. There was no such thing as privacy on board the ship, but he had secured for himself the least exposed place on the 'tween deck. He unwrapped the box from its nest inside his old quilt and held it against his chest. It felt heavy, immeasurably heavy.

By late in the day, the *Sara Maria* was drifting in the gale. Tanner had ordered the anchor dropped, but the boat was in shallow and unpredictable waters. The sailors tried to weigh in the anchor before it struck and punctured the hull, but the anchor line broke. He didn't need to extend his perceptions to sense the crew's state of mind. The look on their faces told him everything. Their anxiety infused into him like a contagious illness.

In spite of the spreading nausea, the passengers retained their calm. For a time, Johannes thought it might be ignorance of their plight, but he soon realized they understood it as well as he did. The sounds of the storm and the shouting of orders from above were all too easy to hear in the 'tween deck. Partly as a distraction, Köster formed a discussion group. A group of the brethren crouched in the circle of lamplight listening to Köster expound.

"*Ophereth* is referred to as wisdom, for a great treasure of wisdom lies hidden there, as in Proverbs, three, nineteen or alternately Job, twenty-eight, six. Wherein—take notice of the word—*Ophereth*, or lead, by the mystical name of Chol, lies the system of the whole universe." Johannes scanned the faces of the listeners: Ludovic Sprogel, Daniel Lutke, the Cassel brothers, Biederman, Van Leer. "Its figure has below a circle, the sign of universal perfection, and over the circle is a cross point, so that you may know that Quaternity lies there, whether you refer to them as sulfur, separator of water, dry water, or the wonderful salt."

Nearby, on the other side of a flimsy sheet, Frau Zimmerman was attending to the embarrassed victims of seasickness and the flux. Each time Johannes returned to the 'tween deck, Köster's group had fewer members, Frau Zimmerman's more.

He looked for Maria and found her sitting with Hilde Lorentz and the child whom the sailors had nicknamed Li'l Bantling. Now that the boy had finally stopped wailing, they all wanted nothing more than to hear him cry again. Christian Warmer came over, carefully balancing a blue porcelain cup from which steam was rising. Maria brushed the hair from her eyes. "*Bitte*," she said, taking the cup from him. There was something affectionate in the look she gave the tailor. There was something equally affectionate in the look Warmer returned. Johannes turned away.

He began to fall apart under his responsibility for the welfare of his thirty-nine souls and his awesome inability to do anything to help.

"When thou passest through the waters, I shall be with thee. Fear not; they shall not overflow thee. Tell him thy people shall be saved by his faith." That thought, with its own strange timbre and tone, coming to him a second time, tore through his depression. He left the passengers and climbed back into the weather to the Captain's cabin. He could hear Tanner inside furiously trading blame with the Swedes. For half an hour, he huddled in his cloak beside the door. The Captain's cabin was the one place on board ship forbidden to the passengers. For half an hour he waited patiently, as he had done so many times as a child beside the door to his father's study, the only room in his home that was forbidden. There had been no matter so important, no need so great as to justify an intrusion. He had learned by the stick.

"Here, you!" The Standing Watch was coming toward him, dragging a limp figure by the arms. "Get this sorry swill-tub below 'fore I throws 'im in the drink."

A red-eyed, dripping wet Daniel Falckner grabbed him by the sleeve. "You and I are going to die, Kelp."

"The lubber's been in the fo'c's'le, drinkin' rum with the Idlers."

He put one of Falckner's arms over his shoulder and guided him toward the hatch. The rain hit the rungs of the ladder. Falckner's foot slipped, and he tumbled down. "*Scheiffe!* Where is Köster?" he demanded. "I need that pompous bastard!"

Köster looked over the heads of the few remaining members of his study group. *"Was zum Teufel...?"*

"I need to make my confession before we die," Falckner slurred.

Johannes felt the look of each passenger turn on him. "Henrich, would you please be kind enough to assist me with our friend?" he asked, trying to feign confidence. Köster got to his feet, reluctantly. The two of them steered Falckner toward the shadowy spot on the low deck where Johannes slept. His neatly folded blankets were getting damp. The hull next to them was beginning to sweat water.

"Daniel Falckner, you have brought shame..."

Falckner pressed his finger against Köster's mouth. "*Halt's Maul!* For once—just for once *in deinem verdammten Leben*—listen to someone else, Henrich!"

"Feel free to speak, Daniel." Johannes put a hand on Köster's shoulder. "Henrich and I are listening."

Falckner's breath overflowed with alcohol. His voice dropped to a whisper. "The Prophetess of Erfurth," he mumbled. "I met her the year I first began teaching. But then she was just Anna Maria. Someone told her I was an expert in Mithraic occultism." Köster made a sound through his nose. "I began to invite her to my home. It was a mistake, I know now. But, Henrich, she was so beautiful and so innocent. I should have known..."

"It is all right, Daniel, there is no need..."

"*Zum Teufel!* What do you know, Kelp? You know nothing! You are the Magister only because Köster couldn't be found." Johannes could feel the eyes of Köster on him. He had been hurt so many times before by drunken words that he felt immune to their sting.

"She told me that since she was a young girl she had had visions and heard voices. They frightened her, and she was in need of someone...someone who would understand and not condemn. I was so moved by her piety. She was gentle and devout and looked up to me as if she were a disciple and I the master. Do you understand, Henrich?"

Köster said nothing.

"One night I was reading to her *The Vanity of Arts and Sciences* of Agrippa. She began to fall into a state of...some sort of trance. She was calling for Jesus, for Jesus to come to her as the Bridegroom. Her chest was heaving and... She tore open her blouse. She continued calling for Jesus to come to her, to enter her."

"*Gott im Himmel!*" Köster groaned and turned his face into the shadows. Johannes, afraid to speak, put a hand on Falckner's arm.

"She lifted her skirt and put her hand between her legs and began to..." Falckner's eyes filled with tears. "I...I was moved to lust... I knew better than to... but I..."

"We are all creatures of flesh," Johannes said, "and our failures are but opportunities to repent. You are not condemned—by us or by God."

"Yes, you are," said Köster. He turned back, pushing Johannes away. "You are condemned by me. You and Francke's little *Hure*. The two of you are condemned by me and the Universal Law to which we are bound. If tonight we die, tonight you will enter eternity in a state of *scelus sceleris!*"

"Henrich, please." Johannes knew too well that the faith of his people was a delicate rosary, held together by the meagerest of string. Conflict was its enemy, one that seemed always to loom, threatening to unravel its thread. Falckner dropped to his knees, crying.

Köster raised his voice and the conversations of the others on the 'tween deck fell. "I hereby excommunicate you, Daniel Falckner. You and the so-called Prophetess of Erfurth! *'Setze ein Messer an deine Kehle, wenn du heiffhungrig bist!'" Put a knife to thy throat, if thou be a man given to appetite.* Johannes knelt beside Falckner and put his arm around him. "Leave him be, Kelpius," Köster ordered. "Let him feel the sting of remorse for the shame he has brought us."

"Please help attend to the needs of the company, Henrich."

"Leave him, Kelpius. I shall not tolerate mitigation of his repentance."

He shall not tolerate? The hand that Johannes held beneath the Magister's robe tightened its hold on the wooden box. "Please, Henrich, return to your study group," he said quietly.

"Did you not hear me, Johannes Kelpius? I shall not relent!" Köster grabbed Johannes by the robe that lay beneath his wet cloak and pulled. In the space of a breath, in a moment's unexpected pause in the wind's fury, the sound of his tearing the Magister's robe cut through the 'tween deck.

Köster's fist fell open. The anger in his eyes vanished, replaced in a blink by the realization of the sacrilege his own hands had perpetrated on the cloth of the Magister's mantle. He teetered backward on his heels, unable to look at Kelpius. Suddenly, as if gasping in horror at Köster's transgression, the storm resumed with a vengeance. Before the party of passengers had enough time to register what had happened, the *Sara Maria* struck bottom. Geissler cried out as he was slammed against the hull by the weight of the cargo, and the passengers' world turned over on itself.

Maria Zimmerman began to sing.

If thou doubtest the verity of the Voice Within, wait upon its thrice return. Magister Zimmerman had taught them the traditional method of distinguishing intuition from imagination by testing its persistence. After the Voice had broken into his mind for a third time, he no longer doubted. It was late, perhaps too late in this crisis, but he knew with a certainty what he had to do.

Above, the rain had stopped, but the deck was slick and dangerously inclined. It was nearly impossible to walk. The ship rose suddenly again and was slammed back down into the sandbar. Johannes fell and slid, slamming into the Captain's door.

"It's one of the Germans." The ship's Swedish Bosun stood at the threshold holding a lantern. Johannes could see into the Captain's tiny room. His furnishings—a wooden sleeping palette, a chart table, a huge trunk—all had been pushed together against the wall. An ink pot lay on its side, dripping black blood from the table.

Tanner had also fallen and was still on the floor, gathering a pile of scattered charts. He had an open bottle in his hand.

"Go back below, son. We're doin' all that can be done."

Johannes struggled to his feet, still clutching the precious box under his robe. "Captain, I beg a word with you."

"He's the leader, Cap'n."

"Well, kick'm out or bring'm in, just close the goddamn door." The Bosun gave Johannes a hand and brought him inside. "What ye want, Herr?"

Johannes crossed the room, sliding on the wet soles of his boots, and steadied himself against the sharp edge of the Captain's table. The Bosun lifted the lantern to his face, blinding him. Tanner stood up. The men were looking at him as though he were a dangerous annoyance, an insufferable distraction at a moment of crisis. Johannes looked into Tanner's eyes. "I have come to offer you help."

Tanner's face was lined in creases that looked painful in the light of the Bosun's lantern. "Well, that's a good thought, Herr. We're doin' all that can be done. Have ye'self a swig, and go below and pray."

For a third time the ship raised up, then fell suddenly. The impact shuddered through the masts and hull. Tanner was knocked off balance, but Johannes clung to the heavy table. The Bosun fell against the cabin wall. His lantern flickered and darkness flashed around the room. Muffled cries of "Jesus, Jesus!" came from the fo'c's'le. "Do you pray, Captain?"

Tanner exchanged looks with the Bosun, whose head began to shake. "I'm an Englishman and a ship's Cap'n," he said, waving his bottle. "Every damn day, I pray."

Johannes felt something unexpected reverberate in his own muscles. It was something coming from Tanner, from the man's voice, from his breath. At first it seemed as if it were fear, but he knew it was more than fear, more than the terror of drowning in the dark waters of the English Channel. It was something far worse—the unbearable weight of Tanner's responsibility for his ship. *Why had I not understood?* he thought. *How could I have been so blind to what should have been so clear?*

Almost as he framed the words in his mind, he knew the answer. His own selfishness had been obscuring his understanding. If he had not been so entangled in trying to ameliorate his own sense of failure, he would have long before realized that here was a man who was feeling a responsibility more awesome than his own. Here was a man who carried the weight of the safety of everything and everyone on board. Here was a man who had been doing his best, making the best decisions he was able, knowing his failures were bringing them all to death. *"Tell him thy people shall be saved by his faith."* The implication of the words charged through his mind.

"If you are no hypocrite," he said to Tanner, "but a man of integrity, which I believe you to be; if you believe that a Spirit can hear your thoughts in English, as well as mine in German, and those of a Chinaman and a Turk; if you believe that this Spirit has the power to understand your deepest longings, then can you, as I do, believe that God will save the *Sara Maria?*"

The Captain reached over and turned upright the ink pot on the table. He glanced at the stained pages on his open logbook. "You're a sort of holy man, an't ye, Herr? Well, I an't as raw a scoundrel as ye may think me be."

"Cap'n…," the Bosun interrupted.

"Stow it!" Tanner shouted. Johannes could see the Captain's eyes welling with tears, and through them, a distant look. "I've done the best that could be done. There an't no more I can do."

It was as if Johannes were staring into a looking glass. Tanner's trembling voice and the guilt-ridden, overwhelmed voice of his own heart blended together into a plaintive harmony.

The message had been meant for both of them.

Johannes moved carefully along the wall to the high side of the room, where he stood taller than the two men. "Your skill might not be sufficient against the power of this storm," he told the Captain. "But if it is strong, your faith can save us."

Tanner turned, looking up at him fully for the first time since they had met along the wharves of the Thames River. For that brief moment Johannes stood as the man, and Tanner the boy.

"In God I do trust," Tanner said to him, "for He be the only hope I ever did have, and I'll have hope in Him yet." He reached up his right hand to Johannes, who took it with his left. The Captain's dry flesh felt barely alive, but Johannes could sense softness beneath the skin. It was a hand that once knew the feel of its partner together in a posture of prayer. Just as he had been vulnerable to Tanner's fears, he now felt Tanner's faith—perhaps less than even a spark, but at least as great as a mustard seed.

A sudden motion of the ship caused them to teeter off balance. The desk slid away from the wall, pushing Tanner along with it. As Johannes fell, the edges of the box he carried dug into his stomach. The room went dark.

The next thing he knew, the Captain and the Bosun were rushing out of the door. The thumping of the grounded hull had stopped. "Make sail!" he heard someone shouting. Footsteps pounded on the deck and across the roof of the Captain's cabin. The ship's pulleys began to creak. The free rocking motion of the ship, the same motion that had made him sick, now seemed infinitely comforting. He got to his feet. The sailors were cheering. The floor of the Captain's cabin was level.

He found the door in the darkness. On the deck, relief overpowered the confusion. Lights were darting as the sailors scrambled to take advantage of the wind that was now easing them back out to the deep water. The suddenness of what had just happened, the confluence of events, and the palpable confirmation of his inner Voice was too much to integrate all at once. He collided with the Captain, who had his eyes on the masts, shouting orders. "Glad to have ye on board, Herr," he said. He slapped Johannes on the back. "Ye proved ye worth as a sailor. Ye weren't afraid at all, were ye, son?"

Johannes smiled for the first time since they had left London. He moved out of the way. The sound of Köster's booming voice leading the company in prayer came from the 'tween deck as he opened the hatch.

"Loben will ich den Herrn mein Leben lang. Er läfft seinen Wind wehen; es rieseln die Wasser. Vertraut nicht auf Edle, auf einen Menschensohn, bei dem keine Hilfe ist!"

While I live will I praise the Lord. He causes his wind to blow and the waters to flow. Put not your trust in princes, nor in the son of man, in whom there is no help.

He knew finally that it wasn't upon his meager, flawed self that the Chapter of Perfection was to depend. It was on the Divine Virtue for which he could only be a channel. And that power was sufficient.

For a few minutes he crouched by the hatch, listening to the song of the faithful. He could pick out nearly each voice—Seelig's forced baritone, Maria's angelic soprano, Geissler's indeterminate wavering, even the slurred tenor of Falckner.

Eventually he stood up and wandered over to the railing. Tiny stars were beginning to appear. From beneath his robe, he brought out the wooden box. The golden hexagonal star glistened in the sailors' lantern lights. He ran a finger over the gold star engraved with symbols that held fast *al Warqa'iyah*, the Dove.

He smiled again.

Part Two

Chapter Thirteen

Saturday, June 23, 1694
Pennsylvania

The De La War River was a lapis lazuli looking glass. In its surface Johannes watched a reflection of lazy clouds and verdant riverbanks. There was no hint of wind in the leaves, but some invisible force was propelling their sloop up the river toward Philadelphia.

He hadn't yet become reaccustomed to tranquility. The voyage from England had been months of continuous motion and continuous noise—water sluicing out the freeing ports, the thumping of waves against the hull, the profanity of the crew. It had been just four days since they had left the *Sara Maria* on the shores of the Chesapeake Bay. And here they were, sailing again. But this time the water and the air were fresh, and the world was welcoming—and quiet.

Something along the bank momentarily disturbed the calm, and a flock of birds nearly darkened the sky. "Passenger pigeons," said the Welshman who stood at the wheel. "A man won't never starve here."

He hasn't noticed, Johannes thought, that we don't have firearms. "I follow a vegetarian diet," he said.

The pilot thought for a moment, translating Johannes' German-accented English for his own Welsh ears. Then he laughed. "Don't worry, son. See them little trees? Miles 'n' miles of blueberries. Those woods'll soon have more walnuts and chestnuts and pecans; ye couldn't eat enough. Then there's Indian corn, what they call maize. Grows faster'n ye can cut it down. Ye can eat it boiled or make it into meal. Now here's a secret hardly no white man knows. Ye take maize seeds, dry 'em, stick 'em in hot oil, and then just look out!" He laughed again.

Johannes smiled at the man's elusive joke and turned to watch the passengers leaning on the railing. During the overland journey across Lord Baltimore's territory, they had tried to wash the smell of seawater from their clothes in a more than symbolic act of ablution. Now they were ready to absorb new fragrances. Their sense of anticipation was overflowing.

He couldn't keep himself from watching. Neither could Frau Zimmerman, who had kept a steady eye on Maria and Christian Warmer since leaving London. There stood the young couple (could he call them that?) pressed together in the huddle of the passengers. Warmer had neither Köster's erudition nor Falckner's cleverness, but he was a sincere man of intense compassion. Like some of the others, Warmer had voluntarily agreed to follow the path of celibacy. For centuries, in mystical communities of different cultures, it had been held that the subtle energies necessary to attain higher consciousness were dissipated by sexual expression. But Magister Zimmerman had not found celibacy a requirement for his spiritual commitment. Now it seemed as if Christian Warmer did not either.

"Where are ye from?"

Johannes avoided the issue of Transylvania. "Saxony," he said. "Germany."

"Are ye a friend of Francis Pastorius?"

It was a name Johannes had heard a dozen times since they had arrived in North America. Pastorius was the agent for the Frankfort Company, the group that had established the most famous German settlement on the continent. But Johannes hadn't even been old enough for the choir in Segesvár when Pastorius had left Europe. "We are planning to journey to his village of Germanopolis," he told the Welshman.

The man laughed again. "There an't no Germanopolis, son. There's a place they call the German Town, but it an't much of a town. There an't more'n a hundred or so, mostly Dutch, livin' up there in the woods. Ye don't have hope of stayin' there, do ye?"

Johannes ignored the twisting sensation in his stomach. The needs of thirty-eight people, plus his own, somehow had to be permanently addressed, and he had no idea where any of them would even spend the night. "We have been given twenty-four hundred acres on which to settle," he said.

"Given by Pastorius?"

"Given by a generous friend in Europe."

The Welshman said nothing but returned his attention to the invisible winds that moved them along. Johannes stared uneasily at the man's weathered face, trying for a long while to unlock the meaning of his silence.

"*Schuyl Kil,*" the Welshman said finally. The sloop was approaching a bend to the east. They waved back to a little fishing boat that had entered the river from a tributary beside a long island near the western bank.

"Hidden Creek?" Johannes asked, translating from Dutch. He squinted to see what he could of the mysterious-sounding river past the overhanging limbs that obscured its mouth. The pristine water that sparkled in the afternoon sun—he wondered from what ancient, uncharted source it originated.

"Up there's where I live. In Meirion, the Welsh Township, a couple of dozen miles upstream, past the falls, across from the Wissahickon."

"What is the Wissahickon?"

"It be the valley of Whitpain's Creek. Funny little gorge on the starboard side of the *Schuyl Kil.* The In'duns call it Wissahickon."

In addition to German, Johannes could speak Latin, Romany, Dutch and English. He could read Greek, Hebrew, Arabic, and Persian. But this word had not derived from any of those languages. The thought set his imagination on fire. He knew the Indians had already had two centuries of contact with Europeans, but that contact had been with men of the world—traders, sailors, and would-be conquerors. The religious beliefs that the Europeans had brought with them were largely those of the Church. The strict orthodoxy of the Puritans, the faith of the Mennonites, and even the openhearted philosophy of the Quakers, all viewed the Indians as raw material to be processed into their own version of Christianity.

"Do Indians live there?" he asked, pointing up the *Schuyl Kil.*

The Welshman smiled. "Son, there be Ind'uns everywhere there's no whites. Up there is *Lenápay* country. *Pahsayung, Kahn-she-hock-keeng, Pemickpaka:* they're all Ind'un villages." His smile turned into a grin, and he took his hand off the wheel to give Johannes' shoulder a squeeze. "Don't worry. They won't be a problem to ye. Not if ye an't makin' trouble. Deal with 'em as a Christian, just as Penn did."

As far as Johannes knew, no European with knowledge of the ancient mystical traditions had yet made contact with the Indians. Zimmerman believed that the Indians were heir to the same spiritual heritage as the rest of humanity. They were at least as deserving as the Europeans and Asians, or likely more so, considering the pure state of the wilderness in which they lived. It would be through the Chapter of Perfection that the mystic "beads of mercury" would be united east to west, and complete the Great Circle of humanity at last. A shiver of energy ran down his arms.

It was Frau Zimmerman who was touching him. Her hand was on his shoulder. Her eyes were darker than they had been a year before and her skin more weatherworn, but her voice was still strong and full of unconquerable faith. "*Gut gemacht,* Magister Kelpius," she said. *You have done well.*

"Let go," the pilot called, and the ship's lad pushed the anchor over the side. The passengers pressed toward the port bow, craning their necks. "Let go the jib sheet and halyard!" The sloop veered toward the bank of the De La War. As the pilot and ship's lad dropped the mainsail, everyone began to talk. Johannes strained to see over the shoulders that pushed him back.

There were no shining towers of a Quaker Utopia. A few hatless stragglers near the shore gawked at them. Past a single dock, an ugly two-story building stood at the waterfront to welcome newcomers. A sign announced the Blue Anchor Tavern.

"Philadelphia!" shouted a voice.

The sloop rammed against the pier. The ship's lad threw a rope over a piling. Then he opened a portion of the railing on the port side and threw a warped plank over the edge. It landed uncertainly on the dock.

"Alright now," called the pilot. "Disembark 'afore the tide turns. Get movin'."

The women, lifting their skirts above their ankles, went first. Then the men followed, their eagerness barely disguised by the sense of decorum the moment required. Johannes was so intently surveying the landscape of their new home that it was only after Köster called his name he realized he was last to remain on board. The pilgrims had gathered in a circle at the end of the dock, waiting for him. Some in their Pietist robes, some in Quaker-style britches and coats, others in the wide-lapel shirts of German students, they were dressed formally for the first time since leaving London. He walked self-consciously to the place in the center, feeling the weight of their esteem.

He knelt down, pressed his fingers into the soft, warm earth, then folded his hands.

Above him, Köster began to pray aloud. He was aware of the voice, solid as always, but it was like gossamer beside the sounds of his own heart. In that moment, in the stench of the wet ground—that strange, foreign ground—all his most secret fears and hopes collided with a paralyzing force. With, or in spite of, his leadership they had all arrived safely, fulfilling the awesome task that the Magister had put in his charge. He had never felt so utterly dependent upon the Power that brought this about. The sense of unreality that always seemed to accompany his strongest emotions overcame him, and it was only with effort he realized he was not, as usual, alone.

He could hear Maria singing and, beneath the melody, the shouts of the sloop's crew as they threw precious cargo from the dark of the ship's hold onto the wharf. But there was also something else.

Johannes opened his eyes. Two men stood beside him, covering him in their shadow. "Who in the name of Jezzus fuggin' Christ are you?"

He rose to his feet, struggling to understand the words and the mind of the man who spoke them. Wiping his eyes he noticed the dirt on his hands. He reluctantly offered one in greeting.

"We are students, having just arrived from a long and arduous journey from England," Köster said.

"England? Y'an't from any part of England I heard of." The man was without a hat, his long hair fallen into his face. Johannes could smell liquor on his breath.

"We are Germans," Johannes said.

"Friends," Köster interrupted. "A group of devout men and women who have left their homeland because of the failings of the German Church and have embraced the simple faith of the Society of Friends. We traveled to these shores at the invitation of the English Quakers."

"Quakers? Ye an't *Keithian* Quakers, are ye?"

Köster was far too quick to be shown up ignorant. "Keithian Quakers? I should say not. I can say with absolute certainty that there is not a man or woman standing before you here that would attest to the manner and worship of the Keithian Quakers. Of those of false doctrine and those who would distort the pure and simple faith, we have had enough..."

Johannes felt that the men were about to have enough of Köster. "We were instructed upon arrival to present ourselves to Governor Penn," he said.

The longhaired man turned to his companion who, not only hatless but toothless, laughed. "Ye better get back on yer sloop." His diction was so poor Johannes could barely understand him. "That fool got charged with bein' a traitor and a secret Cath'lic. He left here nigh two years. He's back in England, probably in chains."

The knot in Johannes' stomach twisted again. Penn, the architect of the great Philadelphian experiment, was the one, they had been told, who would ensure them freedom and safety. "Who, then, is in authority?"

"His Majesty King Will'm," the longhaired man said. "But he an't here either, as far as I know." The other man grinned, baring wide, pink gums. "You mebbe could see Gov'ner Fletcher, but he's gone north to fight the French. There's Dep'ty Markham, but he's one of them Seventh Day'ers and won't do nothin' official on a Saturday. Ye an't Seventh Day'ers, are ye?"

Johannes put his hand on Köster's shoulder. "Your law requires us to report to the provincial government," he told the man. "Is there anyone in the city who can help us?"

The two men looked at each other. "How 'bout Bobby?" slurred the toothless man.

"Bobby Whitpain?" asked his comrade.

"He's settin' in the Blue Anchor."

"Is he sober?" The toothless man laughed.

"He's as sober as you 'n' me."

"Yer in luck, Herr," the longhaired man said to Köster. "Johnny here'll fetch the squire for ye. I'll take ye to his house. It an't but a throw of a brick from here. But ye might want to set some of yer kith here to stay and watch yer goods. Never know who might be larkin' about the wharf."

The home of Robert Whitpain was only a single street from the boat landing. It was large by European standards, made of limestone with glass windows lacking the bars that most Londoners seemed to feel necessary. A fragrant and shady garden to its side and back were also distinctly provincial, showing off the luxury of space that an unlimited continent gave residents of America.

An African servant, dressed in a white lace shirt, answered the door. Yes, he told them, they may come and wait. But just the four of them. Even the master's Large Room could not hold all the visitors. Would the others take rest in the garden? He would fetch them all cool water to drink.

In the Large Room a mahogany clock ticked off minutes beside a portrait of a man who looked annoyed by its sound. A window had been hinged open, letting in warm air and slanting rays of gold that shone across the surface of a long table. A polished silver vase held a bouquet of fresh flowers.

"Good afternoon, gentlemen." A roundish man of about fifty entered the room, adjusting his wig. His eyebrows were thick and wild, giving him a dangerous look of self-confidence. He shook hands with Köster, then Falckner, then Seelig and reluctantly Johannes, whose hands were still stained with soil from the bank of the De La War River. The servant waited at the door until his master was seated in the captain's chair. Then he carefully placed before him a large black book, an inkpot and a great, flowing feather.

"We have just arrived from Baltimore, where we came from London, from Germany," Johannes said.

"Yes, so I have heard." Whitpain opened the book. "How many in your party?"

"Thirty-nine," Falckner said, quick to display his grasp of English. "Nine women, twenty-seven men, three children."

"Reason for coming to Pennsylvania?"

Falckner looked to Köster. Johannes was suddenly filled with dread that Köster was about to launch into an apocalyptic speech about the Last Days and Time. "To help establish an harmonious community according to the *philadelphian* ideas of Peace, Truth, Love, and Plenty," he said, quoting from the seal of the province that was emblazoned on the cover of Whitpain's book.

Whitpain ran a finger around the curve of his ear. From his vest pocket he took a pipe and a small bag. With a deliberate movement, he struck a match across a flint. He puffed a series of violent breaths that sent a cloud into the angled sunlight.

"You fellows got entangled in some sort of trouble back in the fatherland?"

"We are religious pilgrims," said Köster.

"I see," said Whitpain. "Where do you plan to live?"

"Zeigen Sie ihm das Papier," Köster said. Falckner reach into his robe and brought out a scroll.

Whitpain fumbled for a pair of spectacles and unrolled the document. "I can't read this," he said.

"It is written in German," Johannes explained.

"What kind of seal is this?"

"It was notarized in Holland, from where the document originated."

Whitpain moved his eyes up and down through the glass circles on his nose. "I don't see Pastorius' name on here anywhere," he said.

Köster leaned over the table. "My good fellow, there is no need for you to inspect the letter. Its validity is beyond question, as my brother Ludolph has assured me." He reached to take the document, but Whitpain pulled it away. Rerolling the paper tightly, Whitpain stuck the end into his pipe and puffed until it caught flame. He held it up ceremoniously, then let it fall on the carpet where he stomped it under his boot.

For a moment Köster seemed unable to move. "Sir, if you take me for an ignorant itinerant, you are in grave error. I am Henrich Bernard Köster, formerly in the employ of the privy-councilor to the House of Brandenburg. I will not tolerate such brazen destruction of valuable property!"

"Valuable? That little piece of Dutch parchment wasn't worth the trouble it took you to carry it across the street. And as to who you were formerly, there isn't a soul in the province who cares a rat's ass if you used to crap in the Brandenburg privy, or if you used to hump the Queen of Spain. Welcome to America, Mr. Köster." He blew another cloud of smoke and called to the doorway. "Little Joey, come in here. There seems to be a pile of ashes on the carpet."

Köster turned angrily to Johannes. "*Sie müssen handeln,* Kelpius!"

Only the steadiness of the floor beneath him—the tangible reminder that despite all the dangers they had arrived safely in Pennsylvania—gave Johannes composure. *"Gott wird versorgen,"* he whispered to Köster. *God will provide.*

The African entered the room with a broom and dustpan. Johannes looked at Whitpain, wiping the tension from his face. "Where might we find Mr. Pastorius?"

"Well, son, he's just built himself a little house in Germantown. That's a few swampy miles northwest of Fairhill, but you won't have the time to haul all your belongings up there today. We still have some legal matters to go through."

Johannes put a restraining hand on the arm of Köster's robe. "Then we will need to find a church with a beadhouse," he said, "where our people might find lodging for the night."

Whitpain laughed. "You won't find a church anywhere in this whole province. The Swedes used to have one down in

Christiana, before their sot of a pastor let it fall into ruins." He turned to the African. "Little Joey, when you're finished cleaning up, run over to Mr. Markham's house and tell him we need to make arrangements somewhere in the city for forty young Germans for the night. Now, boys, you're going to have to swear a loyalty oath to King William. I trust you're not the kind of Quakers who are against swearing oaths. Are you boys Keithians or orthodox Quakers?"

Falckner seemed to be having trouble following. *"Was ist dieses* Keithian *wieder?"* he asked in a whisper.

"Squire, we have spent the last five months at sea. I am afraid that we do not understand your question."

Whitpain grinned. "You don't know George Keith? Well, boys, it's the sort of story that makes a man glad he's a member of the Church of England, even if only in spirit. I had the pleasure of having dinner with Keith, right here at this very table. Penn sent him 'round once to a meeting of the Assembly. Said he was a brother Quaker, good friend of old George Fox, and so on.

"After dinner Keith and I got talking. Well, it was more like he got talking, and I got listening. Told me all about Christian redemption and the transmigration of souls. How Jesus was a Master of Egyptian Magic, and how it was possible for a soul to resurrect its own body or some rot. Penn being governor at that time, it wasn't polite for me to do anything but listen. Well, even the Quakers had trouble with all this, as odd a lot as they are—no particular offense to you boys. Even though he was a friend of Penn, the Quakers finally tossed him out, but by that time old Keith had himself a big group of followers. They're what they call the Keithians now, and you boys wouldn't believe what a row these More-Peaceable-Than-Thou's can make. Last time I saw Keith, he was skedaddling down the river to grab the first boat back to England.

"Take my advice, lads. Keep a wary eye on your Quaker brethren. All that Inward Light's been flashing around here like a thunderstorm. Now, since I assume you don't object to swearing an oath to the Crown, I'll have you bring your people in here. But you'll need to bring them in two by two. And keep them quiet.

Little Joey doesn't like it when we have too much commotion in the house."

He went to extend his hand again to Johannes but changed his mind. "You boys can clean up in my washroom. I've got a half a hog hanging in the smokehouse and the best wine cellar in America. We'll make a night of it."

The sun had already set by the time all the arrangements had been made, but the midsummer sky remained a rich indigo. About twenty pilgrims walked out of the city along Vine Street, the municipal boundary that led toward what were known as the Liberty Lands. Past the final lonely house, they followed a path into the darkness of the nearby hills.

"Englein!" Geissler's voice caught in his throat. *Little angels!*

The forest was alive with tiny lights that flickered and danced in the shadows. The whole party stopped. "*Nein,*" Falckner said. *"Der Glühwürmchen."*

Daniel Geissler, limping since he had broken his leg onboard ship, dropped down to his knees and clasped his hands in prayer. *"Englein!"*

Seelig laughed and swung his arms into the air until he caught a light. He held it in his cupped hands and brought it to Geissler's face. "Glowworms. Just flying glowworms."

Geissler shook his head. *"'Ich will sie auf einem Weg gehen lassen, den sie nicht kennen, auf Pfaden, die sie nicht kennen, will ich sie schreiten lassen,'"* he quoted to Seelig. *"'Die Finsternis vor ihnen will ich zum Licht machen.'"*

And I will bring them by a way they knew not; I will lead them in paths they have not known. I will make darkness light before them.

Seelig patted him on the back. Falckner helped him back to his feet and they started into the forest. When they reached the top of a small hill, without a word being spoken, they began to gather sticks and pine boughs for the ritual fire of St. John's Eve. Their movement in the underbrush stirred a tremendous flock of passenger pigeons. For a full half-minute the pilgrims stood staring into the fluttering vortex of the birds' flight. It was a stunning demonstration of the natural power of the world that lay before them.

Even after the pigeons had passed, the woods were still alive with a symphony of natural music. Parakeets sang lullabies, crickets chirped in vast choirs, and a mockingbird offered a repertoire of American bird melodies. The air was heavy with fragrance. Falckner struck a flint and the aroma of smoke mingled with holly, honeysuckle, and the richness of an undisturbed forest floor.

"Let us sing a hymn to the Father." Köster invoked the secret words of Jesus. "'And go forth to what before us lies.'" The brethren took hands around the fire. Their faces, eyes closed, gleamed in the firelight.

Johannes' attention had wandered. Hearing Köster's invocation, he entered the center of the circle that slowly began to circumambulate. Through the moving shadows, past the fire's light, past the silhouettes of the forest, he glimpsed a light. Probably, he thought, a reflection from the waters of the *Schuyl Kil*, the hidden river to the city's west.

In Europe, land had been divided and subdivided for so many centuries that there was not an acre that hadn't been subjugated into private property. Here everything was different. On the other side of the *Schuyl Kil* lay the Welsh township. Further west were Indian lands. And beyond that? No one knew how far the wilderness continued, or what secrets lay there unsuspected by a smug European civilization. No wonder some believed that when Christ returned bodily to Earth it would be in America.

He closed his eyes, trying to concentrate on the ritual, but in the quiet of his mind, the strange sensation was strong. He had no doubt that someone else was nearby. He didn't know who it was, nor could he understand what kind of presence he felt. Nevertheless, it was unmistakable. Someone was there, watching them. And waiting.

Chapter Fourteen

Oral report to Lenápay Tribal Elders
Settlement of Okehocking
Autumnal Equinox, 1694

May the Creator put truth into my mouth, so the words I speak may bring blessing and benefit to the People.

It was on the day before this that I arrived from the tribe of Those-Who-Live-Near-The-Waves. But the gift they presented to us I have not brought back, and I shall explain why.

On the last night of my visit I receive a message from Num-ox-oó-mus, my Grandfather. When I was a child, Num-ox-oó-mus would take me into the forest along the high ground between Wissahickon and the river *Mëneyung*. He would tell me that the *Manituwák*, the Spirits, once made a trail there from the Heavens to Earth. On this trail the *Manituwák* traveled, just as we travel from village to village. He would tell me it was here that the wise ones of the People would come to speak to the Creator and receive Food-That-Cannot-Be-Seen.

As a child I would ask Num-ox-oó-mus where this trail is, and say that I wished to speak to the Creator and receive Food-That-Cannot-Be-Seen just as the wise ones do. Num-ox-oó-mus would laugh at me. He would tell me that this Food is a gift from the Creator only for those whom He chooses, and that I have been given other gifts. He would say that, besides, the *Manituwák* moved their trail that leads from the Heavens to Earth, and the place where the old trail used to be is now overgrown and neglected and can hardly be found.

I would ask Num-ox-oó-mus why the *Manituwák* would let this happen. He would say that this was because of the will of the

Creator, who knew that soon *Shu-wá-nackw* would come. *Shu-wá-nackw* must not walk this trail, for he is not worthy and would defile it. When I would ask Num-ox-oó-mus who was this *Shu-wá-nackw*, he would tell me of the white man with his hats and his papers and his guns. This was many summers before I ever saw *Shu-wá-nackw*. Num-ox-oó-mus was one of the wise ones of the People.

Then, in the village of Those-Who-Live-Near-The-Waves, on the last night of our visit, Num-ox-oó-mus returns to me in a dream. I am once again with him on the top of that same high ground. In his hands, he holds *Amimi*, the Dove. Num-ox-oó-mus calls me to him. Then he opens his hands and Amimi flies away into the sky until no more can I see him. I understand that it is because *Amimi* knows how to find the ancient trail of the *Manituwák*, and he is following it into the Heavens.

When I wake from this dream, I know what I must do. With me on my visit to Those-Who-Live-Near-The-Waves is my grandson, Amimi, who next summer will be a hunter. He is strong and skilled, but I believe he also possesses special gifts. I tell Amimi that we are going to travel near the white man's village because I want to fish in the stream of the Golden Valley, where I played and fished as a boy. I do not tell him that Num-ox-oó-mus has visited me in a dream. I do not tell him of the Spirit's trail between the Heavens and Earth.

We cross the big river and sleep outside the white man's village. Amimi is bothered by the smell, and I tell him he must get used to it, as this land will smell like this for a long time. Early in the morning, while Sun is not yet shining, we follow the little valley that comes to the large rocks, and when I see Wissahickon, my heart is so full of joy that tears come to my old eyes. "This is Wissahickon," I tell Amimi." It is here that I am happier than anywhere else."

We see that the leaves of Sugar Maple are changing to yellow, and Wissahickon proves her name as the Golden Valley. I take Amimi to where the waters bend, and we find the very stones Num-ox-oó-mus placed with his own grandfather to trap Catfish and Trout. Amimi is glad to see me so happy, but he keeps looking into the forest instead of paying attention to Trout. I am annoyed at him, but I know that my eyes and ears and nose do not know as much as they once did. I wonder if, in some way, he knows we are near the ancient trail of the *Manituwák*. I have always believed that this boy possesses special gifts. Then I hear something, too. It is *Shu-wá-nackw*.

He is the only creature who comes through the forest without caring who knows he is there. He is one man alone, with a *Shu-wá-nackw* beard. He is clad in the dress of a woman, but it is long and unadorned. He is broad of shoulder and carries the white man's favorite tool—the book in which he keeps marks.

Trout and Catfish hide from the sound, but Amimi and I continue to hold our nets in the water, hoping that *Shu-wá-nackw* will pass by and leave us alone. He does not. Instead, he stops when he sees us, and even my old nose can smell his fear. Amimi has never seen a white man, but behaves as if it were Wolf. He does not threaten but stands unafraid.

For a long time this white man watches to see if we will hurt him. When he is no longer afraid, he splashes into the water as if to frighten Trout and all his family downstream. Even Amimi must raise his eyes at this. When he does, the white man stops and points a finger at his own chest. He speaks only one word, "Kuster." We continue to hold our nets, hoping that *Shu-wá-nackw* has done all the frightening of fish he has come to do. But the white man continues to point at himself saying "Kuster, Kuster, Kuster." I think to myself that this name is not one that is auspicious for the People.

At first *Shu-wá-nackw* Kuster is afraid because we do not speak to him. Then he is angry because we do not speak to him. Then he grows tired of being angry. He crosses the creek and begins to make more noise through the forest on the other side. Amimi is happy that he is leaving us, and so are Trout and Catfish. But I watch *Shu-wá-nackw* Kuster. He is walking up to the ridge between Wissahickon and the river *Mëneyung*, the place where once there was a trail between the Heavens and earth. Amimi does not understand why we must leave our fishing and follow *Shu-wá-nackw* Kuster. I think I might tell him about the trail, but I do not speak of it. I want to wait to see if Amimi knows it is there. I also want to know where the white man is going.

We find the place of my dream, the very place where Num-ox-oó-mus had taken me when I was a boy. Cedar and Chestnut and Pine have been cut down. Now there is a great skeleton of logs in the shape of a white man's house, but as tall as the top of the forest. Upon the summit of these bones of trees is a wooden wheel with four spokes. Many white men are there, but they do not speak. I have never seen white man with his brothers when they are not all chattering like Mockingbird. Most are standing together to form a circle, just like the circles of the People. Into this circle comes *Shu-wá-nackw* Kuster. He puts down his book and takes their hands. In the center of the circle is a small fire, and a tall, thin white man is scattering powder into the fire. I can smell that it is Cedar mixed with powerful medicine.

The eyes of Amimi are open wide. He knows of the white man, but the stories he has heard are not about this tribe. I think that I am seeing a dance of the People, except for the dresses these men are wearing, their soft, unprotected skin, and the hair on their faces. There is no drum, but these white men make a chant. I cannot understand the words, but it is clear to me that these men think they are speaking to the Creator. I laugh inside myself.

Amimi looks at me. I know that he is thinking, "They are not moving the right way. They are not saying the right words. They are not in harmony with the Creator and the Earth." He is young and does not understand that the special knowledge of ceremonies is a gift that has been given to the People. He does not understand that *Shu-wá-nackw* does not have the education and culture that we do. But we wait and watch.

There is a white man in the middle of the circle. He turns around and around and calls out the prayers. He acts like the leader of this tribe, but he does not appear to be much older than Amimi. He turns his palms up and holds his hands toward the Heavens. He is asking for the blessings of the Creator, even though their dance does not have any power. I think that the medicine in their fire is meant to send them on a spirit journey. It is very entertaining to watch them play at this like children, and I understand why the *Manituwák* abandoned the trail between the Heavens and Earth before these men arrived.

It is then that the young man in the center, the leader, turns and looks in our direction. "He cannot see us," I think. "We are hidden in the leaves. We make no noise. Their smoke covers our scent." But then I think, "Perhaps the Creator has told him we are here."

The white men stop their dance. The circle breaks open and the leader walks toward us. He is not tall like most of the *Shu-wá-nackw*. One of his eyelids falls down too far, and because of this he resembles Num-ox-oó-mus. He says nothing to us and stands apart. I do not threaten but stand unafraid.

It is Amimi who moves first. For a moment, I am afraid. I have seen *Shu-wá-nackw* reach for his gun when he thinks he is being attacked. But Amimi walks past me into the clearing, holding his hands to the Heavens, palms upward, as if he, too, were asking for the blessings of the Creator. The white man smiles and does the same. I follow Amimi toward the white men.

"Do you speak English?" asks *Shu-wá-nackw* Kuster.

"No, I speak the tongue of the *Lenápay*," I say.

The white men laugh. They are nervous.

"But you understand English language?" asks *Shu-wá-nackw* Kuster.

Did he not hear me? Sometimes I am surprised by the ignorance of the white man. "Yes," I say. "Do you, *Shu-wá-nackw* Kuster, understand *Lenápay* language?"

The white men laugh again.

The young man with the eyes of Num-ox-oó-mus takes down his arms and puts his hand out toward me in the manner of greeting of *Shu-wá-nackw*. "*Itah*," he says. "My name is Kapé-e-shush. We are your friends. We are *netap*." He uses words the English use when they are trying to speak *Lenápay*. I wonder why he has the name *Kapé-e-shush*, Little Twin. I look around to see if there is anyone who resembles him, but all of these white men, with their long dresses and beards, look alike to me.

"My name is Séh-laak." It is the tall white man who scattered the Cedar-medicine into the fire. I understand why he is named *Séh-laak*, Scattered.

Amimi and I take the hands of the white men. They are still afraid of us, but not afraid that we will hurt them. They are afraid that we will not like them. They look at us with curious eyes and speak to each other in strange *Shu-wá-nackw* tongues. Amimi enjoys the attention of the white men, and I am concerned that he will not learn to avoid them as I have.

They offer us water and food. I do not understand how *Shu-wá-nackw* has the knowledge to build boats that carry a hundred men across the salt water but does not know how to nourish his own body. Their food is curdled cow's milk and cakes that are as hard as stones. Once a white man told me that he believed disease was caused by eating too many different kinds of food. It is this kind of stupidity that makes me wonder how long *Shu-wá-nackw* will last in our land.

Then they lead us to their great construction of logs. They are proud that they have cut down Cedar and Spruce and Pine and are building this tall thing. "I do not understand *Shu-wá-nackw*," I say to Amimi. "I do not understand why he builds houses as if he will live in them forever. Does he not understand that if Life does not make him journey, then Death will?"

"I do not think this is to be a house," says Amimi. "I think this will be their sacred place, where they worship the Creator."

I look at Amimi. I do not know what makes him think this. He does not understand the white man's language.

They have worked a very long time to make this skeleton of a house. I can smell the fresh scent of Cedar and Pine. Upon one of the logs they have hung a wheel with four spokes. It is like the one that is built upon the roof, but this is made of white man's Iron. I think that Amimi must be right. This must be their sacred place.

"Do you wish to see the *Sternwarte*?" Kapé-e-shush asks us. I do not know if I do or not. He invites us to follow into the skeleton. We walk across a platform of logs and climb stairs that wind around in a circle. We climb higher and higher. At the top we come to a small place to stand. In this place there is a table with many of the white man's books upon it. Beside the table is something that looks like a very smooth and straight branch of a tree, standing upon three skinny legs.

Amimi walks to the edge and looks out. We are very tall up in the trees. We can see very far, past the river *Mëneyung*, almost to our own village. Kapé-e-shush closes his eye, the one with the eyelid that falls too low, and looks through the smooth branch that stands upon three skinny legs. Then he asks me to do the same.

At first I can not see because there is white man's glass across the hole. Then I begin to be able to see. I see the waters of Wissahickon as if I were standing there. It is like being Eagle and seeing Rabbit from a cloud. I understand. This is what these white men use to look for the trail that leads from the Heavens to Earth. I am sad. I see the young and eager face of Kapé-e-shush as he shows this thing to Amimi. I want to tell him that the trail is no longer there. But I know that if I could tell him this, it would wound his heart. He has come from so far away. This is a very sad thing.

Kapé-e-shush takes us back down his stairs. We sit in a big circle on the platform near the ground. There is no pipe. The white men are silent. Kapé-e-shush shows me markings from a book. One looks like a star with six points. I think that he is wondering if I know how to read these marks. He asks me many foolish questions. He wants to know about the stars and about *Lenápay* medicine. He wants to know about our sacred things and our sacred words. He is full of useless questions that I do not know how to answer.

At last he says, "We would like to learn about your beliefs and your practices. We invite the wise ones of your people to visit us, to teach us what you know and to share our knowledge."

I smile at Kapé-e-shush, but he does not know that it is a smile of sadness. I am sad for him. He wants to learn so earnestly, but he does not know how. What I want to say to him is this: "If you wish to gain the knowledge of the wise ones, you must come to live with the *Lenápay* as a child. From your mother and father you would learn the things needed to be a Person. Then, if the Creator wills, you might be given the gift of learning from the wise ones. Even then it might take you a hundred moons. And if you became wise, Kapé-e-shush, you might learn things that you did not want to know when you started. That the *Manituwák* have moved their trail that leads from the Heavens to Earth. That you have come so far too late."

Kapé-e-shush makes a signal to his people. He says that they will pray in silence, so that our hearts may meet in a place where there are no words. There is still no pipe, no medicine. They have invited Amimi into their circle even though he is not yet a man. This is not the way to go on a spirit journey, but we close our eyes and sit with them. We sit for a very long time.

When Sun falls down into the treetops, I know it is time for us to leave. I want to cross the river *Mëneyung* and be away from *Shu-wá-nackw's* land before it is dark. I must rouse Amimi from this trance. We leave the white men to their prayer circle.

We are walking away from their sacred house but Amimi stops. I look back and see Kapé-e-shush. He is coming toward us. He holds something. He gives it to me. It is a white man's blanket. He wants to give it to us as a gift.

I look at it. It has very many bright colors. It cannot be worn in the forest. It is not even a single piece of cloth, but is made of many small pieces sewn together. But to Kapé-e-shush it is a thing of value. I do not want to offend him, so I take it and thank him in English.

Amimi looks at me. He is thinking, "It is not right that we accept this gift and have none to offer in return." He is right. I think that I do not have anything of value, but I remember the gift of Those-Who-Live-Near-The-Waves. I reach inside my bandolier bag and offer Kapé-e-shush the shells that were the gift to our village. He tells me that he is grateful for this gift, and that he will treasure it. I think that he is such a good boy, and I am sad again.

We follow the river *Mëneyung* upstream to where we have hidden our dugout. We cross the river. The water is still and blue as the sky. Amimi tells me he knows why the leader of the white man's tribe, the man with the eyelid that falls down too far, has the name Kapé-e-shush, Little Twin.

I ask him why.

"When we are sitting in the white man's prayer circle," he tells me, "I see a light behind Kapé-e-shush. This light does not come from Sun or from a fire. I am very curious about this light. I watch it from closed eyes so it does not know that I can see it. While I watch, this light changes into the shape of a Person. It is hidden behind Kapé-e-shush and I cannot see its face. At first I am afraid, but then I think that this must be a *Manituwák,* a Spirit. She does not move, but just sits behind Kapé-e-shush. I think that this white man's twin must be a Spirit. That is why someone so young can be the leader of his tribe."

For one breath, I think I will tell Amimi about the old trail of the *Manituwák*. Instead, I nod to show that I have understood. We hide our dugout and come home.

Yoconock, Lenápay Elder

Chapter Fifteen

Tuesday, March 23, 1697
Germantown, Pennsylvania, and vicinity

"I will call it *Irenia*, the House of Peace." Köster's voice was warm and bright. It was the only thing warm and bright in the cold and damp morning. Patches of snow still lurked in the edges of the meadow. There was no sun, only a sky like slate that mocked the calendar. "Upon this rock I will build my church," Köster said, spreading his arms. But it wasn't a rock that he held in his hand. It was a land deed.

The ground was too wet to dig a foundation for a building, or even for the two men to want to walk down the hill to the site. Instead, they stood on the high ground, trying to imagine the future edifice. For Köster, it was a euphoric dream. For Johannes, an ironic one. Just four years before, he and Henrich Köster were under threat from the Church. Hadn't they forsaken the continent of their birth to escape a vengeful, sanctimonious institution? Now Köster wanted to erect a new institution.

"It will be the True Church of the Brethren in America, an authentic spiritual community." Köster spoke the word "authentic" without concern that it might be insulting. Köster had never been able to abide well in the Tabernacle in the Wissahickon. And he had never been able to disguise his contempt for it.

Johannes understood. His own ascension to leadership had been at Köster's expense; at least that's how it seemed to Köster.

Zimmerman had been right about one thing—Köster wanted to lead, not to follow. Pennsylvania had presented him too tempting a challenge. It was only the first day after their arrival, after they had learned there wasn't a church or an ordained minister in the province, that Köster began to take it upon himself to lead regular orthodox services. At first, it was just for the Germans, but the charisma of his personality soon brought him the larger following for which he had so desperately longed.

And then there was George Keith. The departure of the radical religious leader had left a vacancy of leadership in his Quaker community. Francis Daniel Pastorius, the principal figure in Germantown, had worked patiently and earnestly to heal the breach created by Keith. By the time the Chapter of Perfection arrived, the Quakers had started to reunite, but Köster couldn't resist the power of the vacuum left by Keith. He entered it vigorously and succeeded in returning Friends to Enemies.

"Kelpius," Köster said, holding up the deed, "I trust it will not be necessary for anyone to know about your generosity in this matter."

Johannes just smiled. If Zimmerman had still been alive, Köster would not have had the courage to commit such apostasy. The truth was, though, that Johannes felt relieved to be freed from Köster's constant hostility. As for land deeds, he was equally happy not be encumbered by such things. In an act of contrition more than generosity, the wealthy Robert Whitpain had offered the Community one hundred and seventy-five acres to use freely—free from deeds and papers and the bounds of ownership.

God had truly provided. The location of the land they had been given was perfect. It was close enough to Germantown for them to minister to the townsfolk, but remote enough to be a natural sanctuary. The high ground between the Wissahickon Creek and the *Schuyl Kil* offered a perfect site for the Tabernacle's astronomical observatory. The forest was a treasure house of provisions, as were the crystal clear waters of the creek itself. The winding valley of the Wissahickon, with its sunlit groves and deep, mysterious glens nearly hidden from the world, was a marvelous geographic anomaly.

But there was more.

Johannes had felt the subtle influences even before he first stepped onto the Pennsylvania soil, although it had taken him weeks to understand. He led the pilgrims through the wilderness to the grove of giant trees along the western ridge, to the magnificent high ground that opened to the heavens, to the matchless site his calculations proved had been ordained for their great Tabernacle. For him, there had been no doubt. The place had been lying in wait for countless millennia for their arrival, protected by the Creator for the realization of His promise to mankind.

The city of Philadelphia, a few miles to the southwest, lay along the seventy-fifth longitude, placing the Wissahickon Valley in the middle of the terrestrial energy line indicated by Zimmerman. The ridge itself—at the location they had chosen for their Tabernacle—was precisely forty degrees north of the Earth's equator—a mathematical confirmation of the numerological perfection of their undertaking.

"Thank you for coming all the way here," Köster said. "Sprogel will take you back to Germantown. I wish to remain here in solitude." For all his study of the human spirit, Köster seemed oblivious to the significance of the moment. He and Johannes had been more than just traveling companions, more than comrades against the oppression of the authorities. They were spiritual brethren, linked together in the ancient chain of students of the mystic arts. But as Köster offered Johannes his hand that morning, it was as if to a stranger. Köster's eyes did not even look at him, but were lost in his own imaginary future. "*Lebewohl,* Brother Henrich," Johannes said.

The way back from Plymouth was optimistically called the Great Road, but here it was barely more than a wide path up and down the hills. Along its trail, snow still showed the tracks the wagon had made earlier, but they were quickly disappearing. The wind was blowing and Johannes pulled in his cloak. He sat in silence in the damp wagon while Sprogel urged the tired horse that pulled it along. Sprogel, like a handful of others, had left the community the residents of Germantown had wryly named "The Woman in the Wilderness."

Even though Germantown had doubled in size since their arrival, there were still fewer than forty houses—functional structures of logs and dark, rough stone. Most had steep roofs, front stoops and trim fenced-in gardens that reminded Johannes of rural Germany. All were huddled along the section of the wide Great Road that had been developed from a muddy path into a full half-mile of cobblestone paving.

Sprogel left him off in town in front of a log house. It belonged to the aged widow Dimmers, whose needs were being met by the members of the Zimmerman family.

"Grüff Gott, Magister Kelpius. Won't you please come in?" The door was answered by Maria—Maria Zimmerman no longer, but now Maria Warmer. Neither was she any longer the young virgin who had endured the journey from Magdeburg to Philadelphia. Her green eyes shone from a face flushed with the life force of her pregnant body, the result of her fleshly union with Christian Warmer. "We have been expecting you."

"Grüff Gott," he said. His own face flushed at her touch. "How does she feel today?"

"She has been waiting patiently for your visit. It is her only relief."

The inside of the house was deadly dark and still. Nothing moved, and even the sound of their footfalls seemed frozen in time. At the end of the house, one door was ajar. "Frau Dimmers?" Maria whispered. "Magister Kelpius has come to see you."

"Grüff Gott, Magister."

"Would you light the lamp, Frau Warmer?" he whispered to Maria.

"I am having..." the woman tried to speak.

"You are having difficulty breathing." There was no doubt it was rheumatic heart congestion, the same affliction that had taken the life of Maria's father.

"Magister, I have seen..."

"Yes."

"I have seen them."

"I understand, Frau Dimmers."

"My sons. My husband."

There was nothing he could do but help ease her transition into the next world. "I will write you the most powerful prayer of all," he said.

Maria stood on the opposite side of the bed, holding the widow's hand. Johannes took from his bag a small piece of paper, a feather pen, and a small bottle of special ink.

"I am the Truth" were Christ's words. This was not the Truth. It was a deception, a foolish compromise with superstitions. The truth would have been to tell this lovely, gentle, suffering soul that the relief provided by the *Essentia dulcis* in his ink would be temporary. At best, it would delay her reunion with members of her family who had preceded her in death. He took a deliberate breath of his own, the strongest ritual he could perform there, and silently invoked the Power that would, at its own bidding, flow through him to the body of the woman whose hand he held.

Then, inscribing Latin words on the paper, he whispered them. *"Fiat voluntas tua sicut in coelo et in terra."* Thy Will be done in earth as it is in heaven.

"Per Dominum nostrum Jesum Christum Filium tuum." Maria spoke the response that Frau Dimmers was not able to make. She took the paper from Johannes, placed it on the old woman's tongue, and gave her water to swallow.

"Benedicat vos omnipotens Deus, Pater, et Filius, et Spiritus Sanctus." How different was this from administering communion? For a moment he thought about Köster and his church. "We cannot take Unconscious Man and transform him directly into Perfected Man," Köster had once said. "That is why the religious path was instituted. It is a necessary stage in moral evolution." Köster had not thought that way before he came to America. He had not thought that way when he was on the outside of the established religion—before he had become his own religious leader. "Blessed Kelpius," gasped the woman, taking his hand between hers.

"Frau Dimmers, it is God who heals. You are much loved by Him." The very last thing he wanted was to be thought a saint. The idea repulsed and shamed him. Service to humanity was part of his work, but his own spiritual path required—no, demanded—the constant surrender of his personhood. He would not allow them to make him into something that he was not—at least, was not yet. "We must pray as Christ Jesus taught. *'Fiat voluntas tua sicut in coelo et in terra.'*"

What more could be done?

An hour later he walked back into the daylight. It was blinding after the asphyxiating darkness of the sickroom. A great wind was breaking up the clouds, sending them across the river into the Jerseys. Pieces of blue sky shone through the cracks. "Thank you, Magister," Maria said, kissing his hand at the door. "We are so fortunate to have you here with us." He couldn't prevent himself from looking at the bulge in her gown. Zimmerman would have enjoyed speculating on the identity of the soul of his coming grandchild. It was a bittersweet thought.

Across the street from the house of Frau Dimmers was the undisturbed lot that the residents had set aside for their market. There was still no money for its construction and no labor for its clearing. In the absence of a proper building, business was conducted in the middle of the wide paved portion of the Great Road. *"Grüff Gott,* Herr Kelpius." Two men bowed to him, with sweeps of their hats. His appearance in Germantown was rare; rare enough to stop the conversations of the men who were weighing flaxseed, bartering tools, or discussing legal affairs.

"I have been holding mail for you, Herr Kelpius. A letter from Germany and a package from London." He greeted Issacs Van Bebber with an exchange of *Grüff Gott.* Van Bebber had arranged food and housing for the pilgrims during their first summer in Pennsylvania. He was a visionary Mennonite, a baker, and one of the original purchasers of land from William Penn. He had presented the mystics to the local residents as people of learning who had come to minister to their medical, educational, and spiritual needs. It was an expectation that was easy for the newcomers to fulfill, and easy for the townspeople to accept. At least it was for most of the townspeople.

"Grüff Gott, Herr Pastorius."

A stocky figure entered the crowd. The cuffs of his broadcloth coat nearly reached his elbows. His shirt was elegantly ruffled—made of the fine local linen for which Germantown was becoming known. A mass of black and gray hair flowed from his three-corner hat down to his shoulders. Even on such a muddy morning, his square-toed boots were impeccably clean.

He greeted each man in the street by name. He bowed slightly to the last one, staring for a moment at the parcel in Johannes' hands. *"Grüß Gott,* Herr Kelpius. How fares she?"

It was an unexpected question, coming from unquestionably the most difficult person in the settlement. Johannes returned the bow in kind. "I am afraid that Frau Dimmers will..."

"I do not refer to Frau Dimmers." There was a polite smile on Pastorius' round face, but it wasn't able to shield Johannes from the contempt that lay behind it. Johannes had done nothing to evoke such intensity, other than to be associated with Pastorius' sworn nemesis, Henrich Köster—other than offering his own education, his own compassion, his own wisdom to the residents of Germantown. "I refer to the Woman," Pastorius said.

"The woman, Herr Pastorius?"

"Yes, of course. The Woman in the Wilderness. How fares she?" There was not even a hint of malice in Pastorius' voice. There was nothing to make an ordinary observer think Pastorius was pleased to hear a muffled laugh from elsewhere in the crowd. His forehead was politely furrowed in concern.

The pilgrims had explained their retreat to the forest in Biblical terms, like the woman in *Revelation* who fled into the wilderness to bear her child, safe from Satan's dragon. It was the best way to avoid questions about an occult term that held significance only to the initiated. They were not there to establish new religious boundaries. They were the seed of the True Church, one that would encompass all humanity. They were of no sect. They had no affiliation. Their spiritual lineage was without name, they had explained to nervous Philadelphians.

The local people had begun to refer to them by the phrase "The Woman in the Wilderness."

"Contented," was Johannes' reply.

"No signs of imminent planetary calamities? No heavenly indications of the dawn of the New Age?" His voice exuded calculated sincerity.

"The Old Age remains in effect, Herr Pastorius," he said, equally sincerely. "But perhaps not for very long."

For a brief moment, for the blink of an eye, Pastorius seemed to hesitate. Then, recovering himself, he placed a firm hand on Johannes' shoulder. "We trust that you will let us know so that we, like the Wise Virgins, can trim our lamps in expectation of the arrival of the Bridegroom."

Johannes would not allow himself to participate in an exchange of veiled jabs. "Good health to you, Herr Pastorius," he said as he tucked his package under his arm. *"Wiedersehen."* He was beyond the reach of conversation before the rest of the men had finished their polite and requisite parting wishes.

The sun was now shining over Germantown. The dampness was disappearing from the air, and puddles of water glistened in the sunlight. On either side of the sixty-foot wide Great Road, Pastorius had planted peach trees. Their bareness was only a deception, as the chartreuse gleam of their branches betrayed that new life was only weeks away.

A group of children ran toward him.

"Herr Kelpius!" It was Christoph, almost fifteen, Frau Zimmerman's youngest son, who bowed with a sweep of an arm. With him were two younger boys and a small girl. "May we walk back with you to the Tabernacle? May we have school today?"

Johannes patted each of them on the head. "The day is half gone, *liebe Kinder.* If you want to come with me, we must leave right now. Your parents would not want you walking home in the dark."

"Herr Kelpius, do you think I'm not old enough to be responsible for myself?" In some half-uncomfortable, half-flattered way, Johannes thought that the look on Christoph's face was one that a son would give to a father. It made him smile.

"Sometimes we must be responsible for each other," Johannes said. He patted the head of the little girl. "Will you lead us, *Liebes Fräulein Lieschen?*"

The five of them walked down the Great Road, the little girl kicking mud on her dress as she skipped ahead. She turned beside the home of Von Bebber, down the path that led along the flax field into the woods, now beckoning in the brightness of the spring day. *"Amo, amas, amat. Amamus, amatus, amant,"* she sang, showing off her Latin conjugations.

The school that Johannes and Seelig had established was the only one in the settlement. In fact it was the first—and only—free education anywhere in Pennsylvania. But it had been a nearly impossible challenge to convince the residents of Germantown of the need of a liberal education for their children. Survival was the first concern, and that nearly always meant tireless work from all family members, no matter how young. Frau Zimmerman, of course, was insistent that her children be educated. Her two handsome and popular young sons had been the catalysts that brought other children to the project, but soon Christoph would be too old for school. And after that?

He could hear them laughing as they ran ahead. The children enjoyed the trip to school more than actually being there. In the valley, they followed the tributary stream that ran past the Rittenhouse Mill, over the rocks, and down to the Wissahickon Creek. The forest floor was dotted with bright green sprouts that pushed up through the humus. Even though snow still hid in protected pockets, the trees were pregnant with foliage. Soon the foliage would cover the naked curves of the valley like a silk garment over the body of a beautiful woman.

It was an hour's walk through the ancient stands of chestnut, elm and pine. Virgin woods had long since vanished from Europe, but in Pennsylvania the forest was redolent with the undisturbed peace of the centuries. There was no challenge, no conflict, no concealed sarcasm. Some, he knew, looked upon the forest with fear for its untamed dangers. Others—and more were arriving from Europe each year— saw profit waiting to be reaped. For Johannes, it was Scripture. The liquid gold of sunlight through infant leaves, the trickles of water across the path, even the designs of pebbles and mud were Revelation of Divine Intent.

Johannes came to the small bridge across the Wissahickon several minutes after the children had already crossed and started up the hill. The water sparkled and sang. He stopped to feel the warmth of the sunshine on his face.

"*Geistes!*" He heard Christoph yelling. The children were screaming. He crossed the bridge, running. *"Geistes!* Herr Kelpius! *Kommen Sie geschwind!"* Ghosts!

The path from the creek to the Tabernacle was well worn but winding, and all uphill. He was out of breath when he found them, fifty yards from the clearing, laughing. Ahead of them were a dozen or more frantically gesturing figures, truly ghostly—faceless beings in hooded robes, suspended in the air. "*Geistes!*" Christoph repeated, but now almost doubled up with laughter.

"Die Wäsche, Christoph Zimmerman," he said. He had been frightened, not for his own sake, but for the children. The joke was disrespectful. For a moment he felt angry, but he couldn't prevent himself from laughing. It did look like a coven of spirits, caught in some demonic, spasmodic ritual.

It was the laundry.

Daniel Geissler appeared from behind the row of robes that swung in the breeze. "If you children don't mind your teacher," he said, "I will free these ghosts to come down and spank you."

Christoph thrust out a stick like a saber. "Let them try!" he called in a voice that was suddenly and remarkably his father's. "I fear no evil. I will vanquish any foe!"

The Community's buildings had been laid out in the forty-times-ten-square-foot clearing that also contained their orchards and gardens. The arrangement was from the drawings left by Zimmerman. The plans were, so the Magister claimed, the same as had been used by ancient spiritual communities. Each building, each window and door, had been painstakingly designed to harmonize with solar and terrestrial angles to make use of the earth's subtle energies.

The grounds were full of activity. Brethren were in the gardens, tilling the weeds of winter into the soil of spring. The air was filled with the smoke of the lime kiln. The rugged banks of the Wissahickon Valley were rich in deposits of calcium carbonate that the brethren transformed into quicklime for agricultural—as well as alchemical—purposes.

The afternoon sun shone through the window of the *Saal,* or Great Room, of the Tabernacle. When Johannes walked in with the children, Seelig was sitting on the floor, teaching a lesson in mathematics to two boys and two girls. Taking off their shoes before entering, three of the newcomers joined them silently. The bareness of the *Saal,* its impeccable cleanliness, and its austere solidity seemed to evoke quiet from anyone who entered. The only decoration at all, the only break in the carefully hewn log walls, was an iron circle four feet in diameter. It enclosed an iron cross. The symbol hung in solemn immobility, waiting to receive the sunset of the equinox through the window.

"A music lesson today, Herr Kelpius?" Christoph lacked his father's interest in higher mathematics, in spite of an exceptional aptitude. It was understandable, as all the adults in his life were more focused on spiritual than worldly goals. In any event, America had no universities for him to attend. But his ability and enthusiasm to play music were a delight to Johannes, and the boy made a satisfying pupil.

The virginal organ sitting on a small table against the east wall of the *Saal* was the only instrument of its kind in Pennsylvania. It was used twice daily, once in the morning for the public devotional services the brethren offered to the residents of Germantown, and once in the evening for private rituals. Johannes sat down next to Christoph, while the latter practiced playing from the Tabernacle's own hymnal. The boy had been so well taught, there was no need for instruction and hardly a need for attention.

Ihr seelen! Die ihr seid Vom schlaff welt erwecket,
Ihr die ihr würlick habt des herren leib geschmecket.

It was through music, an inheritance from his mother, that Johannes was able to find self-expression. The part of him that was stirred by the effects of music was the part he considered his soul-self, his subtle body, the form that existed partially in the Invisible. Through his own music, he sought to reach that same part of others. So he had become a writer of hymns. The words he used were carefully chosen to be compatible with orthodox Christianity, but subtly mystical, and brazenly honest expressions of the pain and hope in his own soul.

Ihr die ihr nur in euch des herren klares licht
Schaut wie im Spiegel mit entdecktem angesicht.
O souls who from the love of this world awaken,
You, who most truly have of the Lord's Love partaken,
You, who have in your Selves the Lord's clearest Light,
Behold, as in a glass, in pure transparent sight.

He would write his verses in the blank book he was given before he had left the bustling, noisy world of London. There he had been a celebrity, at least in the community of religious "nonconformists." Like their counterparts in Germany and Holland, the mystically minded English came from the ranks of the well educated and the well to do. If he had remained with them as they had wanted him to do, his compositions might have found their way into the popular hymnals of the day. His name might have been known to churchgoers and schoolchildren across Germany. Here in the wilderness, he would use them as a lesson for Christoph. Seelig, his dearest friend, would urge him to sing for the handful of curious souls who undertook the walk to attend their public devotionals. Who would understand them? Who would appreciate the language and the poetry? Who would remember them?

It wasn't a melancholy reverie. It was actually satisfying for him to feel how much he had sacrificed for his spiritual path, his exchange of the temporal for the eternal. It was reassuring to feel how little it seemed to have cost him, in comparison.

He hadn't needed prescience to know that the children would stay too long with them at the Tabernacle. The days were growing longer, but not long enough for the children to reach home before dark. Geissler volunteered, as usual, to escort them back to Germantown. Three years after he had broken his leg, he still favored it, but he claimed never to mind following the rugged trail that snaked into town.

Like all communal meals, the evening one was taken in complete silence in the separate dining hall. In the *Sternwarte,* Falckner was filling the Horologium Achaz Hydrographicum, which enabled them to make such accurate astronomical calculations. It was Falckner's turn to observe the movements of the heavenly bodies on that coming clear night. He wouldn't be able to participate in the ritual that the rest of the brethren would celebrate in the *Saal.*

Johannes climbed the stairs to the *Sternwarte* past the second floor where ten of the brethren were in meditation in their tiny prayer cells. "Did you wish to speak with me, Daniel?"

"Magister," Falckner fumbled with the instrument in the flickering light of a lard lamp. "I understand the need to perfect the number of our Circle, now with Köster leaving, and the others. I wanted to discuss with you an idea that I have had to expand our number to that end."

"An idea?"

"We both know that there is a great deal of false rumor about us back home."

"I don't believe we need to be concerned with the gossip of Europe."

"Magister, we must move forward, or else we shall move backward. Today it is Köster and Sprogel. Who will leave tomorrow? If we have an obligation to the children, don't we also have one to ourselves—to the Community that is involved in preparing humanity for the Millennium?"

"What is your idea?"

"I would like to return to Europe, to explain ourselves to those back home, to recruit new members."

Johannes turned to the railing and stared into the sky. "Do you have any motivation other than this?"

"Another motivation? Of course not, Magister. What other motivation could I have? Perhaps I'll locate old Burgstaller and convince him to bestow on us the secret of elixirs before he dies. Or I might visit my family in Zwickau."

"Your family is here, Brother Daniel. We are your family."

"That is easy for you to say, Magister. You have no family. I have a mother and two brothers in Germany."

Johannes let go of the wound and turned back. "Will you return?"

"Of course I will. I plan to return with a new supply of *Essentia dulcis* and twenty-four hundred acres secured in a deed that even Pastorius won't be able to dispute."

"Daniel, we don't need twenty-four hundred acres. We have all the land we need here."

"But we don't have a deed for the property. Even Köster was smart enough to arrange that for himself."

"Daniel, I don't believe that we have come all this way—so safely and purposefully—to have anxiety over matters that have no relevance. It's folly for any man to believe that he can possess land."

"Kelpius, I only want to ensure that we will never be treated as we were in Germany."

Seelig appeared from the top of the stairs. "Magister," he whispered. "It is time."

"Will you investigate all the arrangements?" Johannes asked Falckner.

"I already have, Magister."

In the swirl of incense, in the light of the Holy Lamp, in the crescent of the initiates, Johannes recited, "'I have need of someone who will hear. This Cross of Light is sometimes called the Word by me for your sakes, sometimes Mind, sometimes Jesus, sometimes Christ, sometimes Door, sometimes Way, sometimes Bread, sometimes Seed, sometimes Resurrection, sometimes Son, sometimes Father, sometimes Spirit, sometimes Life, sometimes Truth, sometimes Faith, sometimes Grace. Thus it is the marking off of all things and the uplifting and foundation of those things that are fixed but had been unstable, and the harmony of the wisdom and indeed the wisdom of the harmony.'"

These words had been judged blasphemous and expunged from authoritative Christian Scripture thirteen hundred years before. But despite official injunctions against them, they had been preserved through the secret transmission of Christian adepts whose roots traced back to the very foundation of the religion. They were the words of Jesus himself.

"'But there are on the right and on the left, powers, principalities, dominions and demons, operation, threats, wrath, devils, Satan, and the Inferior Root, from which the nature of transient things proceeded.'"

The brethren moved around him, counterclockwise, step by deliberate step. "Glory be to you, Father! Glory be to you, Word! Glory be to you, Grace!"

"I will be saved, and I will save.
I will be loosed, and I will loose.
I will be pierced, and I will pierce.
I will be born, and I will bear."

"Amen."

Never did he feel more the Magister than in the midst of the call and response rituals. Johann Kelp the Transylvanian scholar fell away and the power of all the spiritual teachers who preceded him transmuted his personality—as from lead to gold.

"I will eat, and I will be eaten.
I will hear, and I will be heard.
I will be understood, being wholly understanding.
I will be washed, and I will wash."

"Amen."

After all the years, there was still an exhilarating sense of freedom to perform the exercise in a way that even the primitive Church had not been able—without fear of oppression. Even with the whispered warnings of "the evil eye," the children being led suddenly to the other side of the street, the brethren were respected in Pennsylvania. They were sought after for their astronomical knowledge, appealed to for medical assistance, and consulted on matters of scholarly importance.

They turned. Faster, yet always in the rhythm that they believed channeled energy from the subtle realm into the physical. According to their traditions, the linking of all their intentions, even with less than the required number of forty, obtained an effect that single devotions could never produce. They turned, as if their efforts were carving out a hollow, a space for the Divine to inhabit. They turned until their final revolutions brought them back into the world.

Johannes was outside the Tabernacle, carrying a candle in a tin lantern, when he remembered the letter and parcel that he had picked up in Germantown. By the time he retrieved them from the organ bench, the brethren had all retreated to the lodging house.

The woods had come alive. For the first time that season, the songs of the crickets and frogs filled the night. Their music accompanied him down the winding path from the Tabernacle that led toward the glens along the creek. He stopped part of the way down, where the song of the creatures was joined by the rush of fresh spring water.

The one compromise he had allowed himself as Magister was his private cell. He had dug it out himself from the hillside, under the shelter of an enormous cedar. He had supported the interior with the ancient rocks of the Wissahickon Valley, and finished it in fragrant wood. The arms of the earth wrapped around five of its six sides, save only for a stone-arched entrance with a doorway to the world. Warm in winter and cool in summer, the only subtle influences inside it were his own. Years of silent communion with his own soul had imbued a sense of peace into the very substance of its walls.

It greeted him that evening with its familiar aroma, all the stronger for the dampness. Nearly sixteen feet long and eight wide, it was a home as well as a retreat. His lantern illuminated two shelves, one with his most precious books, his hymnal and diary, ink and pens. The other held a collection of instruments, a colored glass container that held the *Essentia dulcis*, a porcelain pitcher, a bowl, and a towel. Beneath were a polished copper brazier for heat and a lamp for light. Carefully folded in a corner were his blankets, and under them the small wooden box with the gold star that he slept near each night. Against the back wall hung a small tapestry of Turkish origin, a present from the Philadelphian Society of London.

He took off his boots before he entered. He lit the lamp, extinguished his candle, and sat down to examine his mail. The letter was from Magister Fabricius, his former mentor from the University of Altdorf. *"We understood that you were a Quaker, but also have heard that you have assumed the celibate life. Have you become a Catholic priest, or perhaps a Hindu divine?"* Johannes took off his robe and cap. This was typical of the Scholarly Mind, he thought. It had a nearly unquenchable need to categorize, to have a name for something, so it could be put in a glass jar and studied. In spite of his great intellect, or perhaps because of it, Magister Fabricius wasn't able to understand how a reality could exist beyond a name.

The name of Peter Shaeffer, the young Finn they had met in London, was written on the parcel. Johannes opened it carefully. There was a note.

Blessings accompany this package, Brother Johannes Kelpius. Blessing upon blessing! By the Sound of His Celtic-Hebraic Chophar, I have been summoned unto a Glorious New Dawn. The Lord has instructed me to depart from the company of the Foolish Virgins, to take leave of these Babylonish shores, and join with thee in Anticipation of the Manifestation of Aurora's Herald of the End of Days. I patiently wait upon Him to supply the means of my journey to North America. Meanwhile, as gratitude for my everpresent place in thy Circle, I most humbly offer these gifts.

I remain with cordial embrace in the love of Jesus,

Peter Shaeffer

London, England

Beneath the note were small, wrapped packets of seeds; *Mankun-ruash* poppies, tragacanth, belladonna, henbane, ammoniancum, chamomile. Shaeffer's meaning, albeit oddly conveyed, was not lost on him. Even though the numbers of his group had been dwindling, they were in reality—if not yet in appearance—the seeds of a new garden, a garden whose fruits were the fulfillment of the destiny of mankind. It would be a fruitful garden.

He poured water from the pitcher onto the towel and cleansed his skin. He extinguished the lamp and knelt in the darkness.

He repeated his prayers, aware of the sounds of the forest. They were a reassuring harbinger of the coming season. Then they passed from his consciousness and he followed his breathing, gently guiding it into the meditative pattern he had been taught. Finally, this too faded away and the Tabernacle, the Community, his cell, and even Magister Johannes transformed from solid to ephemeral to transparent.

Here there was no Köster, no Pastorius, no disunion, no strife, no contention. Here there was only perfect peace that surpassed understanding.

And yet, in that place of peace, there was longing. It was a longing so deep, so utterly beyond his reach, that he wanted to deny its existence.

For all his erudite knowledge, Zimmerman had been wrong. The world had not come to an end in 1694. There had been no extraordinary signs in the heavens. The Indians did not have any eschatological beliefs, nor did they expect an imminent dawning of a New Age.

Still, Zimmerman was only a man, an imperfect instrument. If his calculations had been wrong, they were only calculations. After all, Zimmerman had not been the only one to predict the Millennium, the Age in which Christ would manifest through the souls of Perfected Ones. Preparation meant a striving for that perfection—in the body, in the mind, and especially in the heart.

It was in his heart that the longing resided. It was an old longing, much older than his alliance with the Chapter of Perfection. Its origin felt so ancient, it transcended his own life of twenty-four years.

He would call it a spiritual longing, a longing of the separated soul for union with her heavenly Father. He would call it his love for Christ, a need that made the soul despise worldly comforts and achievements. He would pour that longing into his hymns, in unconscious expectation that its expression would free him from its prison.

Yet there, in the silence and darkness of his cave, peace overcame all else, and both he and his longing ceased to have meaning.

Chapter Sixteen

Friday, March 23, 1700
Germantown, Pennsylvania, and beyond

"Yes sir, Master Kelpius. That is what I said. I belong to the governor."

Johannes stared at the young African standing beside the carriage, hoping to connect with the human being behind the man's dark eyes. "Brother Alfred, are you telling me that William Penn considers you to be his slave?"

"It an't a matter of *consider*, Master Kelpius. It's a matter of *is*."

There had never been a slave before in Germantown.

Johannes put his hand out to touch the African on the sleeve of his red wool coat. He wanted to acknowledge the man, but also sense his inner condition. He was fascinated by the reality of slavery and this living victim of its evil. For a moment he fumbled beneath his robe.

"Oh, no, Master Kelpius. An't a need to pay me, sir."

Johannes pressed an English half-crown into the man's hand. God has charged me to deliver this to you on His behalf."

"Master Kelpius, I don't need money."

"One day the need will come, Brother Alfred."

The African stared nervously into the distance.

"Ah, there he is, Governor. I knew he would be on time." It was the unmistakable voice of Francis Pastorius. He was walking across Market Square from the town hall, leading a man whose attempt at a dignified stride was frustrated by pain. "Governor, it is my pleasure to introduce to you Herr Johannes Kelpius, the famous *Einsiedler* of Germantown. Kelpius, our honorable proprietor and governor, Friend William Penn."

The face of the proprietor was marked with blotches. He extended a swollen hand. "I have been looking forward to meeting you, Friend Kelpius. For years I have heard reports of what you have been doing for the citizens of Pennsylvania. They tell me that you are not only a philosopher, but a lawyer, a naturalist, and astronomer—and that you possess extraordinary mystical powers!"

Johannes shook the man's hand gingerly. "You are too kind, Sir William," he said.

"'Sir' was my father's title." When Penn smiled, creases formed at the corners of his protuberant eyes. "I would never abide such vanity. I am merely William Penn, Friend." It was obvious that the great proprietor was struggling—with age and the conflict of living irreconcilable roles. He was overweight for his nearly sixty years, overdressed for a visit to an Indian village, and overly concerned with his own persona.

"It is said that among the secrets of your Tabernacle lies the formula for the *lapis philosophorum* of immortality," he said raising a gray eyebrow.

With practiced care, Johannes allowed his eyes to show only polite indifference. "I am grateful for your invitation, Governor," he said.

"As you know, I have an abiding interest in matters of the spirit, Friend Kelpius. If my circumstances had been different, I might have chosen a life of contemplation and devotion, as you have done." There was nothing in Penn's silk doublet, his carriage, or his aristocratic demeanor to suggest that it was true.

Pastorius put his hand on Penn's shoulder. "We should be getting along, Governor."

"I see that you have been chatting with Alfred, Friend Kelpius," the governor said. "He's a fine and loyal lad. Alfred," he said to the slave, "would you kindly help our guests into the carriage?"

Johannes ignored the African's arm and climbed inside. He was surprised to find a woman no older than himself, holding an infant to her breast. He averted his eyes and sat across and away from her. Pastorius followed him and sat next to the mother and child. "Madam Penn, this is Johannes Kelpius, of the Woman in the Wilderness."

"It is a pleasure to finally meet you, Magister Kelpius," she said.

"The pleasure is mine." He stole a glance at her smiling, girlish face.

With the help of his slave, Penn labored to enter the carriage. Johannes reached to offer assistance, but Penn pressed a hand against the ceiling and settled into the dark leather seat across from his wife. He removed his hat. "Friend Kelpius, have you met my wife Hannah? And my son John? Yes?"

Johannes was looking through the window, watching the African untie the horses from the railing along the street. "Of course, slavery as a concept is quite indefensible," the governor said in his ear. "In the event, however, it is something quite different. I am convinced that a slave, who is considered valuable property, is often better treated than an indentured servant."

Johannes was silent.

"Isn't that right, Friend Pastorius?"

"Certainly, Governor." Pastorius smiled broadly at the small crowd that had gathered in Market Square to investigate the famous man who had recently been reinstated as their governor. Alfred shook the reins and the carriage started slowly down the Great Road. Penn waved enthusiastically through the window. None of the curious returned his gesture.

"It seems to be a strange infection of this New World," the governor said, "that its citizenry often feel as if they owe no allegiance or loyalty to the proprietors whose lands they live upon."

"William!" Hannah Penn shifted her son to her other breast.

"It is true," Penn said to Johannes. "Once these people have a deed of sale, fully paid or not, they become ungrateful to those who made their land available to them, oblivious of those who labored to provide them with the most humane government yet devised..."

Penn's wife interrupted. "Tell me, Friend Kelpius, how is your community faring?"

"It should be quite lonesome, I should imagine," Pastorius said. "I have heard that your comrade Köster has had quite enough of Pennsylvania and returned to Germany." Penn looked back and forth between his two German companions. "Have you not heard of Henrich Bernard Köster, Governor? No? Well, no concern. The province is far better off without him."

"Pray, tell me."

Johannes started to answer. He would have told Penn of Köster's remarkable intellect, of the famous teaching system that he had devised, of Köster's meticulous re-translation of the German Bible. "He was a boaster of the highest order, Governor," Pastorius said. "From the day he arrived in Pennsylvania, Köster began to set Quaker against Quaker and Christian against Christian. Several times I was compelled to rebuke him by printing, at my own expense, pamphlets to answer his follies."

"Indeed?"

"It is sad but true, Governor. Köster's disputations became so onerous that if it hadn't been for my mitigating influence, the people of Germantown might have forcibly expelled him and all his comrades, including young Kelpius. As it was, the hermits asked the man to withdraw to his own retreat, a place he had the hubris to call *Irenia,* the House of Peace. In truth it was *Erinnia*, the House of Raging Contention."

"What became of him?"

"Governor, the man wrote a book and tried to have it published. He sent it up to New York, but it was so full of haughty nonsense that not a printer in America was able to properly proofread it. After that embarrassment, Köster sold his property in order to pay for transport back to Europe, but he was swindled out of the money. I understood that some generous fool finally offered to pay for his voyage. The last time I saw him, he was boarding a ship bound for Virginia."

Pastorius spoke loudly and enthusiastically. Johannes wasn't listening. He stared out the window into the spring morning, breathing the freshness of the moving air. His thoughts were elsewhere, back in the ravages of slavery, trying to comprehend the burden on both slave and slaveholder. William Penn considered himself to be not only the owner of vast estates on two continents, not only the owner of the entire province of Pennsylvania, but the owner of living, conscious human beings. He could sense ruination in the governor's soul.

"Isn't that correct, Friend Kelpius?"

"Pardon me, Herr Pastorius?"

"I was telling Sir William about your unfortunate friend Shaeffer."

"Friend Pastorius was telling me that you cast him as well as that fellow Köster from your Society, Friend Kelpius."

"Not at all, Governor. We parted on the most cordial terms."

"Shaeffer was given to sudden and bizarre peripatetic impulses," Pastorius said. "He appeared one night in Philadelphia at the home of Edward Shippen, frightening to death both the magistrate and his wife. The man claimed that God had commanded him to stay in their home for forty days and forty nights whilst he undertook a fast."

"And he was a perfect stranger to them?" Penn asked.

"Not perfect in any sense, Governor, but a stranger man there never was. The Shippens, being pious Friends, extended their hospitality to the man, but came to regret it, as Shaeffer continually upset them with sudden outbursts of the most disturbing nonsense."

"And is this man still in the province?"

Pastorius gave Johannes a sharp look. "I heard he was last seen in Jersey, but perhaps Friend Kelpius knows better than I the whereabouts of his comrades. For the sake of the province, I hope he has decided to bless us by returning to Europe, as did Köster and Kelpius' other friend, Falckner."

Penn's forehead was furrowed.

"You have been misinformed," Johannes said. "Not only will Falckner be returning to Pennsylvania this summer, but he will be bringing with him a number of new ascensions to our community."

"Excellent!"

"Then I shall anticipate his return," Pastorius said coolly, "with great enthusiasm."

The carriage trembled as they descended a road rutted by winter rain.

"Oh, Hannah, child, look there. John has puked all over your shoulder!"

"It's quite all right, William. I can clean it up."

Pastorius squirmed. "Friend Hannah, may I..."

"No, no." She pulled a rag from between the infant's legs and daubed her shoulder.

"Now your dress will be soiled," Penn said.

"William, I'm certain that the Indians won't mind. They have babies just as we do."

"The Indians are representatives neither of civilization, nor of the Light of Christ."

"Please do tell us, Mister Kelpius," Hannah said quickly, "is your Pietist religion similar to that of the Quakers?"

"Do you share any beliefs with the Anglicans?" Penn asked.

"Yes, Friend Kelpius," said Pastorius. "Do tell us with which of these two faiths you most closely align yourself." He smiled politely, maliciously.

Johannes knew the Founder of Germantown would be delighted to discredit him in front of the great proprietor. The smoldering conflict between the Anglicans and the Quakers was on the verge of igniting, and even Pastorius couldn't blame its flammability on Köster. The smoke had reached as far as London, where Parliament was threatening once again to revoke Penn's charter, this time over the perceived mistreatment of Anglicans. As for Penn, Johannes suspected that his own conversation with the slave had rankled the governor's conscience.

He closed his eyes. The years of quietude, just as much as the years of university study, had given him clarity of mind and an ability to meet a challenge. An old metaphor came into his mind. "I pray that someday," he said, "we all may be made worthy of appreciating the variety of different rooms in the Divine Mansion. I'm certain that no one would be so simple as to think that they should all be of one sort; or that God Himself cared a whit about the system of our architecture."

"That is very true," said Hannah Penn. Pastorius squirmed again.

"I sometimes wonder," Johannes continued, "how many pious people, if they were in pain, or on their deathbed, would be glad to be received in any of those rooms, even those they may have once thought to be heretical."

"Quite correct, Friend Kelpius," Penn said. "It strikes me as evidence of the deterioration of the times in which we live that few have the insight to understand these issues as clearly as we do."

"Insight is a quality much to be cherished," Johannes said. As Penn gave his assent, he added, "Of course humility is a necessary prerequisite to insight, as I'm sure you will agree." Penn, as if momentarily unsure, looked first to Pastorius, then nodded tentatively to the distance outside the window.

The carriage rattled along in silence until Pastorius, not ready to let his opportunity pass, cleared his throat. "You have not yet told us, Herr Kelpius," he said, "if you prefer the Quakers or the Anglicans, or which sect would best find affinity with the Woman in the Wilderness." He looked eager.

"Even though I do not profess myself to be a Quaker, Herr Pastorius, I have deep respect for them, as I do members of every faith, even the Anglicans. I'm sure you will agree with me, Sir William, that the thirty-nine articles of the English Church are very general, and mild enough to be accepted by anyone who is not too narrow-minded."

The governor turned from the window. "You are quite broad-minded with your doctrine of Universal Restitution, Friend Kelpius," Pastorius said. "It is not everyone who is willing to agree with your hopeful assertion that all souls, no matter what their faith, will be redeemed in Eternity."

"There are many who are quick to judge their fellows, Herr Pastorius," Johannes said. "But I pray for all of them. They are not to be blamed any more than blind men arguing over a question of colors. As for the different sects in the world, it is my guess that if each believer were questioned closely enough, we would find there are as many different religions as there are hearts in the world."

Pastorius folded his arms tightly in front of his chest. Hannah Penn began to hum to her baby and to herself.

As they descended into the valley that led to the river, a stench filled the air. "Hannah, my old nose tells me that John requires your attention." The governor's wife laid her baby across her knees and began to unwrap strips of cloth filled with thick, brown liquid. "Friend Kelpius," Penn said, "I believe your choice of a celibate life is quite to be envied."

"William! You would not endure a week of the celibate life!" She and the governor laughed.

The carriage stopped suddenly and Penn fell toward his wife's lap. "Oh, dear God!" she screamed. The ground shook as an uncountable herd of deer fled across the path. A great stag stood apart from the rest, staring intently into the carriage.

"This is Hannah's first visit to the New World," Penn explained. "And we have spent most of it in Philadelphia."

The carriage rolled on again, along a trail toward a wide bend in the river. "Our ferry, Governor." Pastorius pointed out through the window to a small boat near an even smaller dock, jutting out from the weeds into the *Schuyl Kil.* "We will cross the river here, travel by wagon through the township of the Welsh, and then go by foot into the Indian village."

Hannah Penn stared off into the endless bare forest on the far bank and stroked her crying baby's head.

"Sir, there is a fair bit of mud between here and the riverbank," called Alfred. "I don't believe I can bring you any closer."

The governor reached under the seat and brought out a shiny cane, a leather pouch, and a thick English Bible. "I hope that we do not encounter any bear on this journey," he said.

Hannah glanced at her white satin high-heeled shoes, then looked back out the carriage window. "Where exactly are we, Friend Francis?"

"The Indian name for this place is *Kahn-she-hock-keeng,* Friend Hannah. It means 'elegant land.'"

Before they could see the *Lenápay* spring settlement of *Oke-hock-keeng*, they could smell the smoke of cooking meat. But even before the smoke, they could hear the drums. By the time the clearing was just ahead of them, the path narrowed them into single file. Hannah clutched her crying infant.

"Friend Hannah," said Pastorius, "I am certain that the governor has explained the importance of maintaining cordial relations with the Indians. We must avoid doing anything that might antagonize them."

"Both John and I are fully capable of comporting ourselves properly, Friend Pastorius. Even in a gathering of primitives."

"There is no reason to fear." Penn handed his cane to Pastorius. "The *Lenápay* are simple yet accepting people. They will do us no harm. I have found them to be able to sense one's inner motivations and respond accordingly. If you approach them with an honest heart, as I have done, they will respect you. I have worked diligently not only to earn their respect, but also their admiration." He held his Bible against his chest and walked into the clearing with the same painful gait he had used in Germantown.

"Kapé-e-shush! Kapé-e-shush!" A group of *Lenápay* children in their tribal regalia ran past the governor. Johannes raised his hands, palms outstretched, as a greeting, then touched each one on the head. "*Heh! Heh!* Kapé-e-shush," they sang in a greeting. Beyond them, just on the other side of the edge of the woods, stood Amimi. His eyes followed the Europeans as they entered the clearing. Pastorius watched him exchange nods with Johannes.

The settlement of *Oke-hock-keeng* was swirling with smoke and activity. The event was one of two annual gatherings that brought together members of neighboring villages and lasted for twelve days, the number of heavens in *Lenápay* cosmology. Arranged in a circle were several rectangular bark-covered structures that the Europeans called "long houses." In the center was the *wig-wam,* a large, eight-sided building used for tribal and ceremonial affairs. All around, there was a flurry of motion. Women with short skirts and bare breasts, painted men in deerskin pants, barefoot children displaying their parents' beads and feathers, all were jostling, striding, and singing to the overlapping rhythms of the drums.

"Husca n' Lenápay wim." Truly a human being I am.

"Onas!" A wrinkled man wearing a feathered headdress raised his palms to them. "Onas!" The greeting was taken up by the children around Johannes, who led the Europeans into the village as if it were they who had brought them. *"Kula-mul-sęe hech?"* the old Indian asked Penn.

"*Us-kay oret.* I am quite well," Penn lied. "It has been a very long time, Issímlus."

"A hundred moons," the Indian said. "You have brought friends."

"My new wife, Hannah Calloway..." he began, but a tide of *Lenápay* women had already crowded around, eager to see and touch the crying white baby. "Francis Pastorius, the agent for the Frankfort Company, and Johannes Kelpius, but—you know Friend Kelpius?"

Issímlus embraced Johannes. "*Itah,* Kapé-e-shush."

"*Itah,* Issímlus," he answered.

Along with Seelig, Johannes had made many trips to the surrounding villages during the first years of their life in America. They had invited the *Lenápay* to their Tabernacle, prayed with them, questioned them on matters of cosmology, and attempted to connect the *Lenápay* spiritual system to their own.

The strange, sad-eyed Amimi was their most faithful visitor. In the winters, Amimi would appear in the clearing on the ridge above the Wissahickon. The Germans would welcome him as they did the children of Germantown, and allowed him to sit and watch their activity. Seelig was convinced the quiet young man was the incarnation of some great wise soul. It wasn't a concept that was foreign to the *Lenápay,* who believed in the return of souls to earth.

Penn handed his Bible to Pastorius and brought handfuls of buttons and beads from his leather bag. He passed these out to the women and children gathered nearby who, in turn, hurried to share them with their sisters, cousins, nieces and nephews. "Observe the hearts of these people," Penn said to his wife. "They don't think to keep anything for themselves, but want only to circulate wealth through their tribe." Hannah could barely hear him over the flood of attention.

Issímlus led them to the *wig-wam.* The women who were marveling over the quilted stitching on Hannah's dress, the children who were doling out English beads, all suddenly fell back. Inside the *wig-wam* it was warm and unexpectedly quiet. A cone of light shone from the smoke vent in the center of the ceiling. Huddled around its soft brilliance semicircle of *Lenápay* elders sat with the Great Chief in the center, his brown face framed by dangling beads and feathers. Two men with jingling anklets appeared in the light. They sprinkled dust into a circle of glowing embers.

"Onas," announced Issímlus.

The Great Chief said nothing, but simply looked at Penn and raised a hand, palm upward. Penn, again clutching his Bible with his left hand, raised his right. "*Itah*," he said. The men of the circle shifted, opening a space for Issímlus on the Chief's left and Penn on his right.

"*La-má-tah-peekw.*" Issímlus invited them to sit.

Hannah's eyes were wide. She pressed her baby against her shoulder and patted his back. "There are no other women in here," she whispered to Pastorius.

"You are being honored, Friend Hannah," he said. "As the wife of the great Onas."

It was a great joke of the *Lenápay*. Europeans considered the natives to be illiterate, but the *Lenápay* were far from verbally unsophisticated. Onas was what they called William Penn, poking fun at the homonym with the Europeans' cherished writing tool. The word meant feather.

Pastorius gave a wary glance at the woven mat before sitting down next to Hannah. Penn, too, hesitated. He placed a hand on the shoulder of the Chief and dropped into a sitting position, nearly tumbling backward. Johannes took a place furthest down, next to Hannah. Across from them sat Amimi, the youngest member of the crescent of Indian leaders.

A pipe was handed to Johannes, who took a long draught and passed it to the governor's wife. She winced. "Make a pretense," Pastorius whispered. Johannes remembered his first participation in a *Lenápay* circle. The herbs that had powerful effects on the mind, he knew now, were not offered casually to visitors.

"*Husca n' Lenapay wim.*"

It was a familiar song to Johannes, the *Lenápay* version of Creation. Whether it was sung to the drums, or if the drums followed the song—if the two dancers moved to the rhythms, or if the rhythms flowed from the dancers,was impossible to sort out. The effect was intended to be a multi-sensual experience, the meaning of the words being only the smallest part.

"In the beginning of time there was only God, eternal, omnipresent and without precedence," the governor translated. "He made the earth, the sky, the sun, the moon, and the stars to move in harmony. When the wind blew away the fog, islands grew from the water. Then the great God of all gods spoke anew—to all beings, mortals, and souls."

In spite of, or perhaps because of, the incessant rhythms, Hannah's baby finally fell quiet in her arms. The dancers continued, shaking bracelets and anklets, sprinkling dust into the coals.

"Do they know they look positively ridiculous?"

"This is a heathen ritual," Pastorius told her. "It is all these people know. But perhaps in the eyes of Friend Kelpius, it is sufficient to redeem their souls."

Johannes leaned and whispered in Hannah's ear. "Things are not always as they may seem, Madam. Do you see what these men are wearing on their heads? This is the Dance of *Cha-mum-suk,* the Rabbit. In their language, the word for 'rabbit' is a homonym of the word for 'light.' They are honoring light, which is for them Divine. It is perhaps the same Inward Light acknowledged by Quakers."

She watched the dancers, then looked back at Johannes, as if trying to decide if he were foolish, rude, or marvelously wise. Across the circle, Amimi was studying the newcomers intently.

It had taken a long time for Johannes to come to terms with Indian culture. If, as many believed, the *Lenápay* were truly the lost tribe of Israel, they had not brought with them the secrets of the Kabalah. It was a bitter disappointment—only one of many—for Johannes to conclude that the Indians were not an unspoiled race with intact secrets from ancient times. They were certainly not the savages most of the English declaimed, but if they lacked the European advantages of written philosophy and history, they *were* free from a great many European vices. All in all, the *Lenápay* were human, as their name translated. God was moving through them, transforming them from the inside, just as He was doing in all societies. And it was in such as Amimi that Christ, for the Indians, was manifesting the spiritual awakenings of the New Age.

The Chief clapped his hands and the drums fell silent. From somewhere, great heaps of deerskins, beaver skins, and beadwork were laid at Penn's feet. It was far more than would be possible for them to carry back to their wagon. *"Waníshi,"* Penn said. "Thank you."

Issímlus was standing. "*Chit-kwas-sikw!* Onas has come from far away to attend our *kintinka.* Let us listen to his words." He invited Penn to rise.

It was not so easily done. Penn looked as if he were searching for his cane, then struggled to push himself up with his arms. Pastorius came to his rescue. "Your Bible, Governor," he offered, only after Penn was steady again.

Coughing from the tobacco smoke, Penn turned to the page he had marked with a red silk ribbon. He recited from memory, feigning to read. "'Seek ye not what ye shall eat, or what ye shall drink, neither have need of these things. But rather seek ye the kingdom of God; and all these things shall be added unto you. Fear not, little flock; for it is your Father's good pleasure to give you the kingdom.'"

He closed the book and pressed it against his chest. "*Wah-li kishku.* My dear friends, I have come to refer thee to that which has comforted and guided me, namely the Light, Grace, Spirit and Truth of God which is within. This book is my gift to thee, and I charge thee to learn to read and understand it—the Old Testament for history, chiefly, the Psalms for meditation, the Prophets for comfort and hope, but especially the New Testament for doctrine, faith and worship."

A feeling of embarrassment crept over Johannes. He was keenly aware of the respect that his Indian friends held for the great Onas. He watched them as they gazed at the proprietor, flattered that such an important European would join them in their *kintinka.* But Johannes' own presence there at their *kintinka,* in their eyes, validated Penn's credibility, rather than the reverse. It was a validation he wished he could deny.

He and Seelig had been careful to offer the *Lenápay* Christianity in its essential form—stripped of centuries of accretions of church authority. In the absence of any correspondence in symbolism and cosmology, Johannes had used Behmen's concept of God in Nature as common ground with the *Lenápay*. He had tried not to teach, not to preach, not to assume intellectual superiority. His greatest fear for these people was that they would inherit the worst of European society from those who were spiritual in words and not in the heart. From those who were lovers of the world. From slaveholders.

"As soon as thou wake in the morning," Penn said. "I adjure thee to retire thy mind from thoughts and ideas of worldly things and lift up thy heart unto God. Feel His good presence and trust thy whole self into His blessed care and protection. Then rise, if thou are well, and read from the Scriptures. Whatever thou do, in all thy thoughts, words, and actions, place thy trust in His all-seeing Presence. As Christ expresses to us, have no concern for thy worldly comfort, but seek only the Kingdom of God, and thou will be supported in your disappointments and moderated in thy success. When thou close thine eyes to sleep, make the Lord the last thought in thy day."

He coughed again, changing the tone—and direction—of his voice. "Know well, my friends, that the true house of Christian worship is within, where the soul is encloistered. True followers of Christ do not exempt themselves from intercourse with the world. It is merely a selfish invention to withdraw from society, a lazy and unprofitable life to remove oneself from the path of temptation. No thanks are due to those who do not commit what they are not tempted to commit. If thou have faith, then thy ship will be steady at the helm, and not stealing away from the world, leaving those that are in it without a pilot."

Whether or not the *Lenápay* elders understood the agenda hidden in Penn's words, they listened patiently. The governor didn't look at his audience. He stared at the spiraling smoke that trailed up from the embers into the light. Johannes watched his eyes, feeling in empathy the proprietor's bitterness—with his world, his faith, and himself.

"What love is to the heart, silence is to the mind. No man can hear God's voice who is not silent in himself. In the manner of Quaker worship, let us rest our souls in silence, speaking only if stirred by the tender motions of the Inward Light." He tottered. Pastorius rose and helped him back to a sitting position.

What Johannes sensed when he closed his eyes was not the tender motion of Inward Light. It was the cedar smoke of the fire, the rustling of feet outside, the fidgeting of William Penn's infant son. Yet there was a stirring, an energy he could feel rising in the collective consciousness of the group. He opened his eyes in time to see Amimi uncross his legs.

The young Indian who stood to speak was no older than he himself had been when the Chapter of Perfection had arrived in Pennsylvania. Amimi now wore the paint of *Lenápay* men across his chest. His hair was gathered in a thin, tight braid that trailed down his back. His dark eyes no longer looked pensive. His voice no longer sounded hesitant. When he spoke, it was in confident English, seasoned with his own peculiar mixture of *Lenápay* and German.

"Friend Onas, you come into our village from across the ocean to bid us believe in the Creator and Preserver of heaven and earth, but you do not believe in Him yourself, nor do you trust Him. You have made your own the land that we once held in common. Now you worry, day and night, how you may hold on to this land, so no one may take it from you. You are even anxious beyond your own span of life and concern yourself how you shall divide your land among your children—so much for this one, so much for that one.

"The *Lenápay* have faith in God, the Creator and Preserver of Heaven and Earth. He provided for our ancestors. He provides for us, and we believe with certainty that He shall provide for our children. Because of our faith, we do not worship pieces of paper, nor do we need to take constant heed of possessions—who shall own this, who shall own that. We bid you consider the words of your own wise one, so that you might truly have faith in He who preserves Heaven and Earth."

There was silence. The sound that finally broke it was the gentle cry of John in his mother's arms. Johannes looked past him, past the grimacing Pastorius, to the governor who sat with his eyes clenched tightly. It had been an exhausting trip for a man stricken with gout, and it was very warm inside the *wig-wam.* Perhaps, Johannes thought, it was only perspiration that trickled down the governor's cheek.

Chapter Seventeen

Wednesday, December 24, 1828
Christ Church, Philadelphia

It wasn't a decent lamp that the bishop handed to Lydia. It was only a half-burnt candle in an open holder. Lydia knew she would have to keep a hand in front of it as they climbed the draughty staircase. The bishop twisted suddenly into the shadow. When he turned back, he was holding a lighted match.

Back in the sanctuary, with the gray afternoon light filtering through the great arched windows, he hadn't looked as old as she had expected. The Right Reverend Doctor, Bishop William White, had a tenure even lengthier than his list of titles. "I've been at Christ Church longer than the United States has had its Constitution," he told her. They had stopped to listen to the choir rehearsing for the Christmas service. "The loyalties of my distinguished predecessor lay with the Crown. I guess that makes me the first *American* pastor this old Episcopal Church ever had. Founded in 1695. Not me, of course," he chuckled, "the church."

In the darkness at the bottom of the stairwell, in the flickering light of his match, he looked very much his eighty-some years. The shadows made his nose appear long and pointed, as well as his chin. But in spite of his age and the severity of his features, his eyes were bright.

He lit her candle, then his, then put the flame to his mouth. A hazy glow appeared out of nowhere, and the narrow stairwell was overcome with the smell of a cigar. "Now, Mrs. Bielen," he said through clenched teeth, "are you ready to see the library?"

"It's Miss Bielen."

"Oh, forgive me, I assumed…"

"Mr. Kriebel is my fiancé."

"How wonderful! Perhaps you will choose Christ Church for your wedding."

"We are German Lutherans, Bishop White."

"Of course, of course." He started up the stairs, politely ahead of her. The treads creaked under their steps. There was no handrail, only an old rope held into the brick wall by iron pins. It didn't matter. Both of Lydia's hands were occupied, one holding her candle, the other protecting its flame. "Did you know that a German Lutheran figured prominently in the history of Christ Church?"

"No, Bishop." She wished at least that she could hold onto her skirt, to keep herself from tripping in the dark.

"Few people do. It was a young man by the name of Henrich Bernard Köster. I never have been able to discover exactly what brought him to Philadelphia. He certainly wasn't a Quaker."

"But he wasn't an Anglican."

"No more than you are, Miss Bielen. I fear that his sentiments were more against the Quakers than they were for the Church of England. He fell into a row with the Quakers over what I've never heard, and wound up getting on the wrong side of Francis Pastorius—another German, I'm sure you know. Apparently, Mr. Köster took it upon himself to save the Quakers from themselves." He paused at the second landing to draw in a cloud of smoke.

"What did Mr. Köster do that was so awful?"

"I don't know exactly. But Pastorius made it quite clear that there wasn't room enough for them both. Took the skin off the man, figuratively speaking. Drove him right back to the Fatherland." He chuckled. "But Köster had his revenge. Well, here we are." He held his candle to the door and, by its meager light, guided a key into the lock. "Welcome to the Bray Library, Miss Bielen."

The door creaked louder than the steps. Inside was a small room, less than two hundred square feet. It looked more like a storeroom than a library. There were only two windows, both obscured by dust. Lydia saw stacks of books on a long table, books set haphazardly on shelves, and books piled up on the floor. "What you're looking at was intended to be the first public library in America. It even predates Ben Franklin's. Let me tell you, Miss

Bielen, there is a distinct advantage in having a library inside a church. The only reason these relics escaped being pilfered for cartridge paper by the Continental soldiers was the Good Lord's Providence—and the fact that no one knew they were up here!" He set his cigar down precariously on the edge of the table and shone his candle into her face. "So, what makes a bright young lady like you interested in such dull old matters?"

It was a question she earnestly wished people would stop asking her. "*Der Steppdecke*, sir."

"Pardon me?"

"Nothing more than an old quilt, you know. In planning to move after the wedding, I have been gathering together my—oh, I don't know what to call them— my possessions. I came upon an old quilt that my great-aunt gave to me before she died."

"Oh, I'm sorry."

"It was supposed to have belonged to one of the Hermits of the Ridge. I've been curious about them ever since. It was Frau Kriebel..." She paused, thinking how odd the name would soon sound on her. "That is, Mrs. Kriebel, who will be my mother-in-law—she told me she heard that you had something about them in your library down here, or rather up here." She didn't like being this nervous. "But I don't even know..."

"What Mrs. Kriebel heard is quite correct, Miss Bielen. Over there by the window, yes, that stack right there, those are supposed to be the Hermit's old books, or at least those of them that were sufficiently orthodox to be accepted for our library. We've had them up here for somewhere around a hundred years."

"Exactly a hundred years," she whispered. When she opened the musty volume on top, there was a shower of dust. The bookplate inside marked its donation. *Ex dono, Ludovic Christian Sprogel, in Philadelphia, Die Decembris 24, 1728.* She read aloud from the title page, translating from the Latin. "*The Ecclesiastical Astrology* by Gaspar Sciopi, Imperial and Royal Councilor. 1634."

"Hmm? Yes, very valuable, to be sure, to the right person. I'm certain that I've seen—yes, I believe this is what I was looking for." He handed her a thin sheaf of brittle papers, just in time to retrieve his cigar and tap the ash into his palm before it fell to the floor.

"Please take all the time you require. I will relock the door after you leave."

"Thank you, Bishop," she said, staring at the papers in her hand.

A curious report concerning a party of Germans who arrived in 1694 and their subsequent sojourn in Pennsylvania.

Something made her stop. She picked up her candle and rushed to the door. "Bishop White!"

He was nearly at the second landing. "Yes, Miss Bielen?"

She had suddenly remembered seeing that name once before, on the fragment of the journal she had discovered in the remains of the Tabernacle. "Bishop, what was Köster's revenge?"

"Pardon me?"

"Henrich Bernard Köster, sir. You said that before he returned to Germany, he had his revenge upon the Quakers."

He climbed back a few steps, close enough that she could see him blow a puff of smoke up the stairwell. "Mr. Köster used to hold weekly services in English, which he apparently knew very well for someone who disliked the Quakers as much as he did. He also knew the King had arranged that in the event that there was sufficient demand, Penn would allow the Church of England to send a missionary priest to Philadelphia to set up an Anglican congregation. Right in the heart of his Quaker haven. Köster was quite a charismatic fellow. He helped gather a crew, a very miscellaneous crew. It included a great many from outside the province, and some quite notorious characters, I'm afraid."

"You don't mean to suggest…?"

The Bishop laughed. "Yes, Miss Bielen. It was on account of the German Henrich Bernard Köster that the first Church of England was founded in Pennsylvania. I'm afraid, Miss, that the choir is waiting for me to give them attention. I hope you find whatever it is that you are looking for."

A curious report concerning a party of Germans who arrived in 1694 and their subsequent sojourn in Pennsylvania.

It appears that these men, mostly former theological students, cared little or nothing for the Holy Sacraments as instituted by

Scripture. On the contrary, they held to their peculiar interpretation of the Holy Writ, busied themselves with studies and speculations of Theosophical Sophia, that is Divine Wisdom, and at the same time practiced the Black, or so-called Egyptian Arts, also known as Alchemy.

It is held that there was upon the grounds of their community a laboratory, well equipped with sundry profane devices. These were used in experiments based upon beliefs of earlier centuries that it was possible by chemical means to distill from ordinary matter a *menstrum universale,* or *prima materia,* a substance that would prevent sickness and aging, or even death. This was known in legends as the *lapis philosophorum*, or Philosopher's Stone. These men held that the viability of such a possibility was vouchsafed to mankind by Christ. To them, the Lord's resurrection demonstrated not God's redemption of mankind's sins, but a method of triumph of Life over Death that they brazenly believed was henceforth available to all.

The hypocrisy of these apostates was no better demonstrated than in their fascination with instrumentation and invention. Although professing abhorrence for things of the world, these so-called wizards worried over natural observation and the materialistic science. Their true preoccupation was not with things Eternal, as would be expected of true men of spirit, but with Time and Mathematics. It is a matter of record that they busied themselves with the mechanics of clockwork and the construction of musical instruments.

Further extent of the inconsistency of the alchemists is evident in reports that, unlike the devout Christian hermits of centuries past, these German students were driven by a desire for political power and influence. Toward this end, they subsidized the purchase of a printing press (perhaps the first in the province) that remained in use in Germantown for many years, producing many faulty and heretical documents.

I have been shown elaborate horoscopes created by these men, who put their skill in the mathematical arts to use in the service of the proscribed art of astrology. These gruesome charts are full of ancient and pre-Christian symbols, no doubt designed to command the respect of the uneducated peasantry (the gullibility and ignorance of whom are well-known to all clergymen). True, it has been said that a belief in astrology was quite prevalent at that time, and that these men refused payment for these services. However, the fact that they themselves may have spurned the use of astrology as primitive does not excuse them from the sin and error of exploiting its use.

The leader of this group was a young man variously styled John, or Johann, or Johannes, Kelp, or Kelpius. He was described as being of slight stature and having an affliction of one eye. He wore a plain wool robe in the manner of the medieval anchorites, held fast at the top by a clasp, a white cravat around his neck, and a cap about his head. Despite early instruction in Christian theology, he maintained an occult library, which was said to contain works of Jewish, Saracen, and heathen magic. I was unable to discover any records of his origin or fate.

An assiduous investigation into the exact nature of his doctrine and the cause of his apostasy was fruitless. Of the heresies of his associates, material was plentifully available in the form of reliable, albeit thirdhand, reports. However, all I was able to ascertain regarding Kelpius himself was derived from a fragment of a report from the Ephrata community, a German settlement in Lancaster County. As laudable as is the morality expressed, it is singularly indicative that the source of the man's morality was not Christ, but the pagan Marcus Aurelius.

"Kelpius was a strict disciplinarian and kept attention constantly directed inward upon self. To know self, he contended, is the first and most essential requirement of knowledge. He directed a sedulous watchfulness over the temper, inclinations and passions, and applauded very much the counsel of the Roman philosopher, 'Look within, for within is the fountain of good.'"

It was while I was visiting the Ephrata settlement that I lingered in the upper room that housed the community archives. The evening being pleasant, a soporific feeling overcame me until my attention was drawn by chance to an odd manuscript. The effect upon me was disturbing, and I proceeded to transcribe the document into my notes. Although it does not directly refer to the above-discussed German alchemists, it most certainly has some connection to them, as the belief in the supernatural contained therein is representative of their errors. The quaintness of the language itself is evidence of the naïveté of the author. I have tried to preserve this lack of sophistication in my translation:

"June 23rd, being Saint John's Eve, as well as the anniversary of their arrival, the brethren set about to perform the mystic rites incumbent upon them by their ancient order. At a short distance from their house of worship lay a level meadow, guarded by the ancient and lofty sentinels of the forest. The weather was clear and bright, the evening still, and the sky an exceptional blue. Luminous clouds were tinged in gold, as the midsummer sun proceeded toward the west. Feathered creatures of the wilds were hushed, as if in expectation, save for an unseen dove who sang to the brethren in a mournful tone, reminiscent of the soul's longing for Union with her Creator.

"Greater preparations than usual had been made for the evening's rituals as this was their seventh anniversary—the number seven holding special significance. Long were the hours the brethren spent in meditation, strenuous were the movements performed for the purpose of purifying the energies that, according to their strange and incomprehensible beliefs, comprised the subtle or astral body of the human being.

"The Master convened the brethren who then assembled in the glen. The forest to the east was gilded by the setting sun; to their west, an emerald brilliance appeared to arise from the bright depths of the wilderness itself. As the Master entered the circle, an evening breeze disturbed the upper leaves, which began to dance in a shimmer of luminescence.

"The manner of the ritual of the hermits was of initiatory nature, and secrecy was incumbent upon all who were privy to its mysteries. However, it is said that upon that day, the gathering commenced in the following manner:

"'Let us sing a hymn to the Father, and go forth to what lies before us.'

"The assembled took one another's hand and began to circumambulate their Master, responding 'Amen.'

"'I am a lamp to you who see me.

"'I am a mirror to you who perceive.

"'I am a door to you who knocked upon me.

"'I am a way to you, and a wayfarer.

"'He saith, "If you respond to my dancing, see yourself in me who speaketh; and when you have seen that which I do, keep silent about my mysteries! You who dance, perceive what I do; for yours is the passion of mankind which I am to suffer!"

"It was then, whilst the brethren were so engaged, that a white, obscure moving body appeared floating in the air above them. So compelling was the sight, all fell silent. Together they watched as the apparition approached, assuming the form and mien of an angel. The vision receded into the shadows of the forest, only to reappear before them as a splendid being, who surpassed in beauty the loveliest of all humans.

"So profound was the effect of this sight upon the hermits that they, of one accord, dropped to their knees, beseeching their God. After long years of toil and deprivation, after countless miles traversed across land and sea, the Harbinger whose appearance they had anxiously awaited had finally arrived. Great were the hopes and fears the vision engendered upon their tender hearts. Sublime was the sense of confirmation of their mystical expectations. Earnest was their praise, in joyful assurance that the final deliverance of the world was at hand.

"However, as their prayers increased in intensity, the mysterious form vanished. Hope was replaced by alarm. Energized by their holy exertions, the hermits sustained their invocations as the deep shadows of night fell across the glen. The being did not return.

"At last, as the hour of midnight drew near, the hermits lit the fires marking the Eve of *Sanct Johaness Tag*. The flames dispelled the darkness of the forest, reaching as if to heaven itself, until their glow illuminated the strange symbol adorning their tabernacle.

"The hermits chanted their incantations, the heart of each filled with assurance that his voice was being heard by celestial ears. When the fire had been spent, upon a signal from the Master, the glowing embers were scattered down the hillside, flickering in the eerie shadows of the rugged forest.

"The Master enjoined the hermits to return to the house of

worship, where they reconvened. Despite sincere and energetic supplications throughout the night, offered without pause or intermission, no further signs were disclosed. When the rays of the new morning sun illuminated the sky, the hearts of the hermits lay darkened with gloom. Strong had been their joy, yet so was their confusion. The Master was unable to console the despairing brethren. In the bitterness of their disappointment, an explanation was offered for the spirit's disappearance, to wit, that one of their members had committed a sinful act whilst still in their homeland, far beyond the great sea. This the Master would not accept, reprimanding his fellow initiates, and restoring their attitude to one of forgiveness and redemption.

"The following night the brethren reassembled in the glen, their confidence restored. High were the hopes in the reappearance of the divine emissary. Expectantly they watched the skies, which, alas for them, harbored naught but clouds of disappointment. They prayed in earnest until their eyelids became heavy and their hearts weary. The night air brought the weight of dismay, and the brethren retired in silence.

"On the third evening, whilst engaged in their common prayer within the solemn stillness of their tabernacle, a light was seen to appear behind the form of their Master. The holy being then reappeared in her brilliant splendidness. With mounting energy, the brethren offered their supplications. Upon their knees, they implored the angel to enjoin what she would upon them. But rather than attracting the fair deliverer, their prayers always repelled her. At length, she disappeared, never to return again.

"Thus, they remained in seclusion, in patient expectation of the final drama of mankind, which they were to enact in the wilderness."

Lydia turned over the paper but beneath was only a copy of a receipt for a virginal organ, bequeathed anonymously to the church. She returned to what she had just read, running the index finger of her gloved hand over the handwriting. For a moment she wanted to add something to the document, some proof that she had read it, some acknowledgement that this strange, forlorn story had been remembered.

Instead, she gathered the sheets back into a sheaf and laid it gently onto the shelf. She walked over to the window on the north side of the room. The glass was gray, covered in condensation and dirt that she smeared away without regard for her handkerchief. Clean, there was barely any change. The smoke from a thousand hearths touched the sky and hung in the cold air over the city. There was the Schuylkyll River, silver and lonesome on Christmas Eve. Somewhere out of sight, but not six miles away, the Wissahickon Creek ran with ice along its banks, clinging to whatever secrets it held.

Below, probably impatient in the cab, was Joseph Kriebel, the man she was going to marry.

"O shorten the time! Let the hour draw near!
Think on Thy most gracious Promise dear,
So that before the world it shall appear."

The voices of the choir sounded distant and ghostly. She shook herself. What *was* she doing, poking and prodding into the past? Why should she feel as if a part of her lay restless and unfulfilled in a relationship with someone who had been dead for a hundred years? Her whole future lay in front of her in endless possibilities. It was waiting for her, down in the street.

She took the candle and closed the door to the library, softly and reverently, like the lid of a casket.

Chapter Eighteen

Saturday, September 27, 1702
The Wilderness

Johannes woke from terrible darkness. The alteration of his consciousness was so sudden that for several moments he struggled for a sense of who he was. He found himself in the *Sternwarte,* alone in the cool light of morning. It had not been the birds or the sunlight that woke him. It had been the breeze, bringing with it voices he could barely hear, but that carried his own name.

"The Magister has been..."

"*Schwermütig.*" Melancholy.

"I would agree."

"...too much time apart."

"Seems to have lost his interest in..."

He had never before fallen asleep on his watch in the observatory. Not even on languorous summer nights when the flying glowworms danced the forest to sleep. Somehow, even in the bracing autumn air, he had fallen victim to his own inability for endless patience. Now there would be no notation for the previous night's conjunction of the Moon and Jupiter. No one to report the presence or absence of the unusual. The Magister had been sleeping.

He picked himself up, stiff from the awkward position. He tried not to listen to the concern for his welfare in the voices of the brethren below. He looked out over the trees, into the light of the morning. He heard the cooing of a dove. The plaintive sound he heard every morning and evening, he chose to imagine came always from the same creature—an unseen but constant presence in the wilderness. That morning the spaces between the dove's call were filled with the sounds of children who were arriving with their families for the morning devotional.

He climbed down the stairs to the *Saal*. He felt no need to say anything to the brothers whose faces betrayed embarrassed solicitousness. He returned their "*Grüß Gott,* Magister" with a smile. He needed to prepare for the service. They could gain a lesson from their discomfort.

He hurried, unnecessarily, down to his cell. Throughout all the years only once had he ever had cause to be concerned for his secret box. He had been on watch that night, also.

When he had returned to his cell, Shaeffer the Finnish prophet held it in his hands. There had been nothing in Shaeffer's manner to suggest that he was planning to tamper with the box, or indeed, suspected its importance. Still, Johannes felt his pulse race.

"Please give that to me, Brother Shaeffer," he said.

When he had arrived in America, Shaeffer had cut off his hair almost entirely, revealing a round and unpleasantly large head. In the shadows of Johannes' cell, he looked only marginally human. "What is inside?" he asked.

Johannes mustered his voice into politeness. "In our traditions, we allow a special privilege to the Magister, to maintain certain objects and information that are given to students only when appropriate for their development."

"Where did you get it?"

Johannes put his hand on it. Shaeffer was unpredictable, and Johannes was still unsure of the Finn's perceptive abilities. "It was given to me by my own Magister, Jakob Zimmerman."

Seemingly satisfied, Shaeffer released his grip. He went over to examine the Turkish tapestry. "I have no need for a Magister as an intermediary," he said to the wall. "Nor do I have a need for secret possessions or special privileges." When he turned back, neither his face nor his tone displayed a trace of hubris. "I believe that only God, and no mortal teacher, can judge another's spiritual attainments. I believe that only by a man's fruits can he be known. *Matthew*, chapter seven, verse twenty."

Regaining the possession of the box was infinitely relieving. "Brother Shaeffer," he said, "I beg your indulgence. If perhaps because we are not as developed as you, we still hold to such things. While you are our guest, I'm sure that you will accommodate our traditions." He put his free hand on the tattered cape that the Finn kept around his shoulder and led him toward the door. "Perhaps I could convince you to assist us in this morning's service?"

"One thing more," Johannes said as they were on their way toward the Tabernacle. Hearing his thoughts spoken aloud, they sounded more like those of Pfarrer Kelp than his own. "It is not considered appropriate to enter the Magister's cell unbidden."

He later regretted inviting Shaeffer to participate in the service. "We consider the orthodox practice of the sacraments to be empty ritual," Johannes told him afterward. Shaeffer had taken bread from the kitchen, held it over his head, and proclaimed it the body of Christ.

"The Sacrament of the Eucharist was instituted by the Holy Spirit and recorded by the prophets and apostles," Shaeffer said. "Do you place yourself above them?"

Johannes wouldn't let it become a matter for discussion. "We welcome you to our community, Brother Shaeffer. You are free to remain here with us long as you wish. If, however, you were to change us, then we would no longer be the same community. If we were to become something else, we would no longer be able to welcome you in the same way." He tried to smile as he spoke. Shaeffer said nothing.

From his cell, Johannes returned to the Tabernacle. He took his place on the floor, in the circle of the assembled. There was no pulpit. He had agreed to public worship services only on the condition there would be no sect, no name, no hierarchy at the human level. No one would be elevated over another.

The sound of the flute and viol accompanied the song that began the morning service.

"Getreuer Hort! Denk an dein wort:
Errette die Elenden,
Die dir vertraun; doch Jetzobaun

Im fluch mit müden Händen."
Most faithful Lord, think on Thy Word:
Deliver the distressed,
Who trust in Thee, although they be
Under yoke oppressed.

When Johannes spoke at a service, he often did so without preparation, to allow Divine Intention to flow through him as the Quakers did. But he was feeling insufficient to the task—still shackled by his nightmare, still in the past with Shaeffer, still reading the letter that Daniel Falckner had delivered.

"And Thou wilt then, the yoke of sin,
Remove from Thy creation,
And call Thy hosts from every coast
To Sabbath's celebration!"

Christian and Maria Warmer were in the *Saal*, along with their son and daughter. Maria was once again pregnant, so close to delivery that Geissler brought a chair from the dining hall. Klincken and Schumacker stood in the back. The court of Germantown had appointed them to establish a school, which they had—with Pastorius as the schoolmaster. It was a properly orthodox school, purged of Pietistic and esoteric influences. Still, the two men would sometimes visit the Tabernacle, he suspected more out of curiosity than affinity.

There was old Van Bebber with his family. They had made the journey by carriage from Philadelphia where they were now living. The two of them exchanged a nod. Van Bebber did not look well. The supply of *Essentia dulcis* that Falckner had brought back from Germany was already depleted.

Johannes began to address the little congregation, not knowing where his words were taking him. "Three and a half centuries ago, Tauler wrote 'Some men at the present time take leave of symbols too soon, before they have drawn out all the truth and instruction contained therein.' Such men are scarcely, or perhaps never, able to understand the truth aright. For they would follow no one, and lean unto their own understanding, and desire to fly before they are fledged."

His mental vision was flooded with the vision of a dove, unable to either fly or light. He struggled on.

"Let us therefore take and receive example and instruction, reproof, counsel and teaching from devout and perfect servants of God, lest they should say of us, *'Thus they have loved to wander, they have not refrained their feet, therefore the Lord doth not accept them; he will now remember their iniquity, and visit their sins.'*" The clarity of his recall was clouded, and he paused. "*Jeremiah*, chapter fourteen...verse ten," he stammered.

He spoke on the need for the institution of teachership. He said that although the essence of religion was in personal experience, that experience needed to be ripened in the context of a living spiritual tradition or it would decay and become useless. He tried to relate his ideas—as always—to the accepted Scriptures, but he found the nagging circularity of his mind ensnaring him.

After the service was over and he had completed his morning exercises, he found Seelig in the dining hall. "You should eat, my friend," Seelig repeated. There was still food on the table. Perhaps Seelig was right. Was it because of his fast that he hadn't had the strength to complete his watch?

"Perhaps," he said, but his stomach rebelled at the sight of the cold fried eggs.

"Will you come walk with me, Kelpius?"

"I have work to do this morning."

"Today is the Sabbath, my friend. Would you work today?"

"Inner work."

"Excellent!" said Seelig. "Let us do our work, you and I together, while we walk."

So they left the dining hall together, past the Tabernacle and the orchards, across the fence and down into the forest. The morning was exquisitely brilliant, the air cool, dry, and transparent. The valley below was flooded with color. Chipmunks and squirrels, honoring neither the Sabbath nor the two humans, scurried in the underbrush. Less visible were the insects, who droned their peculiar harmonies of the season.

Johannes was grateful for Seelig's company, but also for his silence. He fell quickly into the rhythmic concentration exercise linking motion of the legs, breath and mind. It was nearly an hour until he felt inclined to speak. When he did, he startled himself nearly as much as he did Seelig. "Last night I dreamt of old Zimmerman."

"I hope he was properly repentant for all his errors."

"I had been left in a graveyard to wait for him. When he didn't return as he had promised, I went searching for him. Finally, I found him, tied to a tree by heavy chains."

"Chains?"

"I freed him, pulling the chains from his wrists, but he fell away from me. Below him was an empty grave. The chains had prevented him from falling into the hole. I reached to save him, but I lost my balance and fell after him—into an abyss. Then I woke, in terror."

"A nightmare certainly. Do you think it has significance?"

"Seelig, from where would you say that Zimmerman received his spiritual authority?"

"From Francke, I suppose. It was he who appointed him Magister. Or perhaps Ludwig Brunnquell."

"And who passed on the authority to Brunnquell—or even to Francke, for that matter?"

"Are you asking me to recite the chain of Alchemical Magisters from Hermes the Egyptian to Paracelsus?"

"I'm asking you to tell me how I derive my own position as Magister." He could hear tension in his own voice. "And by whose authority?"

Seelig stopped and looked at him. "Is this what has been has been troubling you? Are you wondering if you are another of the old Magister's miscalculations? He was not so far wrong, Kelpius. It was only his world that came to an end in 1693—not ours."

"I am wondering how are we able to distinguish Divine Guidance from the tricks of an unsettled mind."

Seelig patted his shoulder. "Jesus has already provided you an answer, Kelpius. *Matthew* chapter seven, verse twenty."

Do men gather grapes of thorns, or figs of thistles? Every good tree bringeth forth good fruit; but a corrupt tree bringeth forth evil fruit. Every tree that bringeth not forth good fruit is hewn down, and cast into the fire. Wherefore by their fruits ye shall know them.

Johannes said nothing, regretting the bitterness that he had allowed into his voice. The two of them walked on along the Indian trail that wound snake-like up and down the mysterious hills of the Wissahickon Valley. They startled a group of squawking turkeys in the underbrush. "Are you as thirsty as I am, Kelpius?" Seelig asked. "Let's head down to the creek for a drink."

The terrain dropped off steeply into a bright hollow, through which a tiny stream traced a path down the gorge. They followed it to a place where the rill rushed over rocks and flowed into the sunlight of the Wissahickon Creek. Assured of the privacy of the wilderness, Seelig took off his robe and splashed his face until the top of his undergarment was soaked. "Is it cold?" Johannes called.

"I have always known that you were prescient, Kelpius. But this you must find out by experience!" Johannes did, and Seelig laughed at him as he shivered. Taking a pair of apples from a sack in the pile of his robe, Seelig threw one to Johannes. "You didn't eat this morning, Kelpius. Have an apple."

They sat along the bank eating. The fruit was tart and felt good in Johannes' stomach. Seelig found a place beneath a tree and crossed his legs in a meditation posture. Johannes stepped over a series of stones that led to a flat boulder in the middle of the rushing waters of the creek. He took off his robe, yawned, and lay his back against the warmth of the rock.

One terrible night, three years before, he had allowed Peter Shaeffer to join their circle, only because he had exhausted his ability to refuse. The energy of Shaeffer's presence was undoubtedly powerful. All the brethren sensed it, although no one, including Johannes, knew exactly what to make of it.

Afterward, when the Finn was unaccounted for, Johannes rushed to his cell to make sure his box was still well-hidden. Then, with a lantern, he went looking for Shaeffer in the woods. It was cold and moonless, and he was haunted by his own premonitions. Calling out was an effective way of locating someone who wanted to be found. He didn't think that Shaeffer did.

It was nearly a half an hour later, after Johannes calmed enough to allow his intuition to guide him, that he found Shaeffer. The prophet was crouched in the bushes, upstream where the waters roared over rock. He was naked.

"Touch my body, Brother Kelpius!" he called, even before the light of the lantern was on him. "Touch anywhere upon my body. You cannot cause me to fall prey to sins of the flesh."

Johannes lowered the light. "Come with me back to the *Saal,* Brother Shaeffer. There you can tell me more of Doctor Portage and his thoughts on Behmen."

"*Nein! Nein!* I will not talk about them. Do not attempt to coerce me!"

"It is cold, Brother. We can discuss whomever you wish, but let us join the others."

"Whom I wish to discuss, Kelpius, is *your* brother." Johannes lifted the lantern just long enough to see Shaeffer's face. The Finn's eyes were gleaming in his huge head. "Your brother is dead, Kelpius. He died of consumption four years ago—alone, in Hamburg."

Johannes felt his throat constrict. "I did not know."

"I know, Kelpius, because your brother speaks to me. He wishes me to warn you. 'Tell my brother, Peter Shaeffer,' he says to me. 'Tell him that I have died. Tell him that I have borne the repentance for abandoning him.'"

A chill penetrated Johannes, and his hands trembled. "Please, Herr Shaeffer."

"The Pfarrer, your father, hurt you greatly, did he not, Kelpius? To others, he was a man of God. To you, of the Devil. 'Abandon thy quest for the secrets of life and death.'" Shaeffer's voice rose into a disturbing timbre. "'You cannot return me to thee. From dust we are made, and to dust we shall return. Destroy the stone of immortality, Hans. It is not thine to employ.'"

Something rose in his heart and struggled with his fear and outrage. It was shame, a feeling he hadn't experienced since he had left Segesvár, escaping the town's thinly disguised pity. An infantile impulse rose in him, and he wanted to cover his ears, to shut out Shaeffer's words. Instead, he retreated into prayer.

Fiat voluntas tua.

"Do not close your ears, Kelpius. Do not close your ears to your mother. "'Tell him, Peter. Tell him how I waited twelve years for him, just as Rachel did for Joseph. Tell him of my delight when he was born.'" The strange shrill voice began to break down. "She was not able to complete her gift to you, Kelpius. She wanted to give you a gift of many colors because you were her Joseph." It sounded as if Shaeffer were weeping. "I am cold," he said finally.

By what Johannes considered Grace, he found Shaeffer's cape in the bushes. Compassion overtook his confusion and fear. He went into the bushes and covered Shaeffer's shoulders. "Do not be cold, Brother."

"I cannot stay here," Shaeffer whispered.

"Let us return to the *Saal,* Peter."

Shaeffer's petulance returned. "I mean that I cannot remain in a place where my gifts are not valued. I must leave this faithless circle."

"I understand." He took Shaeffer's hand and started back up the hill. "We have many friends in Pennsylvania. We will find somewhere for you to stay, somewhere your gifts will be valued."

"*Nein! Nein!* Do not try again to coerce me, Kelpius. You are not my Magister." He pulled his hand free. "No one shall command my movements but God! I shall put my feet only in the direction that He instructs."

"Of course, Brother Shaeffer," he said. "God would not have granted you such gifts if He did not have a plan for their use. Everything will be all right for you. I am certain."

By the time Johannes opened his eyes, it was well into the afternoon. He took a long drink from the creek and put back on his robe. Seelig, who had not stirred from his spot along the bank, opened his eyes. "Do you have another apple?" Johannes asked him.

"Look there, yes, in the pile of my robe. And another for me, too, please." Johannes threw an apple to him. "I thought it best to let you sleep. You looked as if you needed the rest."

"Thank you, Brother Seelig. You seem to have taken on the task today of caring for me."

"Sometimes we must be responsible for each other."

They left the creek with its soothing sounds and climbed back up to the high ground. They were halfway to the Tabernacle when Johannes spotted something large and covered in fur. He tugged Seelig's sleeve and pointed. A small brown bear, neither a cub nor full-grown, stood up from the shrubbery and sniffed the air. It looked at them for a moment, then ran off, crashing through the dry leaves. "Seelig, you and I must make a frightening sight," he said.

"I suspect," Seelig said, "that he may have been scared away by the unorthodoxy of our beliefs." The look on Seelig's face was intensely serious before it broke into a grin. For a few moments the two of them stood looking at each other, Seelig laughing like a child.

It was Seelig's laughter—mocking his own self-conscious melancholy—that gave Johannes the courage to speak. In the space of a breath, he decided that he could no longer endure carrying his burden alone, even at the risk of spoiling a rare moment of pleasurable comradeship. "Seelig," he said, "I must tell you something. It concerns Peter Shaeffer."

Seelig raised an eyebrow.

"In the spring I sent a letter to our friend Ulhegius in Sweden, asking if he had any information on Shaeffer—if he knew whether or not he ever returned to Europe. Last week, Falckner came by with a reply. The report was not what I had expected."

"Brother Kelpius, your kindness to the man was greater than he deserved."

"Apparently, Shaeffer had not exaggerated about his education. He truly had all the degrees he claimed. But before he came to America, he had been arrested on a charge of heresy. Several of his comrades were put to death. He recanted and managed to escape. He wandered around northern Germany for several years before he met Mecken and Clerk in London.

"He was the same after he left us as he had been before, unable to stay in one place for long. Somewhere along the way, he experienced a vision, commanding him to return to Finland. He claimed he was instructed to reprimand those who had wronged him, so he turned himself in to the Finnish Consistorium. They spared his life, but imprisoned him in the fortress of Gefle. He died there, insane."

Seelig closed his eyes. "May God grant him a blessed resurrection."

They spoke no more the rest of the way back. By the time they reached the Tabernacle, the afternoon light was gold and the trees were casting long shadows across the orchard. The ground was littered with rotting fruit. "The apples are ripening faster than we can pick them," Johannes said.

"Are you all right, my friend?"

"You needn't be concerned," he said. "I am fine, still just a little tired."

"Then I will meet you later in the dining hall?"

"Yes, but there are some things that I must do, even on the Sabbath."

Johannes left Seelig at the tall fence that surrounded the Tabernacle and crossed over to the laboratory. Inside, he found a pail and, after washing it carefully, walked back to the orchard. For a while he forgot about Shaeffer and went from tree to tree, collecting the ripest of the fruits before they would fall and be eaten by the insects and worms.

Chapter Nineteen

Friday, June 24, 1704
The Wilderness

And when Herod saw Jesus, he was exceedingly glad; for he was desirous to see him of a long time, because he had heard many things of him; and he hoped to have seen some miracle done by him. Then he questioned with him in many words; but he answered him nothing. And the chief priests and scribes stood and vehemently accused him.

It was silence that brought Johannes back from his contemplation on the Passion. For numberless hours he had been lost in his concentrations, in the examination, the experience, and the transcendent meaning of the suffering of Christ.

Despite the worrisome leak in the roof of his private cell, the rain had provided a reassuring backdrop to his thoughts. Its rhythm helped him shut out the world, as it offered an excuse for him to withdraw from its activities. Inside his cell, with the constant drumming on the ground above, he easily found the peace of solitary renunciation. Then all of a sudden, it stopped.

Not since Shaeffer left had there been anyone who would have dared to bother him during his time alone—rain or shine. The week before he had stepped out into the blazing light of a midsummer morning to find that someone had come to visit his cell. Someone had made the walk from Germantown and back, simply to leave a letter on the ground where he would discover it at his convenience. It was written in a familiar female hand. It smelled of rosewater.

To Our Beloved Magister Johannes Kelpius,

The Pleasure of your Company is requested at the Home of Christian and Maria Warmer on Friday, June Twenty-fourth, being the feast of St. John, at the Hour of Six in the Evening to meet with some Friends from Long Island who are traveling to Philadelphia and have expressed a Desire to meet the renowned Magister.

Respectfully,
Maria and Christian Warmer

He hadn't wanted to attend. So many people had come to see him over the years. In the beginning, he had seen it as a proof that he had been made a living medium for the expression of Divine impulses. Then it had become merely his responsibility to share the benefits of his education with those who had been denied such opportunities. Eventually he had come to the bitter realization that those who listened to him did not have a desire to learn anything of the spirit, or of the mind, or even of the world. They were interested in having him validate their own religious prejudices.

They had come from Philadelphia. They had come from New England and Virginia. Some had even come from Europe. They had heard stories about him, some wildly exaggerated. Those stories had inspired so many Seekers of Curiosities that they crowded out the Seekers of Truth. If there had ever been any.

"So many heads, so many opinions," he had written to his old mentor, Magister Fabricius, at the University of Altdorf. His visitors called themselves religious, but their actions proved they were as worldly—in their pride, in their combativeness, in their jealousies—as the ungodly. Perhaps more so. And all his teaching and all his preaching didn't seem to have helped them understand.

Wouldn't Maria forgive him for hoping the rain would continue all day, hard and long enough that he could remain in contemplation? He emerged from his cell, rubbed his eyes, and looked up through the canopy of dripping leaves. The sky was still gray, but the clouds were moving wildly. He wished he hadn't been able to, but he could sense the barometric change in his body.

He shaved, put on his boots, and donned his cap. It was well past five. He found Seelig in the Laboratory. "Are you leaving for town, Kelpius?"

"Seelig, my friend," he began.

"If you have come asking for a companion, Kelpius, please remember that it was your name only on the invitation."

"Yes, but…"

"What would Maria say if I arrived uninvited?"

"I'm certain she would be grateful that I had brought someone capable of reminding me to stop speaking when I had overrun my obligations."

Seelig laughed. "She said her visitors were friends. Do you suppose she meant acquaintances or Quakers?"

"Seelig, if I knew that, I would be the saint they might suppose me to be."

Seelig wiped his hand on the cloth he held. "Is it a directive from the Magister that I attend?"

"It is only a choice, my brother, between hours spent cleaning the lime kiln and an opportunity to engage in religious discourse with travelers from New York."

"I believe I will choose the lime kiln, Magister."

Johannes was across the swollen creek when the light in the forest suddenly changed. The clouds had taken on the shape of mountains, infinitely lofty, with a majestic ray of light flowing from a perfect representation of Heaven. There was something ominous in the sight, something strangely disconcerting in the beauty. A disturbing feeling ran through him until it possessed him entirely.

In the space of a breath, he was half a world away, a small boy outside his father's study. He was staring through the open door at a framed picture, an etching in meticulous black-and-white detail. *Himmel.* Heaven, depicted as the sun breaking through fantastic clouds. He sat on the floor, studying the picture, wishing to be in its safe, comforting splendor. *An Allegorical Representation of All Faiths* was the legend. Bathed in the beatific light were strange men and even stranger symbols that intrigued him with their suggestion of the exotic. And there, with his chair turned to the wall, sat his father, weeping.

He didn't know why the Pfarrer was crying, but it frightened him more than the stick. There were many things that his father was not, but he had always been stoically strong. For every question, Pfarrer Kelp had an answer. For every vagary in life, he knew the moral absolute. Every sorrow was a punishment for sin. What had been his father's sin?

Johannes shook himself and smiled at this odd, bittersweet memory. The leaves were still full of rain that continued to drip and sparkled in the fickle sunshine. There was stillness in the freshly washed forest. Beneath the heavenly beams, the great boulders stood exactly as they had for centuries before his father had ever been born. They would be the same long after he himself was dead. What was a memory of twenty-four years to them?

The clouds rolled back over the sun. There was a rumble of far-off thunder. He left the path and found his way to where blueberry shrubs lined a small tributary stream. He lingered there, filling a basket until he wondered if he were intentionally delaying his arrival at the Warmer home. A nearly filled basket would suffice.

When he reached Germantown, the sun broke out again. The town was bathed in a golden supernatural light with a dark, threatening sky behind it. He followed the deserted Great Road down to High Street, one of the new cross streets in Germantown. A team of wet horses stood listlessly between a well-worn wagon and a trough along the street. There was another roll of thunder and the clouds overtook the sunshine again.

The Warmer house lay on the southeast corner. It was a credit to Christian and his success as a tailor. It was two stories tall, made of stone. Its windows and door were placed in neat symmetry, unlike some of the other housefronts, which had been designed by practicality rather than aesthetics. It lay next to the home of Francis Pastorius.

If the former Ruler of Germantown had seen him approaching through the curtains and quickly hid his face, he couldn't be sure. A flash of movement through the window was little cause for Johannes to take offense. There had been so many more causes—so many more threats—since Falckner had returned from Europe. Johannes had managed to avoid responding to all of them.

"Welcome, Magister. We are so happy that you were able to join us." Maria, standing at the door with her arm around little Christiana and holding her youngest in her arms, spoke to him in English. It meant that her visitors were likely not friends, but Quakers.

"I am grateful for the invitation." For providing an opportunity for self-denial, he thought. "I have brought you some berries, and here," he said, reaching into the basket, "something for Christiana and her brothers." It was an Indian toy, a pair of tiny drums on a stick with two pebbles tied to the end with leather straps. As he twisted it back and forth, the stones beat against the drums. George, the baby, giggled and reached out his hand to grab it.

"Juengchen!"

"It is all right, Maria. It belongs to them now."

Inside, the small parlor was crowded with people standing. "Magister, I would like to present Joseph Palmer and his wife, Sarah. Their daughter, Hester. Samuel Pressman and his wife Ella. Friend Martin and his son, Willard."

"It is a pleasure to meet you," he said, over and over, approaching each one. As he touched their hands, he struggled to ignore the chaos of images and sensations that flooded his intuition. Each stranger brought his—or her—own halo of memories, thoughts, and even portents. They had not come to be told what lurked in the dim corners of their minds or what their destinies were likely to be. He tried to muster the effort to dismiss these impressions, to look them in the eye as if he were unaware, to appear polite and unthreatening. "*Grüff Gott*, Christian," he said, turning at last to his friend. He patted the head of the junior Christian, now seven years old.

"For you—a chair—we reserve." Christian beamed as he demonstrated his English.

"Please," Johannes said, "allow a lady to be seated, and I shall stand. Perhaps you, Mistress Palmer?" He offered the seat to the young lady beside him. She was a plain young woman with light brown eyes beneath barely visible eyelashes. Curly hair slipped unceremoniously from the edges of a worn blue bonnet. She lowered her gaze.

"We would not allow thee to stand, Friend Kelpius," her father said.

Johannes' descent into the ladder-back chair was followed by silence.

"Before thou arrived, Friend Kelpius, I was asking Friend Warmer if there were as many *muskettoes* here in Germantown as we have in Flushing. In the early summer, there are times it is impossible to be outside without being feasted upon by these little demons."

"It is the poisoned weed that is most bothersome to us. My good husband was once prepared to return to England after being overcome with the rash."

The visitors laughed and continued to boast of their unpleasant experiences in the New World. Johannes sat, marveling at the swirl of conversation and its unreality. Once more he had to pull his attention from the images that appeared in his mind—a buried memory of childhood trauma, the moment of a loved one's death, a strange and forbidden sexual desire—these and more came into his awareness from the minds of the people in the room. His extended periods of solitude left him unused to the suppression of intuition that was required to endure human company.

Perhaps it was his own fault for assuming that these good people had traveled from Long Island to meet him. They were on their way to Philadelphia, he remembered that the note had read. Once they had returned home from whatever their real business had been, they could claim that they had met the famous Hermit of Germantown. They would be able to speak of it sometime in the future, at some other gathering, and perhaps never realize they had not truly made contact with him.

"And thou art from Saxony, Friend Kelpius?" He wasn't even certain who had asked the question.

"Magister Kelpius was not born in Germany," Maria said.

"I am from Transylvania," Johannes said. "That is, *Siebenbërgen*." He felt instantly foolish. What would the German name mean to English Quakers? They stood in silence, looking down at him. He tried to think of something else to say.

"It is little known, but a prophecy of the New World was made during the time of Christ." The young lady in the bonnet spoke so softly, her words would have been missed if the room had not been so quiet. They all turned their attention to her. "*'There shall come a time in later ages,'*" she quoted, "*'when the ocean shall relax its chains. A vast continent shall appear, a pilot shall find new worlds, and Europe shall be no more earth's bounds.'*"

The awkwardness compelled Johannes to come to her rescue. "*'Venient annis secular seris, quibus oceanus vincula rerum,'*" he said. "*'Laxet et inges pateat tellus tethys que novos detegat orbes, nec sit terris ultimata Thule.'*"

Her eyes widened. "Thou knowest it, Herr Magister?"

"The philosopher Seneca. It is from the chorus in the second act of *Medea*."

Christiana twirled the Indian drum between her palms, making a sudden noise. "Mistress Hester," Maria asked, "do you suppose that the Romans knew of the existence of the American continent?"

"I think, Frau Warmer, there is a difference between knowing the possibility of something and the ability to make use of that knowledge."

"Hester," said the girl's mother, "we have come here to meet Magister Kelpius, not to hear thy thoughts. What dost thou say, Friend Kelpius?"

Hester Palmer's pale cheeks flushed with embarrassment and she looked down to her feet. She was somewhere in her twenties, probably close to the same age as Maria, who stood by her own hearth, a wife and mother of three. He felt a wave of sympathy for the young woman and could no longer bear sitting while she stood beside him. "I think," he said, rising, "that Mistress Palmer's thoughts are very wise. They echo my own."

"It is quite wonderful," Maria said, "when thoughts are the same. Especially when the thoughts are so wise. I believe that we have kept you waiting long enough. My dear husband, would you help me in offering to our guests some food?"

Two benches had temporarily replaced chairs at the small table in the adjoining room. Johannes sat, shoved in between Hester Palmer and her mother.

"Your food is a special blessing to weary travelers," someone said.

"In a sense, we are all travelers in this world," Johannes said. "As we were speaking of the philosopher Seneca, he wrote..."

"How far is thy hermit's cell from here?" Joseph Palmer asked, from across the table.

"Not more than three miles through the woods."

"Then thou hast not traveled very far."

"The walk was quite pleasant," he said. He decided not to volunteer any more information on the philosopher Seneca.

Christian called for a moment of silence before the meal, in respect to the faith of his visitors who, he said to no one in particular, preferred silence to vocal prayer. Maria then served trout and catfish that had been caught in the Wissahickon Creek. There were bowls of peas and beans from her garden. There was bread but no meat. He was astonished at the energy with which the Quakers ate. His own body was so accustomed to fasting that it rebelled at the endless onslaught of food.

"The blueberries," Maria said, "were provided by Magister Kelpius. They grow in the Wissahickon Valley, down the hill from where the brethren live on the Ridge. Their Tabernacle is the finest house of worship in Pennsylvania. The mystical significance of its location was determined by my father while he was still in Germany."

Hester raised her eyes to Johannes. "I would very much like to see it," she said barely audibly.

"Dost thou think that your Proprietor will ever return to America?" someone asked.

"Governor Penn once made a special visit to Germantown to meet Magister Kelpius," Maria said. "He is an admirer of the Magister's commitment to the contemplative life."

"I was spiritualized by Friend Penn's book, *No Cross, No Crown*," Joseph Palmer said as he ate. "I consider Penn to be one of the most spiritual men of our time."

Johannes remained silent.

"Herr Magister." It was the small voice of Hester. "There has been a division between Quakers in recent times concerning the person of Christ. One group holds to the divinity of the historical Jesus, others worship the spiritual Christ. What would thou say to them to heal this strife?"

The eyes of everyone turned to him. He felt once again acutely aware of an onslaught of sensations. The air was a thick mixture of unfamiliar aromas and unspoken thoughts of the strangers. He wiped the edges of his mouth.

"Mistress Palmer, if your mother had several daughters, and if the many of you came to her and asked which was the most perfect, what do you suppose she would say?" He turned toward her mother. "I think she might say that each had her merits—one more beautiful, one more intelligent, one stronger, and so on. She would say that each had a contribution to make, yet none had a claim to perfection. There are so many sects, and sects within sects, each claiming to perfection. I believe that they all have a contribution to make with their many doctrines, yet when they clamor for precedence they are furthest from the perfection they claim."

"Friend Kelpius," Joseph Palmer said, "these are mere allegorical words. I cannot determine from them if thou art a Christian, a Jew, or even a Turk. Tell us truly what thou sayest of Jesus, the man. Was he, or was he not, the Son of God?"

The words stung him. "Is this not the very ground of the Christian religion, Master Palmer?"

"Dost thou answer each question with one of thine own, Friend Kelpius?"

He felt the pressure of eyes upon him as he weighed his answer. "The Jews say that God is a Spirit," he said, "and cannot beget a man for His son. In a sense, they cannot be blamed for believing this, for truly it is a mystery that surpasses human understanding. Now the Turks, whom you mention, accept Jesus, the son of Mary—that is what they style him—as the Word of God incarnate. They believe that He is anointed by the Holy Spirit above all the Prophets and Mohammed himself. But even they cannot accept that He is the Son of God."

He was aware that his thoughts were outpacing his ability to communicate. None of them, possibly excepting the young lady who stared at him rapturously, wanted to hear what he was saying. He knew all this while he spoke, wishing that Seelig had been there to restrain him, as he wasn't able to restrain himself.

"I say that the true understanding of the question you ask requires a revelation from God, like that of the Father depends upon the reception of the son, and mankind is yet to answer the question: Why Jesus, being God of the very God, came to be man and died?" He felt dizzy, as if he were finding himself in two places at once, both at the Warmer's home yet still alone in his meditation cell. "True, he received his almightiness from his Father, but we know He made no bragging ostentation, but instead He humbled himself even to the cross. He styled himself only as the son of man, or rather, of mankind," he said to the young woman. "The word in Greek denotes both sexes. Wherefore God, by the resurrection, exalted him above all, Lord over all worlds, visible and invisible, this and that which is to…"

The sound that baby George Warmer made was not a cough. It was the sound of a child desperately trying to breathe. His father lifted him from his mother's arms and began hitting him on the back. The child's eyes teared. Someone at the table made an audible gasp, as if it that would somehow help the baby. Maria took him back. She pushed herself from the table, patting his bottom as she lay him across her knees. George made a retching sound and spit out a blueberry, a stem still protruding from its top.

It only took a second for the child to smile again. He wiped his eyes on his sleeve and grabbed for another berry.

"Genug!" his mother scolded.

Christian Warmer rose from his seat. "I believe enough is what all have had."

The others took his lead.

"We are deeply grateful to thee, Friend Warmer, for accepting us into thy home and providing such hospitality."

"Thou art true Friends of God."

"I fear the hour is getting late, and we must find our lodging place in Philadelphia. Willard, fetch the gift we brought for the Warmers."

"We thank thee, Friend Kelpius, for sharing your enlightening thoughts."

Johannes was not only stricken with self-reproach for his carelessness while picking the berries, he regretted that too many solitary days had made him so enthusiastic in company. Did he always need Seelig to signal him to return from the depths of his own mind and consider the patience of his audience? "The gratitude is mine," he said, looking down at his feet, "for your interest."

Maria seemed distraught. "Friend Palmer," she said. "Our good neighbor, Francis Pastorius, is desirous of meeting you and your company before you leave. He is the most prominent Quaker in Germantown and a close friend of William Penn. Perhaps Mistress Hester would be so kind as to remain and converse with Magister Kelpius in the meantime?"

"But, Madam Warmer..."

"Herr Pastorius will be cross with us if you do not."

Like a breeze, Maria swept the company out into the street. "Christiana, *du auch!*" she called to her daughter.

Johannes was not prepared for this. Certainly he did not want to join the others. Pastorius would not have allowed him in his house, in any case. But to be left unchaperoned with a young lady whom he had just met—to be thrust into such a situation, without any prior warning...He turned to her. "Mistress Palmer, it is rather close in here. Perhaps you would wish to step outside to the Warmer's garden?"

She lowered her eyes, looking as awkward as he felt. He was not able to understand what she mumbled, but assumed it was assent. "I would be most grateful if you would accompany me." He motioned toward the door that led to the garden from the side of the house. He followed her outside, past the summer kitchen, past the smell of fish and smoke.

The garden lay behind the house, beside the pasture. Behind that, an ancient maple marked where the wilderness began again. A heavy green light settled over the world, filling the forest with mist.

The aroma of the persistent honeysuckle overtook the air. "It is quite lovely here in Pennsylvania," she said.

"As it is, I'm sure, on Long Island." If he had thought she was plain, he decided he had been mistaken. Her eyebrows were very light, as was her hair. Her nose was small and her cheeks pink from the sun. Hers was not a Germanic ideal of feminine beauty, but perhaps it was closer to an English one. He stared into her eyes, into the soul that lay cowering in the dark void behind her pupils. In its silence he heard an echo of his unspeakable longings. Suddenly, the taunts of his boyhood merged with the whispering of the children of Germantown. His fingers rose to the defect of his left eye as if he could, by touch, redeem it from its curse. "I must apologize," he said, "for discoursing too long at the table. It is one of my failings."

Flying glowworms began to flicker in the woods. Hester Palmer, leaning her arms over the garden fence, turned to him. "Would thou forgive me, Herr Magister, if I asked thee a question?"

Not knowing how to answer, he began first to nod, then shake his head. "There would be no need to forgive," he decided to say, "as you could not possibly offend in the asking."

"I would not presume to ask, but I sense a current of understanding between thy soul and mine."

"I pray that it be so."

She continued to look at him, then half turned her head toward the flowers that lined the garden fence. "I have wondered if the need to remain in the wilderness is a permanent requirement of thy spiritual path, or only temporary?"

He looked back at her, standing beside him in her plain bonnet and travel-weary smock. He marveled at her question and its motive. It was one of his firmest beliefs—one that found no resonance in his world—that the differences of gender were an illusion. He offered his teaching to girls as well as boys, believing both to be equal in potential. He counted as many women as men among his friends. He reminded himself there was no reason for his affection for her to be different than for any other person.

"By that," she said, "I refer to the woman in *Revelation* who, according to John, was to remain in the wilderness for one thousand two hundred and threescore days. Or even Christ Himself—the historical figure as opposed to the spiritual—who spent forty days only in the wilderness."

"Mistress Hester..." He hesitated. "Friend Hester, your question reveals depth of thought and touches on a subject that I have spent much time considering. But I fear that my speech might become so energetic and lengthy that you would tire of it. And of me."

She turned back to him, and for a fraction of a second touched him on his sleeve. "That would not be possible, Herr Magister." She bent her head toward the ground.

"Have you, in your memory, the experience of ever losing your way, Friend Hester?"

She hesitated. "Yes, Herr Magister."

"'Wilderness' is the term we use for a stage in the soul's journey. It is both a literal and figurative place, for the soul must bear the pain of separation from its former false beliefs before it may arrive at the Truth, which is its goal. The experience of 'wilderness' is confusion and loneliness as you, yourself, have known in your heart."

"Yes, Herr Magister." Her eyes still diverted from his, she shielded her chest with her hand.

His agitation was mounting. "Are you certain, Friend Hester, that you wish to hear about my peculiar philosophy?"

"Magister, my parents have raised me in the Quaker faith, yet despite their love and their instruction, I have become lost in my own wilderness, a spiritual wilderness, as you have rightly sensed." She looked up, and their eyes met. "I long to find my way. It is this longing that has emboldened me to approach thee."

"Boldness is not required," he said.

"Then please, Magister Kelpius. Please, help me to understand. Why does God lead us into desperate wilderness, where we no longer feel content, where the thoughts that once gave us comfort only confuse?"

Hearing laughter from the nearby house of Francis Pastorius, he felt an impulse to speak to her of the pain in his own heart. He wanted to tell her of the times of great exultation that had been followed by bitter disappointment. He wanted to tell her how it felt to be abandoned by his brethren and despised by the world. "Friend Hester," he said instead, "the wilderness is but a stage through which we must pass. The wineskin must be emptied of the old to be filled with the new. The Barren Wilderness is but the first of the lands on the journey. This is the Wilderness begotten in the darkness of Egypt, which is ignorance. Here the soul lives constantly in fear of death, and what it fears comes to pass. It falls and dies in the Wilderness before it can reach the Promised Land of Caanan."

"But, pray, tell me that there is a land beyond this."

"Yes, beyond the barren land of ignorance lies the Fruitful Wilderness. The soul there is born from the struggles of the first, but it continues on, because it understands the great mysteries therein."

"And what are those mysteries?"

"Its mysteries are that in the most bitter myrrh there is the most delicious sweet. That to become weak is the greatest strength. That in the darkest sorrow there is the most joyous inward gladness. That in becoming nothing, one partakes of..."

"Herr Magister!" Little Christian Warmer, breathless, skipped toward them from the neighbor's house. *"Es is an der Zeit! Jetzt muss die Dame los!"*

He couldn't shield his heart from her perception. "What is the matter, Magister?"

"It is nothing. I believe your mother and father are ready to take you to Philadelphia."

Her whole body shifted into a posture of submission. "I so much want to see your Tabernacle."

"Perhaps sometime in the future..."

"Yes," she whispered. "The future. Perhaps in the future."

He felt her sadness so keenly, he wanted to take her hand as they walked along the fence toward the front of the house. Suddenly, in view of the small crowd gathering in front of the wagon along the street, she turned and took his. "Would thou, Magister, make me a promise?"

He answered. "Ask, and I shall promise."

"Promise that thou wilt not forget me. Neither in your prayers, nor in your heart."

"I shall not, Friend Hester," he said.

There were tears in her eyes. "I shall not forget thee, Friend Johannes."

The air he breathed on the way back into the wilderness was redolent with the richness of a wet summer evening. The songs of passenger pigeons and parakeets kept him company until they gave way to the drone of cicadas and crickets. He was preoccupied with thoughts of the wilderness—his home, his refuge, his prison. He had been moved by the intense sadness of Hester Palmer. He had sensed it all too keenly, unable to separate her feelings from those of his own. It had left him badly disturbed.

There were so many things he wished he had been able to discuss with her, so many things he had contemplated for so long. He would have told her more about his thoughts on the wilderness, of its significance in history and scripture, of the many levels of meaning that it held. She would have understood him in a way that others could not. Her broad education and gentle, aspiring soul! She was compensation for the others who listened but did not hear. Perhaps their meeting had been intended to be a catalyst for both their souls. Perhaps even more.

The gray-green light seemed to linger indefinitely, so he decided not to return to his cell straight away but instead follow the winding creek upstream along the ancient trail that skirted the steep bank. It was a world of neither darkness nor light, but rich in the sounds of life. The wilderness, in the folds and wrinkles of the Wissahickon Valley, wrapped itself around him. Each bend brought him past another mist-filled vale, filled with tiny, flickering angels beckoning him with what lurked within. He would pause, just long enough to honor the possibilities that existed in the unexplored wilderness—the virgin expression of the love of its unfathomable Creator.

"There is a difference," she had said, "between knowing the possibility of something and the ability to make use of that knowledge."

The stark truth of the statement wounded him. Like all things manifest, he knew there was an end to the wilderness, all the wildernesses. Even eternity had its limits. The original Hebrew word did not signify endless existence, endless suffering, endless waiting. With or without tangible signs, the consummation of all that had come before would arrive. Then all things would be made possible. Then he and Hester Palmer would be together in a way that most human beings could scarcely comprehend. It was a thought that eased the heaviness in his heart. It was the only thought that he was able to hold.

He reached a sharp turn in the creek, where its waters opened up wide and shallow. He sat on a fallen log and removed his boots and stockings. Even with the recent rain, the water was barely over his knees. He held his robe and allowed the rushing coolness to caress his legs. It was a powerful and sensual feeling, free of the seduction that would divert his subtle energy into lower channels. It was the reassuring touch of the natural world from which his physical body had sprung.

It was nearly dark by the time he reached the far bank. He walked up the hill, past the great boulders, toward the ridge. There was no light in the *Sternwarte*. It was too overcast for stargazing and, besides, years of the unremarkable had caused enthusiasm to wane for the endless vigils. Seelig was probably asleep. What would he say to him if he were not?

His cell was the same as he had left it. It wasn't like the lodging house, the Dining hall, or the Laboratory, with brethren leaving traces of their presence and activity. It wasn't like Germantown, with its burgeoning and unpredictable growth. In whatever condition he left his cell, it was the same when he returned.

He lit the lard lamp, took his ink, and started working on his hymn, *A Conversation of the Soul with Itself, Composed in a Pensive Longing in the Wilderness*. He hummed the melody, but hearing his own voice in the stillness was an unwelcome reminder of his loneliness. He cleaned his pen nib and put back his work, untouched.

There, removed from the demands of human companionship that drained him, far from the touch of strangers that brought an onslaught of unwanted impressions, he longed for his intuition to become quiet. He dreaded the voices and the visions, the celestial melodies and lights. The Gifts that had once validated his spiritual efforts now only made him ill at ease in the world and were powerless to help him transcend that world.

He stared at the papers on the Passion and Crucifixion he had been studying earlier. Among them was an etching in meticulous black-and-white detail. It was a gift that Shaeffer had brought from Europe to the community. It portrayed the mother of Jesus and the disciple John standing beneath the crucified Christ. In the countless times he had looked upon it, he had never noticed the features on the face of Mary—the exquisiteness of her beauty, the depth of her compassion, the intensity of her suffering. He ran his finger across the illustration, almost as if he were stroking her hair. The legend was a paraphrase from the *Gospel of John*, chapter nineteen.

Mulier ecce filius tuus. Filium ecce mater tua.

Mother, behold thy Son. Son, behold thy Mother.

He turned his face to the wall and wept.

Chapter Twenty

Monday, June 24, 1850
Borough of Germantown, Philadelphia

Lydia sat in the outer office of the Town Hall, beside the door marked Deeds and Records, thinking how similar her feelings must be to those of her own students waiting to be cross-examined by the headmistress. She reminded herself that her perspiration was from heat and not anxiety. After all, she was the one who was there to ask questions. She tightened her grip on her leather bag.

"Mrs. Kriebel? Please come in." A head had appeared at the door, a balding and spectacled head whose voice had the unmistakable traces of a German-speaking childhood. "Horatio Seidensticker," he said, thrusting out his hand as he waited for her to sit opposite him at his desk. "You are a teacher?"

"I taught in Flushing, Long Island before I was married. I have been at Philadelphia Normal School now for over twenty years."

"And you are interested in the old records of Germantown."

"Yes."

"I'm not familiar with any Kriebels in Germantown."

"I am Bielen by birth, Mr. Seidensticker."

"Nor Bielens."

She felt unexpectedly on the defensive. "My maternal grandmother was a Wüster, her mother a Warner, or rather then, a Warmer."

"Ah!" He looked up over his spectacles. "Two of our most respected families."

"Yes, I know." She instantly regretted not speaking more politely. After all, he had agreed to her request, and presumably it was beyond his normal duties to deal with personal matters such as hers. But he had kept her waiting a very long time. She patted her forehead with her handkerchief for what seemed like the hundredth time.

"What exactly are you here to learn, Mrs. Kriebel?"

She loosened the strap that closed her handbag and took out the small, leather book. "My son recently married..."

"Congratulations, Mrs. Kriebel."

"He and my daughter-in-law are living with us, and in rearranging our house, I discovered something that I had thought I had misplaced forever." For some reason, her hand trembled as she passed the book across the desk. "Do you know what this is, Mr. Seidensticker?"

He tilted back his head, peering through the spectacles that had crept down his nose. He turned through the pages, much more aggressively than she thought appropriate. *"'The Lamenting Voice of the Hidden Love, at the time when she lay in misery and forsaken; and oppressed by the multitude of her enemies. Composed by one in kumber.'* 'In kumber' is an archaic term, Mrs. Kriebel. It means *in distress.*"

"Yes, I know."

A page fell from beneath the front cover and floated down to the desk. Seidensticker picked it up and read. *"'It is of the Lord's mercies that we are not consumed, because His compassions fail not. They are new every morning. Maria Warmer, 1705. In Germantown in Pennsylvania.'* Consumed?" He used a slender finger to scratch the bald spot on his head. Who was spared being consumed—and by what?"

"I asked if you could tell what book this is, Mr. Seidensticker."

"A hymnal?"

She reached to take it back, but he stood up and took it to the window. "A very old handwritten German hymnal, I should say."

"Mr. Seidensticker..."

"I am not a clergyman, Madam."

"It is the work of Johannes Kelpius."

"Kelpius?"

"Yes, do you know anything about him?"

He returned to the desk, placing the book just out of her reach. Then he crouched down at the bookshelf that lined the wall opposite the window. He stood up holding a manuscript bound together in twine. She watched as he took his time, wading through the contents.

"'John Kelpius, the hermit, was a German of Siebenbürgen, of an eminent, possibly noble family and a student of Dr. John Fabricius of Helmstadt University. He came to this country with about forty companions, being generally men of education and learning, to devote themselves for piety's sake to a solitary or single life; and receiving the appellation of the Society of the Woman in the Wilderness. They first arrived among the Germans where they shone awhile as a peculiar light. Having fallen upon an interpretation of Scripture that drove them from the Universities of Germany, they came seeking some immediate and strange revelations they believed would prefigure the Great Deliverance. Kelpius was much visited by religious persons and taught the children gratis. He professed love and charity for all, but desired to live without a name or sect. His holiness was doubtless very remarkable.'" He tilted the folder so Lydia could see the handwritten title. "'Written for the sake of posterity, Christian Lehman, July 21, 1766,'" he read.

"Is that all?" she asked.

"What more do you want?"

"I'm not certain."

He leaned forward. "Are you familiar with *Paul Ardenheim?*"

"Paul who?"

"Paul Ardenheim, The Monk of the Wissahickon," he said. "About twenty years ago, George Lippard wrote a novel based on the legends of the life of Kelpius. Have you read it?"

"I do not read popular literature, Mr. Seidensticker. Particularly not popular literature of the sensational sort."

He sat back down at the desk. "You missed a thrilling read, Mrs. Kriebel. It's the story of a man torn between his vow of celibacy and his lust for a beautiful young woman in whose blood lies the missing ingredient for the formula of immortality. Full of wizards beneath the light of the moon, secret Rosicrucian societies plotting gruesome murders, that sort of thing. Wonderful reading on a stormy night. You might still find it in one of those used book stores downtown on Sansom Street."

Lydia patted her forehead again. "Yes, I'm quite sure. Do you know anything more factual, Mr. Seidensticker?"

"That all depends on what sort of facts we are talking about."

"I don't know, Mr. Seidensticker. I suppose I was talking about the sort of facts you might have here. Was Johannes Kelpius married? Does he have any descendents? Where is he buried?"

"I would be delighted to look through the official records, Mrs. Kriebel," he said, although his tone betrayed his preference for fiction. "If you wouldn't mind having a seat in the outer office, I will return in a short while. May I keep the hymnal?"

She stood up and took it from his hand. "I should think not, sir."

She regretted wearing her church shoes. It made no sense to have assumed that the kind of reception she would receive would be dependent upon her footwear. Her ankles felt swollen and her feet hurt. She played with the idea of taking off her shoes. She thought about tearing off a piece of her skirt to make a replacement for her damp handkerchief. She imagined scolding old Mr. Seidensticker the way she did her erring students. She smiled.

Making sure she was still alone, she opened her bag and once more took out the old book.

Wenn werd isch doch ein anshuauen und Empfinden?
Wenn werd ich in ihm gantz Zerflieseen und Vershwinden?
Wenn fält emin füncklein gar in sein Licht-feur ein?
Wenn wird mein Geist mit ihm nur eine flame sein?
When shall I behold this One and clearly then perceive Him?
When shall I be lost in Him and incapable to leave Him?
When shall fall my spark into the fire of His Flame?
When in spirit with Him shall we be one in the same?

"I'm afraid that our records contain only two official references to Johannes Kelpius." Mr. Seidensticker pushed open the door to his outer office with his shoulder. "I found these in the papers of Francis Daniel Pastorius. You are familiar with the name."

"Certainly."

He handed her an armful of papers, keeping the first sheet. "'Whereas,'" he read, "'upon the recommendation of Mr. Daniel Falcker, the Frankfort Company has made me their Agent, together with the said Mr. Falckner, my circumstances do not permit me to entangle myself in like affairs. I do hereby deliver all the authority which is given unto me in the Letter of Attorney to the same, to wit, Mr. Daniel Falckner, to act in the interests of the said Frankfort Company, as he would alone in the case of my natural or civil death. As witnessed by Johann Gotfried Seelig and Johann Hendrick Sprogel. Signed, Johannes Kelpius, 1700.'"

She disliked feeling unequal to the civil servant. "Mr. Seidensticker, I'm afraid I do not understand the significance of what you have just read."

"What it signifies," he said, "is that whether your hymnist was a scholar or a wizard, he was wise enough not to engage in a fight with Francis Pastorius. I recalled that down in the basement we keep some historical material—material that has been donated to us through the years. I discovered among the papers of that time something concerning the Daniel Falckner who is mentioned. I can't vouch for its authenticity or its source." He tapped his finger on the pile of papers he handed over to her. "But if you have a few minutes, you might wish to look through it. I believe you might find something that will shed light on that legal notice."

It appeared to be a personal letter, the beginning of which was missing. She read:

... leaving you in Erfurth, I traveled to visit Francke who, as you well know, secured himself a position as Professor of Oriental Languages at the University of Halle after his expulsion. He welcomed me with great cordiality, but confirmed what you and others had already told me, to wit, that the situation of the Pietists in Germany was no better than it had been when we left in 1693. In fact, the persecution had only increased, and I found myself grateful for the pettiness of the difficulties I had formerly complained of in Pennsylvania.

Francke was very much involved at that time in the establishment of the Halle Orphanage, which is one of those grand projects that has a humble origin. You know how Francke has always fancied himself in the tradition of the spiritual masters. Soon after he had settled in at the University, he began the practice of handing out weekly charity from his door. There were so many pitiful cases, especially children, that he was finally moved to take one or two of the most destitute into his own home. He explained to me one evening, with eyes wet from emotion, how the more children he took in, the more funds seemed to manifest themselves spontaneously for their care. It seems that when the old alchemist Burgstaller had mixed his final vial here on earth, he bequeathed to Francke his mysterious apothecary, and the secret recipes for their concoction. You would find it difficult to guess how much income Francke realized from all that. I asked him several times to repeat himself, to make certain that I hadn't heard him incorrectly. Whether my old friend was exaggerating or not, he was able to found a permanent institution—one which continues to flourish and rescue so young souls who otherwise would find themselves destined to ruin and waste.

After becoming convinced that I had thoroughly worn out my welcome at the home of Francke and his new wife, I rejoined the others and we made our way back to Rotterdam. As you might guess, the city brought back unhappy memories. When I was invited to dinner at the home of the widow Mariecke Jansen, the very house in which the old Magister breathed his last, I was prompted to decline—a decision that might have changed the course, not only of our community, but of the political future of Germantown as well.

In the event, I accepted the invitation. As I had been throughout my entire visit to Europe (and by you, most prominently!), I was well received. Among the guests was a singular old gentleman by the name of Benjamin Furly. I knew him well, but by name only, as he figured prominently in the financial affairs of the Frankfort Company. He was very interested in both the spiritual and material progress of Pennsylvania, and asked me questions so earnestly that I think the other guests felt eclipsed by our conversation.

When I told him of the loathsome end to which our original gift of twenty-four hundred acres had come, he was extremely upset. He asked if Francis Pastorius (of whom I spoke with a great deal of energy when I was in Erfurth) had been involved in the incident. I told him that he had not, but that I was certain Pastorius would not have declined the chance to applaud Whitpain for his action, and likely give him a kindly slap on the back.

I did not volunteer any evidence to discredit Pastorius, but I did answer all Furly's questions in an honest and unrestrained way. I told him of the many reports to which I had been privy—reports that Pastorius had sold land belonging to the Frankfort Company but had provided no deeds of sale. I told him of the sharp increase in the value of real property in Germantown, the haphazard collection of rents, and the apparent lack of record keeping. I told him of the vindictive insults that had been directed toward my old spiritual comrade, Henrich Köster, and how poor Köster had been driven back to Germany. I also told him of the grand style of life that the agent of the Frankfort Company—that supposed simple and pious Quaker—had taken on in his role of Monarch of Germantown.

Needless to say, Furly became more and more upset the more he heard, wringing his hands until I feared for the well-being of his fingers. When he told me that the Frankfort Company had thus far realized nothing—absolutely nothing—on its investments, I assured him that I was sympathetic. After all, I said, the Great Pennsylvania Experiment was just as much a material project as it was spiritual.

Even after all this, I was stunned when Furly suggested that I be named agent in place of Pastorius. I told him that, as honored as I was, there was great danger in being put in such a position. I did not want to succumb to the temptations of power as unnamed others had done. He then asked if there was anyone else with whom I might share the responsibilities, to be required to act jointly, and thus prevent one or the other from becoming corrupted by the opportunities of authority.

I could not think of a person who was further from the temptations of corruption than my dear comrade, Kelpius.

So it was that when Johann Sprogel, my brother Justus, the others, and I arrived back in Pennsylvania (in August of 1700), I could hardly wait to relay our good fortune to Kelpius. We found him in the *Saal* teaching children, as was his major occupation of the time. We embraced (not in the manner you and I have done!) and he joyfully welcomed us all. I introduced him to Sprogel and the others. It is odd, but now that I think back, I remember him being rather distant to Sprogel. At the time, I supposed that as Sprogel's brother Ludovic had left our community to join with Köster, Kelpius was carrying a resentment. Now that I know better, I have an increased appreciation for the Magister's unusual perceptions.

When I confided the news to Kelpius, he steadfastly refused to cooperate. I was in disbelief. "Magister," I pleaded, "think what this would mean. Under our financial guidance and with the growing population of Germantown, we would soon be in a position to triumph in a way we scarce believed possible. We would have the funds to establish a real school (perhaps this was not so wisely said), or a hospital, or perhaps an orphanage as Francke has done. We could do all of this in accordance with our principles, with the direction of your insight. This could mean the fulfillment of the New Jerusalem of which we have dreamed for so long."

"Brother Daniel," he told me, "the New Jerusalem will not be established in this way. We must persist in our spiritual journey until we have fully arrived. Only then will we be fitting stewards of the Millennium. I realize that this involvement with civil affairs may appear to be an opportunity, but in truth it is only a seduction. I beg you to look away from it, and return your attention to things that truly matter."

I said, "Kelpius, your name is already on the papers. Whether you desire it or not, this honor has been given to you."

"Then I will make whatever arrangements are necessary to decline the honor."

I was convinced that my old friend was spending too much time alone in his cell contemplating the Eternal.

On my first opportunity, I went to see Pastorius. His wife ushered me into the parlor of their elegant little home. "Ah, Friend Falckner," he said. He was in the process of polishing his boots when I arrived. "I see you have returned to Germantown." He didn't even pause from his ferocious brushing. "Did you bring back anything other than the pleasure of your presence?"

"I bring news of interest to you, Pastorius. Read this!" My eye catching the idle stream of smoke coming from his tobacco pipe, I changed my mind. "No," I said, "I think it would be best if I read it to you." It was very lengthy and full of *'hath resolveds'* and *'cum potestates.'* When I reached *'that we do confer full power and special attorney on Misters Daniel Falckner and Johannes Kelpius as our two Plenipotentiaries,'* he dropped both his jaw and his boot brush.

It took him a fair good minute of sputtering until he was able to speak. "Give me that document," he demanded.

"We shall have less of 'give me' and more of 'in your graciousness, permit me, Friend Falckner,'" I said. "However, I shall not give it to you, but will allow you only to look upon it, especially the notarization and the signature of one Benjamin Furly, dated 24 January of this year."

"Where is Kelpius, if he is supposed to be your joint Plenipotentiary?" I explained the Magister's reluctance to participate. "Then the document is worthless," he said.

I calmly instructed him of the true facts, which were, namely, that the paper explicitly stated (and I quoted) *"that in the death of one or the other, he who remains shall have in the best form the Administration of all our goods and property"* and so on. When he protested that Kelpius was not dead, I relayed to him the Magister's own words, which were that he, Kelpius, was preparing to have himself declared *civitus mortuus,* that is, considered dead as far as the law is concerned. Furthermore, I told him, I needed a full accounting of all the Frankfort Company's properties, holdings, rents, allowances, debts, and obligations. For good measure I added, "And I expect this accounting immediately, any sooner putting an unfair burden upon you."

When he declined to shake my hand in a gentlemanly manner, I took my leave. "Be prepared for a battle, Falckner," he said, and I thanked him for caring so much for my welfare as to provide me with a warning. I was not concerned in the least, having had a great deal of experience in combat. After all, I had survived four months at sea with Henrich Bernard Köster.

So therefore I began in earnest to straighten out the tangled affairs of the Frankfort Company. When I say that the condition of the records, the rectification of accounts, and the number of persons involved was far more mystifying than any of Köster's spiritual discourses, you may not be able to appreciate the comparison. But try I did, and that same fall in the local Germantown elections, I was duly elected to the high administrative position entitled bailiff, my dear brother Justus to burgess, and my old friend Geissler as crier of the court. I had successfully won against Pastorius in each and every attempt he had made to discredit me and maintain control of his fiefdom. I felt certain of the final victory, which would prove to Kelpius that the Glorious Millennium would manifest itself in the world as well as in the soul.

My dearest, the fact that I did not write to you was not because you were ever distant from my mind. Dealing with complexities that became more complex the more I attempted to simplify them, left me scarce time for personal matters. My involvement with the activities of our spiritual community lessened, although my inner commitment never waned.

My only help in dealing with the affairs of the Frankfort Company came from one Johann Hendrick Sprogel, who, as I have already mentioned, had eagerly followed me back to Pennsylvania—his brother Ludovic having been one of our original circle. Now, while we were in Germany, this Sprogel had impressed upon me his lack of interest in material matters. His soul was fixed upon the Eternal, and to that end he wished to devote his life to the *philadelphian* ideal of service toward his fellow man.

Looking back, I had no reason not to take him at his word. There was no initiation as there had been with Magister Zimmerman, no required period as a novitiate, no extraordinary perceptions distinguishing the false from the sincere. Matters were based solely on the persuasiveness of your beloved Daniel Falckner, enticing the willing and able into a new life in North America.

Now picture, if you will, your friend Daniel in the Germantown Hall, sorting receipt papers on a dreary and cold

Christmas Eve of 1703. Since you obviously haven't seen the Hall, I will describe it as not so much a hall as a hut, the former residence of old Isaac van Bebber, the Dutchman who welcomed us into his home on the day we arrived in Germantown. At that time it was serving nearly as many different functions as I did (accountant, bailiff, scholar, farmer, astrologer, physician, alchemist, seeker-of-truth, &tc.). The Hall that afternoon being empty, there was no fire lit, and no other sounds to disguise the noise of the windows rattling in the wind. I had just spilt ink across some important correspondence and allowed an unfortunate curse to escape my lips. So when I heard a voice, my first instinct was to think that it was the reprimand of the Angel of Retribution.

"*Stehen Sie auf*, Falckner!"

"*Fröhliche Weihnachten*, Constable Luken," I said, after recovering. "Isn't it time for you to be at home lighting your *Adventlichter*?"

Constable Luken was not smiling. He asked, "You are one Daniel Falckner, born November 25, 1666, Langen-Reinsdorf, Saxony, in Germany?"

I quoted him *Luke*, twenty-two, verse seventy. "'Thou sayest that I am.'"

"Come with me, Falckner," he said. "You are under arrest."

I spent the following days in the new Germantown jail, the very one I had been instrumental in raising money to complete. I suffered not only from ignominy and extreme confusion, but also from severe indigestion caused by the mealy biscuits I was given for sustenance. Kelpius, Seelig, Maria Warmer, and my brother (bless them all) came to visit, bringing edible food, affection, and most of all, hope. As you can imagine, I was distraught. I had narrowly escaped being imprisoned several times back in Erfurth (as you well know), but little did I expect to find myself on the wrong side of the law in the utopian province of Pennsylvania.

Christmas Day that year being a Wednesday, it was not until the following Monday that my friend Johann Hendrick Sprogel came to see me. Now, when I use the word "friend," I use it in a sarcastic manner, one that indicates not just irony, but bitterness.

"*Grüß Gott*, Brother Daniel," he said. *"Guten Tag."* As I have just used the word "friend," so had Sprogel used the word *"guten,"* for it was not a good day that he was wishing me. "I would like you to meet Councilor David Lloyd, my attorney."

Now, perhaps I have been remiss in describing this Sprogel. One of the strictest disciplines put upon us, not just by Kelpius but in the long tradition of Seekers of Truth, is that of cleanliness—it being incumbent upon us to perform ablutions several times a day. Apparently Sprogel did not follow this path. His appearance suggested that he bathed only at the turn of each century, and he had evidently missed the change from the seventeenth to the eighteenth. An odor surrounded this man, one that always reminded me of the streets of London, especially on its warmer days. His attorney, Lloyd, appeared to be well groomed but displayed the worst of English characteristics—an imperturbable belief in his own superiority.

Sprogel said, "Lloyd has in his possession some papers that have recently come to light, Daniel. Papers that are extremely discrediting to you." I asked him *was zum Teufel* he was talking about. Lloyd then spoke to me in English, so slowly that I assumed he took me for an idiot, which I most definitely was.

"I have a document from one Henrich Bernard Köster," he said, "stating that you once confessed to brazen immoral conduct while a student of theology at the University of Erfurth."

"That isn't even Köster's signature," I told them. I was laughing at the time.

"I am afraid that Mister Köster is no longer in Pennsylvania to validate your claim. I would remind you, Mister Falckner, at the risk of dampening your jocularity, that Governor Evans has recently issued a proclamation against immorality."

"Let the governor proclaim what he will. Whatever may or may not have occurred in Germany is no crime here."

"Perhaps, Mister Falckner, but I do not think that you will laugh at this. I have here a letter from a Mariecke Jansen, residing in the Haaringvliet, Rotterdam, Holland. It attests that you coerced one Benjamin Furly by force into signing a document against his will."

By this time they had my full attention. I had seen Frau Jansen's signature on the old Magister's death certificate, but I didn't need to compare the handwriting to know that I was a victim of the most unconscionable evil and deceit. "This is a total and absolute forgery, and what is worse, both of you know it."

"We know nothing of the kind, Mister Falckner. What we do know is that we are in possession of a third document, one that is unfortunately the most damaging. I have here a bill of sale from one Captain Alexander Meredith, formerly of His Majesty's Navy, now a notorious pirate. This document states that on June ninth, the year of our Lord seventeen-hundred and one, he received from one Daniel Falckner of Pennsylvania, fifty pounds of illegal spirits, one hundred pounds of sugar, and other commodities equivalent to a value of seventeen pounds sterling. You realize, Mister Falckner, that Parliament in London has been taking Governor Penn to task on account of illegal trade here in America. It has been pressuring him to enforce the death penalty upon any persons involved in pirating, especially persons of doubtful character."

My mind was flooded with the memory of Kelpius' warning. I resolved right then that should I somehow escape that situation with my life and freedom, I would devote the remainder of my life to Eternal matters and leave Temporal ones to the likes of Sprogel. "Why are you doing this to me?" I asked.

"Mister Sprogel is only interested in justice being done, Mister Falckner." I suggested, if that were the case, Sprogel should permit me to grasp him firmly around the neck. "However, if you were to propose an exchange to Mister Sprogel, I'm certain that he would agree to drop the charges against you." I asked him what sort of exchange. "I believe that I could induce Mister Sprogel to hand over these papers to you, in exchange for—as an example—the properties and affairs of the Frankfort Company."

You must believe me, Anna Maria, when I tell you that if I had been able to foresee the ways Sprogel would use his power, I would have refused to participate in his evil scheme, regardless of the personal consequences. Many of the honest, hardworking people of Germantown have since been forced to repurchase their own land from Sprogel, land for which they had spent years paying.

Furly and the members of the Frankfort Company were very sympathetic when I wrote them of what had happened, but since they never realized any returns for all their years of investment, they were unable to offer me any reimbursement for the years and years I spent working on their behalf. They, as you can imagine, were as distraught as I over Sprogel's heinous machinations.

I had hoped to write to you as a former pilgrim guiding the institution of a New Jerusalem. As it is, I am but a former criminal, who is now destitute and repentant. I am determined to leave Pennsylvania, but I have no desire to return to Europe. A very generous friend (one who wishes to remain anonymous) has offered me a gift in the form of the enclosed money. It should be sufficient for you to come join me, not only in America, but also in marriage. Thinking of you all these years has put me in mind to renounce my vow of celibacy, as Francke has done, as well as Warmer, and Biederman…

Lydia stood up and knocked on the door of Deeds and Records. "Mr. Seidensticker?" After a few moments and the sound of a chair sliding, the spectacled face reappeared at the door. "I want to thank you for locating these papers and allowing me to read through them," she said.

"You are quite welcome, Mrs. Kriebel. Did you find anything in them that was helpful to you?"

Lydia didn't answer, only smiled and asked, "Mr. Seidensticker, earlier you told me that there were two references to Johannes Kelpius in the official records. You showed me only one. What is the other?"

"Did you not find it? There, on that sheet underneath the Falckner document. Yes, that is the one. It is just a mention in a petition by one Ludovic Sprogel to the Pennsylvania Provincial Council of March, 1709. Look near the bottom of the page."

She ran her finger down the page, not having any idea what she was searching for. The sensation she experienced when she found it felt like a chill, but the room was far too warm. There were only four words, set apart by a pair of commas in an otherwise unremarkable paragraph. She was stung by their brevity. *"Johannes Kelpius, now deceased."*

Chapter Twenty One

Saturday, December 24, 1705
Germantown, Pennsylvania

He had not wanted it to be this way. Every breath he took felt as if a knife were stabbing his chest. He would have preferred to stop breathing altogether than to force himself to walk any further. Seelig had him by one arm, Doctor Witt by the other. Somewhere behind them in the darkness was Geissler, carrying *al Warqa'iyah,* and everything else that he had been able to take away from the Magister's cell. It was their way of letting him know that he would be away for a long time.

"Not much further now, my brother," Seelig said. Johannes knew that it hadn't been an easy journey for him either. Desperate in his concern, Seelig had covered him with his own cloak. The difference in their heights had meant that Seelig had to walk hunched over all the way from the Tabernacle.

He had not wanted it to be this way.

"I can see lights ahead. It is Christmas Eve, heh, Kelpius? Everyone has candles in the windows." It was easier for him to keep his eyes closed, to trust Seelig and the doctor. Thinking about where he was only brought him back to his physical body, back to the dizziness, back to the pain.

Where virgin woods had once stood along the way to Germantown, dark expanses of fields offered no protection against the wind. The Great Road was covered with ice. They slid on the steps of Warmer's house. Seelig pounded the door. *"Mein Gott!"* The gasp in Maria's exclamation assured him that Doctor Witt's optimistic assessment had been just a kind deceit.

They pulled him inside. "He needs to lie down," Johannes heard the doctor tell her. "Somewhere warm."

"Can you carry him upstairs? Put him in young Christian's bed."

Johannes tried to open his eyes, but the brightness only made them water. When he tried to speak, phlegm was choking his throat. "It is all right. I have walked all the way. I can walk up the stairs."

"Mein Gott!" Maria repeated. "Seelig, how could you allow him to become so sick?"

"Frau Warmer, I'm sure Brother Kelpius would appreciate some hot tea and a good supply of soft rags on which to blow his nose."

"*Mutter*, what is the matter?"

"Geissler has brought his things," Seelig said. "Doctor Witt thinks he will need to be taken care of for some time."

"*Mutter,* what *is* the matter?"

"Where is Christian? Children, go fetch your father. Hurry, now!"

The stairwell was too narrow for anyone to hold him, so he forced himself to climb alone. Little Christiana was at the top of the stairs with a candle. She pushed open the door of the nursery. It was dark, but he could see young Christian's bed in the center of the far wall. The bed had high wooden sides, protection to keep a restless child from falling out in the night. He dropped to a sitting position. Before he knew it, Christiana was pulling off his boots—his cold, wet, dirty boots. "Bring a chamber pot," Doctor Witt called from downstairs. "He will need it after he drinks the tea."

He had not wanted it to be this way.

He was still shivering, but he did not want to lie down on the clean bed in his wet cloak—Seelig's wet cloak. His fingers trembled as he untied the strap. He threw it on the floor, removed his soaked cap, and lay his body on the straw mattress.

Maria brought in a lamp and hung it on the wall. The light transformed the dark space back into a nursery—another child's bed for Christiana against the wall, a crib for George, and a miniature wardrobe strewn with children's clothes.

Geissler appeared at the foot of the bed. His cheeks were flushed from the cold, and his hair was wet and matted. In his arms, he held Johannes' diary, his hymnal, his books and papers, and—wet from the icy rain—the wooden box with the six-pointed star. "Seelig thought that you might wish to have your compositions with you, Magister."

"Thank you, Daniel. I will work on them again when I am feeling better."

"What would you have me do with them?"

"It does not matter," he said.

The doctor settled uneasily on the wooden edge of the bed. He held a steaming cup. "You must keep warm, Herr Kelpius. Do as Frau Warmer instructs. As you know, my house is just on the other side of Pastorius'. I will come by first thing in the morning with some more medicine and help you celebrate Christmas Day. Until then, take your decoction. It will purge you of ill humours and help you sleep."

Christian Warmer rushed into the room and threw himself down at the side of the bed. *"'Abends und morgens und mittags klage und stöhne ich.'"* His voice broke. *"'Und er hat meine Stimme gehört.'" Evening, and morning, and at noon, will I pray, and cry aloud: and He shall hear my voice.*

Johannes touched his friend's hands, which were clutched in prayer. He tried to smile. It was awkward enough for him, and he could not bear to feel as if he were the center of a shrine. "I will be fine. Truly, I will."

"Of course," Witt said. "It is merely a bad cold. Some warmth and plenty of good food, and, of course my good *mittel.*" The doctor put his hand behind Johannes' head and brought it toward the cup. The liquid burned.

"I'm sure your herbs must be very powerful, Doctor," Johannes said, "or else they would not be so foul-tasting." Nervous laughter trailed around the room.

Maria was bent over a chest. "I received a letter from Hester Palmer the other day, Magister. She told me to send her most ardent affections, and said that she is desirous of receiving a line or two from you. If you wish to write to her while you are here, I will make sure that your letter is mailed."

"I promise to attend to it when I am feeling better." There was something in his words, even as he heard himself say them, that was disturbing.

Maria stood again, holding a bundle in her arms. She carried it to the bed. "Here is something to keep you warm," she said. "I am sorry that it is not as beautiful as *der Steppdecke* your mother made for you. Do you still have it?"

He looked up at the forced pleasantry on her face, no less sincere than his own. He would have liked to explain why he had given it away to the Indians. The only thing he felt able to say was, "No, I'm afraid I no longer do."

"I am so sorry, Magister. This one belonged to Frau Dimmers. It will do nearly as well." She lay the heavy cover over him.

Doctor Witt unhooked the lamp from the wall. "Now," he said to the rest, "we must leave the Magister to sleep in peace."

He didn't want them to leave. "Seelig," he called. "You will take care of everything for me? You will heed my instructions regarding the disposition of our astronomical records?"

The doctor walked to the door and shadows fell across the room. Seelig knelt beside him. "What I will do most of all is pray for your health, my friend."

"I have not spent Christmas with a family in a long time," Johannes said to him. "Let us—you and I—consider this only a visit with Warmer."

Seelig's lips quivered, and Johannes was afraid he would fall into tears. "Do not leave," Johannes told him. Comforting Seelig would require more effort than he could expend. "Until you take back your cloak. I will not need it any more."

Seelig picked up the wet garment from the floor. He took Johannes's hand and spoke something under his breath, something that Johannes was grateful not to hear. "I will return tomorrow, Magister," Seelig whispered.

"'Neque mors, neque vita,'" Johannes said, *"'neque angeli, neque instantia, neque futura, neque fortitudines, neque altitudo, neque profundum, alia poterit nos separare a caritate Dei.'"*

Neither death, nor life, nor angels, nor powers, nor things present, nor things to come, nor height, nor depth, shall be able to separate us from the love of God.

Seelig closed the door.

Lying prone in the terrible darkness, he began to cough. Each time he did, the pain he had felt breathing the night air was increased tenfold. He grabbed the sides of the bed and brought himself to a sitting position. He didn't think he would be able to sleep.

He fished cautiously with his hand along the floor until he found the teacup. His hands welcomed the warmth of the cup, but they shook as he held it to his lips. After a few more sips of Witt's decoction his nose began to run. If Maria had brought him rags as she had been told, she hadn't left them anywhere nearby. He tried unsuccessfully to sniff back, knowing he couldn't live with himself if he soiled young Christian's bed sheets. He pulled off his robe—his Magister's robe—and blew his nose into the sleeve. What did it matter? It was only a piece of cloth.

A chill ran through him. After taking another long draught of tea, he pulled the quilt up over him to his shoulders. For so long he had striven to exorcise himself, to free his self from the illusion of personhood, and this is what it had come to—utter helpless dependency. It was the furthest thing from freedom he could imagine.

Fiat voluntas tua.

With his nostrils clear for the moment, he could smell Frau Dimmers' old quilt. It brought with it a flood of memories of his own quilt, and then of his mother. For some reason he was able to recall her more vividly than ever before. What was it he had said to Geissler? It might have been the emotion in Geissler's eyes—the same defiance of the unacceptable he had felt at his mother's bedside—that had brought back those same ghostly words.

Her long black hair had lain matted and wet, making even more fearful the crimson blotches that shone through her skin like rosy crosses. Her lips were dry and crusted with sores. He was terrified to wake her, even though there was something he urgently wanted her to see. He turned to God, imploring Him in childish desperation to open his mother's eyes before Pfarrer Kelp would grab him away. "Hans," she whispered. He wanted to recoil from the awful stench of her hand, but at the same time cling to it forever. He held up to her face the great backing cloth of the quilt, only half-finished in the colorful patterns of the Romany wheel of life. Her finest needle was stuck into it, holding fast a pile of tiny bright pieces of cloth. She took her hand from his head and ran a finger across the stitches. "I will work on it again," she told him, "when I am feeling better." It was the last thing she said to him.

For a few minutes he lay there in the darkness of the Warmer's nursery, marveling at the memory and its mystery. Then, coming at him with a ferocity that only medicine could evoke, he felt the truth of Witt's prediction. He needed the chamber pot.

His head swam when he stood, and for a moment he thought he might faint. But his nostrils were still clear enough to take a long breath and in a moment he was able to make it to the door. A few inches open was enough to let in the sounds of the family downstairs and enough light to find what he took to be the children's chamber pot underneath the window. It would have to do.

While he sat there allowing Doctor Witt's purgative to perform its work on his physical body, he felt precariously close to death—as if the foundations of his entire being were disintegrating. Finally, after what seemed an eternity, the pain in his stomach subsided. Beside the pot were the rags he had been looking for. He cleaned himself, covered the pot, and staggered back to young Christian's bed.

It took several minutes until the room stopped spinning. The purging had actually made him feel better, even if weaker. His head was still clear and the coughing subsided. The door was open. He felt partly incapable of closing it, and partly disinclined. The sounds that streamed into the room were reassuring. He didn't know at what point it entered his consciousness, but in the swirl of his fevered thoughts, he became aware that there was a presence just outside the door. *"Wer da?"* he asked. *Who is there?*

"Christiana, Herr Kelpius."

"What is it that you want, Christiana?"

"*Mein Püppchen*, Herr Kelpius."

"Pardon?"

"My doll, Herr Kelpius."

"Please come in, Christiana. After all, I am only a guest in your room." The little girl stepped hesitantly into the room, preceded by a circle of candlelight. "Put your light on the stand. It will help you see."

She did so, on tiptoes. "George asked me if you were *Weihnachtsmann,* Father Christmas."

He suppressed a chuckle that he was afraid would stab him in the chest. "I hope that you did not tease him and tell him that I was."

"No," she said. "I told him that you were like one of the wise men who came to Bethlehem to find baby Jesus. That is what *Mutter* said."

"Your mother is too kind, *Liebchen.* I am only like the wise men in that I, too, look for Jesus." He lifted himself up to a sitting position again. "If you would wish to hear it, I will tell you a story about those wise men."

"Is it a story from Scriptures?"

"No, *Liebchen.* This is a story that fell out of Scriptures. It comes from the land of the wise men. It is the story the wise men told after they returned home from bringing their gifts to Jesus."

Christiana, clasping her doll to her chest, climbed onto her own bed, against the cold stone wall. Her eyes, like her mother's, had a peculiar green light. "Was their home in Germany?" she asked.

"No, *Liebchen.* Their home was in Persia. It is far away from Germany, and even farther away from Pennsylvania. Foolish people say that because the Persian people worship fire, they are heathens."

"Like the Indians?"

"Those people do not understand why the Persians worship fire. Would you like to hear the reason?"

"Yes, Herr Kelpius."

"Well, as you know, the wise men, knowing that Jesus had been born in Bethlehem, traveled there to bring Him gifts."

"Gold, frankincense, and myrrh!"

"Yes, *Liebchen.* Gold, that they might know if he were an earthly king, frankincense that they might know if he were God, and myrrh that they might know if he were a mortal man. Now, these wise men were of three ages. The first was an old man."

"Like Herr Pastorius?"

He stifled another laugh. "Yes, *Liebchen.* And the second was a man of middle age."

"Like you, Herr Kelpius?"

"Yes, like me. And the third was young."

"Like me?"

"Well, let us say perhaps as young as your Uncle Christoph. When the youngest went in to offer his gift, Jesus appeared to him as a young man. When the next went in, Jesus appeared to him a man of middle age, and so it was with the oldest."

Her brow furrowed. "Why was that, Herr Kelpius?"

"Well, *Liebchen,* it was because most men wish to see in Jesus only a reflection of themselves. That is why there is so much discord among the Lutherans and Quakers and Anglicans and Catholics and so on."

"Did the wise men fight among themselves, too?"

"They might have, Christiana, but you must remember that they were wise. They decided to all go to Jesus together."

"What did they see?"

"When they put aside their own idols of Jesus, they were able to see the truth of Jesus. And, as a reward for solving the mystery, Jesus gave them a gift. It was a small box, sealed and locked closed."

"Like that box?" She pointed to *al Warqa'iyah,* lying on top of the pile of his papers beside his bed.

"Like that box," he said. "Yes, it was. It was exactly like that box."

"What was inside?"

"That is just what they wondered. Jesus had not told them what was inside. They wondered and wondered, thinking that it must be something marvelous indeed to come from someone as special as Jesus."

"I would have opened it and seen what it was!"

"Well, for several days they carried the box with them along their travels back to Persia. Finally, they could stand to wonder no more. They pried the gold seal from the box and opened it."

Her eyes were wide. "What was inside?"

"It was a stone!"

"A stone?"

"Yes, *Liebchen.* It was a stone. The wise men were very disappointed. They did not understand that the gift was meant to signify that their faith should remain as firm and unchanging as a stone. It was not what they had wanted, but it was what they needed, and that made it the greatest gift of all."

"I would not have liked a stone."

"Well, you can understand what the wise men did. They were very angry, thinking that Jesus had insulted them. They cast the stone into a well. But when they did, a very strange thing happened. All of a sudden, fire burst forth from the well, for the stone had the power to change water into fire."

"It was a magical stone!" she said.

"The wise men then repented bitterly for their foolishness and lack of faith. They took some of the fire home with them and placed it in one of their churches, careful to never let it go out. They wanted the fire to always be a reminder of the gift of Jesus. That is why even today, if you go to Persia, you will see fire burning in the churches. It is the light of very same fire."

"That is a wonderful story, Herr Magister." Maria and Christian stood in the doorway. "But we will have time tomorrow for more stories. Christiana, let us bother Herr Kelpius no longer tonight. Bring your pillow and blanket. You may sleep with us tonight."

Christiana slid off her bed and gathered her things. "Herr Kelpius," she whispered to him, "when you go to see Jesus, I hope he appears healthy and not as a man with consumption."

He squeezed her hand and turned his face away.

It began to sleet again and there was a steady tapping sound against the roof. He ran his fingers along the wooden edge of the bed, thinking how much like a coffin it felt.

Doctor Witt's decoction was beginning to cloud his thoughts.

"Schlaft ein!" He could hear Christian's voice from the other room, telling his children to go to sleep. It was the same tone and

nearly the same voice that his father had used when Johannes sat too long beside the door of the study. *"Schlaft ein!"* It was a stern order, one that seemed insensitive to a child's fear of the dark oblivion of sleep. Yet, in Christian's voice, as there had been in his own father's, there was a counter-harmony of caring and even of love.

Then he began to laugh—quietly to himself, even though the rhythm of suppressed laughter hurt him. He thought that he must ask Doctor Witt what magic had been in the decoction, to free such memories from the locked box of his heart. He laughed, in such pleasurable pain that his eyes watered and the tears trickled down his cheeks.

He finally remembered. Perhaps it had been his own desire to maintain the reassuring illusion that his father was uncaring and invulnerable that had veiled the vision from his memory. Perhaps he had refused to accept it even as a child, preferring the anger of resentment to the heartbreak of pity. But there was the great Pfarrer Kelp, turning his chair from the wall. *"Schlaf ein!"* he had said. His eyes were red that night, but not from wine. Pfarrer Kelp had not been studying the Scriptures. He had been sewing, finishing for his son the present that his wife had not been able.

Johannes wiped his tears from his face with his fingers. A moment later he found himself in the shady graveyard beside the little church in Denndorf. The sunshine fell in lazy patterns across the emerald grass, across the white flowers that lay like clumps of sugar on cake. It fell across the headstones that shattered the soporific splendor with their grim reminder of annihilation. Everything was the same as before. He sat in the soft warmth, waiting beside the cold and rigid stone at his mother's grave, waiting for his father—with the same endless certainty that all would be made right when his father returned.

He was being taken over by the tea.

No—his father was dead, he realized once again. Yet this time someone else was in his dream. He looked up into the fluttering arms of the trees that arched over the graveyard. In the spaces between the hypnotic dance of the leaves, he had a vision of something bright that emerged like a bird from the blue emptiness of the sky. The brilliance of its whiteness blinded him, and it was not in his eyes, but in his heart that he was able to see her. "Why seek ye the living among the dead?" spoke the angel. Her arms—so gentle and delicate and yet so sure, pointed to an empty grave. Georg Kelp was there beside him, alive and redeemed, his own strong arms open wide.

As Johannes was beginning to lose consciousness again, he was once more aware that someone had come into the room. He could sense a light through his eyelids. He was too tired to be polite, or even to pay attention. He told himself that it must be the angel of his dream, there to guard him as he slept.

Chapter Twenty Two

Saturday, June 23, 1888
West Philadelphia

It was not even noon and it already had been a long day. Lydia had been taken at dawn to the railroad depot in Norristown by her grandson. From there she had ridden the train all the way to 30th Street Station. Then she had taken the noisy Woodland Avenue cable car to 39th and Pine. She still had another six blocks to go, and great mountains of clouds were congregating above the city. But she could not stand to wait, pay, and ride again on another mechanical contrivance. She decided to walk the rest of the way to the Sachse house. A student from the University of Pennsylvania helped her find the house number.

"Mrs. Kriebel!" The woman who answered the door threw her arms around her. "*He* has been looking forward to meeting you." The way she spoke the word *"he,"* as if her husband were a divine being, was a notion of youth that Lydia deplored. Seeing the gray in the bun in her hair, Lydia thought that Mrs. Sachse seemed too old for that kind of nonsense. "I am Emma Sachse," the woman said brightly. "Please come in before you are rained on!"

It was dark inside the foyer and almost impossible for her to see. The parlor, though cool for its partially drawn curtains, was not much better. "Please have a seat, Mrs. Kriebel. *He* is upstairs in his study. I'll call him down."

"I'm not too old to climb stairs," she said. "I did come by myself all the way from Schwenksville."

"Of course you did, Mrs. Kriebel. That is why you should sit here and rest. I will bring you something cool to drink. Do you favor ice?"

"Not especially, dear. It gives me a headache." As Lydia's eyes grew accustomed to the light, she noticed that the walls were covered with framed pictures. Many seemed to be photographs, and she remembered her daughter-in-law saying that Sachse worked as a picture-taker for the *Ladies' Home Journal.* But what captured her attention were what appeared to be drawings, although there was no lamp lit, and her eyes were almost useless in dim light. In the corner near the window was a rendering of a building surrounded by a mythical forest. It took effort to lift herself from the cool leather chair and walk over to it. She pulled the curtain from the edge of the window and strained to see its detail.

"Ah, Mrs. Kriebel! You are so kind to come so far to see me." There *he* stood in the doorway—tall, broad-shouldered and elegantly handsome. His beard made him look, if not older, then perhaps more maturely dignified than she had expected. "I am Julius Sachse." He did not shake her hand, but kissed it as she imagined a European might. "I see you are looking at my impression of the Tabernacle in the Wilderness. I drew it purely from secondhand information, of course, as it is there no more."

"I visited it once a great many years ago," she said, comparing the haze of her memory to what she could make out of the rendering. She made an effort to be polite. "You have done very well by it."

"You are fortunate to have had the experience of having seen it, Mrs. Kriebel. When Mrs. Righter passed away, the property was sold to a businessman named Prowattain. He tore down what little was remaining of the structure to construct a suburban residence, one he gave the quaint sobriquet, 'The Hermitage.' I believe it is now leased by a retired colonel."

"My, you seem to know a great deal about it."

"The subject of Pennsylvania-German history is an abiding interest of mine, Madam. Unfortunately, the history of our ancestors in this country has been undeservedly neglected. I believe that is partly because the early Germans excited the envy of their less successful and intemperate neighbors, and partly because so many of their ways of life have been misunderstood—their refusal to become embroiled in politics, for instance, or their pacifism. Do you know, Mrs. Kriebel, that in all my researches into our early history, I have yet to find one example of a firearm or murderous weapon brought into Pennsylvania by a German emigrant?" He turned to his wife. "Ah, here is Emma."

"A lemon squash, Mrs. Kriebel? And a slice of *Käsekuchen?* And here is a fan, in the event you find it too warm."

"Thank you, dear."

"Has my husband let you stand for so long after such a journey? Please take this chair. It is his, but I know that he insists."

"Of course, I insist. I was about to explain to you, Mrs. Kriebel, that I have been searching for information on the Pietists of the seventeenth century with the intention of writing a book on the subject. That is why your note intrigued me so much, and why I have so eagerly anticipated our meeting. I believe you mentioned some items that you believe belonged to Johannes Kelpius?"

She sighed. "You must sit, too, Mr. Sachse. You see, I seem to have a distant connection to the men you refer to as Pietists—or at least to those who knew them. When I was a child, my great aunt Christina gave me a small gold ornament, an old counterpane, and a handwritten book of German hymns. They were said to have been among his possessions."

"Do you still have them?"

She held up her left hand. "Here is the gold. After I was told that it was not likely ever to have belonged to Kelpius, I had it melted down and shaped into a ring, my wedding ring. It has been on my finger for nearly sixty years. The old quilt was already falling apart when I received it. I'm afraid my daughter-in-law gave it to the rag man a long time ago."

"And the hymn book?"

"Yes, the hymn book. *Die Kläglige Stimme der Verborgenen Liebe. The Lamenting Voice of the Hidden Love*. What a strange, sad collection of poetry, Mr. Sachse! Whatever else may be true about the author, he possessed quite an exceptional soul. That was one thing about which my great aunt was quite correct."

"Do you still have it, Mrs. Kriebel?"

"Well, to be honest, Mr. Sachse, it's been ten—no, fifteen—years since it became too difficult for me to read. It is somewhere safe within my house, although it will not be my house much longer. My son is determined to sell my house and everything in it."

"I am sorry, Mrs. Kriebel." He reached over from his chair and patted her hand. "What may I do for you today?"

Lydia could feel her throat quiver. She was not accustomed to revealing her emotions to anyone, and certainly not to a stranger, no matter how kind or distinguished. And yet, his kindness was causing her emotion, and his erudition was causing her to trust. "Mr. Sachse," she said stiffly, "my entire life I have been haunted by the specter of a person about whom I know practically nothing. I do not know why he came here or what befell him, yet his ghost hovers near my heart, always present, but always out of sight. In many ways, my life has been a most ordinary one—" Her voice began to falter. "There has been but one thing—that whispers to me—of something extraordinary."

"I understand, Mrs. Kriebel."

She took her handkerchief and daubed her eyes. "I wonder, Mr. Sachse. I wonder if you do."

"Growing up in Germantown, I have heard many extraordinary tales told about Johannes Kelpius."

"I'm sure you have."

"There was a survival of medieval superstition even in that late day, Madam, which was just the dawning of what we now call the Age of Reason. We may pride ourselves on being modern, but our ancestors brought many superstitious notions with them from Europe."

"Such as a belief in the Philosopher's Stone?"

A breeze came through the window, rustling the curtains and bringing with it the smell of light rain on hot pavement. Sachse ran his fingers through his beard. "It's strange that you should mention that."

"How so?"

He stood up, his height overpowering the room. In one great stride he was standing at a small writing desk along the wall opposite the window. "Just the other day," he said, "I received a correspondence from a man who lives in the ancient German city of Halle. He works in the library in the Halle Orphanage. Among the musty volumes in the archives, he came across a strange old letter concerning that very subject. It is addressed to an Augustus Hermann Francke, the man who founded the orphanage in the late seventeenth century, and whose name is remembered in the Lutheran Church that you yourself may attend in Montgomery County. The letter was written by the Reverend Heinrich Melchior Mühlenberg."

She was puzzled. "The patriarch of the American Lutheran Church?"

"The very same."

"But what connection would Reverend Mühlenberg have…I mean to say…?"

"With the *lapis philosophorum?"* He slipped a dark piece of paper from an envelope and returned to his chair. He placed a pince-nez to his nose. "This is what the Reverend Mühlenberg had to say. 'In 1742,'" he read, "'the year of my arrival in America, I was introduced to a crippled but trustworthy old gentleman of Germantown by the name of Daniel Geissler. Herr Geissler, I had been told, had once been intimately acquainted with the community of mystics that had flourished there around the turn of the century. To my question of what had befallen them, he answered that following the dying wish of their leader, a certain Herr K., the group disbanded—many rejoining the world, a few retreating from communal life into solitary seclusion.

"'When I inquired as the particulars regarding the passing of the young Magister, Geissler told me that, among other things, Herr K. had been of the firm belief that he would not die a natural death, and that his body would not decay, but would be transformed like Elijah and translated into the spiritual world. However, as many years of illness continued, it became apparent that the Magister's health was indeed failing. As his last hours drew near, the Magister spent three long days and nights praying to God, struggling and supplicating that the Lord would receive him bodily as He did Enoch and Elias of old.

"'At last, on the third day, after a long silence, he ceased his prayers and, addressing himself to his faithful friend, said, "My beloved Daniel, I am not to attain to that which I had aspired. I have received my answer. It is that from dust my body came, and it is to dust that it is to return. It is ordained that I shall die like all children of Adam."

"'Herr K. thereupon handed Geissler a small box, which was well secured and sealed and told him to carry it to the deep waters of the creek, and cast it into the water. Geissler took the box as far as the river bank and, being of a somewhat youthful and inquisitive nature, decided to hide it until after the Magister's death, and then possess himself of the secret of its contents.

"'Upon Geissler's return to his Magister's hut, Herr K. raised himself up and, with outstretched hand, pointed to his faithful servant, looked him sharply in the eyes and said, "Daniel, you have not done as I bid. You have not cast the box into the river, but have hidden it near the shore." Geissler, now more than ever convinced of the occult powers of the dying Magister, without even stammering an excuse, hurried to the river bank, and threw the box into the water as he was bidden.

"At the moment the mysterious box touched the river, the *arcanum* within transformed the water and there was an explosion of fire. For a time, flashes of lightning and rumbles like unto thunder emanated from the river.

"'When Geissler thence returned to his master, Herr K. was much relieved, saying that the great task that had been given unto him had been accomplished. It was but a few days later that the master gently and gracefully entered into his rest. His body was carried to an unmarked grave and, upon the moment of sunset, lowered into the waiting arms of the earth. As the corpse was placed into the ground, a snow-white dove was released from a cage. The bird winged its way heavenward, and the brethren, such that had remained true to their vocation, thrice repeated the sacred invocation, *'Gott gebe ihn eine seilige Auferstehung.' God grant him a blessed resurrection.*

"How sad," Lydia whispered. "How sweetly, bitterly sad."

From outside came a rumble of distant thunder. "I am very sorry if I upset you, Mrs. Kriebel. I read it only because it was so fresh in my mind, and is an example of the kind of fascination with the supernatural of that time, even among such as the Reverend Mühlenberg."

Her voice, even to her, sounded thin and distant. "Do you have anything else?"

"Right now, Madam, the only other things that I know about the Pietists of early Pennsylvania are titillating legends and superstitions that were handed down even through my generation. I'm afraid that superstitions can be very persistent."

"But have you nothing else? No reason why young Kelpius came all the way to live in the Wissahickon forest? Nothing more about who he was as a man? Nothing factual—about his doctrine—or his faith?"

"Mrs. Kriebel, I would not let old stories about alchemy and such disturb you. From the letter you sent me, it was clear that your own Christian faith was inspired and strengthened by the poems in that hymnal. I'm certain that they were written by Kelpius, and I'm certain that he was a most devout and pious Christian, despite the accusations that he was an apostate. That is what I was trying to impress upon you—that two centuries ago even the most orthodox of Christians believed in things that you and I would dismiss today. It doesn't mean that..."

"Oh, Mr. Sachse!" She sniffed back tears. "I'm not concerned with what is orthodox and what is not. Who am I—or you, for that matter—to know whether the Philosopher's Stone is a delusion or a signpost of a faith that may be superior to ours?"

"I'm afraid that I don't understand."

She struggled out of the chair. "I do not want to appear ungrateful. You have been very kind. The problem is not yours, it is mine. I allowed myself to become captivated by our Mr. Kelpius a very, very long time ago. The poems in his little book are more than simply pious rhymes. They express a pain so deep that I can only imagine its depths. I have come to appreciate his struggle in a way I cannot quite explain to you, Mr. Sachse, as much as we may both wish it to be otherwise. I suppose, in my own foolishness, that

I had hoped to discover something that would prove that Mr. Kelpius at last found peace—so that I might, too. Instead, all I have found is a bitter end to a romantic tale."

There was a great clap of thunder and the sound of wagons and cable cars gave way to the drumming of rain. He shook his head. "Madam, I can only tell you what I know."

"Mr. Sachse, I promise to look for that hymnal and when I find it, I will send it to you. There is no one in my family to whom it would mean a thing. Perhaps it will help you with your book. But I will be leaving now. Thank you for your hospitality."

Emma Sachse had been standing in the doorway. "Mrs. Kriebel," she said, "it's raining!"

"It's all right, dear. It's only water."

"Madam," Sachse pleaded, "please sit and have a slice of *Käsekuchen* and wait for the storm to pass."

"Thank you just the same. You have been more than kind."

"I insist that you at least allow me to escort you to the cable car—with an umbrella." There was another clap of thunder, this time sharp and loud.

"Perhaps," Lydia said, "if you insist."

Emma Sachse took her by the arm. "He does. We both do."

"I will go find an umbrella." He disappeared up the stairs.

Emma led her to the foyer. "Perhaps you can come back and see us again. He so enjoys the chance to discuss his favorite subject."

"Thank you, dear."

There was a great flash and for a fraction of a second the foyer was lit with brilliance.

"I do wish you would reconsider leaving in this storm, Mrs. Kriebel."

For a moment Lydia was unable to speak. "Do you have a lamp in here, my dear?" she asked.

"A lamp? Yes, right there by the mirror." Emma lit the gas and a tiny light appeared inside a red-tinted glass. Lydia bent toward a framed picture beside the mirror.

"I promise you, Mrs. Kriebel, that I will expend whatever effort, sparing no expense that may be required to discover..."

Sachse came down the stairs, hat and slicker in one hand, an umbrella in the other. "So, you noticed my rendering of the old *Einseidlerhütte.*"

Lydia was squinting. She had seen the picture only for an instant in the lightning and was struggling with it in the flickering of the gas light. "*Einseidlerhütte*?" she asked. "Whatever do you mean?"

"The Hermit's cave—not a natural cave, but the cell Kelpius created for his seclusion. It is where he spent time in prayer and meditation."

It looked to be a glorified spring house set into a wooded hillside. A shaft of light played on the stones of the arched entrance. "I was under the impression that he lived in the Tabernacle," she said, nearly pressing her nose to the glass.

"Well, yes and no. The Tabernacle was where the brethren worshiped and held services and so on. The anchorite cell was the Magister's own dwelling. It was likely where he composed the verses that have meant so much to you."

"And it is there still today?"

"Why, yes it is. I'm afraid that the entranceway has become blocked with debris over the years. I doubt that anyone has entered it in over a hundred and fifty years."

She kept looking at the picture, at first intrigued, then captivated by the romantic whims it evoked in her sense of mystery. "And you say that the property is now leased by a retired colonel?"

"Actually, the city of Philadelphia acquired that particular piece of the Hermit's property right after the war. It is now part of Fairmount Park."

"And one would not need permission to visit it?"

"No, not at all." He smiled. "It is a little difficult to find. I'm afraid you must walk some distance through the woods. But there is a stop on the Ridge Avenue cable car line at Righter Street. From there it's not much more than a quarter mile, just down the hill from where the Tabernacle once stood."

"And it is public property?"

"Yes, I assure you."

She was astonished by what she was thinking. She always had a tenacious resistance to what she considered mechanical intrusions into everyday life. "Mrs. Sachse," she said before she could change her mind, "does anyone in this neighborhood have a telephone?"

"A telephone?" Emma asked. "Whatever for?"

"I would like to place a telephone call to Schwenksville, to get a message to my grandson."

"Mrs. Kriebel," he said, "I would be most happy to escort you..."

"No, thank you very much. You see, my grandson is expecting to meet me in Norristown this afternoon, and I have decided to stay overnight in Germantown."

Sachse stroked his beard. "There are several telephones down at the university. Shall I take you to one?"

There was another roll of thunder. "Yes, I would appreciate that. But first, Emma dear, I believe I will have that piece of *Käsekuchen* after all."

Chapter Twenty Three

Sunday, June 24, 1888
Fairmount Park, Philadelphia

The day was the epitome of perfection. The storms of Saturday were gone and in their place was a Sunday morning bright and alluringly fresh. The man at the Linden Hotel left his station behind the desk to escort Lydia to Saint Michael's. It was not a Lutheran service, but Lydia was more concerned with the building than the strange Episcopalian liturgy. The man from the Linden had told her—and the Reverend Murphy had confirmed—that the very chancel of the church had been built on top of the graves of some of Germantown's earliest settlers. The reverend had mentioned the town's first physician, Doctor Witt, his good friend Daniel Geissler, and, surprisingly, Christian Warmer, Lydia's remote ancestor.

After the service, Reverend Murphy introduced Lydia to a man who claimed a connection to the Wüsters and who treated her as if she were kindred aristocracy. When she mentioned Kelpius, the stranger smiled. He twirled his waxed moustache and inclined his face close to her.

"'Painful Kelpius from his hermit den
By Wissahickon, maddest of good men,
Deep in the woods, where the small river slid,
Weird as a wizard over arts forbid.
Behmen's Morning-Redness, through the Stone
Of Wisdom, vouchsafed to his eyes alone,
Whereby he read what man ne'er read before
And saw the visions man shall see no more.'

"The poet Whittier, you know." He held up his hand, as if to prevent his words from being overhead by the red church doors. "He's a Yankee *Quaker*."

She accepted the stranger's kindness and rode with him in his open carriage past the old mill on Rittenhouse Street, along the winding Lower Wissahickon Drive that followed the creek toward the Schuylkill. After they crossed the Ridge Avenue bridge, he let her off at the corner of Righter Street. He seemed more than willing to wait with her until her grandson arrived, but she insisted that she not take any more of his time.

This would be her last time there. She thanked God that He had provided such a day, so that the memory would shine in her heart as brilliantly as the sun was in the midsummer sky. Old Mrs. Righter was gone, as was her ancient cabin and her wilderness. Soon—Lydia knew all too well—she, too, would be transformed into a memory, at first vivid, then gradually dim until there was not a trace she had ever lived. But the thought wasn't melancholy; it wasn't even the shadow of a bird across the sun. She had not accomplished anything extraordinary in her life, but she had come to understand what Kelpius had meant when he sang:

So let die that which must! Yet breathing still am I.
For what in Love doth burn, will never fear to die.

"Good morning, Grandma." Eli, her daughter's oldest son, stood at the corner while the Ridge Avenue cable car clanked down the hill. Obedient to her request, he was carrying a long-handled shovel. "Please don't laugh," he said, grinning. "I've been given enough odd looks already this morning." He hugged her as if she were fragile. "I told a woman at the station in Norristown I was an undertaker." He did look like one, dark-haired and handsome, and dressed more for a formal affair than an exploration in the woods.

"Nonsense," Lydia said. "An undertaker buries people. Today you are going to help me dig someone up."

"Grandma, please tell me that you are joking, or else I'll take the next cable car home."

"Eli, have you ever known your *Groffmutter* to joke?"

"Only when the truth was too serious, Grandma."

She took his arm. "It's a fine morning for a walk, don't you think?"

"I suppose you will explain this all to me when you are ready."

"Of course, dear. You must be patient with me. I am a difficult old woman."

He squeezed her arm. "At least you are an honest, difficult old woman, Grandma."

They strolled down Righter Street toward the large house that now stood at the end of the lane somewhere, she guessed, near where the old orchard had been. Two women in white Sunday dresses were setting a table outside in the shade. Behind them was a rose garden, laid out in the shape of a cross, blooming red and white in the sun. She could smell its fragrance. She decided that she would believe it marked the place where Johannes Kelpius had been laid to rest, so far from his Transylvanian home.

They stopped a polite distance from the house. Eli waved to the ladies while Lydia struggled to reach through her memory. Nothing familiar had been left behind to help her remember where the Tabernacle had once stood. The cave was near a spring, Sachse had told her, just down the hill from the Hermitage. She pulled Eli's arm and they walked beside a picket fence to a sign that read "Property of the City of Philadelphia—Border Fairmount Park, April 1868."

"I am looking for a cave," she said. "Something that looks like a spring house. It should be down this hill, near a stream."

Eli looked at the wild and thorny underbrush with suspicion. "And the shovel…?"

"It may be partially buried."

"There are blackberry vines in there, Grandma," he said, but she had already plunged ahead of him into the thicket.

The forest was full of the songs of birds. She and Eli were far enough from Ridge Avenue that they could no longer hear the sounds of the city. There must have been days just as exquisite a hundred and eighty years before, she thought. How different could it have been then? Some of the elms and oaks that towered over her were already large at the turn of the eighteenth century. Surely it had not been all that long, as God counted time. And it was God she was counting on for help.

"Grandma, is *this* what you're looking for?"

She followed the sound of his voice and came upon a small creek, stepping over it to where Eli stood leaning on his shovel. He was staring at a stone archway built into the hillside, covered by a decrepit pair of boards, themselves partially buried in a mound of dirt. "Please tell me that I'm mistaken," he said.

There was no mistake. Julius Sachse had a fine hand for rendering. Apart from the debris, it was a life-size version of the picture in his foyer. She felt a chill of excitement. "Eli, you are a wonder! That's it exactly. Now, dear, all you must do is dig the dirt from the door and pry off those boards."

"Grandma, this is public property."

"Exactly, and we *are* part of the public. What do you think will happen, Eli? Are you worried that Grover Cleveland will come along and put us in prison? I'm the only authority you need to be concerned about, dear, and I'm telling you to dig."

He shook his head and thrust the shovel into the pile. "If there's a dead body in there, Grandma, I'll swear to the police that I've never seen you before."

"That's good, Eli," she said. "You were always strong, even as a child. A few more shovelfuls should do it." She waited until he had moved the pile. "Now just tear off those boards."

"Grandma..."

"I don't want to have to spank you, Eli."

"I'm thirty years old, Grandma."

"I'd say one of these little sticks would do well as a switch."

Reluctantly, he stuck the pointed end of his shovel between the boards and pried until they came loose in a small shower of dust and pebbles. He jumped backwards. "Jesus!" he cried. "What's inside there, I don't want to know."

She was too curious to reprimand him for his blasphemy. She pushed by him and peered into the dark recess. "Grandma," he said, "please don't go inside. It doesn't look at all safe. The whole thing might come tumbling down and bury you inside."

"Well," she said, "that would save the family from the expense of hiring a real undertaker." She stepped into the shadow.

It had been her foolish enthusiasm again, this time causing her to forget that she couldn't see in the dark. But even blind as she was, her heart collapsed at what she wasn't able to see. For the past twenty-four hours she had hid her hope from herself—her hope of finding the hidden retreat of a poet, a scholar, and a mystic, perhaps worn by the years, but captive of all that its creator had been.

Instead it was dank and cold. She ran a hand against the wall and could feel nothing but stones. She didn't need her eyes to tell her that it was empty, she could hear how the sound of her feet on the dirt fell back on her ears. It was crushing—too crushing—to think that Julius Sachse was just a man whose desire to believe in the romantic was stronger than his common sense. She had been in spring houses before and they were often built in places such as this. "Eli," she called. The energy and humor had fled her voice.

"I'm not coming in there."

"Please, dear. I can't see. I just need for you to tell me that there's nothing here, and I promise we can go home. Please."

"What do you see?"

"Not a thing, dear. I thought that there might be something here, but I don't think there is. I just want to be certain, and I need for you to confirm that there really is nothing here."

He stood in the doorway, blocking out what there was of light. "You're right, Grandma, it's empty, thank God."

"What's this?" she asked.

"It's just a large stone that's come loose from the side, that's all."

"What's that?" She tapped something with the toe of her foot.

"It's a board."

"Would you lift it up and see if there's anything underneath?"

"Grandmother..."

She bent down and felt with her hands until she was able to pull it up. "Is there anything underneath?"

He stepped inside and lifted her up by the arm. "Broken glass," he said. "You'll cut yourself."

"Nothing else?"

"A great deal of glass and some broken pottery." He kicked the tip of his Sunday shoes into the dirt. He sounded no longer amused. "What is it that you're looking for, Grandma?"

It was the same question she had asked herself for sixty years and now, at the end of her journey, she still had no answer. She took a breath and tried to imagine how she would explain it to him on the way home, explain it without shameful, indefensible tears.

"Do you have a handkerchief?" he asked.

She felt the clasp of her bag and fished inside until she found it. "What are you doing, Eli?"

He had taken her handkerchief and was crouching in the corner. "There's a little box. I don't want to touch it with my hands. Here," he said, rising. "Maybe this has your treasure inside."

She grabbed his arm and followed him outside into the warmth of the sunshine. "May I see it?" she asked.

"It's either locked or else just plain stuck. Uh-oh, the bottom's come off. Sorry, Grandma, it's completely rusted through. Ho, look here, there's something inside." There was a shower of brown particles. "It seems to be an envelope. Here!" He turned away as she grabbed for it. "It will crumble if you tear at it. Let me try to open it—slowly."

"Does it have anything written on it?" Her breathing was short and shallow.

He blew on the envelope and held it to his face. "Deliver to Hester Palmer in Flushing, Long Island."

"Does it have a date or a return?"

"No. Let me see. Here goes. Good Lord, this is brittle. Alright, Grandma, there's a letter inside."

She was struggling to contain her hope. "Is it written in German?"

"No, it's English. Very small handwriting. Shall I read it to you?"

For some reason, the image of her *Tantchen* Christina crossed her mind, the recollection of her smell, the memory of visiting her on Christmas Days. Lydia couldn't recall her face, or the letter she had received just before her great-aunt died, but she knew that the two of them were connected in a way that nothing she had learned or believed could make comprehensible. She also knew that it was the same sort of connection that her *Tantchen* Christina had once had with her own *Groffmutter*, and perhaps—if she allowed herself to be sentimental—that her great-great-aunt Christiana had with the man who came to stay at her home.

She would not allow herself to believe in the transmigration of souls. It was a concept incompatible with her Christian faith, and yet the sensation would not relinquish its hold on her. How else, it repeated in the language of her heart, could a letter composed a century before she was born be intended for her?

She settled herself on the pile of dirt Eli had made beside the cave. The air was full of rich light and the tumble of gentle water from the spring. She was tired, but not from the fatigue of her aging body. She felt as if she had made a long journey, a journey that crossed the very barriers of life and death, in order to receive something that had been meant for her even before she had been born. "Yes, dear," she said. "Please read it if you can."

Dear Beloved Hester, (he read)

What a change the past few hours have wrought, that I am now emboldened to break through the wall that has so long prevented the expression of what has been in my heart. Your wisdom and your beauty, your compassion and kindness towards me, have sustained me during the most difficult years of my life, made all the more difficult as I was unable to fully share the burdens of my heart with you.

If I have not shown you my love, nor flown to your side as lover, it was not from any lack of fervency, but from foolishness and—finally from fever, the manifestation in my body of my heartache. You deserve more than mumbled words sprung from muffled thoughts. You deserve the attentions of a man, one who is able to inspire, support, and accompany you through the marvelous journey of life. Would that I could be that man!

Three days ago I traced the footsteps of the Master to the Garden of Gethsemane. I prayed blindly—and fruitlessly—that God might take from me this burden. You know as perhaps no one else, how long I have longed for the ceasing of self, the ceasing of my longings, for the unceasing belonging in the Self of God. What I have received has fallen so short of that which I longed, but in losing I have found.

My friends that remain are few. Seelig, who is more dear than my own soul, prepared a bed for me, arranged so that I might look out upon the colors and light of the season. This afternoon, while resting from my prayers, my attention was drawn to a light in the forest. At first it seemed to be a trick of sight caused by my fever, but as I watched, toward my hut flew a bird, shimmering and luminescent. It lit, not more than a few feet from where I lay, and assumed the shape of a woman, fair and gentle. Her hair was like that of the substance of light, her dark eyes gentle and penetrating.

The effect of this vision was sudden and intense, and I feared that I had lost my sanity. I began to tremble until the apparition spoke. Her voice touched me in a way that this pen is not sharp enough to convey. All I am able to say is that her words dispelled my blinding wonder, and left in its place a certainty I was being spoken to by the voice of Wisdom herself.

"Johannes Kelpius," she spoke, "dear, painful and pious one. Loosen thy heart from excitement, for it is only the ignorant who confuse fervor of feeling with capacity of understanding. Thou wert abandoned by thy family, misled by thy teachers, and deceived by thy world. Thou hast come so far and sought so earnestly, yet dost thou know what thy efforts have been worth?"

I felt shamed by her pity. "Have mercy upon me, O Emissary of God," I said. "I am without hope."

"Johannes, hope is the cheapest of commodities, for it can readily be purchased at the expense of Truth."

"Then give me Truth, for I have nothing left to spend."

She took my hand and lifted my head from the pillow. "That Truth exists thou art certain, but certainty alone is not sufficient for its attainment. The methods thou hast chosen are the ones in which thou hast found the most comfort—even if they were the comfort of stings and lashes. Thou hast not considered that the words and acts and persons of the past—those which you revere and hold sacred—may belong to their own time and place, and that the needs of thy soul belong to thine own time, to thine own world, and to thine own people."

The radiance of her countenance was dazzling. I implored her to tell me who she was.

"I am like thee," she said, "an orphan. I have been separated from the land of my origin, a place of incomparable riches. Thy people have shunned my kingdom, and built a war of fear around its borders. I was left outside—left to wander through a wilderness of ignorance and poverty of thought. Some like thyself, having heard of my kingdom, have sought its treasures. But deluded by pride and trust in their own judgement, they instead pursue me, and in doing so become lost. Further and further they stray into the most remote wilderness, searching for traces of me, boasting they have attained a glimpse of my raiment."

"In finding thee, Sophia, have I then lost?"

Her eyes shone with a radiance that pierced the veil of whom I had thought myself to be. "It is *I* who have found *thee*, Johannes Kelpius. The depth of your sincerity has attracted me to thee. Hear now what thou should have learned from others:

"The demands of thy heart are not the same as the needs of thy spirit. Knowing in your spirit the falsity of thy outer self, thou hast sought to renounce it, but vain is the sacrifice if self-hate replaces self-love. The end of that path is not knowledge, but misery.

"Union with the Absolute thou can attain, but only in the way that leads to Union, and not by following those who have the form of knowledge, but not the power thereof. Where there is a real need, the true path can be found, but where there is merely a usurping of authority, there is only error. One may seize the Sophic Fire, but one cannot steal the knowledge of how to use it to dispel darkness.

"Thou hast prayed to be spared the annihilation of death. That which belongs to this world must return to it. Release thy anxious gaze upon the shadow of Johannes Kelpius and turn to the truth of Johannes Kelpius, the truth of one who cannot be touched by death. In his light, I shall show thee the Kingdom wherein lie the treasures thou hast sought."

In an instant she was gone, leaving in her place a snow-white bird, soon lost in the forest.

Then, I was visited once more. As if from the air itself, as has always been his gift, my friend Amimi appeared. He had with him a present, *die Steppdecke*, the very same Quilt of Many Colors that I had given to him many years ago. Within its seams was a secret blessing from the man and woman who gave me earthly life. Amimi was not surprised at my condition, as he explained that the *Manituwák* or Spirits (thus he styles his intuition) told him that I would take a journey upon a long-neglected trail, a road his people once believed led from this very place upon the ridge toward a more real world. He said that the souls of those who had made the quilt would accompany me on this journey, and that it was incumbent upon him to return it.

Dearest Hester, how precious are friendships and how difficult are goodbyes!

It is not with regret that I offer you my love, but with hope— borne not at the expense of Truth, but in the interests thereof. I love you dearly, in spirit and in truth, in a way that reaches beyond the short span of time we have been given together. I pray that you will neither mourn nor regret, but grow into a full life of joy as well as wisdom. God asks patience of us, for our time is not His, but I beg you not to defer your life in expectation of some promised tomorrow, for our gift is the present.

As I conclude my letter to you, I hear the approach of faithful Daniel Geissler. He has remained at my side throughout my ordeal, despite his own limitations, desiring only to assist his Magister. Upon my instructions, our project here will be dismantled. I have understood at last that the doctrine and methods of enlightenment are impotent without the presence of one with Perceptions and Authority essential to the process. This world is far too cluttered with remnants of heroic but piteous efforts. I will not suffer another to add to its errors. I have for Daniel but one more task, the disposition of *al Warqa'iyah,* the Dove, for I know now that the spiritual Virtue with which our Circle was once supplied has been exhausted, and I shall not permit its trace to be carried further into useless and repetitive error.

I have at last seen that a new age indeed will come, but it shall not be the age of which I have struggled through so much of my life hoping to bring to fruition. The world will turn its back upon Faith and seek its hope in Reason. Of this age there too will be an end, and my final prayer is that one day, amid the disappointments of the future, the wall that surrounds the Kingdom of Truth shall crumble, and mankind at last be worthy of its treasure. It is in that Kingdom I shall be, awaiting you.

In love undying,
J.K.
Rocksborough, Pennsylvania, 1707

Eli cleared his throat and looked at his grandmother. There was an expression on his face that resembled fear—a sort of troubled reverence, Lydia thought, for her imagined prescience that had led them to such a discovery. She returned his gaze with a smile, one that she hoped would reassure him that she was as surprised—well, perhaps nearly as surprised—at finding the letter.

She sat there in the sunshine, in the dirt, hoping she might catch sight of a dove—a presence from which she could beg forgiveness for the extraordinary length of time it took her to reach her elusive end. Finally, she took her grandson's hand to help her stand. From his loose and absent grip, she took the letter. It crumbled as she tucked it into her bag.

Epilogue

Wednesday, June 24, 1903
Harrisburg, Pennsylvania

When Elizabeth Grayson looked at the clock, she doubted there would be any chance for her to take a lunch break. Her reputation for efficiency in Governor Samuel Pennypacker's administration had been hard won—a necessary victory to establish herself in the male world of politics. But the reputation had come with the price of inordinate responsibility. She had single-handedly been conducting the research for the governor's statement on Pennsylvania child labor, this over and above her regular duties as his personal assistant. She hurried to gather her papers in the unlikely chance the governor would have time to review them with her before noon.

There was no answer to her knocks on his office door, neither her polite tap nor her urgent rap. She turned the knob and stepped inside.

Governor Pennypacker stood facing the window, his hands locked behind his back. The side windows were open and the lace curtains were fluttering with a breeze that carried a smell of cut grass. "Excuse me, Governor," she said.

He didn't turn around, but stared out the window, across the lawn that separated their temporary offices from where the capitol building was being reconstructed. They had inherited an incinerated capitol from the previous administration, and so far there was only the barest outline of what would someday be a magnificent dome. The governor repeatedly told his staff that it was a reminder that American government would always be a work in progress.

"Governor Pennypacker?"

He raised a finger in the air. "Do you hear that, Miss Grayson?"

She listened for a moment—to distant hammering and even more distant hoofbeats from downtown. Then she heard what seemed to have captured his attention. "A bird?" she asked.

"A mourning dove."

She put her files on his desk. The governor had draped his coat over the back of his chair and left his spectacles on the blotter. It was not a good sign. "Yes," she said, "I hear them all the time."

"Do you believe in fate, Miss Grayson?"

His back was still to her, his thin form in silhouette against the long window. "Fate, sir?"

For a few moments he remained silent. "Quite a number of years ago," he said, "back in 'ninety-four, I was home in Schwenksville for a weekend. A fellow named Kriebel was having a sale at his house, and you know I've never been able to resist the opportunity to discover something of historical interest." When the governor exhibited odd behavior, it almost always had something to do with his penchant—in Elizabeth's opinion, his obsession—for history.

"I bought a lot of old books and had it sent to my office in Philadelphia. The ones that looked of value I finally took back home with me, and I stuck the remainder of the lot on top of an old box."

"That's an interesting story, to be sure, sir. Perhaps you can tell me the rest after we've had a chance to review the child labor research."

"When I moved my office, I hired someone to carry all the odds and ends back to Schwenksville. He put everything up on shelves in the garret. That's where it all sat, I suppose just waiting for me to get around to throwing it away." Elizabeth began to tap her foot. "Then a few years ago something took me upstairs—I can't remember what in the world it could have been—and I heard a mourning dove outside. Hearing it must have caused me to remember something that I had seen years before, but my mind hadn't registered. I noticed that among all that rubbish was a manuscript with its front leaves gone and the words *'Der einsamen Turtletauben'* written on one of its pages.

"A foreign book, sir?"

"*'Der einsamen Turtletauben,'* is typical symbolism of a peculiar religious group of the late seventeenth century. *'The moving song of complaint of the solitary little dove in the place of its trial, sung in the still woods of patience.'* "

She had been waiting for the connection between the rubbish in his attic and the identification of bird calls.

"It was dated 1705. An original German hymnal composed in Pennsylvania. It was strange but fortunate that it fell into my possession—and fortunate that it didn't fall out again. It would have been a terrible loss."

"I'm sure it would have been."

"As it turned out, I was able to donate it to the Historical Society where I was serving on the Board of Trustees at the time."

"That was very charitable of you, sir."

He turned, and for the first time she was able to see the distance in his eyes. "Miss Grayson, have you ever heard of Johannes Kelpius?"

For a moment she thought to ask if the man were a Democrat or a Republican, but decided that the governor was not in a mood to appreciate her attempts at humor. "No, sir, I don't believe I ever have," she said.

He sat down at his desk but left his spectacles folded on the blotter. "It's a pity. He was one of the most extraordinary of all our early settlers. Someday, perhaps, his story will become better known. Until then, just leave me your files, Miss Grayson, and I'll attend to them later. Why don't you just take an early lunch?"

"Thank you, Governor." She laid her papers on his desk. After all, she thought to herself, it wasn't the end of the world.

From outside, the call of the dove came in on the summer breeze.

Historical Notes

The following notes are primarily intended to indicate where I have deliberated departed from verified facts, reported facts, or extant oral history. If not otherwise noted, most material is either true or plausible within the parameters of accepted historical fact.

PROLOGUE
Lydia and her great-aunt Christina are fictional characters, although Christina's grandmother, Christiana Warmer, is real. The vision of the angel is not part of reported oral history, but is representative of the beliefs of that time and place, and especially those surrounding Johannes Kelpius. The quilt and the gold star are not actual objects associated with Kelpius. I have used them as symbolic of the personal and mystical life of Kelpius, respectively. The hymnal is real, although I have combined the history of one of the collections of his writings with the content of the other. These are two of only three extant writings by Kelpius. For more information on the two hymnals, see notes for the Epilogue.

CHAPTER ONE
It is not likely that in 1826 the Tabernacle was still in the condition described. This portrayal, taken from George Lippard's nineteenth century novel *Paul Ardenheim* (see bibliography), relates to the Tabernacle as it probably was in the late 1700s. Although Kelpius is claimed by various organizations associated with the Rosicrucians and Masons, it would be of great historical interest to know if there is any written attestation of this prior to Sachse's publication of *Pietists* (See bibliography.) in 1895. The fragment of Kelpius' writing in this chapter is paraphrased from the first page of his actual diary, the third extant original material. The quotation from the Roman philosopher Seneca that begins Kelpius' diary is translated in Chapter Eight.

CHAPTER TWO
The bequest from Count Valentin (Count Valentine Franke) is fictitious, although an inheritance similar to this would explain why tradition held Kelpius to have been a nobleman. The circumstances of the death of Pfarrer Kelp and his alcoholism are invented, but plausible. Johann Valentin Andreæ, the commonly accepted author of the manifestos of Rosicrucianism, later disavowed the works that became a foundation of

much of the Rosicrucian movement according to Fisher. I am grateful to the late Idries Shah for information on the origins of Rosicrucianism. (See bibliography for both sources.) The German hymn that opens the chapter was composed many years after this incident by J.G. Seelig, a friend of Kelpius in his adult life. The translation is roughly: *Where are you, my little dove, my sweet little angel? I am in pain from longing, and my heart cries out for you.*

CHAPTER THREE

All the characters are real, although I have brought them together in a fictitious meeting. Anna Maria Schuckart's ecstatic trances and stigmata were convincing enough for Francke to consider her genuine, although he later denounced her "gifts" as spurious.

CHAPTER FOUR

The circumstances surrounding Kelpius' early involvement in the Pietist movement are not known, although it probably began during his time as a student at Altdorf. The prevailing theory is that he was introduced to new and radical ideas through Christian Knorr von Rosenroth. Many of Kelpius's hymns were written to melodies composed by him. It was with regret that I left this colorful and important character out of the story. For definitive information on Knorr von Rosenroth and his associates, read Fisher's *"Prophesies and Revelations."* (See bibliography.) For the name of the "Cobbler of Gorlitz," I have chosen the spelling "Behmen," which was commonly used at this time. He may be more familiar to modern students of European mysticism as "Boehme." The philosophies that Francke expounds are simplifications of various mystical concepts that I have used for narrative significance. In the absence of any historical information regarding the first meeting of Kelpius and J.G. Seelig, I have placed it at this time for literary reasons.

CHAPTER FIVE

Puffendorf, the spy for the Ducal Consistorium of Würtemberg, is fictitious, but I have named him after a contemporary theologian who was a zealous opponent of Zimmerman. In an interesting twist, the military incursion of the French into Würtemberg that Zimmerman claimed to be Divine retribution for his expulsion was the very reason that young Johann Kelp decided not to attend Würtemberg's University of Tübingen (Kelp's first choice in education), but selected instead the University of Altdorf in Bavaria.

Zimmerman's sermon is drawn from the writings of Philip Jakob Spener, considered the first exponent of the Pietist movement in seventeenth century Germany. The intriguing "Dial of Achaz," now in the collection of the American Philosophical Society, does indeed demonstrate a "reversal of time" through its calibrations for refraction of light through water.

CHAPTER SIX
There is only speculation regarding the first meeting of Kelpius and Zimmerman, and of Kelpius' original association with the Chapter of Perfection. The spirit of the atmosphere in Erfurth that I describe is authentic, however the specific words and rituals of the Chapter of Perfection (being initiatory) are only plausible fiction. In this case, I have derived them largely from Sachse's description of German Rosicrucian mysticism (see bibliography) with my own addition of the Arabic. The lines of the hymn sung in the church are translated at the very end of the chapter. They are from Kelpius' "*Bitter Süſse Nachts Ode,* Bittersweet Night Ode" verse 5, undated.

CHAPTER SEVEN
The descriptions of Benjamin Furly and his library are taken from a firsthand account (regarding the very book mentioned here), but from decades later. Symon and Mariecke Jansen are real, but did not necessarily fulfill the role I have given them.

CHAPTER EIGHT
The Chapter of Perfection traveled to Holland in two separate groups; likely Zimmerman led one group and Köster the other. Daniel Geissler was probably not a member of either group, but joined with Kelpius and his comrades later in America. Zimmerman's thoughts on his emigration to America are inventions of my own, although I believe them to capture the essence of his motivation.

CHAPTER NINE
The tale of the seer in the forest comes from a story regarding Conrad Matthäi, a Swiss mystic who joined Kelpius' group in America around the turn of the century. He is another fascinating character who was left out of this book with great regret. The tale, likely derived from oral sources, is found in Sacshe's *Pietists*. (See bibliography.) It is my own belief that the mysterious "dove" referred to in Kelpius' diary was a play

on words for the sound-alike Arabic word for rosary, associated with the concepts of the "rosy cross."

CHAPTER TEN

The exact date and circumstances of Zimmerman's death are not known, although the church records of Bietgheim record his death in Rotterdam in 1693. The hymn is from Kelpius' *"Gespräch Der Seelen Mit Sich Selbst,* Colloquium of the soul with its self over her long purification," verse 32 (1698).

CHAPTER ELEVEN

Other than Kelpius' association with the members of the Philadelphia Society of London and others of like inclination, nothing specific is known about his six month's stay in London. The group did receive a prophesy of success from some unidentified "seer," but I have made him the Finn Shaeffer (who returns to the story later) for narrative reasons. Comments in a letter Kelpius wrote years later to Heinrich Johann Deichman, the secretary of the Philadelphia Society, were the inspiration for the invented incident involving Mecken and Clerk (M. and C.).

CHAPTER TWELVE

Not only did Kelpius keep a diary of the events of his sea voyage, but Seelig also described it in an open letter published in Europe. This is the best-documented event in the book. The incident that Kelpius describes as "the memorable excommunication of Falckner by Köster and that of Anna Maria Schukart, the Prophetess of Erfurth" appears in Kelpius' account at the very end of the voyage. The details of the "misdeeds" are mine, although confusion between religious and sexual frenzies was not uncommon. The hymn sung by Maria is from Kelpius' hymn, *A Comfortable and Encouraging Song,* verse 7 (1706).

CHAPTER THIRTEEN

In a major departure from historical reality, I have combined the character of Christian Warmer with that of Ludwig Biederman, the first member of the Chapter of Perfection to marry and the actual husband of Maria Zimmerman. In doing so, I have given the role of Christiana Warmer, the "ministering angel" of the mystics, to Maria Zimmerman. Because Robert Whitpain's name was associated with the Wissahickon Creek, I have given him a role of antagonist that he likely does not deserve. It was probably Deputy Governor Markham (a cousin of

William Penn) who performed the swearing-in ceremony. It is not known if Kelpius possessed any written documents concerning the gift of twenty-four hundred acres, but for unknown reasons, the promise was never honored in Pennsylvania.

CHAPTER FOURTEEN

There is a tragic lack of information about the Indians of southeastern Pennsylvania. The accepted spelling of the name of these people is "Lenape" but for phonetic accuracy I have used "Lenápay." The Lenape language is as authentic as possible, but the legend of the Trail on the Ridge is a romantic invention. For obvious reasons, the Lenape had no word for "gold." I have attributed the translation of "Wissahickon" to "Golden Creek," although the Lenape root word "*wissa*" signifies "yellow."

CHAPTER FIFTEEN

The hymn is from Kelpius' *"Die Macht Der Liebe,* The Power of Love which conquers the World, Sin, and Death," verse 120 (1705).
The words of the mystics' ritual come from the *New Testament Apocrypha*, the Acts of John.

CHAPTER SIXTEEN

Kelpius recorded the Lenápay's public rebuttal to William Penn in a letter to his college mentor, Magister Fabricius, in 1705, although he does not specifically state that he acquired the information firsthand. Kelpius dates the incident as possibly occurring in 1701, but I have moved it up earlier in Penn's brief second visit to Pennsylvania.
Most historical characterizing of Penn and Pastorius has been much kinder to them. At the risk of displaying them at their worst, I have chosen to portray these men as I believe Kelpius and Falckner perceived them.

CHAPTER SEVENTEEN

The account of the angelic vision comes from Sachse, who found it among the archives of the Ephrata community, a religious settlement founded by German religious nonconformists a generation after Kelpius and the Mystics of the Wissahickon. Although I have expanded the details of this unusual incident, it is essentially faithful to the original report.

CHAPTER EIGHTEEN

The poetry is from Kelpius' "*Von Der Ruhe,* Upon Rest, As once in Poverty and in the Wilderness I had been made Weary with Labor," verse 7 (1697). I am grateful to Elizabeth Fisher for her insights into the influence of Peter Shaeffer's eccentricities on Kelpius. (See bibliography.)

CHAPTER NINETEEN

Kelpius attributes his connection to Hester Palmer to one M.B., whom I have taken the liberty of assuming was Maria Biedermann, or as she appears in this book, Maria Warmer. In a letter to her, he makes reference to this interruption in a prior personal conversation.

CHAPTER TWENTY

This chapter take place a few years prior to the incorporation of Germantown into the city of Philadelphia and before the construction of the noted Town Hall building which still stands today. It is not known if Germantown at that time had such an office as Deeds and Records. The quotation from Christian Lehman, which I have paraphrased, is the source of information on Kelpius used by John Watson in his *Annals of Philadelphia,* which in turn has been used as the source for most subsequent research.

The hymn is from Kelpius' "*Das Paradoxe und seltsame Vergnügen,* The Paradox and Seldom Contentment of the God-loving soul," verse 19 (undated). The actual document that revoked Pastorius' role as agent for the Frankfort Company named a third partner, Johann Jawert, to act with Falckner and Kelpius. Jawert later became a Quaker and sided with Pastorius in his conflicts with Falckner. To the best of my knowledge, the specifics of the false charges against Falckner are not known. The actual identity of the woman Falckner married is not known. He moved to New Jersey and assisted the efforts of his brother Justus, the first Lutheran minister to be ordained in America.

CHAPTER TWENTY-ONE

The tale of the Wise Men from Persia comes from the *Adventures of Marco Polo* and was likely known to Kelpius.

Dr. Christopher Witt, an Englishman, was a prominent associate of Kelpius and the brethren during the last seven or eight years of Kelpius' life. It was into his possession that the Horologium Achaz Hydrographicum likely came following the dissolution of The Woman in the Wilderness. Witt then gave the device to Benjamin Franklin who eventually donated this remarkable instrument to the American Philosophical Society.

CHAPTER TWENTY-TWO

Of the two collections of Kelpius' hymns, *The Lamenting Voice* was known to Sachse well prior to the composition of his definitive work on the subject.

CHAPTER TWENTY-THREE

If Kelpius had any further correspondence with Hester Palmer after May 1706, he did not transcribe a copy into his journal.

The message of Sophia was, in part, inspired by this extract from Idries Shah's *Knowing How to Know.* "People can start to learn when they are willing to accept the possibility that the very evidence of 'something higher' in themselves may in fact not be reliable, and may even be screening them from real perceptions."

The cave in Fairmount Park that bears Kelpius' name has never been authoritatively verified as his meditation cell. It may never be proven one way or the other.

EPILOGUE

Of the three extant writings attributed to Kelpius, two are collections of hymns. *Die Kläglige Stimme der Verborgenen Liebe, The Lamenting Voice of the Hidden Love,* contains the poetry that has been quoted throughout this book. The German hymns and the music were written on the left-hand pages, presumably copied by Christina Warmer from Kelpius' loose manuscripts while he recuperated in her home during the winter of 1705-1706. On the right-hand pages, Dr. Christopher Witt made an heroic but awkward attempt to translate the poetry into English. I am grateful to Dr. Witt for providing me with a foundation for my original translations.

The other collection of hymns, generally known as *The Hymn Book of the Hermits of the Wissahickon,* which contains compositions by J.G. Seelig and H.B. Köster, was the book that suffered unknown vicissitudes and was recovered by Governor Pennypacker. The song of the Little Dove that caught the attention of the governor was written by Seelig. It introduces Chapter Two.

A book entitled *A Short and Easy Method of Prayer* was translated into English by Dr. Witt and bears Kelpius' name as author. The first editions of this interesting book have never been recovered. Sachse asserts that this was a reconstruction of an earlier German work by Augustus Hermann Francke. Although I am certain that Francke's book was in Kelpius' possession and in harmony with the latter's philosophy, I think it probable that the authorship was attributed to Kelpius posthumously.

The most revealing original material that we have of Kelpius is his journal, a small book that he brought with him from Europe. In it, he kept a record of the events of the long sea voyage to America and copies of some of his correspondences. I am deeply grateful for his efforts, as this story would not have been possible without them.

Notes to the graphics

PROLOGUE
Adapted from the title page of *Il burato librode recami*, Alessandro Paganino, 1518.

CHAPTER ONE
Sachse introduces his book, *The German Pietists of Provincial Pennsylvania,* with the acronym DOMA (Deo Optimo Maximo Altissimo) taken from the title page of a Rosicrucian manuscript.

CHAPTER TWO
A 1550 woodcut illustration from the *Rosarium philosophorum*, a work of symbolic alchemy.

CHAPTER THREE
Illustration from Eleonore von Merlau's *Glaubens Gespräche mit Gott*, 1686.

CHAPTER FOUR
From the title page of *Tractatus Theologo-Philosophicus* by the English physician, alchemist, and Rosicrucian Apologist, Robert Fludd (De Fluctibus), 1626.

CHAPTER FIVE
From the end page of a mathematical treatise by Oronce Fíne, 1530.

CHAPTER SIX
From the title page of Robert Fludd's *Utriusque Cosmi Historia.*

CHAPTER SEVEN
Images by Nicolaus Häublin from *Helleluchtender Hertzens-Spiegel*, a work of alchemical philosophy based on the writings of Tauler and Behmen, compiled by Paul Kaym, 1680.

CHAPTER EIGHT
Diagram taken from the Horologium Achaz Hydrographicum (used with permission of the American Philosophical Society, Philadelphia).

CHAPTER NINE
From *The Testament of Cremer*, an English account of alchemy attributed to a fictitious Benedictine monk. Part of the collection, *The Hermetic Museum*, 1678.

CHAPTER TEN
From the *Rosarium philosophorum*.

CHAPTER ELEVEN
Adapted from the cover page of Knorr von Rosenroth's *Kabbala Denudata*, 1663.

CHAPTER TWELVE
Adapted from a Dutch print of the *Sara Maria.*

CHAPTER THIRTEEN
From the allegoric and alchemical work, *The Book of Lambspring*. Part of the collection, *The Hermetic Museum*, 1678.

CHAPTER FOURTEEN
Design of wampum belt presented to William Penn by Lenápay leader, Tamanend,1682, in acknowledgement of their treaty.

CHAPTER FIFTEEN
From the title page of Robert Fludd's *Anatomiae Amphithea*, 1623.

CHAPTER SIXTEEN
From *The Book of Lambspring.*

CHAPTER SEVENTEEN
From the title page of Robert Fludd's *Tractatus Theologo-Philosophicus.*

CHAPTER EIGHTEEN
Illustration by Hans Weiditz, from the title page of Oth. Brunfel's *Herbarum,* 1530.

CHAPTER NINETEEN
From *Dye Zaigungdes hochlobwirdigen hailigthums* by Lucas Cranach, 1509.

CHAPTER TWENTY
Images from the title pages of Robert Fludd's *Tractatus Theologo-Philosophicus* and *Meterologia Cosmica,*1626.

CHAPTER TWENTY-ONE
From title page of Robert Fludd's *Integrum Morborum Mysterium*, 1631.

CHAPTER TWENTY-TWO
Pen and ink rendering of Kelpius' cave by Julius Sachse, 1894.

CHAPTER TWENTY-THREE
A composite of allegorical images from alchemical texts.

EPILOGUE
Fragment of *Die Kläglige Stimme der Verborgenen Liebe,* the hymn book of Magister Johannes Kelpius.

Major Bibliographic Sources

Carr, William. *Travels through Flanders, Holland, Germany...containing an account of what is most remarkable in those countries...*, London, 1725.

The Committee on Historical Research of the Pennsylvania Society of the Colonial Dames of America. *Church Music and Musical Life in Pennsylvania in the Eighteenth Century,* Vol 1. Lancaster, PA, Wiskerham Printing, 1938.

Croese, Gerald. *The General History of the Quakers*. London: John Dutton, 1696.

Einaudi, Giulio (editor). *The Travels of Marco Polo*. New York: Orion Press, n.d.

Fisher, Elizabeth W. "Prophesies and Revelations: German Cabbalists in Early Pennsylvania." *Pennsylvania Magazine of History and Biography,* CIX: 1985.

Harris, J. McArthur, Jr. " The Enigma of Kelpius' Cave." *Germantown Crier*, Summer 1983.

Hocker, Edward W. *Germantown 1693-1933*. Philadelphia, 1933.

Jones, Horatio Gates. "John Kelpius, the Hermit of the Ridge," *The American Historical Record*, 1873

Kelpius, Johannes, Journal (manuscript) 1694 -1707.

Keyser, Naaman H., et al. *History of Old Germantown,* Germantown, Pennsylvania: Horace F. McCann, 1907.

Lippard, George A. *Paul Ardenheim: Monk of the Wissahickon,* Philadelphia: T.B. Peterson & Brothers, 1843.

Martin, Willard M. *Johannes Kelpius and Johann Gotfried Seelig: Mystics and Hymnists on the Wissahickon,* Pennsylvania State University. (monograph) 1973.

Myers, Albert Cook, editor. *William Penn's Own Account of the Lenni Lenape or Delaware Indians*. Wilmington, Delaware: Middle Atlantic Press, 1983.

O'Meara, John. *Delaware-English/English-Delaware Dictionary.* Toronto: University of Toronto Press, 1996.

Pennypacker, Samuel W., Seelig, Johann Gotfried, et al. *Johann Gottfried Seelig and the Hymn-Book of the Hermits of the Wissahickon*. Philadelphia, (manuscript) 1901.

Sachse, Julius Friedrich. *The German Pietists of Provincial Pennsylvania 1694-1708*. Philadelphia, 1895.

Sachse, Julius Friedrich. *Pennsylvania: The German Influence in Its Settlement and Development, Part XXVII, The Diarium of Magister Johannes Kelpius.* Lancaster, PA: The Pennsylvania-German Society, 1917.

Schell, Ernest. "Hermit of the Wissahickon: Johannes Kelpius and the Chapter of Perfection." AHI, n.d.

Seidensticker, Oswald. "The Hermits of the Wissahickon." *Pennsylvania Magazine of Biography and History*, XI.

Seneca, Lucius, Campbell, Robin (translator). *Letters from a Stoic (Epistulae Morales ad Lucillim).* Harmondsworth: Penguin, 1969.

Shah, Sayed Idries. *The Sufis*. London: The Octagon Press, 1964.

Thune, Nils. *The Behmenists and the Philadelphians*. London: Upsala, 1948.

Tinkcom, Harry M. and Margaret B. *Historic Germantown*. Philadelphia: The American Philosophical Society, 1955.

Waller, Maureen. *1700: Scenes from London Life*. New York: Four Walls Eight Windows, 2000.

Weslager, C.A. *The Delaware Indians: A History*. New Brunswick, New Jersey: Rutgers University Press, 1972.

A portion of the proceeds from the sale of this book
will be donated to conservation efforts in
Philadelphia's Wissahickon Valley.